DARLING OF DEATH

MADELINE DEVANEY

Contents

1

CHAPTER 1

"Derick," Ariel let out a soft moan as her boyfriend wrapped his arms around her thighs, hoisting her up in his arms as he opened the door to his apartment. He nuzzled his nose in her neck, breathing in the soft cheap perfume that emanated from her skin and pressed debauched kisses down her collarbone.

She gasped, letting out a giggle as they stumbled through his somewhat messy apartment and landed on the bed clumsily. "I've been dying to see you all day."

Ariel laughed, breathlessly yanking her shirt over her head. Derick's brown eyes darkened at the sight of his beautiful companion and he roamed his wide hands down her curved body. "Who would've thought that your grandmother practically left you rich?"

Derick bowed down, peppering soft, sensual kisses up and down her stomach as his hands lowered down to her skinny jeans and began unbuckling them.

"She left us," the naïve girl corrected him, "rich."

The twenty-one year old boy nodded, taking a hold of her neck and pulled her upwards for another kiss. Now that he knew how much money Ariel would have he needed to hurry up and ask her to marry him; there was no way in hell that he'd miss out on so much money.

Ariel giggled, her melodious laugh ringing throughout the room as Derick struggled with his jeans. She unbuckled her bra, making him groan until his pants were finally off and he began to her toned curves.

For a seventeen year old girl, she had the curves of a completely grown woman—and Derick adored it. She was beautiful in every aspect—and rich. Very, filthy rich.

Derick slid his hands down her thighs, squeezing them gingerly before returning to her lace underwear and grinning up at her deviously. Ariel let out a breathy moan, tightening her hold around his dark curls and pulled him closer as he slid his palm in her heat.

Her green eyes closed in pleasure as he rocked his fingers against her femininity, bringing about glorious orgasms. Her back arched as her mouth dropped open and squealed like moans escaped her lips as she reached the heavens.

He chuckled lowly, enjoying the pleasure he was clearly giving her and pulled away to grab a condom from the drawers next to the bed. Ariel frowned; feeling a bit disappointed that that was all the foreplay they'd have for the night.

She thought that since they had been almost the entire day without seeing each other, Derick would want to please her more. She had, after all, just turned into New York's fifth richest person.

Weren't rich people supposed to get a bit more than what Derick was giving her?!

"Derick," she playfully moaned, sitting up to wrap her hands around his neck, "let's take it a bit slower tonight. I want to really enjoy it."

"You will," he shrugged, squinting his eyes to look down at the silver wrapper.

Ariel frowned, crossing her arms over her chest. She had snuck out of her house so that she could spend the night with Derick but he was making her feel like it would just be an ABCD a.k.a another-bang-cum-depart session.

Her school friends were always telling her of how their boyfriends took care of them before they went on to finish their business; Derick was never like that. He always finished first and left her to complete her satisfaction.

She was hoping that tonight was a different story.

"Come on, Derick," she pouted her lips and batted her eyelashes as she wrapped her arms around his neck, "let's do this my way for once."

He glared down at her, taking her small hands in his and gently pushed them away. "No, I'm the guy; I make these decisions."

She rolled her eyes, feeling completely out of the mood and reached for her shirt to put it on. Derick quickly grabbed her hand, realizing what she was intending on doing, but she shrugged him off and tried to put her white shirt on.

The next events scarred Ariel for the rest of her life.

Derick raised his hand again, to grab her but Ariel pushed his chest, glaring at him as he stumbled and fell on the floor. His hands flew up to his chest and he widened his eyes, gasping for breath like a fish out of water.

Ariel raised her eyebrows, thinking that he was feigning whatever he was going through, but quickly realized that he wasn't. Blood began to drip down his nose and she reached for him, making his brown eyes widened in fear.

"G-get away from me!" He spluttered out blood, grabbing unto his chest as he crawled away from her and began coughing blood violently.

"Derick!" Ariel fell to her knees, trying to figure out what was wrong with him, but the more she touched him, the more blood he'd cough.

Suddenly his eyes lost their glint; they became dull and lifeless as he stared up at her in fear. His lips parted as more blood was coughed out and Ariel cried hysterically, not sure of what to do. She reached for him, trying to give him some type of comfort, but as soon as their hands came together, fire would course through her veins.

Ariel gasped, feeling power running through her body as she touched him and a blinding white light flashed through the room as Derick lost his last breath. Her hands shook uncontrollably as she tried to feel for his pulse but found none.

Derick was dead and she came into realization that it had been her fault.

She killed her boyfriend—and she didn't know how.

2

CHAPTER 2

The young girl shuddered as the cold leathered gloves slid in her fingers. She clenched and unclenched her fists, staring down at her small hands, enclosed in her only protection from the world.

A single tear slid down her freckled cheekbone and she wiped it away with shaking fingers. Her bright green eyes stared back at her reflection as she softly applied thick red lipstick to her plump lips. Her long black hair fell to her waist completely straight, adorning her soft-like features and made her seem almost surreal.

She was one of the most beautiful women in New York, but she was also the deadliest. It wasn't by choice; neither were her choice.

Ariel set her lipstick on the bathroom sink, taking a deep breath as she stepped back to admire her features. Over the past three years she had matured enormously. Not only physically but mentally as well.

She had forced herself to disappear from her mother's life and made a new one for herself. She was now the lady with the black gloves, as so many people had called her. They all believed she was afraid of people touching her. "Maybe it's a phobia, son," parents said to their kids many times.

It wasn't a phobia; no it was worse than that. It was reality. The power that emanated from just the touch of her fingertips was horrendous; her touch literally left people breathless and not the good kind.

After what occurred with her ex-boyfriend, Ariel swore not to touch anyone ever again and so far she had kept to her promise. For the first year, she had continuous nightmares of Derick's dull eyes haunting her as she sobbed over his dead body.

Derick didn't have any family, that she knew of, except herself, so it made her running away the much easier. No one could pin his death on her, no one found a body. Ariel didn't hide it, she panicked.

She was only seventeen years old at the time, her mind wasn't exactly pure, but it wasn't that of a murderer. She fled the crime scene and booked the earliest train ticket to New York, where she claimed her grandmother's inheritance and resided in a gorgeous one-room flat.

Now at twenty, Ariel acted older than what she really was and her only companion was the music player on her windowsill. She spoke with people, but they were curt short sentences, in which she was only being polite.

She dared not get close to anyone; she couldn't endure the excruciating pain of losing someone again. She wouldn't let herself live if she killed another innocent life.

"Oh, I'm sorry for blaming you, for everything I just couldn't do and I've hurt myself by hurting you," Christina Aguilera's voice sang softly in the background, opening wounds that Ariel gladly tore open.

She was a masochist when it came to pain; she believed that for all the pain she must've caused Derrick that horrendous night, she had to feel it a thousand times stronger. She had contemplated a gory suicide, but she wasn't strong enough to take away her life.

The worse pain she could bring herself was to live with the guilt. She owed Derrick that; she owed him her life for taking his. One life for another.

Another tear slid down her chin and her leathered-covered fingers wiped it away gently. She knew she was beautiful, she didn't need to be told twice, but she was also deadly; a rose with more thorns than petals.

Ariel took a deep breath, turning away from her pained reflection and walked out of the bathroom and into her room. Most of the time she spent watching TV; that was the only normal thing left in her life, music and TV.

She clicked on her music player for it to change songs and closed her eyes as Gabrielle Aplin came on. She was one of her favourite singers. Ariel loved soft music; it was almost sweet and enchanting.

It took her out of her nightmare of a reality and took her far away into a beautiful dream. She was a dreamer, a hopeless romantic dreamer. Ever since she was little she dreamed of the day that a man would kneel down in front of her and ask for her hand in marriage.

She was somewhat old fashioned and believed that her marriage would be the first and last. She hoped to die with her husband and never feel the soaring butterflies she would feel with her husband with another man.

"Please don't say you love me 'cause I might not say it back. Doesn't mean I'll stop skipping when you look at me like that," Ariel susurrated the words under her breath as she closed her eyes and began dancing around her room, "there's no need to worry when you see just where we're at. Just please don't say you love me, 'cause I might not say it back."

A soft smile grazed her lips as she raised her hands over her head and pirouetted around her bed. She had taken ballet classes since she was five and it was her passion; she loved to dance and lose herself in the music, but ever since she ran away she barely practised.

When the song ended, she took a deep breath and let out a quiet giggle. It was moments like that that made her feel human. Those were the small moments that she lived for. Ariel took another deep breath, patting down her hair and fixed her black dress.

It was almost time for her nightly walk down the park. Walking at night always seemed to relax her and there weren't lots of people present to make her feel uncomfortable. She didn't need to fear killing someone because they were all inside their homes.

The young woman walked towards the wooden table, picked up her house keys and placed them in her small clutch. Then she took a hold of her coat and buttoned it up, to make her way down the cobble stone pathway.

Bright stars adorned the sky beautifully, making another smile grow on Ariel's lips as she looked up at the moon. It was exquisitely beautiful. She adored nature, she found that she wasn't such a monster if she simply admired from afar.

Ariel didn't know why she was capable of taking away life with just her fingertips, but she was afraid to look for answers. She did try researching for others like her, but the internet simply gave her results of Wolverine. She wasn't exactly Rogue but she could be just as deadly.

The streets of uptown New York were somewhat quiet. There was the occasional siren here and there, but it wasn't something that bothered the ear like the buzz of a bee. The air didn't exactly have a certain type of scent, it was just...air.

A sleek red sports car drove by her, startling the girl out of her thoughts and she shoved her hands in her pockets. Ariel looked down at her black flats and kicked a pebble out of her way.

The moon was shining was so brightly that it made it seem like the light posts were unnecessary. Ariel walked past a trash can, stepping off the street to walk by it and then got back on the sidewalk. She had learned that although it was uptown New York, people drove wildly.

She kept on walking down the silent street and began to softly hum a tune under her breath; she couldn't remember the name of the song or the lyrics, but she loved the melody.

Suddenly a hand wrapped around her arm and she widened her eyes, opening her mouth to let out a shriek but the burly hands clamped over her mouth. Ariel struggled against the person, her cries coming out muffled because of his obtrusive hands and she kicked her legs up in the air, trying to put up a fight.

The man groaned when she jabbed her elbow into his stomach, but he didn't loosen his hold on her, he simply wrapped his arm around her waist and kept walking down the street effortlessly.

Ariel wasn't afraid of what he would do to her, no, she was afraid of what she could do to him.

"P-please," she sobbed, "don't touch me. I'll give you all the money you want but please let go of me."

He rolled his eyes, hoisting her up in his arms as he made a turn into an alleyway and in a gruffly voice muttered, "Gross, I'm not going to touch you like that and I don't want your money."

Ariel frowned, jabbing her heel on his foot, but he didn't flinch. "Please! I don't want to hurt you!"

"Oh," he chuckled, "you helpless, little girl. You think that you can hurt me?"

"Please?" she whispered one last time, as she clenched her fists and hoped that he wasn't stupid enough to actually try and violate her.

"Here you go," He threw her into the dark alleyway, rubbing his hands against his jeans as he looked at the cloaked man behind Ariel and said, "now where's my money?"

"It'sss in your houssse," he hissed, sounding like a snake.

Ariel deepened her frown as she stood up and turned to look at the man. Her heart thudded deep in her chest, making it feel like it was going to run out of her and into the night. Her hands were sweating in her gloves and as much as she wanted to take them off and protect herself, she couldn't bring herself to kill another person. Even if they wanted to kill her.

Her captor nodded, walking away as if it was the most normal thing to do and she gulped loudly. The cloaked man chuckled, low and throaty, making chills run down her back.

"W-what do you want?"

He stepped closer to her and she took two steps back. "Well I want you dearie, of courssse."

Ariel rolled her eyes, glaring at him and said, "Why do you want me?"

He let out another chuckle, sounding as menacing as he looked and stared up at her with piercing yellow snake-like eyes. Ariel dropped her jaw open as he slithered his thin snake-tongue out of his mouth and hissed, "Becaussse I know what you did and what you are, Ariel Lockhaven."

"What the fu-" she squeaked as she turned around to run away, but was interrupted by another voice.

"Let her go, Demos."

$$3$$

CHAPTER 3

The snake-man chortled, throwing back his head, resulting in his cloak revealing his identity. Ariel widened her eyes, her fingers flying up to cover her mouth before a loud gasp would escape her lips.

His skin was a pale sickening green with yellow scales overlapping each other. His lips were a darker mint green but completely chapped and thin. He slithered his snake-tongue out, making a hissing noise as he stepped closer to Ariel and she tripped backwards.

Her back pressed against the brick wall behind her and she breathed in quickly. The snake-man eyed her slowly, his yellow eyes glowing with mischief and want. "Who are you to tell me what to do, scoundrel?"

The man behind them let out a loud chortle, sounding cold and completely humourless. "My identity is of no importance to you, Demos. Now let the girl go before I call upon the Praxidike."

For a moment, Ariel swore she saw "Demos'" yellow eyes widening in fear and he bowed his head, gritting his teeth and muttered something in a language that she could not understand. "You do not get her that easy, human."

"You think I am human?" The man stepped closer, enabling Ariel from seeing his face-and to say the least, she was disappointed.

From the way he carried himself and spoke with such authority, she was expecting a tall man with burly arms and a glare that could kill anything on his way. But her saviour was the complete opposite.

His golden curls would put Goldilocks to writhe with jealousy wherever she was and his eyes were so blue, she thought she was staring at a day's sky. He was about inches taller than her and although he might have had muscle underneath his garments, he seemed lanky. Short and lanky.

Ariel rolled her eyes, realizing that now she'd have to save herself and her wannabe saviour from the snake-man.

Goldilocks stepped closer, walking past Ariel and stood right in front of the creature. "You think you can go above a God, Demos? I will have Ares skin you alive and use you as a rug."

"You?" The creature laughed, holding unto his stomach with thin, long, almost skeleton-like fingers, "A God? You humour me. Nonetheless, I'll let you have the girl. I've more important matters to care for, just know I'll come back and I won't let you keep her."

In the blink of an eye, the creature disappeared, leaving behind a green coloured mist and a stench of burnt rubber. Ariel crinkled her nose and began to slowly step back from Goldilocks before he turned to her and smiled brightly.

"Hi I'm Herm-" he cleared his throat, realizing that he was going to reveal his identity to her and finished off plainly, "-an. I'm Herman, what's your name?"

"Uh," Ariel forced out a smile, still walking backwards slowly and said, "I've got to go. I need to feed my uh, turtle."

Herman rolled his blue eyes, placing his hands on his hips and turned to her with an annoyed look on her face. "You've no turtle in your home."

She frowned. "How do you know-you know what? I don't even want to know how you know that. I'm just going to go home and forget this strange night ever happened."

He tsk'ed his tongue, shaking his head as he walked behind her slowly, but not menacingly, "Ha-" he cleared his throat, once more, "Haynes won't be pleased, milady."

She turned to look at him, scowling and said, "Will you stop following me?! I will call the police."

He shrugged. "They won't do a thing for they cannot see me."

Ariel sighed, walking a tad faster and decided that this was by far the strangest night she had ever encountered. And to top it all off, she didn't feel intimidated one bit by Goldilocks, whom was still walking behind her, muttering things under his breath that she couldn't understand.

"How can they not see you when I see you?"

"Well," Herman began slowly, clasping his hands as he walked up to speed with her, "I am letting you see me, therefore you can."

She narrowed her eyes at him, strangely not feeling uncomfortable by his presence-and believing him. "That's not possible."

He sighed, running his fingers through his hair and said, "It's possible if you're-" He cut himself off, speaking to someone else, whom apparently Ariel couldn't see. "Well if I don't tell her, she won't come with me and if she doesn't come with me then-well then you pick her up!" he crossed his arms over his chest, glaring at nothing in particular and hissed, "Then don't complain about my methods; I'm telling the girl who I am."

Ariel raised her eyebrows, finding him somewhat interesting and realized that they were already at her apartment. She stood outside the gates awkwardly, waiting for him to finally walk away so that she didn't need to be rude, but Herman didn't seem to get the memo.

"So...this is it. I'm going inside, thank you for being there when that creature-thing tried to abduct me."

"That's all?" Herman raised a quizzical eyebrow, "You're not confused or curious as to why Demos looked like half-man half-snake? Or why he wanted you?"

She grimaced, silently hoping that he wouldn't bring that up. If she didn't think about it, then maybe it would all go away and never bother her again. "He was probably some psycho that went to a costume party."

He rolled his eyes and muttered under his breath in another language. "Child, you've much to learn. Now, let me introduce myself properly. I am Hermes, the God of boundaries, travel, communication, language, and writing."

Ariel laughed, holding unto her stomach as she giggled, making her sides ache and wiped away her imaginary teardrops. Not only had she met a weirdo with an obsession with snakes, but she had also met a mythology geek. "Where are your flying shoes?"

"Hermes" frowned, glancing down at his shoes and muttered, "You humans lack imagination. I do not wear my "flying shoes" when I need not fly."

She sobered up, feeling her throat dry up when she realized how serious he sounded and sighed. "Look, I don't know who you are or why you're here, but please just go. I've been staying up so late lately that I've began to hallucinate."

He frowned, turning to look up at the sky and groaned, "Why are you humans so difficult?! You are not hallucinating and you do know who I am; I introduced myself."

She rolled her eyes, looking in her clutch for her key and said, "There's no way that you can be a God; they're supposed to be intimidating and old."

"Oh," he chuckled dryly, "so she has no problem believing in gods, but she fears I am not who I say I am because of my looks. Darling, you need not be so judgemental. If I were to show you my true manifestation you'd go blind and die instantly."

This guy needed a new brand of fruit loops, she thought inwardly. "Look, as much as I'd love to chat about gods all night with you-"

Hermes frowned, crossing his arms over his chest and said, "We do not have all night. You need to be with Haynes by tonight, Ariel."

"I didn't tell you my name," she squeaked out.

He sighed, narrowing his eyes and said, "Let's enter your home, I'll explain the rest later and if you say one thing about me being a stranger and entering your abode, I will personally ask Aphrodite to make you fall in love with a turtle."

Ariel frowned, opening the gate and stared at him expectantly when he didn't enter. Hermes rolled his eyes, placing most of his weight on his right foot. "I need permission to enter; I am the God of boundaries, I cannot simply break my own rules."

She sighed, shaking her head as she gave him permission and they walked up to her apartment. If it were any sane human, they'd call the police and turn Hermes'-wannabe in, but Ariel was not a sane human. She was a woman that could kill anything with the mere touch of her fingertips.

If he tried any funky business, she'd have to add someone else to her list of casualties.

"Alright," he clasped his hands together once they reached her living room, "I believe that I cannot tell you every detail of why you need to come with me, but it is for the best."

Ariel gave him a look, carefully taking her flats off and placed them neatly in her closet. After shrugging her coat off, she turned to "Hermes" and said, "If you cannot explain to me why I'd be going with you someplace, then there's no way in hell that I'd be going with you."

He gave her a slight smile, mirth shining in his eyes. "Funny you speak of hell, you're-" he cut himself off, staring past her with now-grey eyes, "I know what you said! But I'm the one taking her to you, so I think I get to-you know what? I am closing this communication portal until I am done speaking with the girl. I will only contact you if I believe your services are needed."

She sighed, walking towards her fridge and grabbed a water bottle. She turned back to Hermes to offer him one, but he shook his head and stared at her quietly as she opened it and took a sip. Ariel flushed, feeling uncomfortable under his curious gaze and he smiled easily.

"Sorry, the man whom I'm supposed to take you to keeps interrupting me and I had to close him off."

Ariel nodded, sitting in front of him slowly and said, "So..."

"Oh, right," Hermes cleared his throat, "well there are rumours going on in the upstairs kingdom that someone is planning on using your powers to kill some immortal beings."

She frowned, staring down at her covered hands and said, "But...I will never use my powers to hurt someone again."

He smiled sorrowfully at her and said, "Child, there are things that we do not wish to do, but our destinies are shaped a certain way and we must complete them."

Her hands shook slightly as she tried to erase the horrible memories of Derick entering her head. She took a deep breath, blinking away her tears and clenched her fists. "So why are you taking me with you?"

"Well," Hermes continued, "the Gods decided that if they have you under their surveillance and closer to them, they'll be able to stop whoever is trying to kill them."

Ariel gasped, widening her eyes and whispered, "There are people trying to kill the gods? That's stupid; they're immortal!"

Hermes chuckled, sitting back in his seat and said, "Your powers are greater than you think, with the right amount of concentration you can wipe out anything you wish to take down."

"But," she whispered again, sounding pained.

"We know," he spoke softly, "you swore that you'd never hurt someone again, but you know how cruel people can be and when they want something they get it. Now," he smiled, "are you ready to go to your new home?"

Ariel shook her head, staring at the delicate white peony as a table adornment. "I just want to sleep and wake up from this crazy dream."

Hermes slid his hand down his face, letting out a small groan and said, "You really don't believe me?"

She was quiet for a couple of seconds, searching in her mind to see if she really didn't believe him. But the problem was that she did. Somehow, in the insanity of her mind, she believed everything that Hermes was telling her.

She knew that she had to leave with him in order to keep her safe, but she also knew that she'd never hurt anyone with her touch again.

A slow smile grew on Hermes' lips. "Oh that's not the problem," his smile grew, "the problem is that you do believe me but you don't understand why you believe me. Is it not?"

Ariel looked up at him slowly, giving him a weary smile. "It's really creepy that you know those things about me."

Hermes shrugged, giving her a boyish smile and then looked down at her hands. She blushed, slowly hiding her hands underneath the table. "Can you really...?"

She nodded, following his gaze and muttered, "Yes."

"Can I see?" He spoke quietly, but his blue eyes shone with so much excitement that it frightened Ariel. He had finished telling her about the danger she had placed the gods in, but now he wanted to see her "powers."

Heaving out a sigh, Ariel grabbed her leather gloves and unbuttoned them from her wrist's latch. She slid her right hand out of the only thing keeping her from hurting anything in her way and slowly caressed the petals of the peony.

Hermes watched with wide blue eyes as the flower slowly began to wither and wilt, until the stem was completely black and the petals were so shrivelled up they turned to dust. A soft sigh echoed through the room as the flower turned into dust and they both stared at it silently.

"That's...incredibly scary."

Ariel cracked a small smile, quickly sliding her hands back in her glove and said, "And dangerous."

He nodded in agreement, standing up and held his hand out, "Which is exactly why we need to leave right now before another thing tries to take you."

She frowned, shaking her head as he grabbed her elbow and she tried to yank herself out of his reach. "Wait, no, stop; where the hell are you taking me?!"

Hermes chuckled, stepping away from her as he reached his destination; Pluto's headquarters. He was taking her to hell.

Ariel slowly turned around, letting her jaw slack in surprise and amazement as she took in her surroundings. Beautiful gemstones shone throughout the palace, adorning the black polished walls and golden chandeliers hung on the high ceilings, illuminating the eerie yet enchanting place.

Black curtains covered the windows, preventing her to see the outside of the palace and a ruby red coloured carpet ran up ending its length at the feet of the grand throne atop the smooth black marble tiles.

She didn't need to be told where she was; she knew. She was in the Underworld and as she glanced up at the man sitting on the throne, the only thing that could enter her mind was writing a letter to Disney about his depiction of Hades.

He was not grey, or ugly, nor did he have fiery blue hair.

No, the man sitting on the throne was a complete and utter God at his finest.

4

CHAPTER 4

Ariel gulped, staring at the God on the throne with wide eyes and turned to look at Hermes. He smirked behind her and then up at Hades.

"Hades," Hermes bowed his head in respect and motioned at Ariel, "she's here safe and sound."

"Indeed," Hades spoke quietly, his eccentric blue eyes shining curiously as he stared at the girl beside Hermes.

"Y-you," she stuttered, staring at the handsome man sitting on the sleek black throne, "you're..."

He rolled his eyes, waving his hand impatiently and said, "Hades. Come on, say it with me. Ha-des."

"Hades," Ariel breathed out, still not believing the sight before her. Every picture she had seen of the gods had not depicted Hades' beauty. The god sitting before her was not a crusty old man with a white beard; no, he was a Calvin Klein model.

"Yes," Hades clasped his hands together and grimaced, "the God of Death and riches; that's me." Ariel nodded, still refusing to believe but knowing she had to and Hades' grimace turned even bitter, "And you, darling, will be staying with me for quite some time."

Ariel gulped slowly, biting her bottom lip as she turned around to look at Hermes, but frowned when she noticed that he wasn't there. He didn't even say farewell! He simply disappeared the same way he had vanished both of them from her home.

Her green eyes travelled back up to the throne and she breathed in sharply. The God's beauty was so overwhelming that all she could do was stare at him with wide eyes.

His hair was black, the ends curling a bit around his neck and they looked extremely soft, as if they'd melt underneath her touch. His jaw was so refined and muscled that her fingers itched to trace them.

Light facial whiskers embellished his face, making him look rugged and completely dangerous. His soft pink lips were slowly turning upward in a smirk as her eyes travelled lower. He was dressed in dark silk robes, long enough to cover his entire body, but the neckline was low enough to give away to the imagination.

Even through the dark expensive-looking robe, one could notice the muscles protruding underneath. His collarbone was strong and his shoulders broad, making Ariel bite her lip even harder to keep herself from falling at his feet and beg him to bed her.

It had been three long years that she hadn't touched another person and to feel someone touching her, the way she wanted Hades to touch her, would be unfathomable.

"Are you done staring?" Hades sneered, his facial features not changing whatsoever. Even when he scrounged up his face in disgust, he seemed gorgeous.

Ariel blushed, turning her head away from him and looked down at her hands. "Forgive me, I didn't mean to make you uncomfortable."

He shrugged, standing up from his throne and slowly walked down to her. "I'd stare at myself too if I were in your place; I'm just so handsome, are I not?"

She frowned, looking up at him in confusion. He spoke words of boast, yet he sounded as if he was testing her. As if he wanted to see what she'd respond and humiliate her in return. She couldn't understand why he didn't like her; he didn't even know her, but his voice was cold and unnerving.

"I spoke to you," he whispered menacingly, stepping closer to her, "I expect an answer."

Her eyebrows slowly rose and she scowled at him. "You did speak to me, but the way you spoke was rhetorical, therefore you do not wish an answer."

Hades stared at her, his eyes expressionless as they scrutinized her face slowly and her cheeks began to slowly turn a shade of pink. He turned away from her abruptly and began walking away.

Ariel frowned, turning around on the same spot to see if she had missed something.

"Are you coming or not?" he snapped, sounding quite impatient.

She gritted her teeth, her bare feet making soft padding noises as she tried to catch up to him. Even though the God of the Underworld was colder than the freezing temperatures of Antarctica, his palace was surprisingly warm.

She spoke quietly; "Are you going to tell me why I'm here with you?"

Hades clenched his jaw, eyeing her through the corner of his eyes and crossed his arms over his chest. Maybe he had done it thoughtlessly or maybe he had done it on purpose, but when he crossed his arms over his chest, his muscles seemed to tighten and look more mouth-watering than before.

Ariel gulped once more, tearing her gaze away from his muscular arms and ran her fingers through her hair. She looked up to catch Hades looking at her hands with interest.

"Why do you wear those?"

She rolled her eyes, crossing her arms on her chest as she walked beside him defensively and said, "You just answered my question with another one; I don't like that. And if you are a God how come you don't know why I'm wearing these?"

Hades opened his mouth, turning to look at her and his eyes glazed with such ferocious anger; she could feel it emanating from his skin. "You dare question a God?"

She bit her bottom lip, trying to keep her tongue from speaking words that would cause her trouble. "I am not questioning the way you think I am. I am allowed to ask questions, no? All you had to do was answer it."

"Same goes for you," he hissed, his low voice, deepening with the anger coursing through his body, "all you had to do was answer it and not talk back."

Ariel glared at him, clenching her fists and said, "I wear them so I don't kill everything I touch. There. Now answer my question; why am I staying with you?"

Hades seemed a bit taken aback, but he didn't let her catch it. He obviously knew why she worse them, he just wanted an answer out of her. But he didn't expect her to be as childish as she was being. If she weren't a threat to the other Gods, he would've sent her straight to Tartarus.

When he didn't answer her right away, she figured he was too angry to answer her, but it wasn't her fault he was being so difficult. She would have tried to be nice, but the God was making it harder than the Sunday crossword puzzle in the newspaper.

Ariel was generally a nice person, curt, but respectful. She just figured that if she was too nice, people would get attached to her and cause her unwanted pain. It was easier for her to push everything and everyone away and prevent her heart from shattering once more.

She couldn't even own a pet without fearing the worse.

"The Gods," Hades cleared his throat, still walking past every room they passed and then yanked her elbow to push her up a set of stairs, "they called a meeting. As you know, there is someone trying to get rid of us by using your powers. They figured that if you were here with us, then whoever is trying to exterminate us would have difficulty reaching you."

He shrugged, "I offered killing you, but apparently even the God of Death can't kill you."

Ariel frowned, staring at him with wide eyes. "Wait you wanted to kill me?!"

"Of course not," he huffed indignantly, "I suggested-"

She interrupted, her voice raising a few octaves as he guided her through more hallways. It seemed that the palace was as big as Bill Gates bank account. "But you just said that you offered to kill me!"

Hades rolled his eyes, holding the urge to smack some sense into her and slowly spoke, "I offered to kill you, but Zeus and the rest of my damn family thinks that its best you stay alive. It has something to do with your ancestors and since I'm no history professor, I won't go into those gritty details."

Ariel huffed; hugging herself to keep from smacking him upside the head and stomp her feet like a child. He was making her so livid that she wanted to throw a tantrum and return to her small apartment in New York.

"I can't believe you offered to kill me," she hissed, realizing that they stopped in front of grand obsidian black doors.

Hades sighed, running his fingers through his black hair and said, "Whatever, you're staying with me because as the God of the Underworld, I'm the only lucky one that won't die by your touch."

She slowly blinked, a small smile growing on her lips. "You mean..."

"Yes," Hades glared at her, "I'm the one that gets stuck with you. I wanted to keep you with Athena, maybe she'd find a way to keep you from killing them or even Poseidon for suggesting you stay with me, but Zeus thought it was a splendid idea." He rolled his eyes, muttering something under his breath that she couldn't quite catch, "So here you are, human; this is your room."

Ariel rolled her eyes at the name and looked at the doors curiously. "This is my room?"

"Do I really need to repeat myself so much with you?" He sighed exasperatedly, "Because if that's going to become a thing, we won't have many conversations."

"It's not like I want to exactly converse with you," she muttered, covering her mouth quickly as she realized she spoke her thoughts out loud.

Hades laughed, the sound completely cold and humourless. "The feeling is mutual."

"I'm sorry," Ariel grimaced, feeling a tad guilty for speaking to him that way. Then again, he did offer to kill her...

The God rolled his eyes, completely ignoring her apology and pushed the doors open. They squeaked in protest a bit and light dust flew behind, making Ariel sneeze. Yet again, the beauty from the place left her breathless.

The room was completely beautiful. Purple curtains hung on the walls, dancing with the soft wind that entered from the oval-shaped windows. A grand queen sized bed sat in the middle, with four high posts and a grey covering on top.

Expensive-looking red quilts adorned the bed and golden coloured pillows were scattered evenly across the top. Ariel gasped, entering the room slowly as the exquisiteness of it all was more than she could handle at a time.

Yes, she had been very wealthy in New York, but she had never seen a room like this. It was eerie with strange décor, but it was beautiful nonetheless. A black dresser stood tall against the wall, different coloured gemstones adorning the sleek piece of wood.

"This is beautiful," she breathed out.

Hades raised his eyebrows. What did she expect?! "Of course it is; I made it."

Ariel rolled her eyes, squealing inwardly as the soft carpet tickled her feet the further she walked in.

The God sighed, running his fingers through his hair uncomfortably and said, "Before I let you get comfortable there are a few rules we need to establish."

She turned to him with a sour expression and waited for him to continue.

"You cannot leave this room without an escort. Wherever you wish to go, I must be notified of. You cannot wander around without supervision because even though my kingdom is extremely hard to get in, rats still manage to steal the cheese from traps." She frowned at his strange comparison, but waited until he finished making her his prisoner. "You cannot go to any of the rooms without my permission, when you're hungry, let one of the servants know and they'll bring it up to you. Do not talk to anyone other than Adrianne and for the love of Cerberus do not whistle."

"Are you done?" Ariel raised her eyebrows, standing in the middle of the room. Hades glowered at her but nodded. "Apparently I'm no guest, I'm your prisoner."

"That can be arranged," he spoke quickly, a mischievous smile growing on his delectable lips.

Ariel scowled at him in response. "Who's Adrianne?"

As if on cue, a dark haired girl walked in, bowing her head in respect at Hades and muttered something softly. Hades motioned with his hand at the girl and said, "This is Adrianne your personal helper. Whatever you need, she'll get for you."

"Milady," Adrianne spoke gently, smiling softly and waited for further instructions.

Ariel shook her head, smiling in return and said, "Call me, Ariel, please."

Adrianne nodded, bowing her head and Hades sighed. "Go rest, I believe it is night in your world and you must be exhausted. We will speak in the morning about the rest of my rules."

Before she could retort an answer, Hades disappeared, leaving behind a black mist, which made Ariel roll her eyes at how clichéd it all seemed. Then again, it wasn't every day that a girl got taken to the Underworld because the Gods feared her.

"Do you wish for anything, mi—Ariel?" Adrianne spoke so quietly, she barely heard her.

Ariel shook her head, walking towards the bed and yawned, suddenly feeling more tired than she had ever felt in her life. "Tomorrow you can tell me why the heck the God of the Dead is an asswipe."

5

— • —

CHAPTER 5

The next morning, Ariel awoke with a jolt. She widened her eyes, unable to recognize her surroundings and let out a quiet squeal as she shut her eyes and hoped with all her might that the previous day had been but a dream.

It wasn't.

No matter how many times she pinched her elbow, she didn't wake up from her dream. With a loud groan, she fell back unto the comfortable pillows and smacked her hands on her face, covering it as she tried to assemble her thoughts.

There was no way in hell that she was with the God of the Dead, it just didn't make sense. Out of all the people she could've been with, they sent her to the God of Death. It was ironic and painful; it reminded her of the pain she could cause to those around her.

Ariel sighed, running her fingers through her hair and grimaced at the excessive oil that it had produced. She needed to wash her hair and take a shower quickly, before she killed herself by the horrendous smell escaping her pores. Well it wasn't exactly horrendous, but she was accustomed to taking showers every morning.

Her green eyes stared up at the canopy of the bed. The grey covering made her feel imprisoned in a way. It obscured a clear view from the ceiling and she suddenly felt suffocated. Of course, she could simply yank the grey net off, but the thought of something [or someone] keeping her prisoner terrified her.

She glanced down at her delicate fingers, no longer hidden in the leather gloves and she sighed, tracing the ridges of her hands gently. What she would give to have someone touch her hands and not die was indescribable.

She loved the bare touch of petals against her fingertips; she longed to touch something soft that would not wilt at the mere touch of her fingertips. She longed to touch the face of a lover, feel his smooth cheekbone underneath her hand and caress him lovingly.

But she could not do that, for she couldn't think of enduring the pain of loss again. Her heart was shattered as it was, she couldn't break the pieces any more than they were.

Ariel breathed out, running her hands up and down the smooth quilt underneath her and smiled. It was so soft it literally felt like it would melt in her fingers. The grouchy God surely had a nice taste in fabrics.

The girl slowly slid herself off the bed, closing her eyes in pleasure as her bare feet came into contact with the plush black carpet. At the sound of someone knocking on her door gently, her eyes snapped open.

Adrianne walked in the room pushing a silver cart with silver platters, she bowed her head at Ariel and smiled, "Milady," she bit her bottom lip, remembering Ariel's request to address her by her first name, but at the girl's friendly smile, she continued, "I brought you some food. Master Hades didn't know what you preferred to eat so I took the liberty to pick out a few fruits."

Ariel smiled in return, walking towards the cart and looked down at it curiously. "I also brought you some towels and a robe so you can shower. Master Hades also said to provide you with a tooth-brush."

"Thanks, Adrianne," she took the bathroom necessities and set them on the table before walking back to the cart and slowly uncovering one of the plates.

Freshly picked strawberries and grapes were scattered in the plate along with kiwi strips and oranges. Ariel breathed in sharply loving the fruity scent that filled the room and licked her lips as her mouth watered.

She quickly grabbed a fork and bit into a strawberry, moaning in delight as all the juices danced with her taste buds.

Adrianne grinned, walking over to a door across from the bed and opened it. "Here is your bathroom, Ariel. I shall prepare you a bath if you wish...?"

She nodded her head quickly, gorging down the exquisite fruits in the plate before her. "Please?" Red strawberry juices slid down her jaw and she wiped them away with the back of her hand as she stabbed the next fruit with her fork and moaned at the glorious taste.

Ariel always loved to have fruits for breakfast, they were usually accompanied with a bowl of oatmeal, but she wasn't going to complain. Besides the fruits were literally the best she had ever had. They tasted completely fresh and mouth-watering.

"Done," Adrianne walked back, smiling as she looked at Ariel eating the last piece of mandarin orange. "Did you like your breakfast?"

"Yes," Ariel licked her lips, "those fruits were delicious!"

Adrianne chuckled, placing the silver lid back on the plate and said, "I shall tell the chef that you loved his fruits. He has a fruit garden and he's obsessed with them. I think he'll be very happy once I tell him that you liked them."

"Thanks, Adrianne," Ariel stretched her arms over her head and let out a yawn, "I'm going to take a shower now."

As she began to make her way to the bathroom, Adrianne followed suit, making Ariel frown in confusion. The smiling maid quickly widened her eyes, as she realized that her 'master' wasn't content.

"Is something the matter, milady?"

Ariel blushed, shaking her head and scratched her neck awkwardly. "It's just that...you're following me into the bathroom."

"Oh," Adrianne lowered her brown eyes in embarrassment, "I did not mean to make you uncomfortable, miss. It is just that in my time, we helped our ladies into the shower and washed their hair and such."

She raised her eyebrows as she walked in the bathroom and said, "And when was this time?!"

"Fifteen hundreds," she grinned, "I assisted many Duchesses before a pirate came and took my life."

Ariel gave her a sorrowed look. "That kind of sucks..."

Adrianne laughed, shaking her head and said, "Oh not at all! Master Hades is one of the best Master's I've ever had. He really is nice and quite understanding."

She snorted, shaking her head as she let Adrianne zip down her dress. The girl turned around, letting her step out of her close in some privacy and she quickly stepped into the white bathtub. "The God of the Underworld is anything but nice! I don't know if we're talking about the same guy here but the one I met yesterday had something up his arse."

Adrianne giggled, folding the black dress and placed it on the countertop as she began looking for liquid soaps and rose petals to pour into the water. Ariel leaned back, closing her eyes as she wallowed in on the refreshing water and felt her muscles slowly relaxing.

After finding the rose petals, Adrianne began to pour them over the water, startling Ariel as she felt a featherlike touch against her cheek. The girl mumbled out an apology to which Ariel grinned in return and went back to enjoying herself.

All of the showers she had ever taken were standing up, so for her to be sitting down, with her legs hidden underwater, felt amazing. Not only did she feel pampered, but she actually felt wealthy. Something that even though she had been, she didn't feel.

Ariel raised her leg out of the water, watching droplets travelling down her calves and wiggled her red-painted toe nails in the air.

"Do you wish for me to wash your hair, Ariel?"

She shook her head, grinning up at Adrianne and said, "No thank you, I think I can handle that myself."

"Humph," Adrianne frowned, crossing her arms over her chest as she pouted like a small child.

"What?" Ariel frowned in return.

The girl rolled her eyes, giving her a pointed look. "Master Hades appointed me to serve you, but you do not like me helping you. It is my job to do these kinds of things, why don't you let me?"

"Because," Ariel whined, feeling her cheeks heating up once more, "I don't feel comfortable with you doing things that I can do for myself. It's just weird...I've never had a butler or anything;

I didn't need one and now that you want to do these things for me...it's just strange."

Adrianne sighed, standing up and said, "Very well, do as you wish. I will be outside if you need anything, yes?"

"Thanks!" Ariel nodded, closing her as she slid deeper into the bathtub, until the water covered up to her nose.

She splashed her hands on the water, letting out a girly giggle and then began to slowly wash herself, loving the smoothness of her skin. She was careful not to touch the petals, but was surprised to find that they didn't turn to dust in her hands and watched as they stuck to her skin.

The bathroom was simple but beautiful. It had a sink with a huge oval mirror over it and next to it was a dark cabinet with about a hundred perfumes and liquid soaps for her to use. There was a small toilet near the tub with a cute red covering over the lid.

Ariel let out another content sigh, loving how her morning had begun. She wondered if every day would be like that because she could so get used to eating the exquisite fruits for breakfast and even lunch and dinner; they were that delicious.

She sat forward; squeezing what looked to be some type of lemon scented shampoo and began to scrub her scalp gently. She closed her eyes, letting her lips part in pleasure as her fingernails scratched all the right places on her head and she grabbed a nearby bucket with water to wash away the soap.

She didn't know if the water was for that but it smelled and looked clean enough to be used for her needs. After adding conditioner to her soaked her and washing it off, Ariel looked around for her towel and forced herself out of the bathtub before her skin became wrinkly.

The girl carefully stepped out of the water, making sure not to slip and crack her head open and wrapped the white towel around herself tightly.

"Adrianne, what can I-" Her eyes widened as she noticed that Adrianne wasn't in her room, but she did have another visitor, "what are you doing here?!"

Hades rolled his eyes, forcing his eyes away from her inviting skin and snapped, "It's my castle; I can be wherever I want."

She scowled at him, panicking as she couldn't find her clothes. "Haven't you ever heard of privacy or are you too high and mighty for that too? You need to knock on people's doors before barging in like a psycho pervert!"

He chuckled, admiring the way her slightly wet cheeks began to turn pink and her long damp black hair stuck to her face. "I could be a pervert it you wish."

She glared at him, tightening her hold on the towel until her knuckles turned deathly white and seethed, "What the hell do you want?!"

The humour vanished from his alluring blue eyes, turning into anger as he clenched his jaw and growled, "Do not speak to me that way!" Ariel simply rolled her eyes, but shut her lips, "I came to tell you that you have to get ready for tonight."

"What's tonight?"

He narrowed his eyes at her, running his fingers through his smooth black hair. "If you impatient human had let me finished, you would have known." She breathed out loudly, making him grit his teeth in annoyance and said, "The Gods are throwing a celebration tonight. Something about not being in harm's way anymore or whatever; you have to go because you are the guest of honour."

"I'm not going," she began, but the God cut her off.

"Yes you are!" His voice boomed and she swore the walls shook in complaint of his anger. His blue eyes glazed with fury as he stared at her, somehow looking more alluring than ever before. "The Gods command you to."

Ariel rolled her eyes, crossing her arms over her chest as she stared at him with narrowed eyes. "You cannot tell me what to do; I am not your prisoner."

In less than a second, Hades was before her, merely inches away from her face as he hissed, "Like I said yesterday, you being my prisoner can be arranged."

Ariel gulped, forcing the strangely tempting smell of the furious God out of her system before she did something that she'd later on regret. She blinked repeatedly, trying to clear out her thoughts and cleared her throat, yet her voice still cracked. "I cannot go to this party-"

Hades raised his hand to grab unto her jaw and make her oblige to his command, but she rushed out, "-because I've nothing to wear!"

He frowned, lowering his hand slowly and cleared his throat. "You, uh, you what?"

Ariel sighed; cocking her hip as she stared at him annoyed and said, "I don't have a dress. I'm not going to a party without clothes."

"Oh," Hades stepped away from her, unable to keep her mouth-watering scent out of his fogged thoughts, "yeah. I'll...I'll get someone for that."

"Thank you," she mumbled out as he turned around and slammed the door behind him. Ariel sat down on the bed, releasing out a breath that she didn't know she was holding and bit her bottom lip.

She couldn't exactly say why, but the way Hades' gorgeous blue eyes raked over her body angrily made her feel hotter than Tartarus. She wanted to drop her towel and beg him to take out his frustrations using her body sexually.

She was never one for pain and pleasure, but the God made her feel angry at horny all at the same time. And she had only been with him for a day and a half! What would happen to her if they spent any more time together?!

"Milady?" Adrianne walked in, holding a white robe in her hands and smiled, "Here, you can wear these until your tailor arrives."

Ariel nodded, taking the robe in her hands quickly and waited for Adrianne to turn around so she could slide it on. She breathed out, hanging the towel on the chair before the vanity mirror and sat down on the bed. "Honestly, why is he such a jerk? I haven't even done anything to him and he just treats me like I'm trash! Is it because he hasn't gotten laid?"

Adrianne puckered her lips, frowning as she tried to figure out something in her head and then slowly said, "Well...I guess that could be part of the problem."

She laughed, sitting up to look at the girl and said, "Are you serious?! What happened to Telephone or whatever her name was? Isn't she his wife?"

Adrianne shook her head, pursing her lips and whispered, "It is forbidden to speak of it, Ariel; I'm sorry."

"Aw," she frowned, "come on! You're my aid; you're supposed to tell me things like these."

"I cannot," she shook her head again, walking over to the bathroom and said, "my loyalty to Master Hades is beyond what you believe. I cannot break his rules."

Ariel groaned, curiosity eating at her insides like a starved animal. Curiosity killed the cat...but she was already in the Underworld...it couldn't exactly kill her, right? "You make it sound like you owe him your life!"

Adrianne shrugged, sitting on a small chair near the door and said, "I don't, but if I break his rules then my family will suffer in Tartarus for my sins. So please, milady," she begged, "do not ask furthermore."

Ariel sighed, nodding her head but before she could speak, the door opened once more to reveal a gorgeous woman with curly black hair and a warm smile.

"Ariel is it?" She nodded as the woman walked further in the room, "I'm Athena; my grumpy uncle called me down here because he said you needed a dress for tonight's party." A grin overtook her lips as she stood in the middle of the room, "Lucky for you, I am the world's best seamstress."

6

Chapter 6

"Alright," Athena knelt down, grabbing a silver needle from the floor, before piercing it through the gorgeous silk fabrics that hung from Ariel's body. "Turn around really quick; I need to see the back."

She did as she was told, careful not to step on Athena's masterpiece and began to look around the room aimlessly. The Goddess of Wisdom was beautiful and very reserved; she hadn't spoken much after introducing herself and the silence was making Ariel's skin itch.

Athena asked what colours she would like her dress to be, but she did not ask her about the design, leaving Ariel curious and grouchy. She was tempted to ask why Hades was such an asshole, but Adrianne's presence prevented her from doing so.

Ever since she questioned her about Persephone's presence, Adrianne refused to talk to her much. The sentences were curt and short, somewhat like Ariel spoke when she was in New York, but now that it was done to her, she didn't favour it.

"Well," Athena stood back, running her fingers through her hair before tying it back into a ponytail, "it's all done, but you can't look until after Adrianne is done with your hair."

Ariel frowned, biting her bottom lip and muttered, "That's not fair...what if I don't like it?"

The Goddess let out a loud chortle, shaking her head as she waved her fingers slowly and the needles slowly slid out of the fabric. To her astonishment, she felt the fabric strings tying themselves together, wrapping around her curves and Athena clasped her hands together.

"Adrianne, will you please go and fetch some hair products Aphrodite left in the foyer?"

She nodded, bowing her head and slipped out of the room quietly. Once Ariel knew she was out of hearing distance, she cleared her throat and looked at Athena. "Why is Hades so...?"

"Ignorant? Impatient? Misunderstanding? Grumpy?" The Goddess finished, grinning goofily.

"Yeah," Ariel laughed, "that."

Athena sighed, sitting down before the covered vanity mirror and turned to face Ariel. "It has to do with my uncle's ex-wife." Ariel frowned, finding that the Gods divorced, to be humorous, "Persephone is a cold bitch," she whispered, "and it is forbidden to speak about it, but since you live here now, I might as well tell you."

Ariel nodded, biting the inside of her cheek in excitement and she continued. "Well about a decade ago, my uncle found Persephone cheating on him with some mortal man. Mind you, my uncle is very faithful and he had only done everything he could to make Persephone happy, so when he found her betraying him, he was heartbroken."

She widened her eyes in surprise, completely taken aback at the information. She was mostly surprised to know that Hades was faithful and he had been heartbroken. "But," she frowned, "I thought that he was going to cheat on Persephone with a nymph?"

Athena laughed, shaking her head, "Those are silly mortal tales; my uncle is the only faithful man up here," she frowned, a quirky smile on her lips as she mumbled, "or down here, whatever," she cleared her throat, "so Persephone was lucky to have him. He would shower her with precious gemstones every day, making sure that she received only the best, but that bitch," she spat, "turned her back to him."

Ariel blinked slowly, awkwardly standing in the middle of the room uncomfortably. She had been standing for only ten minutes, since the Goddess worked extremely fast, but she had been in awkward poses most of the time.

"And she didn't cheat on him only once," Athena scoffed, "she betrayed him with almost all the gods, even Aphrodite."

"What?" Ariel felt her jaw falling open.

"Yeah," Athena rolled her eyes, "Aphrodite doesn't discriminate, when someone offers her sex, she takes it. Anyways, Persephone left my uncle and he's been heartless ever since. He hasn't looked at a woman or even desired her; they are all useless to him. So don't take it personal if he's an asshole."

"Wow," she breathed out, feeling her cheeks heat up with unknown embarrassment. Just as she was to open her mouth and continue the conversation, Adrianne pushed the door open, smiling widely as she entered with the beauty equipment.

Her jaw fell open. The woman in the vanity mirror was not her. There was no way she could be so beautiful and unrecognizable.

Her long black hair was curled almost to perfection, the ringlets falling over her shoulders beautifully. On her head she wore a thin flower crown with dark green leaves and light purple peonies.

A long thin golden coloured tunic hugged her body, adjusting to her curves majestically. The dress was sleeveless but had thin straps tied around her neck. The fabric shone softly with glitter and felt so smooth under her fingers, she feared it'd melt.

Ariel blinked slowly, turning to Athena with wide eyes. "This...this is so beautiful!"

Athena laughed, happiness glistening in her grey eyes and she held a box up to her. "Of course it is, child! What'd you expect?" Ariel grinned, taking the box in her hands and timidly opened it. The Goddess peered down at her, a slow smile growing on her lips as she whispered, "I thoughtyou might want a pair."

"Thank you," she breathed, loving the feel of the elbow-length gloves. They were as delicate and beautiful as her dress and coloured a bit lighter than it, almost a champagne colour.

Adrianne emerged from the bathroom, holding three bottles of perfume and placed them in front of the girl. "Here, milady," she smiled, "smell these and choose your favourite."

Ariel nodded and sprayed each of the perfumes on the air once. The second one was her favourite. The first one was too rich and musky; almost making her feel like an older woman and the third one was too fruity.

Her choice felt perfect; a mix between fruits and flowers. The smell made her feel delirious and content.

"Are you done?" Hades pushed the door open, startling the three women with his sudden entrance. As his eyes fell on Ariel, they widened, slowly raking over each of her features.

Her green eyes were extremely accentuated by her eye shadow, almost making them seem beautifully surreal and her lips had a soft natural pink colour to them. She almost looked like one of his own; a goddess.

"Master Hades!" Adrianne chastised, "You mustn't enter a lady's room without her consent!"

His eyes snapped away from the beautiful woman and to his servant. The small girl had her hands on her hips, glaring up at her Master with a playful yet serious tone underlying her voice. He cleared his throat, scratching his neck awkwardly and mumbled, "It's my castle."

Athena laughed, shaking her head and said, "Uncle, what if Ariel was naked?"

He shrugged; his icy blue eyes making shivers run down the girl's back, making her truly feel naked. "Then, she'd be naked. It's not like I've never seen a woman's anatomy before."

"Yeah," Ariel snapped, glaring up at him, "but this woman wants a bit of privacy. So please learn to knock on the darned door before you barge in. At least warn me so I can cover myself with the nearest thing."

Hades stared at her, his blue eyes turning darker with anger and in a clipped tone of voice, replied, "It's not like you have anything I'd like to see."

Before Ariel opened her mouth to put him in his place, Athena sighed, sliding her hand down her face and said, "That is not the point, uncle. Just knock on the door before you enter, alright? Now, do you like what Adrianne and I made?"

He shrugged, seeming disinterested and said, "She looks decent. At least she won't stick out."

Adrianne huffed, crossing her arms over her chest and glared at him. Ariel blushed, wishing she could say that his words did not affect her. Even if she didn't like the God, he was an extremely attractive man. It kind of hit her ego a bit.

"Fine," Hades rolled his eyes, acting more like a child than the god he truly was, "the human looks pretty nice. Now can we go? My chariot isn't going to wait for her forever."

Ariel gritted her teeth, wanting to smash his head unto the bureau and slid her hands in the gloves. Everyone in the room watched silently as she enclosed her hands and she wished they would stop staring.

She held her head up high in confidence, feeling like the Queen she seemed and walked past Hades brusquely. He widened his eyes, watching her retreating figure and wondered how a mortal woman could be so gorgeous and so deadly at the same time.

Ariel stopped a couple of feet away from the room, an annoyed look crossing her features as she turned to look back at Hades. "Were you not rushing me?"

His eyes snapped away from her voluptuous curves and he nodded, gritting his teeth in anger. Anger at himself and at her. Inside he was a hurricane of emotions; he wanted to grab her and ravish her delectable body while at the same time, he wished to crush her with his bare hands.

Hades led the way, never glancing behind to make sure she was still following or opening doors for her. He wasn't behaving like the gentleman she wished he was. He wasn't behaving like the ridiculously good-looking man he was; a pig fit more of his actions.

And only his actions. His looks were far too godly to be compared to such a low animal.

His jet black hair was slicked back, exposing his strong forehead and straight nose. His icy blue eyes were accompanied by long eyelashes and light facial whiskers. He was the epitome of dangerously handsome.

Ariel inhaled a short gasp, widening her eyes as she halted in front of a magnificent chariot, standing right in front of Hades throne, exactly where she had first met him. It was black with gorgeous grand stallions and a plush purple seating. Hades narrowed his eyes at her astonishment and took her gloved hand in his as he pulled her up the stairs.

"Looking at something won't get you anywhere," he glowered at her.

She sighed, biting back her tongue and placed her hands on her lap. Her small feet were enclosed by a pair of comfortable champagne coloured sandals and her toes were painted a light purple.

"Close your eyes," Hades commanded, his voice powerful but soft.

Ariel nodded, closing her eyes and whispered, "Why?"

He spoke in a language she did not recognize softly, commanding his horses to make their journey above his kingdom and turned to her. "There are certain things that a mortal cannot see and you'll most likely pass out from how fast we're travelling."

She gulped visibly and tightened her hold on her fingers. She was tempted to open her eyes and sneak a peek, but the slight movement of the chariot forced her to follow the god's order. She did not feel air brushing past her cheeks or heard anything, other than the soft gallop of the horses.

With her eyes closed, she frowned. "You don't have reigns on your horses...why?"

Hades watched her, wanting to ease the crease between her eyebrows and clenched his fist in anger. She was a mortal, a woman. He couldn't let himself get persuaded by lust for a woman again. "They are wild animals; they require no usage of reigns."

"Then how do you control them?" she bit her bottom lip, making his blue eyes darken with lust. She seemed so delicate and soft, his hands wanted to travel all around her body just to feel if she really was as soft as she seemed.

"I put my trust in them and they trust me. We are sort of like...one. I give them directions of where to go and I let them run freely to this place."

Ariel pouted her lips, wanting to open her eyes to look at him, but wasn't sure if they had reached their destination. "That doesn't make sense..."

Hades sighed, fixing his black suit jacket. "They are my horses, human, they follow my orders and in exchange, I let them run freely and be their own 'person.' It's a win-win situation."

She nodded, still not understanding his logic but decided not to press the matter further. Hades looked away from her, watching the different colours of the human world speed by him and then glanced at her.

In the soft glow of the moonlight, she almost seemed surreal and his lust for her augmented, making his ethereal-like blue eyes, swirl with different emotions.

"I've something for you," he cleared his throat, the rim of his ears turning a light shade of pink as he dug in his pant pockets for the jewellery box. Seeing that she was still looking away from him, with her eyes closed, Hades growled lowly, making the hairs on her arm stand. "Look at me."

"Are we there yet?" She squeaked, feeling her heart thudding quickly in her chest.

"Yes," Hades snapped, glaring at her as she looked at him. "Here, it'll protect you in case of danger. If anyone wishes to harm you, you'll be sent straight to your room in my castle."

Ariel nodded, lightly tracing the beautiful necklace.

It was a simple black chain with a dark ruby pendant hanging from the middle. It looked almost normal, until she placed it against her skin and it glowed a soft red. Not too noticeable to ruin her elegant look, but enough to warn anyone whom wished to harm her.

"Thank you," she whispered sincerely as he took her elbow and pulled her out of the chariot.

Hades nodded, grunting in return and took a deep breath. He could only hope that the gathering would end quickly so he wouldn't need to see the splendour of the young girl. At least in his castle, he could escape from her presence.

She frowned, looking around in confusion. The room they were at was dark and empty. For a moment, she feared he had actually taken her out of his kingdom to kill her, but as Hades began to speak some words in his native tongue, under his breath, torches began to lighten the suite.

A sly smirk grew on his lips as she gasped in astonishment. The place was gorgeous with high ceilings and an extravagant golden chandelier hanging from it. Exquisite and intricate paintings adorned the walls and a red wine carpet added the finishing touches to the pale-yellow room.

Hundreds of gods and goddesses danced around the room, livening up the place. Loud rhythmic music echoed throughout, vibrating against Ariel's body and she grinned up at Hades. Sweet aromas filled the air, almost making her feel lightheaded with delight and he wrapped his arm around her, pulling her upright against his body.

He forgot that the sweet scent of ambrosia to mortals was strong and almost suffocating. It would take a bit to adjust but for Ariel it would be like a drug that she didn't necessarily mind.

The Moirai stared at the young woman, their eyes following her and the god of the underworld as they made their way further into the room. A slow smile grew on Clotho's lips and she grabbed the thin silver thread from her coat.

"Oh she'll do," she whispered affectionately as she turned to her sisters, "we've found the other half."

Lachesis rolled her eyes, pursing her thin, chapped lips and croaked, "Are you sure she's the one, this time?"

"Yeah," Atropos chimed in, "last time, we messed up big time!"

Ariel widened her eyes, feeling overwhelmed by how beautiful everyone seemed. She felt like she had stepped into a room filled with drop-dead gorgeous models.

Some of the gods she could recognize by their actions.

Dionysus, the God of wine was standing on a table, drinking a beverage from a red bottle and dancing to the Macarena. He was wearing dark jeans and a loose Hawaiian shirt and even in his comfortable and non-casual attire, he was extremely handsome.

Ares, the God of war, was dressed in his full armour, the bulging muscles of his arms looking intimidatingly attractive. His eyes were dark and a long scar ran down the side of his face, yet it did nothing to affect his beauty.

He let out a loud cry of triumph as he slammed down the arm of his opponent in arm-wrestling and laughed contagiously, when the men surrounding him patted his back congratulating his victory.

Aphrodite was wearing a gorgeous red gown, revealing most of her body as she strutted down the aisle of watching men. Saliva literally poured down the side of their mouth as she smiled sultrily at them, obviously leaving a long-lasting effect on the poor souls.

Her gorgeous golden hair was style into a crown, adorning her head with a diamond tiara sitting atop her hair. Her thick lips were fully glossed with a dark red, making her look so beautiful; Ariel almost felt a pang of jealousy. After all, the goddess was the deity of beauty and love.

Poseidon, the God of the sea, had a beautiful woman standing next to him, Amphitrite. He was wearing a long blue tunic, almost looking exactly like the sea and the woman next to him wore a similar dress, except more feminine and with pearls around her waist.

Hades pulled her further into the room, nodding courteously at his family members and led his companion to the drinks. "Would you like anything?"

Ariel shook her head, still looking around the extravagant suite and smiled at Hermes, whom began walking towards her. "Hermes!"

He laughed, dimples appearing on his cheeks and said, "I didn't think you'd be so happy to see me. After all, I did leave you stranded in hell."

She rolled her eyes, letting out a small laugh as Hades narrowed his eyes in annoyance. Hermes laughed at his expression and patted his shoulder playfully. "Oh, lighten up, Hades, this is a celebration! Now," he turned to Ariel, "would you like to dance?"

She bit her bottom lip, leaning more towards a negative answer, but Hermes pouted his lips, trying to persuade her to say otherwise.

She sighed, rolling her eyes with a small smile on her lips and said, "Fine. But not too much, I haven't danced in a really long time."

The girl turned around to look at Hades, who shrugged and drank his ambrosia quietly. The jealousy he felt eating his insides was absurd. Hermes was one of his own; Ariel wasn't. He shouldn't feel so territorial over a girl he had just met.

"So," Hermes began as he placed his hands on her waist, "how's Hades treating you?"

She shrugged, not wanting to badmouth the god and said, "I barely see him. I spend most of my time with Adrianne."

"Mm," he cocked his head as he looked down at her, "really? I figured he'd make your life miserable. He was not content when Poseidon suggested that you'd stay with him."

Ariel pursed her lips, placing her chin on his shoulder and muttered, "Does he hate me that much?"

Hermes shook his head, trying to fasten his pace as the beat began to quicken and said, "No, Hades doesn't hate you. He's just very..." he trailed off and cleared his throat, "How do I put this? He hates everyone."

She laughed, her cheeks turning a slight shade of pink as Hermes winked down at her playfully and said, "I just think that his hatred for me is bigger than the rest."

He shrugged, spinning her away from him and then back. "Mm, I don't know. They do say that the line between hatred and love is extremely thin..."

Her cheeks turned an even darker shade of red and she widened her eyes, almost choking on air. "W-what? Heaven forbid! Hades looks like the type of man that could never love anything other than himself."

"You'd be surprised," Hermes muttered quietly, seeming deep in thought.

"Did someone say heaven?" A tall man with broad shoulders and a thick Grecian accent chuckled, grinning down at the couple.

"Zeus!" Hermes laughed, releasing Ariel to clasp his father's hand and gave him a light hug. "This is Ariel. Ariel," he turned to the blushing girl, "this is Zeus."

She smiled, bowing her head in respect and said, "It's a pleasure to meet you, Zeus."

"Don't flatter him, darling," A woman chuckled beside him, "or his head might explode. I'm Hera, this idiot's wife."

"Hey," he frowned, pouting his lips down at his wife and puffed out his chest, "I'm a manly idiot."

Hera rolled her light grey eyes, smiling warmly at Ariel and said, "How are things with Hades, darling? Do you need me to put him in his place?"

She laughed, shaking her head and said, "No, ma'am. He's been...the nicest he could be."

The goddess laughed, flipping back her chocolate coloured hair and winked her way. She caught the hidden message. Before she could keep on conversing, a shy woman linked her arm with hers and pulled her away.

"Will you ask her to dance?" Eros raised his eyebrows, taking a sip from the red wine.

Hades widened his eyes, glaring at him and said, "What?"

He rolled his eyes, nodding towards a laughing Ariel and said, "Are you going to ask the girl to dance?"

"Why would I do that?" He scowled, gulping down the goblet of wine.

Eros gave him a look, narrowing his eyes and said, "Hades, there is a reason why I'm the god of love. I'm good at what I do and you, my friend," he nodded his head at him and then at Ariel, "want that girl."

"I do not!" He spat, looking completely disgusted. "I don't even know her! Besides she's a mortal woman. I don't mess with her kind."

The god snorted, shaking his head at the naivety of the king of the underworld and said, "Hades, there are some things that we're good at, right? Ares is good at destroying anything on his way. Dionysus is good at getting drunk and throwing a good party. You're good at keeping the souls of the dead in your kingdom and me?" He gave a light chuckle, "Well, I specialize in these kinds of things. Trust me, man, no matter how much you try to deny it, you want her."

Hades growled, tightening his hold on the golden goblet and hissed, "I don't want her, Eros!"

"Fine," he shrugged, running his fingers through his thick blonde hair, "if you don't want her, then ask her to dance."

"I will!" Hades stood up, stalking over to Ariel and realizing half-way, that the god of love had tricked him. He turned back, glaring at Eros, whom chuckled and raised his cup in the air.

"Told you," he mouthed, turning back to fill his cup with more wine.

Hades rolled his eyes, tapping Hermes on his shoulder and cleared his throat awkwardly as the couple turned to look at him. "Want to dance with me?"

Ariel widened her eyes, her heart beating quickly in her chest and blinked quickly. Hermes laughed, literally handing her over and winked at the girl. She bit her bottom lip, slowly nodding and croaked, "Y-yeah."

The god nodded his head once, awkwardly placing his hands on her small waist and growled silently at the warmth that quickly spread throughout him. She felt almost perfect, but so had Persephone and it left him heartless.

At the thought of his ex-wife, Hades tensed, making Ariel clear her throat and tilt her head to whisper in his ear, "Are you alright?"

"I don't like dancing," he replied, glaring at Eros who began making kissy faces.

"Oh," she frowned as he dipped her and then spun her around the dance room. His hands wrapped around her waist again, pulling her into his muscular chest and she felt her heart soaring.

The feel of his masculine chest was amazing. She hadn't been so close to a man in almost four years and now that she was, it had to be with a man that couldn't stand the sight of her.

They danced for a while longer, swaying to the upbeat music and even laughed a couple of times at the foolishness of Dionysus. Hades even cracked a few jokes, surprising the girl with his humour and laughter. If there was a possibility that the god of the dead could laugh more, he'd be even more beautiful than he was. It almost hurt Ariel how gorgeous he was.

He didn't leave her side a lot. He actually liked being near her. She was warm and quiet, the complete opposite of what he thought she'd be. She even seemed to enjoy his company and Hades could only smile in triumph.

While the god grabbed another alcoholic drink, Zeus kept the girl company, sparking an interesting conversation.

"I don't get it," Ariel began quietly, looking at Zeus confusedly, "if I am such a danger to you guys; why don't you just kill me?"

"Yeah," a female voice spoke from beside them, "why don't you just kill her, Zeus?"

The God rolled his dark blue eyes, turning his body so it wasn't facing the intruder and muttered, "Persephone, what a pleasure."

The woman laughed, throwing back her fiery red hair and said, "Oh come on now, Zeus, don't be such a stranger!" She pressed a lingering kiss to his cheek, leaving a deeper meaning behind as she stared at him with dark eyes. "Are you going to introduce me to the 'guest of honour'?"

He adjusted his tie, clearing his throat uncomfortably and motioned to Ariel. "Ariel, this is Persephone, the goddess of spring growth. Persephone, this is Ariel."

Persephone turned to her, forcing a smile on her lips and said, "I'm guessing you're Hades' new toy, eh?"

Ariel raised her eyebrows, letting out a soft chuckle and surprised herself as she spoke confidently. "Sorry to disappoint, but I don't take sloppy leftovers."

The goddess pursed her lips, visibly angered at the mortal woman standing before her and turned to Zeus. "Well, if you'll excuse me, I'm going to mingle with the rest of the family."

The god nodded, grimacing as she walked away and turned back to Ariel. "Sorry you had to deal with her. Persephone isn't the...nicest person at first; especially since you're staying with her ex-husband."

She shrugged, taking a sip of the delicious wine and said, "Don't apologize, I've encountered much worse."

Zeus raised his eyebrows at her, watching her carefully before clearing his throat and said, "We cannot kill you because there is no use. The power you hold is etched unto your soul, which cannot be killed. Therefore, if we kill you, we will do nothing but free your soul to what could be dangerous hands."

"Oh," Ariel frowned, staring down at her gloved hands and nodded slowly, "that...yeah. I understand."

"Would you like to dance?"

"Uh," she smiled up at him kindly, bowing in respect and said, "if you don't mind, I want to sit for a bit, my feet hurt." She actually just wanted to spend time with Hades; he had surprisingly been a lovely company through the night.

He nodded, muttering a goodbye and made his way to his wife. Hera grinned at him, waving at the young woman. Usually the goddess would have been jealous that her husband spoke with other women, but she could tell that neither was interested in each other more than friends.

Ariel sighed, searching through the crowd of frenzied gods for Hades. She wanted to start heading back to the castle, if she was allowed. Her feet couldn't take any more suffering and her body craved the soft feeling of her bed.

Just as she was going to ask someone for help, her eyes found the jet black hair that seemed to stand out from the crowd. Hades was facing away from her, speaking heatedly to a person that Ariel couldn't make out.

She squinted her eyes, trying to make out the mysterious woman and felt herself gritting her teeth. The only redhead in the entire place was placing her hands on the god, making a strange sense of jealousy boil deep within Ariel's centre.

Persephone grinned wickedly at her, her brown eyes shimmering in triumph as she kissed her ex-husband.

Ariel rolled her eyes, returning the grin and flipped her off.

7

CHAPTER 7

Ariel placed her hands on her stomach, entwining her fingers together as she closed her eyes and began to reminisce about the previous night. A smile grew on her lips slowly as she remembered how Hermes managed to uplift her spirits after she saw Persephone kissing Hades.

She did not know why she felt envious or even sadden by their actions since she was nothing to him, except a burden, but nonetheless, she still hurt. She felt angry at herself for feeling jealous and even wanting to claw Persephone's eyes out for rubbing it in her face that she had the gorgeous god.

But she was also proud at herself.

She didn't show Persephone how she truly felt. She smiled and flipped her off, clearly angering the Goddess, who figured she'd receive a different type of outcome.

She was also grateful for the company of Hermes. He was one of the nicest gods present and he treated her like an equal, which surprised her. She'd figure that he'd think of her as a lesser person, but he explained that she was humble and powerful; he admired that quality of hers.

Adrianne entered her chambers, pushing a silver cart and smiled at her, "What's got you in such high spirits, milady?"

Ariel grinned, swinging her legs to the side of the bed and said, "Good morning, Adrianne! And I'm just really happy, I mean, here I am; living another beautiful day."

The girl laughed, shaking her head as she poured orange juice on a cup for her and unveiled the silver platters. Ariel squealed in delight at the sight and smell of the delicious fruits she had so quickly grown fond of and stood up to walk to the cart.

She popped a piece of freshly cut strawberry in her mouth and let out a moan. Her day had begun so amazing; she could only hope it kept getting better. This was a few of the first times she ever felt this happy.

Ever since the incident three years ago, she forced herself to be miserable, but now she felt alive; content. Ironically, she was in the kingdom of the undead. Maybe that was why. She was deadly, maybe she felt at home with death so near.

"Well," Adrianne tucked back her curly hair, "I am glad you are content. I haven't seen many happy people around here for a long time; it's refreshing."

"Of course you haven't," Ariel pointed out, swallowing back the delicious kiwi strips, "this place is super dull. You guys have no music and the king of this place is a grumpy man."

The servant girl gave out a quiet laugh, genuinely feeling grateful that she had some company other than the other workers and said, "Hopefully things will begin changing for the better."

Ariel shrugged, licking her lips as the juices of the fruits began to slide down her fingers. She let out a content sigh, unable to keep the smile off her face and walked over to the vanity mirror. "This décor is so gorgeous; even though he's an ass, Hades has great taste in decorating."

"Well, he wanted the best for his wife," Adrianne shrugged, slowly widening her eyes as she realized what she said.

She frowned, slowly turning around to look at her and cleared her throat. "W-what did you say?"

Adrianne shook her head quickly, grabbing the silver cart and began to walk out of the room. Ariel glared at her, gritting her teeth and a little more forcefully said, "Adrianne, what did you say?"

"N-nothing," she stuttered, gulping loudly. She should have been watching what she said more carefully. Now she had angered the girl and Master Hades would be pissed as well. Way to ruin her friend's day.

"This was Persephone's room?" Ariel hissed through gritted teeth, clenching her hands at her sides.

"Yes," Adrianne sighed, dejectedly, "it is why the décor and soaps are so nice. Mrs. Persephone designed the room to her liking and after she left, Master Hades didn't bother to change it."

"So," she said, "he gave me his ex-wife's room?" The anger in her tone was clearer than water. Adrianne could practically feel the angry waves emanating from her pores. Her bright green eyes were shining with such anger, they almost looked glazed; her pupils were smaller than normal.

"That…that repugnant asshole," the more she spoke, the louder her voice became, "gave me the room where his whore-of-a-wife slept in?! Is he trying to say something by that?!"

"Milady," the quiet girl quickly began, "it is not that bad! I cleaned it before you got here and it's been vacant for ten years! Please do not give it much thought."

"Take me to him," Ariel crossed her arms over her chest, her heart beating about a thousand miles per hour. Her hands were sweating and trembling as the unusual emotion took over her. She suddenly felt suffocated by how angry she was. It may have been childish, but she was tempted to throw a hissy fit because she knew no other way to release her anger.

"Mi-"

"Take. Me. To. Him," Ariel gritted out. Her teeth were so suppressed against each other; she feared they might shatter under the force, but her anger overcame any other feeling she could have possibly felt.

If Persephone had been a nice woman, Ariel wouldn't have minded residing in the room, but the goddess was far from nice. She had only spoken to her for a couple of seconds and automatically received the vibe: bitch.

Even a blind man could see that the Goddess despised her—and she knew not why. Another benefactor to her anger could have been the jealousy she felt the previous night.

Persephone had kissed Hades in front of her as if trying to get a point across and that made Ariel angrier than ever before. She was not usually an angry person, but she was jealous. The two went hand-in-hand in that situation.

Adrianne nodded, letting out a soft sigh and lead her to Hades' throne.

The God sat comfortably in the sleek black seat, looking extremely concentrated as he read some papers in his hands. If she hadn't been so infuriated at him for making her sleep in his ex-wife's room, she would have thought him to be attractive, but she was too irritated.

She crossed her arms over her chest, resting most of her weight on her right foot and glared up at the attractive God. "Ahem!"

Hades slowly looked up, his blue eyes boring into hers as he searched for a reason for her intrusion and let out an annoyed sigh. "What do you want?"

Ariel muttered obscenities under her breath, holding back the urge to snort and took a deep breath. "There are a lot of things I want, but if I tell you, we'll be here all eternity and I'm sure as heck that we don't want to spend that much time with each other."

He rolled his eyes, folding his papers and they disappeared with a flick of his wrist. He then stared at her, resting his chin on his fingers as he looked down at her with a bored-like expression. "The feeling is mutual, human, and unlike you, I actually have all eternity."

She bit her bottom lip, wanting to curse at him for making her feel inferior, but knew that she was not going to act like a child. "It's a good thing that not all the gods are like you."

He scowled, still looking as attractive as he could be and said, "What?"

Ariel shrugged, nonchalantly waving her hand around and said, "Oh, nothing. I just said that luckily for you, the rest of the gods are extremely nice."

"What the hell is that supposed to mean?" he bit out.

"No one would worship them if they acted like you," she grinned cheekily, feeling triumphant as Hades growled and glared down at her as if she were the dirtiest scum in the world.

"Just because I don't act like Hermes does with you," He glowered, "doesn't mean that I'm not nice. I am nice, just not to people I don't like."

Ariel let out a laugh, crossing her arms over her chest again and said, "What does Hermes have to do in any of this?" A slow mischievous smile grew on her lips and she cooed, "Is the big bad God of the Underworld jelly?"

"Jelly?" He scoffed, "I am not a topping."

She rolled her eyes, biting the inside of her cheek to prevent from laughing. He looked genuinely lost and it made him even more attractive than he already was; it was unbelievable. "You're jealous."

"Jealous of what?" Hades raised his eyebrows, staring down at her with interest.

The girl shrugged, running her fingers through her hair and said, "I don't know; you tell me. You're the one that's bringing Hermes into his conversation."

"Whatever," he muttered. "What did you come here for?"

The anger that had vanished for mere seconds, suddenly returned, fuelling her insides with such hatred that she trembled. "The room I am sleeping in."

He raised a perfectly arched eyebrow, running his fingers through his dishevelled hair and said, "What about it?"

"What about it?" Ariel repeated incredulously, "I am sleeping in the room of a shrew!"

Hades clenched his jaw, his muscles visibly contracted, making it look stronger than it already was. "What?"

She rolled her eyes, glaring up at him and hissed, "Oh you heard me! Don't play dumb! I want you to give me another room. There is no way in hell that I am sleeping another night in there. The longer I breathe that air, the more I feel myself susceptible to diseases."

"Funny," Hades said, "you are in hell."

Her glare intensified, making him chuckle at how adorable she seemed. She wasn't taller than 5'5 and her height made her seem even more childish than her actions proved. In her eyes, she was a child that knew nothing of what she spoke.

But what she truly felt was different.

If he wasn't immortal, she'd kill him with her glare. There was nothing than infuriated her more than someone not taking her seriously.

"Just get me another room," she hissed out, clenching her fists at her sides.

"No."

"What?!" She widened her eyes in disbelief. "I'm not asking you for another life, dammit! I just want a fucking room that Persepho-bitch hasn't been in!"

"Persepho-what?" He chuckled, his eyes shining with mirth.

Ariel felt her cheeks turning red in embarrassment and mumbled, "Persephobitch."

"Who's that?" His grin widened, amusement clear in his face as he watched her curiously.

She rolled her eyes, scowling up at him and said, "Your ex-wife, you know? The woman you were making out with yesterday?"

His amused smile quickly disappeared and he scratched the back of his neck uncomfortably. "You, ah, you saw that?"

Ariel gave out a cold laugh, shaking her head in disbelief and said, "Honey, even the blind people thousands of feet underneath me, saw that."

Hades rolled his eyes at her sarcasm and cleared his throat, "That was a stupid mistake, she threw herself at me."

"I don't care," she hissed out, but her heart skipped a beat and she chose to ignore the butterflies that began to soar within her stomach. "Just give me another room."

"No," Hades repeated, scowling at her, "there are no other available rooms."

"This is a damn castle for Pete's sake! How can there be no more rooms available?!"

He shrugged, tracing the armrest of his throne and challenged her with his eyes. She was kind of cute when she was pissed.

"I don't care!" Ariel cried out, the veins at the side of her neck popping out, "I don't care if I have to live inside the janitor's closet, but I'd rather live there than in her chambers! I'll probably catch some type of disease!"

Hades clenched his jaw, his fists closing at his sides and glared at her, "What are you insinuating?"

She rolled her eyes, throwing her hands up in the air and said, "Oh do you really need me to paint it out for you? Your pumpkin woman-wife-shit cheated on you and probably gave you AIDS! You expect me to sleep in the same damn room you locked her in?! Hell to the fucking no!"

In the blink of an eye, the infuriated God was standing in front of her, his hand wrapped around her neck and her back was pressed against the wall. His blue eyes were glowing so bright they made shivers run down her spine and his voice came out between a growl and something otherworldly.

It sounded nothing like she ever heard before and it terrified the hell out of her.

"Don't you ever dare disrespect a god! Do you understand me? I will have you thrown in the deepest, darkest depths of Tartarus—alive. I will make sure that you regret ever being born."

Ariel gasped for air, clawing at his hands and felt her face turning bright red. The anger coursing through her veins was preventing her from thinking clearly. At that moment, she wished he'd throw her in Tartarus; anything but being near him. "I already do."

Hades released his hold on her throat, widening his eyes at the red fingerprints he left behind and mentally scolded himself for allowing his inner beast to lash out at the innocent girl. She had just caught him at a bad moment! "Ariel..."

Her shaking fingers wrapped around her aching throat and she glanced up at him with wide green teary eyes. At that very second, she wished that he wasn't so damn good looking; it just made hating him all the harder.

It happened so fast, she didn't catch herself doing it and Hades didn't see it coming. She slapped her hand unto his cheek, leaving behind her fingerprints and croaked out, "Fuck you." Then she collapsed on the floor, allowing the darkness to envelop her.

Hades widened his eyes, quickly wrapping his arms around her and grunted as he pulled her up. A remorseful sigh escaped his mouth as he swung her up in his arms and tightened his hold around her waist.

He looked down at the girl, biting his bottom lip into his mouth and sighed again. She was truly a beautiful and magnificent creature; he just wanted to sit down and watch her, care for her—and these thoughts angered him.

She would certainly do the same thing Persephone did; she'd steal his heart and shatter it like it wasn't worth a penny. Ariel hadn't given him a reason to believe she'd do so, but he knew. All women were the same; the girl in his arms was no different.

Adrianne bowed her head in respect and quietly said, "Master Hades-"

"I know," the God interrupted, gulping as he continued to walk down the hallway, "I shouldn't have done that. I was justso angry, Adrianne! She's confusing the hell out of me—literally! I've not been able to focus on any of my obligations ever since she's arrived. What kind of king am I if I can't focus on my responsibilities because of a mere mortal woman!?"

The servant girl stayed quiet, not knowing what to say to the troubled man. He was in pain and the confusion growing within him just turned everything he felt into anger; she knew that much. But he also had to let go of his past and embrace what the Fates had given him.

A better second chance.

"Will you move her room?" She asked quietly.

Hades sighed, nodding and cradled her closer to his chest. She felt warm and perfect in his arms; he didn't want to let her go. It was as if she belonged to him—and he to her. "I am truly sorry for what I did, Adrianne. I did not mean to touch her that way; I've never hit a woman in my life. Not even Persephone. She just," he groaned, searching for the words that seemed not to reach him, "she confuses me! I don't...I don't know what I'm feeling when she speaks to me."

Adrianne bit the inside of her cheek, hoping that he couldn't notice the small smile growing on her lips and said, "Master Hades, it is not me whom you need to apologize to," she glanced down at the sleeping girl in his arms and whispered, "it is her."

He nodded, entering the small chamber and gently placed her on the bed. Ariel's head fell to the side uncomfortably and Hades gingerly adjusted her head to a better position. He sat next to her, tracing his strong fingers against the side of her face and sighed.

They lowered to the place where he assaulted her and he closed his eyes, feeling his heart aching and the confusion grew. He didn't know her; he shouldn't be feeling so protective and attracted to her.

Yet it had been ten long years without the touch of another woman. Maybe that's why he desired her so much or even felt like it was his responsibility to make sure she was safe. Clearly he needed a revaluation on what safe was because almost choking her to death was not it.

"Will you get me a wet cloth?" he whispered, not taking his eyes away from the sleeping girl.

Adrianne nodded and cleared her throat before whispering, "Perhaps you should speak to her, Master Hades, she seems to have a certain fancy towards you."

"Really?" He chuckled, gently caressing her high cheekbones.

"Yes," she nodded, "just apologize for almost killing her."

His eyes darkened and he nodded, tensing his shoulders and abruptly stopped the contact between his fingers and her wounded skin.

He couldn't describe how amazing it felt to touch her. Even when she just looked at him, he felt satisfied, even if her eyes were shining with hatred, she was at least looking at him. And it left him pathetically content.

A sigh rolled out of his lips as Adrianne returned with the cloth and left the room to leave them some privacy. Hades pressed the cloth around her face gently, wanting to erase the memories she had just experienced with him.

He had that power, but he couldn't bring himself to do so. He just wanted her to forgive him, not forget what he did. He respected her far too much to tamper with her memories; they belonged to her for a reason.

Hades pressed a soft kiss to her forehead, almost brushing his lips against her skin as soft as a loving whisper. "I am truly sorry for what I've done to you, human. I swear it wasn't my intention to hurt you. You just came to ask me at a wrong time; I was angry at Persephone for thinking she could just kiss her way back into my damn life. You were right, if gods could catch diseases," he chuckled softly, "she would have them all."

His fingers caressed her cheek gingerly, stroking the small pieces of black hair that would get caught around her face. She almost looked angelic underneath him and for a moment he knew that neither Pandora nor Helen of Troy were the most beautiful mortal women in the world; Ariel was.

"When you awake from your slumber, I swear on the river Styx to make it up to you. If you are going to be with me for a long time, we might as well try to be friends." Hades let out a soft sigh, holding back the urge to press his lips to hers and wished her a sweet sleep in his native tongue.

As he walked away, leaving her to her new room, Ariel smiled.

8

CHAPTER 8

Ariel groaned, feeling her muscles stretching to accommodate to her new position and grimaced once she heard her bones cracking. As she pulled back, she sighed contently, wiggling her toes in front of her.

It had been a long time that she had done her ballet stretches and she almost forgot how amazing it felt to stand in her pointe shoes. She wouldn't lie, the first day she wore them again, felt like hell. Her feet had grown accustomed to regular shoes and she hadn't forced her entire weight on her toes for years.

After a week, she managed to familiarize herself with the hard feel of her pointe shoes and was pirouetting around the small room admirably. To the unprofessional eye, she was as graceful as they came, but she knew she was far from her high standards.

Her toes wouldn't point the right direction or her knees were bent too far apart; there was always something wrong with her position, but the stringent thoughts helped keep her busy. Busy from thinking of him.

She closed her eyes, releasing a soft breath as she slowly stood up and placed her foot on the bed. She didn't have a barre to exercise with so she had to improvise with the limited amount of objects in her room.

She had no music to dance to, so she made her own. She sang, hummed and even imagined music to help her stay sane. Being stuck inside a small room for a week was far beyond pleasant. She was tempted to sneak out of her room, but she didn't want to anger Hades anymore.

That lesson was learned and the faint fingertips around her neck reminded her of her place. He didn't have the right to almost kill her, but she was overreacting. In her eyes, it was his fault as much as hers.

He should've placed her somewhere that Persephone hadn't been in. No man was stupid enough to commit that mistake, but Hades never ceased to amaze her. He was filled with surprises; pleasant and unkind, but surprises nonetheless.

After their horrid altercation, he moved her from Persephone's old room, but also stopped speaking to her. She hadn't seen him for an entire week and she was beginning to feel lonelier than she had when she actually lived alone.

Adrianne was usually quiet and was too afraid that something would happen to them, if they angered Hades again. It made Ariel feel like a child that needed a nanny. She had taken care of herself for three years; she could certainly do so for the rest of her life without any aid.

"Milady?" Adrianne knocked on the door gently, before pushing it open and smiling at her widely, "How are you? Would you like any lunch yet?"

Ariel shook her head, breathing out slowly as she used her entire upper body strength to pull herself upwards and stand en pointe.

Adrianne grimaced, watching as the woman managed to stand on the tip of her toes and begin walking around the small space in circles.

She bit her bottom lip, watching with cautious eyes and whispered, "Milady, I do not understand how you can possibly find that relaxing."

Her head fell back as she laughed and had to stand back on her feet to balance herself. "Why not? It helps me calm down and understand my emotions."

"But it looks painful," Adrianne scrounged her nose up and shook her head, "in my time, women wouldn't dare stand in that torturous position."

"Yeah," Ariel kept on laughing, "but they wore tight corsets and thick layers of dresses even if it was hotter than Tartarus."

The girl gave a small smile, watching as she began to unbutton the pale pink pointe shoes. Adrianne handed her a wet cloth to pass over her pained feet and waited for her to sit down on the bed. Ariel motioned with her hand for her to join and she sat down, waiting for further instructions.

"Adrianne," Ariel sighed, falling back on the small bed, "how was it like in your time? Like, how did you live? Did you like it? Were you ever in love?"

A knowing small grazed her lips and she found herself lying next to Ariel, with her hands over her stomach. Their bodies were in a parallel position, but their heads were next to each other's.

"It was nice," she began, "the smell was bad, compared to now's society, at least. But it was alright. I guess that if I had been rich, maybe I'd think that life back then wasn't as hard, but I unfortunately have been a servant all my life."

"Does it suck?" She genuinely asked, wanting to somehow comfort her.

Adrianne shrugged, closing her eyes as she tried to imagine her old life, but found it extremely difficult. Each life she lived began in a new body. She was reincarnated every time—and every time she had the same fate; death by a loved one.

"I do not believe it truly sucks, I can barely remember. I've been reborn so many times; it's a tad hard for me to keep track of all my lives. But I know that my first life wasn't very pleasant. I fell in love with a man and we planned to escape our peasant life. I didn't know how, but he said we would."

Ariel turned her head slightly to the left, watching as Adrianne spoke quietly of her past life. She was completely enthralled with the servant girl's, story that she wished Adrianne could remember them all. Her favourite subject had always been history.

"I faintly remember asking my Lady to lend me some curtains so I could sow my wedding dress. She surprisingly agreed and I happily began to make my dress. When Benjamin saw it, he became enraged. He had been drinking and tore it to shreds. He said that I deserved better than a curtain for a fabric. I was infuriated that he would rip my masterpiece to shreds, but I was so naively in love with him, that I didn't stand my ground. Besides, it wasn't in my nature to stand up to him. I belonged to him as soon as I said we could get married; that's how our laws worked."

She nodded, gasping at Benjamin's audacity to tear her dress apart, but understood the different customs in the time period.

Adrianne sighed again as she shrugged and whispered, "Benjamin came to our little home one night and told me he had become a pirate." Ariel gasped, suddenly remembering how she had been killed. "I told him that he needed to drop the job immediately, that I wouldn't be able to lose him to the damn sea. He got angry and…" she trailed off, blinking away her tears and cleared her throat as she forced out a smile.

"And what?" Ariel croaked, clearing her throat as she found herself teary with emotions.

"Let's just say that he took advantage of me and then disposed of me."

"What a bastard," she wiped away her tears, biting her bottom lip and said, "he deserves to rot in hell for that, Adrianne!"

A phantom-like smile appeared on her lips as she sat up and said, "Master Hades made sure that his punishment fit his crime. That is why I am so loyal to him. He has taken care of me and my family in the afterlife and all I have to do is work for him."

"Where is your family?" Ariel sat up, crossing her legs and pulled them up to her chest.

"They are in Elysium, they were very nice people and Master Hades said I could go with them until I have paid off his favour."

She nodded, biting her bottom lip again and said, "You really like him, don't you?"

"He's like a father to me," Adrianne shrugged, standing up and dusted her skirt off, "I admire him greatly and I mean it when I told you yesterday that he is very sorry for what he did that day."

Ariel sighed, looking away and mumbled, "I know, I just…I don't know what to say to him. He made me really angry, but I know I made him angry as well. I just don't want him to hit me again because I know that even though I can't kill him with my hands, I'll find a way."

Adrianne laughed, shaking her head and said, "Milady, just speak to him. I could find him for you and bring him here so you can converse, but I'm sure he's rather busy with his kingly duties. Ever since you've arrived, he says he's fallen behind."

She frowned, tucking back her black curls and said, "Uh, what? Why after I got here?"

She gave her a knowing, mischievous smile, shrugging and said, "I do not know, why don't you ask him yourself?"

The girl rolled her eyes, feeling her cheeks turn red and muttered, "Never mind."

Adrianne giggled, pulling her out of the room and pointed at Hades retreating figure. "Go; try to catch up to him and talk!"

Ariel shook her head, nervousness bubbling inside of her as the girl pushed her out of the room and locked the door behind her. A loud groan left her lips and Hades snapped his head up, looking back at her.

She blushed, forcing herself to catch up to the curious god and smiled nervously as she reached him. "Hi."

"Hello," he nodded his head respectfully and raised his eyebrows in confusion as she began to quickly apologize for her behaviour.

"I'm sorry! I know I shouldn't have overreacted over the whole room situation but I was angry because it's your ex-wife's room and she isn't exactly the nicest one out of your bunch."

Hades laughed, shaking his head down at her and raised his hand to halt her slurred speech. "It's alright; I should be the one apologizing for touching you inappropriately. It wasn't my intention to hurt you, I just...I wasn't thinking. I swear it will never happen again. I swear it on the river Styx; and those oaths cannot be broken."

She nodded, a slow smile growing on her lips and her cheeks turned a slight shade of pink. "Well I promise to try and be less dramatic over things you do."

He chuckled, placing his hands in his robe pockets as he began walking down the hall alongside her. "I've something for you."

"Really?" She frowned.

"Yes," he smiled, "it's the least I could do for our incident."

Her green eyes lit up in excitement and he led her to the room. "I know you like dancing ballet a lot and since I didn't have a dance room to let you practise, I figured I'd let you use this room." He pushed the door open, revealing a completely dark and empty room.

Ariel raised her eyebrows turning to look at him confusedly and said, "Uh...thanks...?"

He laughed, motioning to the room with his hands and said, "This is the domátio efchón. It was a gift from Hecate for my victory over the Olympics many centuries ago. I never used it because as a god, you don't really see the need for these kinds of things, but I'm sure you'll put it to much better use."

"Uh, Hades, it's really sweet of you to want to give me something, but...this is an empty dark room. How could I possibly put this to use? Unless you're giving me a chance to renovate it and make it my own!"

He laughed again, shaking his head and said, "Human, domátio efchón means room of wishes. Close your eyes and make a wish."

She shrugged, doing as he asked and wished for a pair of purple pointe shoes. She counted to three and then opened them. Her jaw fell open as a pair of purple pointe shoes appeared in front of her. She turned to Hades with wide eyes and an opened mouth and then at the shoes.

"That's freaking awesome!"

He nodded, chuckling at her excitement and watched as she closed her eyes and wished for something else. Suddenly the room changed. Wide tall mirrors adorned the walls all around and a portable barre appeared before them as well as barres around the room.

The cement floor turned to hardwood floors and the room suddenly seemed brighter and more spaced. As she opened her eyes to see, Ariel let out a squeal and almost threw her arms around the God to pull him in for a tight embrace.

"Thank you for this!"

He shrugged away her thanks, the rim of his ears turning a slight shade of pink and he smiled. "I'm glad you like it. Would you like to join me for lunch?"

"Yeah!" She nodded quickly, "I'm not really hungry, but I'll keep you company."

Hades nodded, leading her towards the dining room. Ariel widened her eyes at the extravagance of the room and beautiful décor as she sat down on the black chair that he pulled out for her. A grand golden chandelier hung above the middle of the table and shiny emeralds were studded unto the lovely ornament.

"This is beautiful!"

"Persephone used to like it," he muttered more to himself as he sat down and sighed.

"Hades," she began softly, her hand slowly wrapping around his rigid one, "I know it's not my place, but you have to-"

The god clenched his jaw, his icy blue eyes staring at her intently. The joy and humour that once shone through them was completely gone; in their place stood the coldness and hard façade he forced upon himself. "If you know it's not your place then why are you going to bring it up?"

Ariel sighed, taking back her hand from his and gritted her teeth as she looked down at the black mahogany table. There were a million curses running through her mind, but she managed to control her anger and thought of what to say before it would place her in a horrible position.

"I just...I think that you should just let her go. Supressing your feelings and pushing everyone away isn't healthy. Persephone was an idiot to let you go. You're not as horrible as you think you are."

Hades watched her quietly, his long fingers tracing patterns on the table and Ariel squirmed under his gaze. Minutes went by, making everything around her become extremely enhanced as she waited for him to burst out or laugh in her face.

But what he did, could have possibly, hurt her more.

"How dare you," he whispered, "say something like that?"

She frowned, biting her bottom lip and stuttered, "I-I don't u-understand what you mean."

"How can you judge me when it was you who pushed away everyone in your life after killing that repugnant human? You locked yourself in your home for three years, avoiding people like if they had some sort of terminal infectious disease. Who gave you the right to judge me?"

Her bottom lip trembled as tears began to well in her eyes and she tried to blink them away quickly. But to no avail, the salty substance began to slide down her cheeks, mocking her as they revealed how she sincerely felt.

"I didn't," she choked, "I wasn't judging you."

"No," Hades bit out, "you were being a hypocrite. You were telling me that I needed to let go of what happened with Persephone, but when are you going to let go of that rat?"

Ariel raised a shaking hand to her face, wiping away her tears with trembling fingers and whispered, "Don't call him that. Derick wasn't a rat, he cared for me more than any man ever had."

The God chuckled staring at her with incredulous eyes and stood up. The black robe he wore adjusted to his muscles nicely, but let a bit of room to give away to curious eyes. Hades glared down at her, the cold laughter that left his lips, making shivers run down her back.

"Is that what you really think? How naïve are you, human, to think that that man ever cared for you?"

Her jaw trembled as she contained the turmoil of emotions within her and whispered, "At least he didn't cheat on me."

His eyes flashed such a bright blue colour that they almost seemed surreal, his pupil darkened as he growled out, "What did you say?"

Ariel wiped away her tears and louder, bit out, "At least he didn't cheat on me!"

"Is that right?" Hades growled, his voice sounding as if he were trying to control his anger. His eyes spoke what he felt. They were shining with so much anger she could practically feel it prickling her skin and there was no one that could save her from his wrath—not even him.

"Yes."

Another loud chortle left his lips, almost making the walls shake and she swore the gran chandelier above the table almost collapsed on it. "Why don't you see for yourself what an asshole of a man you were in love with, huh? Why don't we ask your beloved Derick how he truly felt about you?"

Her eyes widened and her heart began to quicken, almost making her feel faint. She could hear it thudding in her ears as she gulped and wiped her sweaty hands on her jeans. "Y-you can do that?"

"Of course I can," he thundered, throwing his hands up in the air for emphasis, "I'm the God of the fucking Underworld. And just to prove to you, that your scoundrel of a boyfriend was indeed, cheating on you, I will fetch him for you."

Ariel gulped, as she watched him muttering something under his breath. His eyes were wild and bright, terrifying her to the core as he stared at her but didn't look. It was as if his eyes were going straight through her and staring right into her psyche.

Hades summoned Thanatos in his native tongue and ordered him to bring forth the soul of Derick Mathias Emerson. The God of death appeared immediately before his superior, bowing his head in respect as he acknowledged his king.

"Thanatos," Hades growled, unable to calm his anger, "did you bring him?"

"Yes, my King," Thanatos nodded. He stared at Ariel with dark curious eyes for a second, interest flashing across his eyes for a minute until Hades silently threatened him and staked his claim on the young woman. "As you requested," he snapped his fingers, a white mist forming from his fingers until it transformed into the shape of a man, "Derick Mathias Emerson, bow down before the King of the Underworld."

Ariel widened her eyes, feeling her jaw slack open as her ex-boyfriend appeared on his knees before her. A million feelings coursed through her body as he looked up at her, but she quickly learned that her loving feelings were not reciprocated.

"You," Derick seethed, anger shining in brown eyes, "you should be dead! You should be in my fucking place, how are you still alive?"

She blinked slowly, trying to grasp everything thrown her way and gulped. "D-Derick...?"

The irate spirit rolled his eyes, forgetting about the other two presences in the room and hissed, "You killed me, you bitch, you should be rotting in hell; you should be in my place."

"Enough!" Hades boomed, making him shut his mouth and glare at him. The god rolled his eyes and Thanatos watched with an amused look on his face as Hades motioned to the spirit before him. "This piece of shit is what you loved."

"Piece of shit?" Derick began, letting out a laugh as he opened his mouth to insult the God. "Let me tell you-"

Thanatos cleared his throat, cutting him off and said, "Watch what you speak, Derick Mathias Emerson, you are in the presence of the king of this realm, you have already been placed in Tartarus for your sins concerning Ariel Marie Lockhaven. You do not wish to anger the king more than he already is."

Ariel stood wide-eyed, still unable to process much and coughed out, "I-I didn't...Derick, I d-didn't mean to hurt you. I didn't know what would happen. I-I...oh my god, I am so sorry!" Tears began to stream down her face as she began to walk to him, wanting to wrap her arms around him dand beg for forgiveness.

But Hades held her back. His warn hands wrapped around her waist and he pulled her away. "He's dead, you cannot touch the dead or you'll meddle with the balance of how things work down here. Besides," he glared down at Derick, "he doesn't seem to want to touch you much."

"Touch her?" He let out an enraged laugh, "This bitch killed me! Why the fuck would I let her touch me again? All I wanted was her fucking money and it cost me my life! She wasn't even good for the sex; I had to go and get it elsewhere!"

"What?" She breathed out, feeling her chest constricting with immense pain that left her almost gasping for air.

His brown dull eyes stared up at her and he dug his pale fingers on the carpet, making a horrible noise with his nails. She couldn't understand how his spirit could touch inanimate objects since he was dead, but his skin also looked almost see-through.

It was such a sickeningly pale white colour that he seemed transparent. The hair she once loved to comb with her fingers was now split and dishevelled as if he hadn't taken a shower in years, but he also smelt of burnt rubber. It was such a horrid smell it was making her eyes go teary.

"Told you I wasn't lying," Hades smirked, his eyes shining with a triumphant emotion as he showed her how much of a hypocrite she really was.

"I hope you rot in hell, Ariel," Derick spat, the green substance eating the carpet away as if it had been acid, "you took my life away, you killed me. It's only fair that you pay for that."

Hades watched uncomfortably as Ariel shattered. Her eyes were glossy with tears and her shoulders were shaking with emotion as she struggled to pull herself together. Somehow she felt that in the back of her mind she knew all along. Derick had cheated on her with multiple women and she chose to ignore it.

"That's enough," he said, but the deranged spirit kept insulting the young woman, tearing apart the miniature pieces of her heart ever further. "That's enough!" He spoke louder, finally shutting him up and in his native tongue sent Thanatos with Derick away.

A sob broke through her chest, almost exploding within her as she turned away from Hades and walked away. He scratched the back of his neck awkwardly as he stood in the middle of his dining room, contemplating on following her or giving her some space.

The further she walked, the quicker her pace became until she was fully sprinting away from the scene. Thousands of horrible thoughts ran through her mind, making her go numb with pain as she found herself in the room of wishes.

She locked the door behind her, wishing in her mind that no one would be allowed to enter until she wanted someone to comfort her. Adrianne, having witnessed the repulsive words spoken to the girl, ran after her, only to be locked out of the room. She slammed her hands on the door, begging for entrance, but received no answer.

Ariel walked around the room, staring at her broken reflection and wished for her pointe shoes to be tied securely around her foot. She forced herself on the tip of her toes, grimacing at the slight sting of her earlier blisters and wished for music to be played.

She would dance her pain away. Dance her way to death.

She poised herself with her head held high; kicking her legs up in the air as she began to dance to the melancholic music that began to fill the room and felt tears streaming down her face as she silently cried her pain.

The barre standing across from her was completely forgotten off as she began to spin around the room, losing herself to the music.

Her hair whipped forcefully across her face, prickling her as she turned rapidly.

Human by Christina Perri blared through the speakers and she laughed at the irony of her situation. The humourless laugh that left her lips, simply made her feel more broken as she pushed herself harder, further into numbness that she quickly embraced.

Sweat dripped down her forehead as she jumped across the room, extending her legs high in the air as she gracefully landed on her feet in second position. As she tried standing en pointe again, her legs gave out underneath her, her body desperately begging her to stop the assault, but she would not listen to herself.

Outside the room, Hades and Adrianne watched with wide eyes. Adrianne begged her Master to enter the room, but he couldn't. He knew she needed to release her emotions somehow; she had kept them bottled up for three years—and he hadn't exactly helped her find out in the nicest way.

"Master Hades," Adrianne pleaded, feeling her heart shattering at the sight of Ariel tumbling and pushing herself to a point that even people who watched could see her body couldn't take any more strenuous pressure.

She got up, ignoring the aching feeling on her knees and ran before jumping and split her legs horizontally in the air, performing a grand jeté. Ariel tried to land her fall gracefully, but the blood seeping through her pointe shoes, made her slip and she collapsed on the floor.

The broken danseuse began to sob hysterically. Her shoulders moved up and down as she cried, releasing all her pent up emotions and begged any gods that would listen to take her pain away.

She had been used most of her life by a man that didn't care for her and she had been willing to give him her all. She had truly given Derick everything she could, even her virginity—yet he was clearly not pleased. Even in the afterlife he hated her.

For three years she had tortured herself. She had forced herself to belief that no one could get past her emotional walls, but that's what she needed the most. She needed someone to support her and help her see that the man she cried over every night, was definitely not worth it.

"Master," Adrianne whispered again and he nodded. The door opened slowly as he pushed it away and walked towards the girl in the middle of the room.

"Ariel?" It was the first time he called her by her first name, his voice was soft and caring, making her feel pathetic. "You're bleeding," he widened his eyes as he looked at her feet. Her light pink pointe shoes were drenched in blood and the floor she was lying on, had blood smeared on it as well.

"Please," she whispered, the pain in her voice piercing his heart, "just kill me. Get it done with. I've nothing to live for...I...please, Hades. Out of all the hate you feel towards me, please just do me this small favour and kill me."

Hades shook his head, carefully pulling the trembling girl up in his arms and hoisted her up as he cradled her against his chest. "Don't say that."

"Please," she sobbed as if she was in a mantra, "you're the god of death; it should be easier for you to do it."

"I cannot kill you," he spoke quietly, but firmly as he made his way to her room, careful not to bump her head into any of his décor or walls. "You have surprisingly grown on me, little human, I cannot force myself to do such a thing."

Ariel didn't understand him. She hid her face into his warm masculine chest; not really realizing whom was carrying her and focused on the steady beat of his heart. It helped her to calm down, she found herself humming along to it as the tears dried on her eyelashes.

Even in her broken state, Hades saw her strength. She was a beautiful warrior, delicate, but she was strong. She was almost fragile like the petal of a rose, with the poisonous thorns of an exotic plant.

And even though he knew she was dangerous, he wanted to cherish the gorgeous flower. Because the most beautiful flower, in his eyes was almost the most delicate and strong.

He ordered Adrianne to fetch some healing water Apollo had gifted him years ago and tended to her feet. She was mostly delirious through the process, mumbling incoherent words of despair as he tried to wipe away the blood from her aching feet.

It had been a difficult process as she continued to jerk her feet away from the soothing water, but the God didn't give up on her. He fought her stubbornness with his own.

Hades wrapped his arms around her, wanting to stand up and leave her alone, but couldn't bring himself to do so. After all, it had partially been his fault. If he had never brought Derick up, she wouldn't have tried to dance herself to death.

"Please stay," she whispered, closing her eyes as she tightened her hold on his strong forearms, loving the comfort he provided with just his presence. She had ironically found comfort with death. She had literally danced her way to Death.

He kissed her forehead lovingly, a whisper of a sigh escaping his lips as he leaned his head on the headboard and revelled in the warmth that radiated from her trembling body. He pulled the covers over her, careful not to push her head off his chest and gulped as his fingers subconsciously wrapped around hers.

What terrified him more than comforting the human, was the feeling of comfort she gave him. He felt at home with Ariel in his arms and their hands moulded together perfectly. The Fates must've been fucking with him once again.

9

CHAPTER 9

The smell of spicy woods and crisp fresh sheets faintly awoke her senses as she felt something stirring underneath her. Ariel widened her eyes as memories of the day before came rushing back like a cold bucket of water and she froze.

Her hand was entwined with a stronger, larger one and she felt fingers stroking her backside gently. Blood rushed to her cheeks and she bit her bottom lip hard enough to draw blood. Her head slowly rose with Hades' chest as he inhaled slowly and she tried to feign sleep.

"How did you sleep?" His voice rumbled through his chest, sounding deep and hoarse. Ariel closed her eyes, trying to frantically ignore the emotions he was rousing with simply his voice. It was soft and almost baritone-like.

She looked at their entwined hands and whispered, "How did you know I was up?"

Hades smiled, running his free hand through her soft hair and said, "Your heart is beating against my side; I felt it beating faster and your breathing changed a bit."

"That's creepy," she mumbled, hiding her face on his chest. He smelled evocative, almost mouth-watering. She didn't know if it was a natural smell or if he had left to bathe, but it was making her delirious—and addicted.

After a short moment of silence, her stomach grumbled and Hades chuckled. He slowly let go of her hand and gently placed her on the bed to sit up. "I'll go get you some fruits. You freshen up and meet me at the dining table."

"Wait," she sat up, looking down at her hands. He had touched her and didn't die. He did tell her he wouldn't, but how did he know that? "You touched me..."

He raised his eyebrows, his blue eyes shining with confusion. "And...?"

"How come you...I mean you told me you wouldn't die," she stuttered, stumbling over her words as she tried to figure out how to express herself, "but how did you know?"

He looked down at her for a second, completely silent and then cleared his throat, "I didn't.

Ariel dropped her jaw open, watching as he nodded his head once and left her room. She gulped slowly, looking down at her hands and clenched them. A slight pang of fear whirled inside of her and she covered her mouth as her mind began to think of the worse.

Hades was nothing special to her, but if she had awoken and he was dead in her arms, she wouldn't be able to live with herself at all. The day before, she had broken down due to Derick's heartlessness and she begged the God to take her life away. And he declined.

Now that she was calm and less frantic, she realised that she wants to live longer, grow old, fall in love and try to gain back those three years that she forcefully tried to bury.

But if Hades had died because of her, she knew she wouldn't be able to cope with it. She would've killed another person—or God.

She sighed, running her fingers through her tangled hair and grimaced at the feel of tears dried on her cheeks. She lightly traced her cheekbones as she walked to the small bathroom and stared at herself in the mirror.

Surprisingly, her green eyes were bright and vibrant. She wasn't one to boast, but her eyes were one of the most beautiful attributes she had. They were almond-shaped with thick eye-lashes and specks of light brown around her pupil. With the right colour of eye-shadow, they'd look surreal.

She stepped into the shower, closing her eyes in appreciation as the warm water enveloped her body and began to scrub away the sweat that had caked on her skin from her ostentatious and emotional dance.

After brushing her teeth, she tied her hair up in a high ponytail. Her fringes fell to the side, untucking themselves from her ear by how long they were. It was time for a haircut.

Ariel sighed, rummaging through the small drawers for something to decent to wear. At times, she missed the room Hades had placed her in before. But then she'd remember who it used to belong to and the feeling would dissipate.

She finally settled for a red blouse and a knee-length flowy black skirt. As she looked at herself in the mirror, she smiled and stepped into her sandals. Every time she checked the closet, there was more clothing.

Adrianne had told her that Hades had ordered some of the best designers that had already been dead, to create clothing for her. She didn't believe the girl because Hades had no reason to care for her that way, but slowly clothing began to appear in her closet.

Nothing too fancy, but Adrianne said that the extravagant clothing was being kept as a surprise for her.

Although the castle was enormous and extravagant, she found her way to the dining room. But what she saw wasn't anything she expected. Her eyes widened as he ran to Hades. He was coughing and holding his throat as his fingernails dug unto the floor.

"Hades! Oh my god, what's wrong?!"

He looked up at her, his eyes flashing different shades of blue and snarled, "Get away!"

She frowned, ignoring him and repeated, "What's wrong?"

He growled, the sound coming deep from within his chest and sounding feral. "Get. Away. Now."

"Hades," she rolled her eyes, kneeling beside him and said, "what happened? Who did this to you?!"

"Aphrodite," he coughed out, deepening his voice to sound so husky that shivers began to run down her back, "poisoned me."

Ariel deepened her frown, looking around for the goddess of love and said, "Where is she? What do I do?"

He shook his head, staring up at her with hungry eyes and growled, "She left. You need to leave. Tell Adrianne to tell the rest of the women in the castle to leave, it'll go away."

She huffed, not understanding anything and said, "Will you die?!"

"No," he narrowed his eyes, his voice sounding sweet like honey and she suddenly felt more aroused than ever before, "it'll go away eventually, but every woman near me will become desirable."

"What?"

Hades sighed, sliding his hand down his face and whispered, "Aphrodite is the goddess of love, right?" She nodded, "She's also the goddess of sex and beauty. Whenever she has a certain emotion, those around her can feel it as well. If she wants you to feel sexually frustrated, you will. If she wants you to feel hate, you will; she controls emotions."

"So," she raised her eyebrows, "she made you feel like every woman around is sexy?"

He held unto the table, holding himself from jumping her and stared at her with dark predatory eyes. "No," his voice was so alluring, she was mesmerized and she slowly found herself inching towards him, "she made the sexual beast that I've been holding back for a decade come out."

Ariel looked at him, realisation slowly dawning on her. It was a funny way of telling her that he was horny. "So you're...horny?"

He growled again, tightly holding the table and said, "That's a mild way of putting it. Right now you are like an aphrodisiac. Your smell is a thousand times more enhanced than it usually is and it is driving me insane. You need to get away from me before I do something that we'll both regret."

She sat away from him on the floor, but didn't move like he ordered her to.

"Ariel!" He snarled, igniting something passionate deep inside of her.

"How can I help?"

"Unless you're willing to be pinned down to my bed and used as my sexual release, then I suggest you get the fuck out of here. You need to go. I can't hold myself back much longer."

She didn't know why she did it. She didn't know why she wanted to help him, but she did. His words didn't scare her; they aroused her.

The thought of the virile God kneeling next to the table, grabbing it so tightly his knuckles were turning deathly white, taking her like she was fantasizing in her head, was more than she could imagine.

Every single attractive attribute he had, seemed more attractive than they already were. She didn't know what to compare him to; he was already a God.

She gulped, her heart beating about a thousand miles per hour as she crawled closer to the trembling God. "Let me help you," her voice was soft, barely a whisper as she placed her shaking hand to his cheek.

Hades closed his eyes, the feel of her soft hand against his skin made the excruciating sexual adrenaline rushing through his veins, worse. He breathed in sharply, his eyes opening and glowing a darker colour than they already were. "Please, leave."

He no longer sounded in control or demanding. Now he was vulnerable, his voice was weak and trembling; he had no will left in him to fight her. His lust was demanding him to take her up on the offer, but he knew that once Aphrodite's spell would abscond, he'd hurt her.

He didn't want to hurt her anymore.

Ariel shook her head, stubbornly and stood on her tip-toes. Hades closed his eyes again, gulping as his last bits of restraint disappeared. She tilted her head, closing her eyes when she was inches from him and pressed a gentle kiss to his lips.

She pulled away softly, licking her lips after their feather-like kiss and stared at him with cautious eyes. He looked down at her, losing himself in the lust and in the blink of an eye, had her pinned against the wall.

"Why didn't you just leave?" His voice came out growled, sexual and powerful.

Her eyes widened, but she was surprisingly not afraid. Instead she shrugged and whispered, "I told you, I want to help you."

The lust-filled God pressed his forehead against hers, his breathing becoming erratic as he tried to fight himself from ravaging every bit of her. "I'll hurt you." He spoke so softly, she almost missed it.

Ariel gulped, placing her hand on the side of his cheek and whispered, "I'm a big girl, Hades, I can handle it. Besides, it's not like I haven't done it before."

A smirk grew on his lips and he pulled away to look at her. His eyes were bright, almost ethereal and it made a pleasurable shiver run down her back. It was as if she knew what was coming and it brought her such a thrill that it almost tore her apart.

"I wasn't..." he shook his head, "I didn't mean it that way. I meant that I'd hurt you," he placed his hand over her heart and tapped it, "here."

"I," she breathed, feeling completely emotional as he stared down at her. The colour of his eyes was mesmerizing her, she felt lost for words. She just wanted his lips on hers, on her. "I can take care of it, Hades."

He nodded, closing his eyes as his mouth pressed against hers. The kiss began slow, gentle and teasing. His lips felt so soft against hers, she thought it was all a part of her imagination, until his hands wrapped around her waist and he deepened the passionate lock of their lips.

Their mouths moulded together perfectly. His tongue hesitantly swiped her bottom lip and she opened her mouth, wanting him to do what he wished with her. She was at his sole mercy and she didn't mind. Maybe she wasn't thinking, but sometimes it was nice to not think.

To just let life guide you, even if it's a mistake, you'll be living it to the fullest.

A gasp left her lips as he pressed his entire body against hers. Every curvature and firm line was pressed against hers and she could feel all of the strong muscles underneath his clothes. Sparks of undying promises lingered on their lips as they continued to passionately speak in a way that words could not.

Hades grunted as he hoisted her up in his arms, helping her to wrap her legs around his waist and pressed her against the wall, urging their bodies even closer. Ariel wrapped her arms around his neck, holding him tightly as they continued kissing.

As if reading her mind, he pulled away, but his lips didn't stop touching her. He trailed a sensual line of kisses along her jaw, reaching her neck and began to suckle on her skin hungrily. Her hand wrapped around his hair, loving the soft feel of his mane and she moaned, opening herself to him.

She trembled in his arms with pleasure as he continued to kiss her soft spot, eliciting moans from her. It felt strange for him to finally be with another woman, it almost hurt how good it was. But he was enjoying it.

Enjoying the warmth radiating from her and the short gasps that her mouth would form as he tugged at all the right places.

Hades kissed the slender column of her throat, his hair tickling her jaw in the process and she arched her back off the wall, pressing herself closer to him as his lips continued their loving attack on her gentle skin.

"Hades," she gasped out, her voice so filled with lust that neither of them recognized it as hers.

A passionate growl escaped his lips, vibrating against her skin as he kissed her hard enough to leave love bites. The sounds of his name leaving her lips was sinfully delicious; it almost hurt him how much he desired her.

His strong hands caressed her thighs, but they never went higher. He just kept teasing her, igniting a passion so erroneous deep within her, that she thought she'd shatter in his arms. He brought his mouth back up to hers, pressing a long, liquid kiss that rushed lust through her and melted in his arms, unable to do anything but want him.

Her hands caressed the strong muscle of his jaw, trying to mesmerize every line of his face with her fingers. She was finally doing what she longed to do; touch a man with her bare fingertips and not be afraid that he'd die in her arms.

Hades sighed against her mouth, feeling the control over his lust slowly return to him, but he continued kissing her. The taste of her mouth was sweet and addicting, he wanted to continue the assault on her mouth until he couldn't breathe.

The thought of kissing her for eternity flashed through his mind and startled him. It was like a nudge from his subconscious to stop. She was human and fragile; she didn't have all eternity to spend with him.

No matter what her fate was, if he was in it, he'd break her. He'd end up hurting both of them. And she didn't deserve that. He wouldn't allow himself to shatter the bits that were left of her heart.

And he wouldn't allow her to shatter his already torn heart. Persephone had already done so; nothing stopped Ariel from crushing it as well.

He slowly released her hold on her, placing the breathless girl back on her feet and almost reluctantly pulled away from her heavenly lips. "I already hurt you enough, Ariel; I don't want to do it anymore."

She frowned; trying to focus but the tingles that were left all over her body was making it impossible to concentrate. "Why do you keep talking about hurting me? What makes you think that you will?"

Hades sighed, sliding his hand down his face and stared at her with light blue eyes. They finally returned to their normal colour. "There's a reason why I'm the God of the Death, Ariel; I destroy everything I touch."

10

CHAPTER 10

Ariel gritted her teeth, breathing in sharply and hissed, "Are you being serious right now, Hades?"

The God frowned, turning to look at her and said, "This is not something to kid about, human; of course I am serious."

"Don't call me that!" She snapped, glaring daggers at him, "Don't call me 'human'! I have a fucking name for Pete's sake! Call me Ariel!"

He restrained the urge to reprimand her for speaking to him disrespectfully and took a deep breath. "I am being as serious as I could possibly be, Ariel."

"How," she began, her bottom lip trembling with anger as she stepped closer to him, "how can you tell me that you destroy everything you touch? You may be the God of Death, Hades, but I kill anything I touch."

Hades widened his eyes at her outburst and watched as she stepped closer to him, poking his chest with her finger with every word. "Don't be so damn selfish! D-don't try to control me and tell me that you're trying to protect me; I can do that myself. I have for three years; there is nothing you could possibly do that could hurt me."

His eyes flashed a bright colour and he grabbed her forearm, staring deep into her eyes as he growled, "You don't know what I am capable of doing, Ariel."

She narrowed her gaze, stepping closer to him and whispered, "And neither are you. I am not asking you to bind your soul to mine, Hades. I just want you to do this."

"What? What's 'this'?" He clenched his jaw, his Adam's apple bobbing up and down as he gulped.

"I-I," she stumbled over her words, "I don't know!"

He closed his eyes, placing his hands on her waist and began to slowly move them around her soft skin. Ariel closed her eyes, leaning closer to him and breathed in deeply. She felt alight wherever he touched her; it was an inexplicable feeling.

Every inch of her skin screamed and burned with desire for him. It was so grandiose that it was engulfing her mind, preventing her from thinking intelligently. At that moment she was at his sole mercy and he didn't even know it. She all but melted at his feet.

"If you don't know what you want," he whispered, his minty breath brushing past her cheekbone, "how do you expect me to give it to you?"

Ariel glanced up at him, her eyes filled with so much lust it almost poured from her soul. Her fingertips tingled with want and power as she placed them against his cheeks and pressed her body closer to his.

Every curvature of her body was firmly pressing against his. She could feel his heart hammering inside his chest and his erratic breathing against her cheeks. He was warm and his touch felt inviting.

She wanted to feel the assertive touch of his lips against hers again, devouring her completely. Her mind, body and soul begged for the release that was suddenly overbearing any thought that she could possibly have against the God.

"You do know what I want you to give me," she whispered, standing on her tiptoes to brush her lips against his.

Hades growled, the noise rumbling deep from within his chest and he bit her bottom lip teasingly, making her moan. "You don't understand that after Aphrodite's spell leaves, you won't feel this anymore; I won't feel this anymore. I don't want us to make decisions that we'll later on regret."

Ariel rolled her eyes, tilting her head backwards as the troubled God began peppering kisses down her slender throat. "Life is all about taking decisions that we might later on regret; we just have to make sure that we learn from them."

He gave a light chuckle, sliding his hand down to the curvature of her ass. He gave her a light squeeze, making her groan in delight at the domineering gesture and brushed his lips against her skin as he whispered, "I am not going to touch you because of a spell. Aphrodite—"

"Okay," A voice snapped them away from their intimate position, "as much as I love to hear people talking about me, you have got to stop bringing my name into this shit, uncle."

Aphrodite grinned, revealing pearly white teeth and red luscious lips. Her golden hair seemed to float around her head, making her seem so beautiful it was almost painful to see. Her eyes were a striking blue and her features seemed to be carved out of pure stone.

"Aphrodite," Hades narrowed his eyes, speaking her name as if it was acid on his tongue and gently placed Ariel on her feet.

The goddess rolled her eyes, walking towards them slowly. She wore a wine red off-the-shoulder dress that made her moving seem like she was gliding across the floor as gracefully as a gazelle. "Hades, you don't seem pleased to see me."

He rolled his eyes in return, raking his fingers through his hair and stepped away from Ariel, giving her some breathing space. "Well you're not exactly my most favourite person right now; you tried to poison me."

"I did not!" She gasped, giggling lightly as he muttered something under his breath.

Ariel watched her with wide eyes, feeling completely enthralled by her beauty. It almost made her jealous how beautiful the goddess was, but Hades seemed completely unaffected by her beauty and charm.

"Just leave, Aphrodite, I don't need another episode of this," Hades muttered, gritting his teeth as the goddess continued to smile cheekily.

"What," she cleared her throat, "exactly, do you think happened seconds ago?"

The God sighed, sliding his hand down his face and said, "You poisoned me with one of your love potions. That's why Ariel seemed so attractive and I couldn't hold myself back from..." he trailed off.

Blood rushed to her cheeks, making her entire face heat up in embarrassment as the goddess scrutinized her face slowly and then turned to Hades, with the corners of her lips slightly turned upward, in a half smile.

"So you're saying that without the 'poison' I supposedly gave you, you wouldn't find this mortal attractive?"

Hades blinked slowly, feeling completely taken aback by the question. He cleared his throat, scratching his neck awkwardly and looked away from Ariel's curious green eyes. "I didn't...I don't..."

"Tell me, uncle," Aphrodite placed her hands on her hips and cocked her head to the side, "you're saying that you, almost fucking the brains out of this poor girl, is my fault?"

"Do not speak that way in front of her," he almost growled, his blue eyes flickering a lighter shade of blue.

Ariel bit her bottom lip, the power radiating off both gods almost suffocating her. She felt a million emotions stirring within her and it all confused her. She wanted to feel angry at Hades for not abiding to her sexual prowess, but she also wanted to kiss him for somehow wanting to keep what was best for her in mind. The sexual tension building inside her was also pissing her off.

Aphrodite waved her hand in the air, as if wiping away his comment and said, "Stop blaming this on me, uncle. I did nothing but open your eyes. I did not 'poison' you, like you believe."

"Then, what did you pour on me?"

She gave a light giggle and whispered something in their native tongue. Ariel frowned as Hades glared at his niece and growled something in return. The anger coursing through his body simply turned her on further. There was something about the way his eyes shone with any emotion that she simply adored.

"I refuse to have this conversation with you, Aphrodite," he hissed, "you can do whatever you please, but don't you dare lie to my face. You poisoned me, just admit it."

The Goddess rolled her eyes, sliding her hand down her face and muttered, "For a God he surely acts stupid."

"I can hear you," Hades snapped, making his sister purse her lips.

"Hades," she clasped her hands together and stepped closer to them, "I didn't 'poison' you with any love potions. I made a bet with Eros that—"

The God shook his head in anger, slamming a chair out of his way and stormed off. Ariel widened her eyes as he kept walking down the hall further away from them and contemplated on staying and speaking to the Goddess or running to her room to forget about her rendezvous.

"Fine then," Aphrodite muttered, "don't listen to me." She looked up at Ariel and said, "I guess I'll just tell you. Eros and I made a bet that Hades wouldn't be able to resist you for too long. I said he'd take less than two weeks and I refuse to let Eros win."

She looked up at her, blinking slowly and said, "So...you poisoned Hades into wanting me so you could win your bet?"

"Heavens no!" Aphrodite shook her head, walking over to a chair and sitting down. She looked down at her ruby coloured manicured nails with high interest and said, "If I had poisoned Hades into wanting you, you wouldn't be speaking to me right now, child."

"What?"

The Goddess laughed out sultrily and said, "Hades and you would be breaking havoc in your room; my magic wouldn't have failed, darling."

Ariel frowned, walking over to the dining table and placed her hands on a chair, gripping it tightly. "So you didn't poison him?"

"No," she shook her head and waved her hand in the air, "and stop using the word poison! You make it sound like I'm trying to kill my uncle and I most certainly am not. I'm just trying to help him. We're fucking tired of him being an ass because he hasn't gotten laid; that's why you're here with him." She shrugged, looking up at her with mirth shining in her eyes, "The part about you not killing him is just a bonus."

"Then, what did you give him?" She whispered.

Aphrodite stood up, staring straight into her eyes and said, "I opened his eyes, darling. I made him have what he has been desiring these last couple of days. I did nothing more than push him a little over the edge so he'd finally give in to that beast that has been tormenting him for nights."

"I don't," Ariel blushed, shaking her head confusedly, "I don't understand."

The Goddess sighed, flipping her hair behind her shoulders and cocked her hips. "My uncle wants you; he's just too stupid to realize it. So," she grinned, "that means you'll have to seduce him into giving you what you both want."

"What?" Her cheeks, if possibly, turned even darker.

She muttered something under her breath, shaking her head and said, "You'll have to seduce Hades into having the best sex in the world, honey. Not only will sleeping with a God blow your mind, but hopefully he'll stop acting like he walks with a fucking stick up his ass. It's kind of like a favour to all the Gods for placing you with someone so attractive."

Ariel bit her bottom lip, choosing to ignore most of her comments and said, "How do I even seduce him? He can't even see me without feeling sick."

"Are you serious?" She clicked her tongue, sighing as she walked towards the young woman. "Listen to me, you are a woman. The gods gifted you with many, many gifts; seduction being one of them. Here," she tapped her heart, "lays a seductive prowess, you just need to unleash her."

She squeaked. "How?"

Aphrodite gave out an incredulous laugh, tapping her fingers against her jaw and said, "Seconds before I came in, you had Hades at the palm of your hand. If I hadn't stepped in, you'd be screwing on the damn dining table. So don't you dare tell me that you don't know how to seduce the man."

Ariel licked her lips, running her fingers through her hair and said, "I honestly don't even know how I did that..."

She grabbed her shoulders, shaking her slightly. "Look him in the eyes; make sure you have a straight connection. Give him a light kiss, say something sexy and walk away. You'll have him like putty in your hands and you'll be screwing each other like horny bunnies. Now if you'll excuse me, I have to go tell Eros to pay up; you better not fail me, Ariel. I do not look good in neon orange."

She frowned, watching as the goddess of love disappeared and shook her head. The day was turning out crazier than she had imagined.

"Milady," Adrianne timidly walked up to her, slowly smiling, "Master Hades was wondering if his niece has left."

Ariel nodded, wrapping her arms around herself and cleared her throat, "Y-yeah, she just left." Before she had the chance to say anything else, a voice from behind them startled them both.

"Ariel!"

She widened her eyes, her lips slowly turning into a smile as she recognized the voice to belong to Hermes. "Hermes? What are you doing here?"

The God shrugged, running his fingers through his hair and said, "Oh I was just helping some souls get to Charon and decided I'd stop down here for a visit. I wanted to see if Hades had given you a tour of the Underworld yet."

Ariel laughed at his goofy expression and shook her head. "No, he hasn't; he's been kind of busy..." she blushed, "running things so I haven't asked him."

Hermes grinned, straightening his stance and said, "Would you like one? It would have to be—" His gaze fell on the girl besides Ariel and he slowly trailed off. His light blue eyes glimmered with an unknown emotion and he stepped closer, bowing his head in respect and took the servant's hand. "Milady," he kissed her knuckles, "by what name do you respond?"

Adrianne widened her eyes, quickly glancing at Ariel for help and she stepped in.

"I don't believe the two of you have met." She pointed to Hermes, "Hermes this is my friend, Adrianne." She pointed to Adrianne, "Adrianne, this is my friend...? Hermes."

"Adrianne," Hermes spoke quietly, murmuring something else in Ancient Greek and slowly let go of the young woman's hand, "that is a beautiful name. It is a pleasure to meet you, milady."

She bit her bottom lip, gulping and felt her cheeks burning up. Her entire face was coloured pink by her embarrassment and she tried desperately not to make a fool of herself in front of such an attractive man. "The pleasure is all mine, sir."

Ariel grinned, liking how enthralled Hermes seemed by her and cleared her throat, trying to gain his attention. "When would you give me a tour, Hermes?"

The God blinked slowly, stepping away from Adrianne and turned to Ariel. "Tomorrow; I can get someone to guide the souls and give you a quick tour. Of course," he smiled, "it has to be alright with Hades."

Noticing that his eyes would continue travelling towards Adrianne, Ariel nodded her head and mischievously grinned. "Alright, I will ask him for permission right now. I will let you know what he says."

"Yeah," he spoke, sounding distracted as his eyes scrutinized Adrianne's physique, "you go and...do that."

She gave out a little laugh as Adrianne turned to her with wide, terrified eyes and before she could open her mouth and ruin her chances with the curious god, Ariel hurried down the hall to find the king of the Underworld.

At first she realized that she had no idea where the God was, but her feet seemed to have a mind of their own and she found herself entering the room where they first met.

Hades was sitting on his throne, looking as handsome as ever with his chin resting on his hand. He seemed to be lost in thought as he stared aimlessly at the grand marbled pillars and didn't notice her entrance.

Ariel slowly walked up to his throne, staring up at him in awe and quietly cleared her throat to gain his attention. His eyes snapped down to her rapidly, the blue colour seeming as beautiful as ever and she felt captivated under his gaze.

There was something about his eyes that enthralled her, left her breathless and powerless against anything he'd throw her way. She felt a prisoner to the ethereal blue irises—a willing prisoner.

"Did Aphrodite leave?"

She nodded. "Yeah, she left a couple of minutes ago."

Hades relaxed, slouching his shoulders into his comfortable seat and then stood up abruptly. He walked down the steps and stood before her, wanting to say a million words that all got caught in his throat. "What did she tell you?"

A mischievous smile grew on her lips as she remembered the Goddesses words. Ariel had never tried to seduce a man, let alone a God, but there was something about Hades that brought out the adventurous side of her.

He not only made her feel alive, but he also made her feel. It didn't matter what emotions they were, but he made her feel something other than a walking void. He also managed to awaken the powerful lust-filled beast within her.

It was something she could not control—it was out of her reach. She knew she should stop speaking to the God as if he could not hurt her, but she felt comfortable with him. Comfortable enough to disrespect him at times, but comfortable nonetheless.

The God just aroused that from her; anger and lust. There was something so deliciously carnal about him that she couldn't seem to grasp or want to understand; she simply wanted him to make her feel the rest of the emotions he was capable of evoking from her.

"It's a secret."

Hades rolled his eyes, stepping closer to her and said, "You are in my kingdom, Ariel, and I hope that I don't need to remind you, whom you're speaking to."

She grinned, staring deep into his eyes and whispered, "I could say the same thing about you."

"Don't," he growled, his eyes flashing another shade of blue as the emotions began to explode within him. They shone an eerie blue, almost making her dizzy with desire.

Ariel widened her eyes innocently, tilting her head as she stepped up to him and placed her hands on his chest. "Don't what?" The sexual prowess Aphrodite was speaking of was definitely taking over her actions and she didn't know whether to fight it or give in completely.

He looked down at her, the feel of her hands on his chest making him go mad with need and he enclosed his hands around her frail wrists. "Just tell me what she told you."

"Oh nothing," she sighed nonchalantly, "but I was wondering if Hermes could give me a tour of the Underworld." Ariel stood on her tip toes, surprising herself as she bit on the God's bottom lip and grinned up at him wickedly, "I want to see how big you are—I mean your kingdom is."

With a wink, she writhed away from his touch and began to walk away. A shuddered breath escaped her lips as she tried to pull herself together and tried to encourage herself to keep walking and not look back.

Her charm worked like magic.

Hades grabbed her arm, spinning her around and wrapped his arm around her waist to pull her closer. His strong fingers wrapped around her jaw and with a deep voice, he growled, "You cannot simply do what you just did without accepting the consequences."

Then he pressed his lips to hers.

11

CHAPTER 11

A loud thud echoed throughout the room as the passionate-filled couple struggled against each other's desires. It was flowing through their body like a stream of forbidden and everlasting lust. Hot and desperate; it was almost suffocating.

Ariel gasped, groaning loudly as Hades kissed her mouth ferociously. His lips were sweet yet demanding; there was no tenderness behind his touch. She wasn't sure she wanted him to treat her like a fragile doll.

What she wanted and desired was something that he was willing to give; a quick reminder that she could still feel something.

Hades grasped her thighs, pushing her into the wall as he continued to assault her mouth with debauched kisses. Wherever he touched her, he left perilous flames behind. She was burning with such a passion that she could barely breathe and although Hades was causing her to be breathless, he was also the only person able to relieve her of her condition.

"Dammit," he growled against her lips, biting them teasingly as he slid his hand up and down her silk-like skin. She felt so soft and warm underneath him. He craved that feeling, missed it, wanted it.

It had been ten long years that he hadn't touched a woman the way he was touching Ariel—and now he couldn't seem to stop himself. He wanted to devour her, strip her of whatever she was offering and even take more.

She was willingly offering herself to him and he was alacritous. There was nothing stopping him, but the thought of not satisfying his sexual beast. Ariel was clearly enough to satisfy whatever he desired, even just by looking at her, one could see how amazing she was, but he was afraid he'd want more.

More. And more. Until there was nothing left to offer and she would want everything he stripped her off, in return.

As if reading his precarious thoughts, Ariel took his cheeks in her hands and stared deep into the hypnotizing eyes she was growing to adore. "Look at me, Hades."

He breathed harshly, wanting to continue but knowing his fears would stop him. She shook her head, tracing his bottom lip with her thumb and whispered, "Stop overthinking it; I want this. You want this. Let's just help each other out."

The doubting God opened his mouth to talk them both out of their zealous affair, but she was a step ahead of his game. "Enough Hades," Ariel leaned forward, rubbing her front against his rough bulge, her body giving him plenty of promises, "stop thinking about later and just think of now. Lose yourself in the now and we'll face the later when it comes."

Hades nodded, capturing her mouth with his and kissed her deeply. They fought for control, for the dominant position that she desperately wanted him to take, but also wanted to tease him for. A sly grin grew on her lips as he growled in complaint and began to rip her shirt off.

Ariel moaned, leaning her head on the wall behind her and curled her fingers in his soft hair. The God growled against her neck in return and in one swift moment slid his hand in her underwear; for someone who hadn't slept with a woman for years, he surely knew what he was doing.

She gasped, millions of sparks exploding within her as he stared down at her with dark, possessive eyes and began to rock his fingers into her centre. At first a slight pain prickled her core, but as she grew accustomed to the welcomed intruder, a forgotten but loved sensation began to build in her stomach.

Hades stared at her, capturing her gaze with his as he pushed a second finger inside, loving the feel of her tightness. A smirk grew on his lips as he bit down on her bottom lip, making her groan and whimper a low moan.

Her hands wrapped around his shoulders, holding unto him tightly as he pushed a third finger and she writhed in his arms, fighting the urge to scream her pleasure.

Whenever Derick would begin something sexual between them, she'd always end up last, but as Hades bowed his head to lick the tender skin of her throat, she realized that that time would be different.

Her body shook in his arms as a maelstrom of emotions erupted inside her, leaving her limp and breathless in his arms. She arched her back off the wall, tightening her hold around his shoulders and mumbled a long string of incomprehensible words.

He hadn't even taken her clothes off and she had already experienced an earthshattering örgasm.

Hades grinned mischievously; his blue eyes shining deviously as he slowly slid his fingers from her and surprised her as he popped them in his mouth. Her jaw dropped open as he continued watching her with predatory-like eyes and something dark snapped inside of her. "You are definitely sweet, my Ariel."

She blushed, biting her bottom lip and gulped. The further they got, the more she'd lose her confidence, it was as if Hades taking control was leaving her dumbfounded. She was used to Derick taking control, but she wasn't used to wanting to be controlled.

At that moment, she wished for Hades to do with her what he pleased—and he pleased to do with her many things.

Her fingers fumbled with the buttons of his shirt and with the blink of an eye, Hades had her pinned down on the carpet, as he pulled his shirt over his head. Her dark green eyes grazed every inch of his godly body, trying to memorize every fine line and inch of muscle he displayed.

Ariel raised her shaking hands, somewhat timidly tracing the hard muscle of his abdominals and counted each square. With one quick movement, she pushed herself from underneath him and straddled his waist, sitting atop him with a wicked grin on her lips.

A ragged breath exploded through his chest as Ariel pressed soft kisses on the eight squares carved unto his stomach. His body seemed like no other; it was strong and every line was so defined it left her breathless.

He was truly a god because only they could be as dangerously beautiful as Hades.

The God growled something underneath his breath, pushing her unto the carpet and pinned her wrists down to prevent her from escaping. It wasn't like she really wanted to go anywhere.

Light perspiration travelled down his jaw, adding to his rugged-ness and his dark hair fell over his eyes. Ariel stared up at him;

not believing what was happening between them and was violently snapped away from admiring him when he ripped her underwear off.

Her eyes widened as the splitting of the fabric echoed throughout the room and he chuckled down at her. His voice was deep, sultry and unrecognizable. "They were in my way."

Ariel nodded, as if in a trance and gasped once he pulled her in for another breathless kiss. His warm tongue swiped her bottom lip, ordering her to open her mouth for him and then he suckled on her lips hungrily.

She tasted sweet like fruit and he was becoming addicted to her taste. She had become his very own aphrodisiac. He tangled his fingers in her hair, biting her lips and quickly removed his pants.

Ariel closed her eyes, tilting her head away from his lips as he began to kiss her with his tongue down her neck. Her eyes were half-opened, but she could make out the upside down furniture and recognized it as her own room.

How they arrived there was a mystery that she did not necessarily want to uncover at the moment.

She could only focus on how amazing it felt when Hades would swipe his tongue down her neck and suckle hard enough to leave love bites behind. She didn't care what marks he left behind as long as they were pleasurable and so far everything he had done had been fantastic.

Hades looked down at her as he rid himself of his boxers and lowered his body over hers. His warm hands cupped her breasts and she whimpered under his touch. It was gentle, but domineering all at the same time. It was making her go frenetic with tangled emotions.

"You will not get any sexually transmitted diseases from me," he whispered near her breast before slowly brushing his lips against them, "or bear a child from me; for I am a sterile god."

A frown grew on her features but before she could question him on the subject, a gasp escaped her lips. He had not warned her about their joining, but once he entered her, she felt as if though he almost ripped her in half.

He wasn't monstrously oversized, but his package would put any erotic film star to shame. It was thick and long and definitely reaching all the right places.

Ariel squealed, shutting her eyes in pain and covered her face. Hades grimaced, almost collapsing on her from the extreme sensation he was feeling and tried to let her accommodate to his length.

"Just," she hissed through gritted teeth, "move!"

He didn't abide to her command, knowing that she was in pain from the intrusion, but it was almost killing him. Persephone hadn't even been that tight their wedding night and she had cried like the virgin, he knew she wasn't.

Yet the young woman underneath him simply had her jaw clenched and her eyes shut tightly as she breathed in deeply. Her eyes snapped open and she tightened her fingers on his muscled forearms. "Move!"

"You are hurting," he grunted, losing the last bits of restraint he had left. He couldn't explain how amazing it felt to be so intimate with her. It was tearing him apart how marvellous it felt to be with a woman and not be able to ravage her like he was dreaming on doing.

Ariel glared up at him, digging her nails into his shoulders and hissed, "I am literally lying almost naked underneath you because I want you to do this; the least you could do is fück me like you mean it!"

Hades' eyes flashed a dark colour, losing the millimetre of restraint he had left and they both moaned once he began to thrust his hips forward. Ariel grabbed tightly unto him, letting her head tilt backwards and gave herself to him.

He grabbed unto her legs, pushing them further apart as he began to rock her hips into hers with such speed, she almost lost feeling in her legs. It was like a white hot fire was burning inside her, overtaking any emotion she had left.

Her mind went blank as she could only concentrate on Hades masculine physique towering over hers as he slammed his hips into hers. Her hand knocked down on the carpet and she curled her feet as mind-blowing sensations burst in her.

The harder Hades pushed into her, the louder she'd moan and gasp his name. A liquid fire of lust and unknown emotions rushed throughout them as they continued their joining, whispering dark obscenities in each other's ears.

Hard long kisses were exchanged along with sweat, which was the only separation between their bodies, along with the mediocre bit of clothing they had left on. Her white bra was halfway off and her shirt had caught around her arm, but they continued ravaging each other like wild animals.

"Shĭt," Ariel gasped, almost passing out by how powerful the passion was. She breathed in quickly, trying to help the flow of oxygen through her lungs and somehow wished that she could stop everything just to concentrate on the blissful feeling Hades was bringing her.

Breathing included.

Hades growled in a language she could not recognize, sounding hotter than anything she's heard before and he bit down on her shoulder, wanting to keep his pleasured grunts just for them to hear.

The savage couple completely forgot about the rest of the personnel in the castle. At that moment, even the dead could hear them and Hades couldn't care less.

Her nails ran down his back, leaving long red marks against his white creamy coloured skin. "Just..." she groaned, wrapping her legs around his waist tightly, "a little...harder!"

And he surrendered to her wishes.

"God," she moaned, "right there!"

The ardent and passionate joining for them felt like hours, but in reality they had only spent ten minutes together—and they had been spent extremely well.

Hades grunted loudly, leaning his forehead against her chest as he exploded inside her and left her shuddering in his arms. As if they had put their bodies in sync, they reached their climax at the same time, moaning each other's name and words that they could not understand—and chose not to listen.

Loud ragged breaths echoed through the room as Hades pulled away from her and fell on his side. His chest rose rapidly as he tried to regain control of his breathing and Ariel watched him silently.

There were many words to describe him, but the only one she could think of at the moment was: beautiful. Well, there were a plethora of words she could definitely use to describe him, but that was the only non-sexual one she could think of.

A yawn escaped her lips and Hades turned to look at her, he grabbed the comforter from her bed and pulled it down to wrap it around her. She snuggled into his side, placing her head on his chest and slid her leg in between his.

"Not so bad for a man who hasn't slept with anyone over a decade."

The God chuckled, shaking his head and wheezed a laugh. "You are something else, little Ariel."

"I'm not that little," she muttered, butterflies wreaking havoc inside her as she realized what they had just done. Not only had they just finished fücking, but it had been the best sex of her entire life!

Aphrodite definitely wasn't lying; and that was only the beginning.

"So," she said after a couple of seconds of silence, "are you going to let Hermes give me a tour of the Underworld?"

Hades was quiet for a bit and with a monotone voice, replied. "Why would you want him to give you a tour? It's my kingdom."

Ariel laughed, entwining her fingers with his and places a soft kiss to his jaw. "He offered to give me one, King Jelly. Besides, I know you're busy with your kingly duties and whatnot."

"I'm never too busy to show off my riches," he muttered, clearly disappointed that she hadn't asked him for a tour of his home, "and I am not 'jelly'."

"Fine," she rolled her eyes, a small smile grazing her lips, "you give me the tour then. But I have to let him know right now; I left him alone with Adrianne and he seemed to catch quite the liking towards her."

Hades watched silently as she sat up and fixed her shirt, not really caring about his nephew's rendezvouses as long as they didn't involve any her. His eyes returned to their normal colour, but pain flashed across them as he noticed the red marks on her back. He gently touched her back, startling and he sat up to press soft kisses to them.

"I hurt you," he whispered.

Ariel rolled her eyes, ignoring the now gigantic butterflies in her stomach and straddled his lap as she bit his bottom lip sexily. "It was a good kind of pain."

He gave a light chuckle, placing his hands on her waist and said, "Oh really?"

"Yes really," she winked down at him, laughing out sultrily, "I might just want you to do it again when I get back."

Before she stood up, Hades cupped her cheeks and kissed her tenderly; the second soft kiss they had—and first of many. "Then you better hurry."

12

CHAPTER 12

"**S**o," Hermes began as the couple entered the room, "are you letting Ariel come with me Hades?"

He shook his head, placing his hand on the small space of her back and said, "I'll be giving her the tour; after all it is my kingdom."

"Very well," he grinned, as if he knew something that they didn't. "Since you're coming, I guess we can have the tour today. I left someone in charge of the souls."

Ariel narrowed her eyes and winked at Adrianne who had dark red cheeks. She smiled timidly, looking down at the floor and stood by her side as the Gods argued on which route it would be best to begin.

"So..." Ariel grinned, "what do you think of Hermes?"

She shrugged, watching as the god threw his hands in the air and glared at Hades. "He's nice, extremely flirtatious, but he's nice."

"Do you like him?" She nudged her with her elbow playfully.

Adrianne laughed, shaking her head and snorted. "Hermes is almost the exact counterpart of Aphrodite. He has more than a 100 wives and I am not looking for that. I want a man that will stand by my side and just my side. Not three hundred others."

Ariel giggled, lowering her voice to a whisper as both men continued to argue and said, "You know...guys can change."

"Psh," she snorted, shaking her head, "Hermes is definitely not one of those men."

"Aw come on!" She grinned, "He's adorable and he totally has the hots for you."

"So?" She narrowed her eyes, "He just met me today. Contrary to the rest of the women he's been with, he'll have to earn my heart."

"It's my kingdom!" Hades bellowed, sounding like an impatient child, "I think I know which of the routes are best to take."

Hermes rolled his eyes, crossing his arms over his chest and said, "I spend more time travelling around it than you do!"

Ariel sighed, shaking her head and turned to Adrianne. "How about we just go by ourselves and leave the boys and their arguing alone?" She nodded, following the young woman down the stairs, to what she believed, were the doors to the exit.

As they neared the high obsidian doors, Hades and Hermes stopped their immature arguing and appeared at their sides. Before either could begin their fight again, Ariel smiled at them and said, "How about I decide where I want to go?

They nodded obediently, biting back their tongues to keep from arguing with her. She rolled her eyes, letting out a quiet laugh as Adrianne winked at her.

The large black doors opened slowly and Ariel took a deep breath, feeling nervous and excited. She expected the Underworld to be dark and eerie like Hades' castle, but as the doors continued opening, her jaw dropped open.

Again, she could only think of writing a very long letter to Disney about his depiction of Hades and the Underworld. In fact, anyone who had described the Underworld had not been correct, for the kingdom was beautiful.

"Oh my god," Ariel breathed, blinking slowly as she took everything in.

Green long fields of grass and tall trees adorned the outside with beautiful roses of every kind adding to the finishing touches. The location of the sunlight was impossible to make out, but it was there. It felt good and warm against her skin for she hadn't been outside in a long while.

She breathed in slowly, closing her eyes as the sweet aromas caressed her senses and she took a slow step forward. It was as if she were afraid that the beautiful mirage before her would disappear in the blink of an eye.

Hades watched proudly as she walked towards a neatly trimmed bush near a marbled bench. She sat down; hesitantly raising her hands to touch the red rose that shimmered numinously on the bush. Just as her fingers were inches from the petals, she closed her hands and pulled them away.

The roses were too beautiful to destroy. Hades sat next to her, slowly taking her hand in his and whispered, "You can touch them, if you'd like to."

Ariel shook her head, forcing a smile and said, "They're too pretty for that."

He chuckled, taking the rose from the bush and held it out for her to grab. "It's not a real rose, Ariel. This is made from gemstones, my realm is of the dead; I can't exactly have living things lying around."

She let out a laugh, staring at him with bright, excited eyes. "So...I can touch them?" He nodded, handing her the rose.

It was delicate but heavier than a real rose. The petals were smooth and thicker than the real ones and she let out a surprised giggle as the gemstone flower began to smell like the real roses. "It smells!"

"It does," Hades chuckled at her awed tone of voice and watched as she smelled it, a content smile lighting up her face.

Ariel squealed again, breathing in deeply and sighed, "It smells so good! Like it's really rich and...just amazing. I'll even say that it smells better than the real flowers."

Hades smiled, feeling captivated by her dazzling smile. She wasn't even trying and she had him at the palm of her hand. He blinked slowly, snapping himself back to reality and pointed to the nymphs dancing in the distance. "They do all of this."

She looked up and watched as the beautiful women danced around the vast garden. They pirouetted and jumped across, moving as graceful as they could. Ariel watched for a bit before turning to Hades and said, "They're beautiful."

The nymphs were dressed in light green dresses and many flowers adorned their heads as crowns. They wore no shoes and had long intricate swirls decorating their bodies.

The pleased God took the rose from her hands and placed it on her hair, tucking it right on her ear. Ariel felt her cheeks turning a slight shade of pink and she grinned up at him. "They used to be wood nymphs. Some turn into trees or something relating to nature, but others choose to come down here. Those who still love gardening and such, grow my garden and watch over it."

"That's really cool," she stood up, lightly touching the rose in her hair to make sure that it was still there.

Hermes and Adrianne were watching them quietly, satisfied smiles growing on their lips as they realized that Ariel was warming the God's heart. He was smiling a genuine smile and his eyes were shining brightly.

"So," she turned to Adrianne, "where should we go next?"

Hermes chipped in, "Elysium is right next to us, we could just go there...?"

Ariel turned to look at Hades, whom nodded and she grinned. He placed his hand on her lower back and led her through the enormous garden. Many bush statues of people she didn't recognize were scattered around the garden, adding an Edward Scissorhands look to it.

"You know what those things remind me of?" She pointed to the nearest statue.

Hades shook his head, helping her up a set of stairs and said, "What do they remind you of?"

She smiled knowingly, unable to keep her lips from widening and said, "Edward Scissorhands."

"Who?" he furrowed his eyebrows in total bewilderment.

Ariel sighed, shaking her head in disappointment and said, "We're going to have a movie date night and we're just going to watch a bunch of movies so you can understand the things I say."

The God chuckled, pushing the silver gate open and said, "It depends on what films we watch."

"Movies," she pressed, not liking how formal he sounded and said, "we are definitely watching Hercules; you need to see how people think you look like."

Hades turned to look at Hermes, whom was trying to help Adrianne but she stubbornly pushed him away and continued to follow the couple in front of her. Hermes shrugged, muttering under his breath about how difficult the girl was being and pouted his lips like a kid.

Ariel gasped as they entered the beautiful fields of Elysium and whispered, "Oh my goodness, this is gorgeous!"

Children ran around, laughing and singing. Couples walked hand-in-hand down the hills and others danced with the soft breeze that enveloped them. It all looked like it belonged in a picturesque photograph; it made her fuzzy and giddy inside.

"People are so afraid of death," she began, "but it looks so pretty here!"

Hermes pursed his lips and said, "Well, this is only for the privileged people whom have been nice during their life. Heroes, children and respected elders are allowed in Elysium. If you don't fit either of those categories, you're most likely stuck in Tartarus or Asphodel."

She looked up at Hades whom was watching a family play with their dog. "Are we going to see Tartarus today?"

He clenched his jaw, shaking his head and tore his gaze from the happy family; something he would never have. "We're not going to see Tartarus today or any other day, for that matter. One of the reasons being, that you cannot go by Cerberus or he'll rip you to shreds and the second reason is that it's called The Place of Torment for a reason. Unless you want to have nightmares the rest of your life, I suggest you take that thought out of your pretty little head."

She frowned, crossing her arms over her chest and muttered, "I'm not little."

He smiled at her expression and continued to guide her past the rivers. They crossed the Acheron River to reach the Asphodel fields and continued south to visit the Place of Judgement. The line of dead people waiting to be sentenced seemed to never end and since Ariel was growing hungry, they decided to speed up their tour.

Hades promised to take her on another, more detailed tour of his kingdom whenever she wanted and she obliged as long as it was just the two of them. As much as she liked Hermes' and Adrianne's company, she felt uncomfortable with them so close whenever she had the urge to kiss the God of death.

She didn't know what their relationship was, but she didn't necessarily want a term placed on them. Whatever they were doing felt extremely good and unless Hades cleared their status, she wouldn't bring it up.

They travelled down the Styx River and as they neared Tartarus, Ariel hid behind Hades for the screams, although muffled, were heart wrenching. He wrapped his arms around her waist, pulling her close to his chest and commanded Charon to speed his rowing.

The cloaked man didn't show his face and didn't say a word. He simply held out a black bag for them to pay for his trip and nodded in respect as his King entered the ferry.

Words could not express how thankful she was that they were able to leave the outskirts of Tartarus and she tightened her hold on Hades for reassurance as they halted multiple times for more souls.

They finally returned to his castle and as the obsidian doors came into view, Ariel and Adrianne let out content squeals. The day had been eventful, but also extremely tiring. Hades spoke about the different ways that the souls were judged and the different places in Tartarus.

At the mention of punishments in The Place of Torment, Ariel remembered Adrianne's murderer and asked Hades to explain what he went through, but he simply told her that he'd tell her once they were conversing privately.

Adrianne bid her goodbyes to Hermes as she walked down the hall to find something for Ariel to eat and he watched after her longingly until she was out of sight. Hades zoned out, in what Hermes explained was a conversation between other gods and Ariel looked around the grand palace.

Hermes turned to look at her and grinned mischievously before whispering, "You smell like Hades. Whatever he did with you, is alerting all the gods that you're his. It fades if you don't continue the joining so," he winked at her, making her blush, "have fun!

She definitely didn't want the smell to fade away.

Ariel watched as his strong fingers wrapped around hers and he began to trace her hands. Her cheeks slowly began to turn a light shade of rose as she realised that someone was touching her delicately and they weren't dying from her touch.

Hades continued caressing her soft hands, loving the feel of her delicateness. He could feel her reddened cheeks, warm against his naked chest and a sly smile grew on his lips. "Why are you blushing?"

She snuggled closer to him, closing her eyes so she wouldn't have to look him in the eyes and said, "I'm just amazed that you're the only person that I can touch. Ever since that happened, three years ago, I thought that I would never be able to do this."

He furrowed his eyebrows in confusion. "Do what?"

"Touch someone the way you're touching me," she mumbled.

He smirked. "Are you complementing my sexual skills?"

Ariel rolled her eyes, laughing at his attempt to lighten the mood and flicked his hand, before letting him squeeze her fingers gingerly. "No, King Jelly; I meant that I never thought I would be able to feel someone else's skin with my fingers. I didn't think I'd ever be able to let someone caress my hands; I like it."

He smiled, stroking her long black hair out of her face and kissed her forehead gently. "I do not want to get your hopes up, but I was conversing with Athena and Hecate and they think there is a possibility to train you."

"Train me?" She frowned.

"Yes," Hades nodded, "we have to speak to one of your ancestors. They think there is a way to control your powers."

She sighed, hiding her face into his strong chest and mumbled, "Don't call them powers; I am not helping anyone with them. This is a curse."

This curse brought you to me. Hades bit back his tongue, not wanting to spark an argument after the amazing day they spent and simply sighed. "As you wish."

Ariel grinned, lifting her head from his chest and pressed a soft, flirty kiss to his lips. "But your sexual skills are pretty freaking amazing."

Hades wheezed out a laugh, making her head shake up and down with his and he shook his head at her bluntness.

"What?" She muttered, feeling embarrassed now that he laughed at her.

He raised his hand up to her cheek and gently caressed it. Then, whispered something in a language that she couldn't recognize and pressed a kiss to her forehead. "You are very amusing."

She frowned, looking up at the ceiling and said, "Why do you do that?"

"Do what?"

"Speak in another language," she huffed, "you know I only speak English. You're probably insulting me and making fun of me because that's how mean you are."

The God raised his eyebrows in amusement, the corners of his lips turning upward as he began to run his fingers through her hair again. "Ancient Greek is my native language, when I think of certain things; I just say them that way. Only the Gods speak it correctly so it's kind of an easy way for us to keep things from people."

Ariel entwined her fingers with his, sliding her leg in between his and snuggled into his side. "You mean to keep things from me."

Hades grinned, nodding his head. "That could be one of the reasons."

"So did you lose your accent?" She traced her finger down his stomach, memorizing the strong abdominal muscles and scars he had.

He shook his head. "No, it just comes out when I speak Greek."

She grinned, turning to look at him with bright green eyes and said, "Say something in ancient Greek."

He laughed at her enthusiasm and spoke the first thing that came to his mind. You are beautiful. Ariel squealed, making him chuckle at her expression and she kissed him as she climbed on his lap.

"That has got to be the sexiest accent in the world and I don't even know what you said!"

Hades bit his bottom lip as she swiped her tongue across his neck and grunted, "You have a very high libido."

She winked at him as she began grinding her hips into his and whispered, "It's been three years, I have to catch up on all that missed time."

He wrapped his hands around her wrists, turning them around so he was above her and nipped at her neck as his growing bulge began sliding past her thigh. His eyes began to flicker between his normal eye colour to a darker blue as they raked over her gorgeous body.

"Funny you say that," he growled, biting her neck hard enough to make her moan but not to cause extreme pain, "I have to catch up on ten years."

Ariel moaned, desperately wanting to press her lips to his and slid her hands in his hair tightly. She raised her body off the bed, feeling liquid fire rushing through her veins at the feel of him thrusting into her again.

She had become addicted to his sexual touch.

"Dammit," she gasped, feeling the desperation growing profusely in the pit of her stomach. She needed Hades to push himself so deep inside her; she would be content for the next hour.

He kissed her hungrily, biting her lips into his mouth and swiping his tongue across her lips to leave her breathless. It was as if she was his oxygen and he was running out of it.

"Hades," she pleaded, staring up at him with bright desperate eyes. He growled, aligning himself with her centre and just as they would satisfy their voracious beasts, shouts began to come from outside of the room.

"She took my room," Persephone cried out, the anger in her voice made chills run down her spine, "and now my fucking husband?! Come out of there you little whore and give me back what you took!"

13

—— • ——

Chapter 13

Ariel pushed Hades off, the anger that was growing inside of her overcoming her lust for the god. She cursed under her breath, searching for her clothes and began to yank them on. "That bĭtch can eat her heart out."

Hades breathed out, quickly getting up from the bed and tried to stop her from leaving the only thing that was protecting her from his ex-wife. "Ariel," he cajoled, reaching for her arm, but she shrugged him away.

"Don't try to stop me," she tied her long hair up in a sloppy ponytail and searched for shoes, "I'm not someone to be fücked with; I'm not some damsel in distress; I will fück her up."

"Ariel," he said a bit louder as he zipped his pants up, "Persephone is dangerous; she's a goddess. You cannot just go out there and fight her, she will kill you. This is not some game."

He wrapped his arms around her waist, trying to stop her from shaking so violently and she hissed, "And interrupting my örgasm isn't some game either! Who the fück does she think she is?"

"I can hear you, bĭtch!" Persephone bellowed, tightening her hold on the alcohol bottle she was swinging in the air.

"You were supposed to hear me, whöre!" She tried pushing Hades away, but he tightened his grip on her and placed her in front of him.

"Listen to me," he spoke quietly and with authority, "if you go out there and mess with Persephone, no one knows what she will do. Let me just calm her down and then you guys can talk about-"

Ariel rolled her eyes, crossing her arms over her chest and pouted her lips like a child. "I don't want to talk to her; I want to rip her hair out for stopping us."

He chuckled, pressing a soft kiss to her lips and said, "As soon as she's gone we can continue, I told you; I have a decade of missed sex to catch up on."

She smirked, giving out a small laugh and said, "Look what you've done to me. I'm willing to go out there to fight a goddess because she interrupted us."

He winked at her, pulling his shirt over his head and said, "I'd do the same. Now be a good girl and stay put, okay? I'll be right back."

She rolled her eyes, looking away from him and huffed under her breath. Hades chuckled, shaking his head and opened the door. Ariel looked down at her nails and began to scratch off the cracked nail polish to keep her mind occupied.

"Persephone," Hades began, clenching his jaw as soon as he saw her, "what are you doing here?"

She glared at him, tilting her head to look behind him and said, "Where is she? I'm going to kill her." Her speech was becoming slurred and she took more swigs of the alcohol. "Hades," she whined, sounding pathetic, "she took you from me. Let's just kick her out of our home and I'll give you that kid you always wanted."

"That's enough, Persephone," he gritted his teeth, staring down at her with disgust, "just leave before I do something we both regret."

"Like what?" she cried, stumbling towards him, "Bring a whöre into our house? Sleep with her and then replace your wife?!" Tears began to slide down her face as she moved closer to the infuriated god and said, "She's tearing us apart, Hades. We have to stop her before it's too late."

Hades clenched his fists at his side, stepping away from her and said, "You need to leave right now, Persephone. I am not going to repeat myself. Leave before I make you."

Persephone growled, a sound so inhuman it startled Ariel, whom had her ear pressed against the door as she tried to make out what was happening. She slapped her hand across his face, leaving behind red fingerprints and she began to curse him out in Greek.

"You püssy-sucking bĭtch!" Ariel hissed, slamming the door behind her as she glared daggers at the intoxicated goddess. She looked up at Hades who tried to pull her behind him and pushed his hands away, "How dare you come into his house like a drunk idiot demanding that I leave?!"

"This is my house!"

"Your house my ass!" The infuriated young woman snorted, "It stopped being 'yours' the day you left him. The day you cheated on Hades was the day that you dropped everything he gave you. So do me a favour and get the hell out before I force-feed you the shit you've been saying."

Persephone turned to Hades, whom was looking down at Ariel with an amused look on his face and said, "You're just going to let her speak to me that way?!"

"I do not own Ariel," he shrugged, "she speaks however she wants."

The goddess threw the bottle down the hall, her brown eyes shimmering with hatred as she hissed, "She is your whöre, you should control her!"

Hades rolled his eyes, crossing his arms over his chest and said, "Ariel isn't a whöre and she isn't mine either. She does whatever she pleases."

Ariel blinked slowly, not liking the strange feeling that began building inside her. She didn't know if she liked that Hades said she wasn't his or if she wanted him to claim his stake on her.

"Fine," Persephone wiped the back of her hand against her mouth and said, "if you don't control her; I will."

She laughed, throwing her head back and crossed her arms over her chest. "What could you possibly do to me? You're the goddess of spring growth. Are you going to turn me into a flower? Oh my," her voice gained a slight Southern accent, "I just about tremble with fear."

The goddess growled, her eyes glowing maliciously as she clenched her fists at her sides and hissed, "You do not know what you're getting yourself into, mongrel. I can have any god I want, torture you. I am above you. Just because you can kill people with your hands, doesn't mean that I am afraid of you."

Ariel smirked, placing most of her weight on her right foot and said, "And just because you make flowers grow, doesn't mean I am afraid of you."

She let out an enraged cry, slapping Ariel across the cheek with such force that she fell to her knees. Hades stepped forward to help her up, but she pushed him away and growled out a sound that was foreign to even herself.

Persephone blinked once, a slight flash of fear appearing in her eyes as Ariel glared at her with glowing green eyes. Her voice didn't belong to her; it was a legion of sinister voices that brought chills to the drunken goddess. "I am going to fücking murder you!"

Ariel lunged at her, wanting to wrap her fingers around her neck and leave her completely breathless, but arms wrapped around her waist and pulled her back.

"Ariel, stop!" Hades ordered, "That's enough!"

She growled at him, pushing his hands away and stood up. The anger she felt was even stronger than when the Goddess had interrupted them. The hatred shredding the bits of humanity she was fighting off was overcoming anything she could have possibly felt before. "Fück you."

Hades sighed, holding Persephone behind as Ariel slammed the door behind her and said, "You need to leave right now. I am not kidding when I say that I will have Cerberus come for you, Persephone. You leave my realm and never come back. You are not wanted nor welcomed here."

"I'm the Queen-"

"-of the shrews," he finished for her, "now leave before I lose the speck of patience I have left."

She muttered something incomprehensible and vanished before he could do something worse. "I'm not done with her; I will kill her, Hades. Even if it's the last thing I do."

He wanted to open the door and speak to Ariel, but he knew that she was fuming and his presence would probably worsen the situation.

The infuriated young woman took a deep breath, trying to calm herself down as she paced angrily around her room. She pressed her fingertips against her temples, the massive headache growing in her head made her feel like someone was beating her with a hammer.

She needed protection from Persephone and the only person she could think of, could help her was the God of war: Ares. She could've asked Athena for help, but somewhere in the back of her dark, feminine, jealous mind, she wanted to provoke Hades for silently choosing sides.

If he at least felt something for her, he would show some type of discomfort with the thought of her being with another man in very intimate positions. If he didn't, then she knew that whatever she felt for him was one-sided.

Her face turned into a frown as she tried to figure out how to summon him and began praying as best as she could. "I think this will do. Er, Ares? If you can hear me I have a request to make. It kind of deals with your whole shah-bam, so I hope that you will answer me."

Ariel scratched the back of her neck awkwardly and squeezed her eyes tightly. "Please answer me, it's kind of urgent and I hate too many people to ask them for help. Do I have to like sacrifice a virgin now? 'Cause I don't have one..."

"You look amusing doing that," A man with a chiselled jaw and an extremely toned physique spoke from the middle of her room. "What do you need my assistance for?" He watched her with curious dark eyes, almost making her feel completely naked under his gaze and leaned back on the wall.

Ariel cleared her throat, completely unfazed by his sudden appearance and blushed as she clenched and unclenched her fists. "You're the god of war, right?"

Ares nodded his head, just watching her silently. It was making her feel uncomfortable, she felt like she was his prey and he was bound to strike any minute; a starving cobra. "Everyone knows that."

The arrogance in his voice made her roll her eyes and she stared at him with an emotionless gaze. "Can you train me?"

"Instruct you?" He frowned, now more interested than before. "In what?"

"Combat," she shrugged, sliding her hands in her back jean pockets. "I want to learn how to defend myself."

Ares snorted, a cunning smirk growing on his lips as he crossed his arms over his muscular chest. "What? Your hands aren't defence enough?"

She gritted her teeth, running her fingers through her tangled ponytail and said, "That is beside the point. Can you do it or not?"

"You've got quite the mouth," he noted, raising his dark eyebrows as he began walking around her. "Of course I can train you, it's my forte. Now the question is; how?"

She frowned. "What do you mean how?"

The God sighed, motioning towards her hands and said, "Have you forgotten that not all of us are immune to your—hands? If I am to train you, I will need to touch you and so on."

"I can wear gloves," she said in a matter-of-fact tone.

He opened his mouth to say something else, but then shook his head and then nodded once. "Very well, we can start as soon as you'd like-"

"Tomorrow," she interrupted, "the earlier the better."

Ares ran his fingers through his long curls, pushing them back to expose his strong forehead and said, "Is there something I should be notified of? Are you going to be in any type of battle?"

"No," she answered curtly, her cheek burned as a reminder of Persephone's slap flashed through her mind, "but Persephobĭtch wants to kill me. Hades won't always be there to protect me and I don't exactly need the gods thinking that I'm trying to kill them if I defend myself from her with my curse. That's where you come in, if you teach me how to defend myself, I can at least have a chance."

He was quiet for a couple of minutes and then said, "You're smart. I will train you. Does Hades know about this?"

Ariel gritted her teeth at the thought of him standing by his ex-wife's side and croaked out, "No; he doesn't own me. I do as I please." She repeated his earlier words, her heart tugging in her chest as she spoke them.

Contrary to what she said, she wanted to belong to him.

Ares tilted his head to the side, eyeing her and said, "You smell like him; you must've had some type of sexual contact, which means that you do belong to him."

"I belong to no one," she snapped, glaring daggers at him, "I have been spending the last couple of weeks here. Have any of you stopped to think that maybe, just maybe that's why I smell like him?"

He rolled his eyes, a small smile growing on his lips and he said, "That's a different type of smell, darling. But I will let you believe what you wish."

"Thank you."

The God nodded in response, bowing his head respectfully and said, "I will see you tomorrow morning, Ariel. Wear something comfortable, we will be going over basics and such."

"I will," she sighed in relief, "thank you, Ares. I owe you big time."

He chuckled, winking her way and said, "There are many ways to repay me, but I feel as if though Hades would have a paroxysm if you did."

She laughed, shaking her head and said, "Not to be rude, Ares, but you're not exactly my type."

"Ah, yes," he grinned, "you like them tall, pale and dead."

"More or less," she laughed, watching as he grabbed the doorknob and waved before disappearing afore her eyes.

She breathed out, sitting down on the bed and stretched her arms over her head. If Persephone wanted a battle, she'd get a war.

"You know," Hades spoke quietly as he entered her room, "you could've asked me to help you."

Ariel pursed her lips, slowing pulling her hair tie off when she stood up and said, "How many times will I have to tell you to knock before coming in? I could be naked-"

"-and I've seen you naked before, Ariel," he walked up to her, placing his hands on her shoulders. "I know you are angry, but you have to understand that we were married for decades before all of this happened."

She walked towards the bureau, placing the hair tie on the drawers and stared at herself on the mirror. "She slapped me," she whispered, "no one has ever touched me that way; not even Derrick. All you did was stand by and when I went to defend myself you pulled me away." She turned to look at him, hissing out as her anger returned, "Fück yes I am angry!"

"I am sorry," he said emotionlessly, "but I cannot just let you kill her. I loved her, Ariel. You have to understand."

"Ugh!" She groaned, closing her eyes and took a deep breath. "That's the problem, Hades. You love her; you still do. Otherwise you wouldn't have stopped me. And it's fine whatever, we had sex it was great; now it's over."

Hades rolled his eyes, turning her around to look at him and cupped her cheeks in his hands. "Listen to me, human and listen to me good. I do not love Persephone. There is not one bit of love left in me for her."

"Then why," she hissed through clenched teeth, "did you stop me?!"

He sighed, torn between smacking some sense into her or kissing her for being so adorable when she was angry. "I didn't let you kill her because I care for you. You are not a murderer, if you had killed Persephone, you wouldn't be able to forgive yourself."

Ariel opened her mouth and then closed it, not knowing what to say. She sighed, crossing her arms over her chest and muttered, "I hate you."

The God chuckled, pressing a soft kiss to her forehead and said, "The feeling is mutual, human."

She narrowed her eyes, stepping away from his embrace and said, "Stop calling me 'human,' I already told you that I have a name."

He rolled his eyes, but nodded, taking her cheeks in his hands again and caressed the faded red imprint. He leaned forward slowly, pressing a gentle kiss to the mark and whispered, "I am sorry for not stopping her before she hurt you. I will never let it happen again."

The millions of emotions whirling inside of her heart were indescribable. She didn't know if she was happy that Hades seemed to care for her or if she should've been afraid of her own growing feelings. It was a mixture of desire and confusion and she didn't know which one to choose.

"You are my guest, I should-"

"-just kiss me," she breathed, the desire she felt making her lose all rationality.

Hades smirked, bowing down to her level and pressed his lips against hers slowly. As he spoke, his lips brushed against hers teasingly and she almost melted by the vehement lust coursing through her veins. "It would be my pleasure."

14

— • —

CHAPTER 14

"Okay," Ares sighed, pinching the bridge of his nose with his forefinger and thumb, "next time don't twist your body to the right. If your attacker is paying attention, they'll see it coming and dodge it."

She nodded, panting for air as she crouched to her knees and raised her hands over her head, stretching her muscles. Drops of perspiration ran down her face, sticking some loose strands from her hair to her face and made the odour of deodorant thicken to hide the smell of sweat.

The God held his hand out to her, pulling her up to her feet and she groaned in complaint. For the past two weeks Ares had been pushing her to the limit.

In the beginning she thought she'd pass out from the exertion her body was going through, but he reminded her that in combat, her opponent wouldn't wait for her to 'catch her breath.'

"Contrary to what people have told you or taught you," he began, walking around her in a circle. He would try to distract her and if she wasn't paying attention, he'd charge and tackle her; she had to listen to his lesson, but be alert of his actions. "You do not want to focus on blocking your opponent's attacks."

Ariel frowned, her green eyes watching him cautiously as she stood in defence, waiting for his attack. "Why?"

Ares smirked, raising his hand to grab the back of her neck, but she quickly spun around, pushed his hand away and straddled his waist. She held her elbow at the base of his neck and tightened her legs around his.

"Because," he breathed out, smiling up at her proudly, "you will start worrying about what he will do instead of focusing on what he will do." He took a deep breath, waiting for her to climb off him and stood up.

Ariel nodded, tucking back loose strands of hair and said, "Got it."

Ares ran his fingers through his damp curls and pulled at the ends of his shirt to unstick it from his perspiring body. If it weren't for the smell, the sight wouldn't be bad to watch. Through most of their lessons, Ariel would ogle the God, for he had the body of one.

His shoulders were wide and broad. Whenever the muscles flexed on his back, it was a sight worth drooling for. His abdominals were so pronounced she could feel them through the fabric whenever their bodies pressed together—it was truly a sin.

"What are the parts of the body that you can do easier damage?"

Ariel wiped away the droplets of sweat sliding down her face and wiped her hands on her shorts. "The eyes, ears, nose, uh neck, groin, knee and legs."

He nodded, stepping away from her to give her some breathing space. "Correct."

She closed her eyes, trying to focus back on their lesson. At the moment, fighting someone was the least thing on her mind. Her primordial thoughts were on something equally physical but far more pleasurable; intercourse.

It had been two longs weeks that Hades hadn't even glanced at her and the aching in between her legs was growing more and more every day. She longed to be touched once more and the intimate positions Ares would place her in, weren't helping her desirous mind.

Her dark eyes glanced up to Ares, whom watched her carefully. He could tell she yearned for something, he just didn't know if his eyes were deceiving him or if she, indeed, wanted him. The way her eyes would darken whenever he placed his hands upon her was a dead giveaway, but he chose not to mention anything in respect for Hades.

Ares also knew that Hades was refuting his relationship with Ariel up in the realm, but that was a matter for her and the God to discuss; not his.

He cleared his throat, trying to clear the awkward atmosphere growing in the room and Ariel walked up to him. She lost all rational thought; her pupils were dilated and her voice wasn't recognizable.

"Help me," she whispered, sounding so vulnerable it hit a special nerve within the God. "This fire," she placed her hands on his broad, muscular chest, no longer caring if she seemed desperate, for she was, "it's eating me inside. I can't sleep anymore; it's like-"

"-like a never-ending craving...?" Ares whispered in return, a light sarcastic chuckle rasping past his lips. He placed his hands over hers, capturing her gaze with his glazing dark eyes and whispered, "You've no idea what you're getting yourself into, little one, walk away before things get messy."

Ariel rolled her eyes, feeling almost breathless with anticipation and stood on her tiptoes to level her lips with his. "I know exactly what I'm getting myself into; relief and sex."

The God threw his head back and gave out a laugh, placing his burly arm around her waist and pulled her closer into him. "What about Hades? What will you tell him?"

"What about him?" She bit out, "He refuses to face me after the last time we did anything; he clearly doesn't give a shit if I get my fill from someone else."

Ares grinned maliciously, the smile made him look sinfully gorgeous and the heat growing in her underwear was getting hotter and hotter by the second. He grabbed her jaw, biting her bottom lip into his mouth and she moaned at the sensation.

He bit down harder, sending shocks of delicious electricity down to her core and she moaned, wrapping her arms around his shoulders. She trembled against him, almost melting at the satisfaction she was feeling.

"What happened the last time?" Ares stepped away.

Ariel gritted her teeth, clenching her fists at her side and hissed, "He fücked the living breath out of me and then left—right away. He literally finished and got dressed then left without a word; hasn't spoken to me since then."

He grimaced, heaving out a sigh and said, "I am not going to take advantage of you. You are angry and you're craving sexual attention; whether you know it or not, Hades has made it clear that no man will touch you." He lowered his voice to a mutter, "Of course he denies wanting you, but we all know better."

She raised her eyebrows, crossing her arms over her chest, "He's denying me? What do you mean?"

He shrugged. "A god or goddess will ask if he has slept with you or claimed you, but he denies even entering your room. Of course, we know he lies but-"

"What an asshole," she hissed out, gritting her teeth in anger and said, "this is why he's still fücking single. He definitely knows how to treat a woman. Okay," she bit out, "I think that we're done for today. Thanks, Ares and sorry about what just happened."

He chuckled, saluting her with two fingers and said, "No worries, little one. Just try not to be too rash or it'll cost you in the long run."

Ariel nodded, turning around and walked out of the room. The anger that was coursing through her being was greater than the lust she felt minutes ago. She was sick and tired of Hades treating her like she was some fragile doll whenever they weren't joining in intercourse.

She slammed the door to her room as she entered, making the vanity mirror in front of the bureau tremble and she growled out. The more she thought about it, the angrier she got and after she showered, she found herself walking towards his throne room.

She ran different scenarios through her mind, to maybe stop herself from entering a suicide zone, but none of them ended so fatally. The worse he could possibly do was deprive her of any sexual relief; and he was already doing that.

"Hades," she called out as she pushed the obsidian doors open and gritted her teeth to keep from saying something she would later on regret. "We need to talk."

Hades raised his eyebrows at her sudden entrance and shook his head. "I'm busy at the moment, Ariel. I can't-"

"I'm not stupid, Hades," she huffed, crossing her arms over her chest and glared up at him. "I know when someone is avoiding me."

If he wouldn't stop to talk to her, she would make him listen.

He narrowed his eyes, "I'm not-"

Ariel gritted her teeth, holding her hand up to silence him and said, "Okay then you're just leaving the room any time I come. Let's call it that, instead, okay?"

He sighed, rubbing his fingers against his temple and said, "I've just been really busy with work and my duties as a king."

"We haven't spoken in two weeks," her face turned red in anger, "I know people die every day, but goddamn! A simple hi would suffice, you know?"

"Ariel-"

"I know I am no one to you. Just your sexual relief but you've locked me up and the only person I have to speak with is Adrianne. Don't get me wrong, I love her and all but I need to talk to other people as well!"

Hades opened his mouth again, to try and explain his reasons for not being by her side for two weeks, but she was too irritated to listen to his apologies.

"And don't get me started on the last time we slept together," she glared at him, "you literally fücked the life out of me and then left me. Like whatever, it's no big deal. Is that a thing that you gods are notorious for? Goodness gracious I'm not asking for much!"

"Ariel," he widened his eyes, but she kept interrupting him.

She threw her hands up in the air and said, "I know that I'm just your fück buddy, but I'd like to talk to you. You know? Be friends? Because, excuse me, but telling you to go harder is not a conversation long enough for me."

"Yeah, Hades!" A voice spoke from behind her, "Try to talk to the poor girl because you got the sex down!"

Her eyes widened and she could feel all the blood in her body, rushing up to her cheeks. She covered her mouth and squeaked, "They've been here all this time?"

Hades sighed, running his fingers through his hair and nodded. "I tried telling you, but you just kept going."

Eros winked at her, wiggling his now-hot-pink eyebrows and said, "It's fine, we prefer talking about this more than what our meeting was about."

"I," she whispered, turning around to look at all the Olympians sitting in the round table. "I'm really sorry. I just..." Her voice came out like the squeak of a mouse, "I was angry at Hades for...and I didn't know he was...I'm sorry!"

Poseidon laughed, loud and exuberant. "Well at least we know that our brother is finally doing something right!"

Zeus chuckled, saluting the embarrassed God. "Congratulations, brother. It's been quite a while! Were you able to last long?"

Hera rolled her eyes, slapping his arm and said, "Zeus! You do not ask that in public!"

Aphrodite laughed, shaking her head and said, "Well I, personally, am proud of my uncle. It's about time that he got some!"

Hades groaned, covering his face with his hands and muttered curses under his breath. Ariel grimaced, forcing out a smile and searched the room for the nearest exit. She could've just left the same way she entered, but for some inane reason, she couldn't remember the direction it was in.

"Of course you'd be proud," Eros muttered, "you're not the one sporting hot pink hair."

The Goddess of beauty giggled, poking his hair and said, "You look like a cotton candy ball."

He glared at her, slapping her hands away and said, "I am never betting against you again."

"Because you'll lose," she said in a singsong voice.

Eros rolled his eyes, turning to Hades and said, "You should've kept it in your pants a little longer, man."

Hades glared at them, slamming his hands on the obsidian table and said, "Enough about this! We have more important matters to discuss! There are people threatening her safety-"

"Her?" Ariel frowned, "Threatening whose safety?"

"Ariel," Hades sighed, standing up in front of her, "someone sent us a message."

She shrugged. "And?"

"They're threatening to kill you to obtain your soul."

Her eyes widened and she let her jaw slack open for a few seconds before regaining her composure and clearing her throat. "D-do you know who it is?"

"No," he clenched his jaw and sat back down, running his fingers through his hair in an annoyed manner. One of the things the God couldn't stand was not being in control. This was way out of his control; he didn't know who he was up against and merely thinking about Ariel's fate made his stomach churn with the utmost anger.

"Oh," she whispered, feeling like an idiot.

"That's why I haven't been with you much; we're trying to find out who did this and how to stop them," Hades continued, sounding as tired as he felt.

"But don't worry," Athena grinned, "we're going to do our best to protect you."

"Even though," Dionysus frowned, "it'll cost us the celebration we-"

Hades held his hand up, glaring at his brother and hissed, "We spoke about this, Dionysus! As long as there is a threat to my guest, I am not hosting a damn party."

"What's the celebration on?" Ariel ignored Hades' warning glares and turned to Dionysus for answers. This was the first time she spoke to him and she felt giddy, he wasn't intoxicated, but he seemed a bit—happy.

Dionysus grinned at her, taking a sip from his golden cup, "We celebrate the dead," he pursed his lips and said, "I know it's not something to be so happy about, but a party is a party nonetheless; I like partying."

Ariel laughed, liking his response and said, "Kind of like Halloween?"

"Yeah, I guess," he shrugged, "however, it's better!" His smile fell and he sighed, "But...Hades wants to cancel it this year."

"It sounds like fun," she noted, turning to the frowning God, "I don't think you should cancel it, Hades."

"You're my guest," he said through gritted teeth. "I'll-"

"I'm not just your fücking guest, Hades!" She exploded, turning red with anger, "We fücked for Pete's sake, stop treating me like I'm some fücking fragile doll! I've been taking care of myself and Ares has been training me. I think I can handle if someone tries to do anything, besides you're a god! If worse came to be, then use some of your voodoo shït and take care of it, dammit!"

All the gods stared at her in silence. Hades blinked multiple times, not expecting her outburst and tried to recollect himself.

Ariel growled out in frustration and threw her hands up in the air. "Ugh, just forget it! Do whatever the hell you want; you've clearly been doing a splendid job at it. Now if you'll excuse me, I'm going to see if I can seduce the statue outside to please me."

"Ariel," Hades cajoled, turning to his family and sighed, "excuse me for a moment." They all nodded, somewhat content that their brother/uncle was finally showing some emotions other than arrogance and hatred.

"Ariel!" He grabbed her hand, spinning her around to face him as she opened the door to her room. "Will you stop and listen to me?"

She glared at him, wiping away her tears and tried will all her might to not cry in front of him. "What?"

"I do not know why you're angry, I really don't. Just tell me what I can do to make it better. I do not wish to fight with you right now."

"You know exactly what you did, Hades," she narrowed her eyes, pulling her hands from his grasp and entered her room. As she sat on her bed, she bluntly said, "We had sex and you left me."

"Well I-"

"-what," she interrupted him, "bothered me more was that you stopped speaking to me. It made me feel like I did something wrong and I clearly didn't. I mean, correct me if I'm wrong but I don't think that you've slept with your other 'guests'. It makes me feel like I'm not returning the favour you give me whenever you give me earthshattering örgasms."

Hades chuckled at her infuriated expression and shook his head. Her words simply inflated his huge ego. "So I make you feel good?

Ariel rolled her eyes. "You know you do, but I, apparently, don't make you feel good."

He frowned. "Why would you ever think that?"

She gave him a deadpanned look. "You avoided me like the plague this past two weeks."

He sighed, sitting next to her. "I was not avoiding you, Ariel. It's just hard for me...you're so young and full of life—and I'm not."

She snorted, rolling her eyes again and said, "That's a bunch of bullshit, but you clearly don't want to tell me why you're avoiding me."

"I wasn't avoiding you," he insisted.

Ariel sighed, placing her feet on his lap and laid back on the bed. "Whatever floats your boat best, mister. But because you did that, I almost rapéd Ares."

"What?" His eyes turned black, a colour she had never seen before and his hands tightened around the white sheets.

"I threw myself at Ares. My goodness, I've never been so desperate for a man in my life that I had to throw myself at one. See what you do to me, Hades? I don't even know what the heck is wrong with me."

He whispered, "What did he do?"

"Turned me down," she replied bitterly, "am I that hideous? Like damn, I just want to get laid."

The God sighed, placing her feet on the bed and crawled over her. "You are not hideous, Ariel. He was respecting you," he leaned forward, pressing soft, sensual kisses down her neck and whispered, "and me, for you are mine."

"I am no ones," she gulped, entwining her fingers into his hair and pulled him closer.

He chuckled, darting his tongue out and caused her to tremble with pleasure. "If you wish to believe that, alright, but know that no man will touch you as long as you are-"

"If you say my guest," her voice came out hoarse, "so help me god, I will knee you so hard, you'll be in bed for two weeks."

Hades laughed, sliding his hand up her thigh, making her squirm underneath him. "I was going to say living with me, but that works too."

Ariel grinned, pushing him down on the bed and straddled his waist. She grinded her front into his hard bulge and whispered, "Well if no other man is allowed to touch me, you better make up for that."

He groaned, biting her lip and swiped his tongue over it. "You're a little freak."

She laughed in return, pulling her shirt over her head and said, "You call me a freak like it's a bad thing." She leaned forward, kissing him passionately and whispered, "Now show me why I shouldn't go out there and seduce that statue outside your throne room."

He growled in response, making her clothes disappear from her body and kissed her deeply. It was a desperate long kiss; he felt as if though she was the oxygen that he needed in order to live and he couldn't get enough of her.

Whether he liked it or not, Ariel was the fire in his life that had been washed out by the mistake the Moirai had so wrongfully placed in his life. And although his life thread was resistant to others, Ariel's had a special sort of magic that allowed the Fates to entwine them together.

It would take time, but they would eventually allow each other to create a bond so tight, that not even death itself could tear them apart.

15

CHAPTER 15

"Ah," she giggled, clapping her hands delightfully, "look!" She pointed to the flower and almost felt herself exploding with excitement. "It didn't die!"

Hecate laughed, nodding her head as she walked around the young woman to look at their experiment. For weeks they had been practising Hecate's theory of Ariel's 'curse.' She was the goddess of magic; after all, it was her forte.

The Goddess believed that she could control the power that emanated from her fingertips if she merely concentrated her emotions on enjoyment. If she felt anything other than positive emotions, the curse would overpower her will and she'd destroy the life source at hand.

"You have, child! I knew you could do it."

Ariel caressed the soft petals of the white peony in her hands and squealed once more. "I never thought I'd be able to do this! They're so soft!"

Adrianne entered the room with refreshments and snacks for her to consume and smiled, "What's got you in such high spirits?"

"I did it!" Ariel ran towards her, about to wrap her arms around her friend, but Adrianne stepped back with wide horrified eyes.

She shook her head and smiled reassuringly, "No; it's okay! I am learning to control them."

"You have improved immensely, Ariel, but do not get too comfortable; we are still running on risky waters. We need to take it one step at a time, alright?" She pouted her lips in disappointment and nodded. "Now, our lesson for the day is complete. I believe I will be seeing you two beautiful ladies in the ball tonight, correct?"

Ariel grinned, sliding on her gloves and nodded, "Yeah! We're waiting for Athena and Aphrodite to get here so we can get ready."

"Remember to wear Hephaestus gift," Hecate nodded, patting down her golden blonde hair and winked before disappearing into a light blue mist. She turned around to look at Adrianne and squealed in excitement. "It's going to be such a fun night! I haven't been to a party in so long!"

"Well get ready!" Adrianne winked, with a devious smile growing on her lips, "The Gods throw one heck of a party!" She giggled louder, slapping herself on the knee and sighed, "Ah get it? Heck and we're in hell? No...? No? Okay."

"Hades is going to die when he sees you," Aphrodite laughed, "and he's the god of death, so imagine how that'll play out."

Ariel laughed, shaking her head as she stared at herself in the mirror and admired Athena's masterpiece. The Goddess never ceased to amaze her.

The dress that hung to her body was short, revealing her beautiful toned long legs and accentuated her curves. It was red with diamond studs [courtesy of Hades, of course] and showed no cleavage. She looked beautiful, sexy and elegant wrapped up in one package.

Blood red stilettoes adorned her feet and her hair was curled neatly to the side. Her bangs were pinned away from her forehead, opening up her face and beautiful mystical makeup decorated her appearance.

Her eyes were accentuated by light gold eye shadow and Egyptian styled eyeliner. To finish off her look, her lips were coloured deep ruby red, brightening her already gorgeous smile and adding a seductive aspect to her look.

"If this doesn't knock Hades' off his feet," Athena began, "then I don't know what will! You look stunning, Ariel!"

She blushed, feeling more admired than she had ever felt in her life. "You guys did it all so you should be patting your backs."

"I think I will do just that," Adrianne laughed, spinning in front of her to show off her lovely green cocktail dress. "How do I look?"

"You know," Aphrodite began thoughtfully, "when Hermes told me that he was interested in you, I thought it was because he's interested with anything that has a beating heart and legs," Adrianne blushed darkly, "but I must say; you are pretty gorgeous! You must be one of my descendants."

The four women laughed, joking on about how stunning they all looked. Even Athena, who was mostly modest and not searching for a counterpart, looked beautiful in a black V-neck dress with a revealing slit down her left thigh.

Aphrodite managed to make a curtain with cat hairballs look fashionable; she wore a golden chic mermaid dress that hugged her curves tightly, but not in an inappropriate look. She managed to add an almost elegant look to it, looking like the true goddess she was.

"When Hephaestus sets his eyes on you, he's going to have a heart attack!" Athena laughed, shaking her head in disbelief.

Aphrodite winked in return and flipped back her luscious long hair. "When doesn't he? I mean, I am the goddess of beauty!"

"Yeah," her sister laughed, "but not the goddess of conceitedness, so stop being so damn full of yourself."

"I can't," she whined, "the mirror likes looking at me."

Ariel laughed along with Adrianne who was adding the finishing touches to her lips. Aphrodite turned to Adrianne and grinned, "I don't know why you're laughing so much; Hermes won't take his hands off you for the entire night."

Athena laughed, cleaning up the materials they used to create the dresses. "Ah, it's alright! She finally gave him the time of day!"

"What?!" Aphrodite gasped, "How come I didn't know of this?! I'm the damn goddess of love! I should know this!"

"It's not love," Adrianne mumbled shyly, "we're just friends."

"That used to be Zeus' excuse," Athena scoffed, making them go into a fit of laughter, until tears were sliding down their cheeks.

A soft knock on the door startled them out of their laughter and they quickly sobered up. "God," Eros groaned from the other side of the door, "entering a room filled with women is like eating figgy pudding."

Ariel giggled, rolling her eyes as she grabbed her clutch and said, "What's up, hot-pink-stuff?"

He rolled his eyes in reply, clicking his tongue in distaste and said, "The party already started about an hour ago. Hermes is sitting by himself waiting for Ms. Hard to Get. Hephaestus is playing with some metals and Hades looks like he's going to start killing people; you ladies need to grace those desperate men with your presence."

Before they walked out the door, Ariel turned around and ran to her bright neon green gloves. Aphrodite stared at them in pure horror and looked like she was about ready to bust a fuse.

"What. Is. That?!" She pointed at them with shaking fingers.

Ariel rolled her eyes, sliding the gloves on, much to the goddess dismay and said, "Your husband made these for me. They turn invisible when I put them on," she wiggled her no-longer-green-covered-gloved hand and said, "see? It's neon green so I don't lose them."

"Oh," the goddess sighed in relief, "okay; ladies, we may proceed!"

Loud upbeat music boomed throughout the castle's courtyard, making the ground shake slightly. Hundreds of gods danced along, grinding their bodies into each other and others almost sucked their mouths out of their faces.

Most of them, Ariel didn't recognize, but she paid no attention to it, for the man that had engrossed her was smiling brightly at her. Hades was dressed in a dressy black suit; he could've been wearing a trash bag and he'd still look as edible as he did then.

She breathed in sharply, turning to her friends for support but found that she was alone and the god of death was making his way to her. She surprisingly panicked, searching for the nearest way out, but her feet seemed glued to the ground and her eyes were captured by his.

"Wow," he breathed, lightly caressing her cheek, "you look absolutely stunning, milady."

Ariel giggled, feeling like a schoolgirl as he kissed her knuckles and took her hand in his. "You clean up well too, Mr. Death."

Hades snorted, rolling his eyes as he led her through a crowd of cheering gods [Dionysus was having a chugging contest] and said, "I always look handsome, human; otherwise you wouldn't look at me with those wide eyes all the time."

"Puh-lease!" She scoffed, "I like looking at ugly things too!" He laughed, handing her a glass of punch and waited for her to take a sip. "This ambrosia thing, you guys drink, is so freaking delicious!"

"Yeah," he placed the cup she had just taken back on the table, "but strong and if you drink too much, not even Dionysus will beat you in drunkard of the year."

Ariel rolled her eyes, feeling her cheeks go warm as he took her hand in his and stood in front of her; just looking at her, with his hypnotizing blue eyes.

"Would you like to dance?"

She nodded, breathing out in relief as he looked away from her, but was surprised when he cupped her cheeks and kissed her lightly. Butterflies began to flutter in her stomach as a nervous giggle blurted past her lips and he winked down at her.

"Since I'm dancing with you," she whispered shyly, "can I take my gloves off? I like touching you."

He laughed, winking down at her. "Of course you do; go ahead, I don't mind. Just don't touch anyone."

She nodded and placed the gloves in her clutch.

Hades placed his hand on her lower back, spinning her around in circles to the beat of the music. Ariel squealed as she recognized the song as Classic by MKTO and left Hades surprised as she began dancing freely. She moved her hips lively, laughing as she sang along and dazzled him with his beauty.

"I'mma pick you up in a Cadillac, like a gentleman, bringing glamour back. Keep it real to real in the way I feel, I could walk you down the aisle."

The God rolled his eyes, spinning her back into his chest and brushed his lips past her earlobe as he whispered, "That's being a gentleman? I'd pick you up in my chariot."

She laughed; loving the feel of his muscular arms wrapped around her waist and threw her head back as they continued dancing the night away.

"You know," he mumbled into her hair after the hundredth song they had danced to had ended, "I was really against having this celebration thing after the threat they sent us, but I'm glad I did. It was fun."

Ariel grinned, wrapping her arms tightly around his shoulders and kissed his chest, "I had a lot of fun too and I'm glad you decided to-" She frowned, pulling up away from him and said, "Hades, what's wrong?"

His eyes were wide, shining a bright blue and he tensed up against her so rigidly, he felt like a statue. "Something's wrong."

"What?" She looked around, trying to see what he meant. "Everything looks fine-"

"No," he repeated, "something is wrong. Cerberus saw something that didn't belong in my realm coming this way." He unwrapped his arms from around her waist and just as he opened his mouth to send her into the castle, a loud booming noise exploded, creating a chaos amongst the gods.

"You got to go!" Hades growled, searching for someone to protect her, "Go into the castle and lock yourself in a room. Hit anyone you don't know and don let anyone in. I'm going to keep you safe, okay, love?"

"Hades-" she began, panic bubbling up her chest.

Adrianne ran towards them, grabbing her hand and said, "Come on, milady! I know the perfect place to hide."

Ariel nodded, turning back to look at Hades and dropped her jaw open as he transformed into something so godly, she couldn't believe her thoughts. She wanted to bed him! He wore traditional Greek armour that made Brad Pitt in Troy, a laughing stock compared to him.

"Pretty sexy, right?" Adrianne winked, laughing as she pulled her through frenzied gods. "That's what I thought when Hermes did the same thing. My goodness, can they rock those armours! I was tempted to go into battle just to see him!"

She grinned in return, snapping her thoughts back to the panicked and screaming gods and said, "What's happening?"

"Watch out!" Adrianne pushed her out of the way, gasping in pain as an arrow pierced her skin and pushed her on the floor. Ariel widened her eyes in fear as Adrianne forced her to lock the castle doors behind them and suddenly collapsed on the floor.

"Adrianne!" She gasped in horror, "You-"

"Can you take it out?" She groaned in pain, whimpering as she touched the blood darkening her beautiful dress. "Athena's going to kill me for this."

Ariel rolled her eyes, searching for her gloves and felt her heart dropping to the pit of her stomach. "I can't!" She cried out, frantically searching for her gloves. She couldn't locate them and she swore she had her clutch in her hand that entire time. "Dammit, where is it?!"

"A-Ariel," Adrianne coughed, the thick red blood oozing down her jaw simply terrified the young woman further, "it's okay. You have to pull the arrow out...I can't breathe..."

She shook her head, warm tears sliding down her cheeks as she knelt beside her friend. "I can't pull it out! I can't find my gloves and I don't know where everyone else is at. Please you have to fight for me."

"It's poisoned," She smiled, so angelic and comfortingly, that it tore her further apart. How could she look so happy when the arrow that was slowly killing her was poisoned?! Her heart was shattering, feeling a type of sentiment that she hadn't felt in a long while; hurt. "Can you at least put pressure? It'll lessen the pain."

Ariel sniffled, wiping the back of her hand against her nose. Her hands shook nervously as they hovered over her friend's body and she sobbed loudly. The chaos erupting behind the obsidian doors that protected her became louder and louder each second and Ariel feared the worst.

She felt helpless and useless. The only way she could help her friend was with gloves and she couldn't find those. As for controlling her emotions, she felt like a hurricane was rummaging them all, disabling her control over the curse.

Adrianne was the closest person she had to a friend; she couldn't lose her when everything was becoming so chaotic in her life. She needed the support a friend could bring and Adrianne was extremely good at lending a shoulder to cry on.

"P-please," Ariel sobbed, holding unto herself for support, "please, Adrianne, don't do this to me. Don't leave."

Hot tears slid down her cheeks as she watched Ariel's heart breaking. A tremendous fire was erupting deep within her stomach, were the poisoned arrow was immovable. Her brown eyes widened as she felt more blood crawling up her throat, leaving a gross iron taste behind.

"It hurts," she whimpered, "I just want it to end now."

Ariel ripped a large piece off her dress, wrapping it around her hands as best as she could and frantically fought against time to save her best friend's life. "No, don't say that. Hermes and Hades need you...I need you..."

"Don't make this any harder, Ariel," she whispered, blinking away her salty tears, "I died with honour; I saved your life. Master Hades hired me for that; it was my destiny to do that."

"Fuck destiny!" She roared, wrapping her other hand, "You're not going to believe all that shit they try to feed you about fate! You control that, not some ugly witches that share one eye."

Adrianne gave out a coughed laugh, wanting to hug her friend tightly. "Those aren't the Fates."

"Well whatever, you're not going to die today. Not by some stupid poisoned arrow, not if I can help it."

"Ariel," she sighed, gritting her teeth as the fire began to grow throughout her body. She felt as if though a thousand needles were pricking her back and tearing her apart from the inside out. As her heart quickened its pace to pump much needed blood, she felt herself going lightheaded, but the pain simply augmented. "Please end it?"

She sat up; using the last bits of strength she had left in her as a massive spasm exploded in her back. Adrianne gritted her teeth, clenching her fists as more blood gathered in her mouth, making her feel as if though she was drowning. "You're just making me die a slow p-painful death."

Ariel's bottom lip trembled and she felt herself shattering, losing the battle to despair. "This is why I don't let people in; I hurt them."

"You didn't hurt me, I saved you. Please, just repay me that favour with a small one," Adrianne reached for her head, but she recoiled almost instantly. "Ariel," she sat back on the floor, holding unto her wounded stomach with shaking fingers, "tell Hermes that in my next life, I'll be waiting for him."

"No," she shook her head; the tears that were running down her face began ruining her make-up, making her look like a red raccoon, "you won't have to do that." She choked on her tears, wanting to do so much, but not finding the strength to be able to, "You're going to be okay," she took a deep breath and wiped her tears away.

Ariel took a deep breath, forcing out a smile and grabbed the smooth wooden arrow. "I'm going to pull it out, okay? That way, you're going to be able to tell him that he won't have to wait. You're going to love him and...and," she sobbed, placing her hand on her stomach and stared at the weakening girl before pulling on it.

Through the small opening of the dress that the arrow had ripped through, Ariel's fingers lightly brushed on her skin, making the dying girl drop her mouth open as the pain she felt, almost tore her apart.

Ariel didn't notice.

Adrianne gasped, her last breath of life wasted on a thankful goodbye.

As the realisation that she had sped her friend's death, Ariel cried out. The sound was so raw and pure; it released a beast that she had buried years before. It trembled throughout the castle walls, silencing any chaos that could possibly be occurring outside and startled the frightened gods.

"No!" She gasped, almost choking on her tears as she brought her bloodied hands up to caress Adrianne's pale cheeks. "No, I didn't...I didn't touch you. Please, don't...Adrianne!"

Her shoulders trembled brokenly as she sobbed, denial running through her mind. Her hair fell around her face, sticking to her salty face and she cried like never before. Not even for her boyfriend's death had she cried so hard.

"Ariel!" Hades ran in the room with other gods running in behind him. He widened his eyes in fear at the sight before him and tentatively stepped towards her.

The broken young girl cradled her deceased friend in her arms, rocking her gently as she continued spilling hopeless tears. "For me," she whispered as Hades placed his hands on her shoulders, "she died for me and I repaid her by killing her."

"Hades, what's going-" Hermes stopped mid-sentence, feeling his heart skip a beat as the familiar long black locks of his beloved came to view. "Adrianne?" He whispered, walking towards them and in a fit of rage, pushed Ariel away. "WHAT HAVE YOU DONE?!"

Tears quickly began to fill his eyes, preventing his vision from seeing clearly and he held her tightly, wanting to desperately save her of her fate. "You bloody murderer, you killed her! You killed Adrianne...my Adrianne..."

Hades growled menacingly, wrapping his arms securely around Ariel and pulled her away. He placed his warm hand against her cheek, trying to take her attention away from Hermes' accusations and whispered, "Ariel?"

"He's right," she whispered back, in a monotone voice, tears still sliding down her cheeks as the God desperately tried to comfort her, "I killed her; I'm a murderer."

He hugged her tightly and closed his eyes, wishing to take her pain and remorse away. "You are not, Ariel."

She sniffled, staring down at her bloodied hands. "That arrow was meant for me…and she got in the way; they should've killed me. Hermes is right, I'm a monster."

Hades growled again, tightening his hold around her and forcefully said, "Do not listen to my nephew! You are not a monster!"

Ariel placed her hands on her lap, leaning into Hades' chest for support as her body began numbing and closed her eyes, welcoming the cold darkness that welcomed her to their realm. Slowly she came into the realization that the thorns of a rose could rip its petals apart; and in the end, the rosette would just wither.

16

CHAPTER 16

"Ariel," Hades whispered, lightly stroking the side of his hand against her face, "a⊠á⊠, look at me."

Her bloodshot eyes continued looking at Hermes' backside as he cried over Adrianne and she felt another tear sliding down the side of her face. Hades sighed, standing up and cradled her into his chest. He bid farewell to his family, whom were all watching Hermes with sorrowed eyes and turned to walk away.

"Hermes...I'm sorry," Ariel managed to croak out, but her voice sounded so hoarse only Hades heard her. She closed her eyes, spilling more silent tears and held unto Hades for dear life. At that moment, Ariel felt lost. She felt mixed emotions and her mind could only think of one thing.

Taking her life for taking her best friends.

As if he could hear her gory plan, Hades shook his head, wanting to say something about it, but decided against it and placed her on his bed. "I'll be right back; I'm going to get you a cloth to clean up."

She nodded, turning on her side to hold unto one of his pillows and stared in awe at the grandeur of his room. She had never been inside his chambers, whenever they did anything sexual, it was always in her mediocre room.

The bed dipped underneath Hades' weight and she turned to look at him. His lips tugged upward into a very small smile as he began to clean away her dried tears. Ariel closed her eyes, feeling confused by his light touch.

Whenever Hades touched her, it was sexual. He was never careful or gentle—and it was angering her. She didn't need him to feel pity for her; she already pitied herself enough.

"Stop," she whispered, pushing his hand away.

The God frowned, placing the damp cloth in a bucket and pushed it away from the bed with his foot. "What's wrong?"

Ariel opened her eyes, staring at him with an emotionless expression. "How are you so calm?" Anger began fuelling her, tormenting her thoughts even further. "How can you sit here and just try to act like nothing is wrong?! I just killed someone, Hades! I killed my best friend," she sobbed, gritting her teeth as she tried to hold back her tears, "and you're just sitting there as if nothing had happened!"

He watched for a few seconds, his dark eyes bore into hers and he cleared his throat, "What would you like me to do then? Would you like me to mourn over her? I can't do that."

She sat up abruptly, angrily wiping her tears away. "Adrianne admired you, Hades! She told me she saw you as her father and you're telling me that you can't fucking mourn her death?!" She tried kicking the comforters off her legs, but he held her down.

"I cannot mourn someone who isn't dead, Ariel."

"W-what?" She stopped struggling his grasp, staring at him with confused watery eyes.

Hades sighed, standing up from the bed and faced away from her. "Adrianne is reincarnated every time she dies; she's not dead."

Ariel frowned, placing her hands on her lap feebly. "I don't...I don't understand. I mean, can't you just bring her back? We won't have to wait until she grows up and whatever." Her eyes began shining with ideas and she smiled as she climbed off the king sized bed.

"Hades, please bring her back! I'll do anything, just please bring her back." She placed her hand on his shoulder, hugging his waist with the other.

"I can't," he replied, emotionlessly.

"What do you mean you can't?!" She gritted her teeth, letting go of him as she took a step back, "If it has to do with the balance of life you can just take mine instead! You know? Kill me and trade my life for hers?"

Hades turned to look at her, his blue eyes glazing with bright anger as he grabbed unto her shoulders and shook her, "Do you not understand that I cannot do that?!" She looked up at him with wide eyes, his outburst taking her by surprise. "I don't have that power, Ariel. What you're asking of me is impossible for two reasons."

She looked down at his fingers that were digging deeply into her shoulders as he held her and he reluctantly dropped his hands to his side. "I am the God of Death, Ariel. My realm, my power, my being is of the dead. I cannot bring back life. I meant it when I said that everything I touched; I destroyed."

"B-but you're a god," she whispered, her voice breaking hopelessly, "you should be able to do that."

"The most I can do is reincarnate her. I can let her soul be reborn into the mortal world and allow her entrance to the Underworld once she reaches appropriate age."

Ariel wiped her tears away, sitting on the side of the bed and stared down at her hands. "What's the appropriate age?"

He sighed, running his fingers through his dishevelled hair and said, "I'd have to wait for her to pass the mortal laws. She'd have to reach 18, but that doesn't mean she's allowed entrance here. She has to remember everything and sometimes it takes time for her to remember. I don't decide that; the Fates do."

"Can't we ask them to hurry the process?"

He shook his head, turning to look at her and said, "I already made that deal with them. I can't alter it any further for I am already transcending their boundaries."

"Oh," she whispered, lowering her eyes to her hands and began to play with her fingers idly.

Hades sighed, kneeling before her and took her hands in his. He pressed a light kiss to her knuckles and whispered, "I am sorry, a□á□□, I know you miss her terribly and I wish I could do more, but I can't. If there was a way to speed up the process I would, but even us gods have laws that we must follow."

She nodded, blinking away her tears and whispered, "I killed her, Hades. I killed someone else and this time she was innocent."

He sat beside her and pulled her in for a hug. "Ariel, you did not kill her. Whoever let those mongrels into my kingdom did. The arrow that hit her? It was poisoned with an incurable toxin. It is a poison that Cronus had created to destroy his kids. Our mother found it and hid it, which is why he swallowed us."

Ariel frowned, turning to look at him. "Wait, your father really swallowed you?"

He smiled down at her and nodded. "You mortals have some facts of mythology right."

"So, can that poison kill the gods?"

His smile froze and he stared at her with expressionless eyes. "N-no, we're immortal. Only Rhea knew where it was hidden and she hasn't been seen for a long time. She was one of the few Titans that were allowed to live among us."

Her frown deepened and she bit her bottom lip. "Then, how did those people get the venom? And who were they?"

Hades sighed, running his fingers through his hair again and then slid his hand down his face. When he opened his eyes to look at her, they were no longer shining or vibrant; they were dull and tired. "They were mortals, about 15 of them. They all committed suicide before we got to them."

"Can't you just ask their souls?"

"That's the problem," he whispered, "their souls are nowhere to be found. When I heard you screaming, I was looking for the souls with Hermes and Thanatos, but it's as if they just disappeared into thin air. I've never had that problem. Whoever they're working for, knows how my laws work."

At his defeated expression, Ariel felt her heart tugging in her chest for him. She pulled him in for a hug, stroking his hair gently and kissed the top of his head. "You're going to figure it out and when we do, I want to personally deal with the person who killed Adrianne."

"Revenge is a dangerous path, Ariel," he sat up, looking at her with serious eyes, "I know you are hurting, but once you go down that road, there's no coming back. And you won't be able to live with yourself."

She stared at him for a couple of seconds in silence and whispered, "I killed my best friend, Hades. You can't bring her back, no one can and Hermes is hurting. He probably wants to kill me and I understand why. Revenge might not be the best way to go, but it's the only thing that makes me want to keep on living."

He gritted his teeth, standing up and forcefully said, "You did not kill her, Ariel. You simply took her out of her misery; the poison was spreading slowly and bursting her insides. Would you have preferred she suffered through that? A true friend would've done what you did."

"Then why do I feel guilty?!" She cried out, no longer able to cry for her body was too tired to produce tears. "Why does Hermes blame me? Because if I hadn't touched her, she would still be alive and maybe Apollo or someone else could've healed her!"

"Hades!" Someone pounded on the door, startling the couple out of their quarrel.

The God frowned, walking over to the door and opened it. Athena pushed him away, closing the door behind her and began speaking in Ancient Greek. Whatever she had told Hades were clearly not good news, for his eyes flashed a bright blue colour and he growled.

"Stay with her," he pointed to Ariel, "if anyone comes in, kill them."

Ariel frowned, standing up from the bed, but Hades shook his head and said, "Stay here, Ariel. Please, do me that favour and stay here."

She scowled. "What's wrong? I want to help!"

"Believe me, you'll be lots of help if you stay here."

He muttered something under his breath, summoning his sword and held it in his hands defensively. To say that he looked like a god would be the understatement of the century.

Ariel knew that gods were supposed to be beautiful, but there was something about Hades that distinguished him from his family.

He had a certain splendour that made him more beautiful than he already was.

She turned to look at Athena, whom was wearing her armour as well and whispered, "What did you tell him?"

Athena sighed, sitting beside her and said, "One of the minor gods began an uprising. A small group think that they are being placed in danger by keeping you here. They want to kill you so that it buys us more time against the group that are threatening us."

"B-but I didn't," she whispered, fear crawling up her back, "I don't want to kill any of you."

"We know that," she sighed again, eyeing the door, "but the idiot, Bathel, thinks that you killing Adrianne, was a warning of what you'd do to us."

Ariel gritted her teeth, forcing herself to speak the words that Hades told her. "I didn't kill her! And I would never kill any of you."

The Goddess smiled comfortingly and pulled her neon green gloves out of her bag. "We know you wouldn't, Ariel, but like I said, they are idiots. Here, one of the mortals that entered the realm had these."

She frowned, sliding them on and said, "How did they even get these?"

"It must've fallen during the commotion," she shrugged and sat down next to her, pouting her lips. "It kind of sucks being stuck here. Don't get me wrong, you're nice to talk to and all, but I want to know what's going on outside."

Ariel nodded, standing up and said, "Then let's go. Hades told me to stay here, but not you. If I go with you, I'll be okay."

Athena chuckled, shaking her head and said, "Your plan has way too many holes, but since I want to know too, we can go."

She grinned and they walked out of the room. At first everything seemed calm, but as they neared the throne room, the commotion and screams, made her arm hairs stand in point. Ariel gulped as Athena slowly opened the door so that they could hear things clearer.

Through the small crack, Ariel could see Hades standing before hundreds of gods and he did not look happy. His face was so livid, she felt afraid of what he was capable of doing.

"Enough!" He roared, silencing the room, "I have heard enough! And all I will tell you is this; if any of you even dare to come near Ariel with wrongful intentions, I will skin you alive. I may not be able to kill you, but I can make you suffer."

A short blond man, stepped forward, scowling at Hades and said, "You would stand against your own family for a mortal?!"

Hades snarled, curling his lip over his teeth and the god who spoke up, visibly gulped. "If I have to fight the entire army of Titans to protect her, I will. Do you all understand me? If any harm comes to Ariel, I will not cease to take matters into my own hands. I don't give a damn if there are laws against hurting your own kin, none of you will hurt her as long as I live and I'd be damned if any of you try to kill Death."

Zeus stood beside his brother, placing his hand on his shoulder and whispered something in his ear. Then he looked at the gods before them and said, "I second my brother's warning. The girl is powerful, but she is not a threat to us as long as she is kept safe. She has no intent on hurting us; we should be trying to keep her protected from those who want to turn her on us."

Poseidon nodded, standing alongside them and raised his sword. "I stand by my brothers; no harm shall come to the girl as long as we are able to fight."

The short blond god glared at them and spat, "No wonder people are trying to kill us, you have gotten soft with the humans."

Ares walked over to the three gods, holding his sword out and said, "Are you threatening us Bathel?"

The gods that stood beside Bathel, all took a step backwards, looking at the four gods in utter fear. Bathel turned to them, shaking his head and turned to Hermes after all the Olympians stood next to Hades—all but one. Hermes.

"Will you protect her too or did her killing your beloved have no effect on you?"

In the blink of an eye, Hermes appeared before him, grabbing his collar tightly as he hissed something in a language that Ariel couldn't understand. She turned to Athena, who smiled proudly and whispered, "He's telling Bathel not to speak of her."

"And yes," Hermes spat as he threw Bathel to the ground, "I do stand by my brothers and sisters; Ariel didn't kill her. The group of incompetent mortals did; and they've started a war."

Ariel turned to look at Athena with wide eyes, but she entered the throne room. "And if they want war," she turned to Ares, who winked at her as if they shared an intimate joke, "they've earned it."

Hades nodded his head in respect and turned to the rest of the gods. "Do I need to take precautions against my own kin?"

Bathel snarled, disappearing before their eyes and the rest of the gods shook their heads. A small woman with long green hair took a step forward, bowing her head and said, "I apologise for my brother's attitude. One of his mistresses left him and he's all edgy lately. I assure you, we mean no harm to your Queen, King Hades."

The God forced back a smile, liking that they all knew his intentions with Ariel; make her his Queen. "Thank you, Zariah." He turned to the rest of the gods and spoke with power, "You may all be dismissed from my realm; if you see anything out of the ordinary do not hesitate to notify me."

Hades walked over to Athena and sighed, "Where's Ariel? I thought I told you to stay with her."

Ariel pushed the doors opened and ran towards Hermes. His eyes widened as she threw his arms around him and hugged him tightly. Tears brimmed her eyes, threatening to spill over as she whispered, "I am so sorry about Adrianne, Hermes. It wasn't my intention to hurt her!"

He tensed up against her, not returning the embrace and whispered, "It is alright. I am sorry for the things I said to you. I did not mean what I said; you are not a monster, do you understand me?"

She looked down at her hands and muttered, "I feel like I am. If it hadn't been for me, she might've been able to speak to you."

Hermes shook his head, pulling her in for a tight hug and brushed his lips against her hair. "They poisoned her, Ariel, no matter what you would've done, she would've died. Now," he forced out a smile, "we just have to wait for her to come back to us and make sure that this time, she stays for good."

"Thank you," she wiped away her tears and he nodded, releasing her from the embrace.

The God turned to look at his family and cleared his throat. "I meant what I said, I will protect Ariel, but...I need some time to myself. I have to see if there is a way to find those souls."

Hades nodded. "I will go with you."

"No," Hermes shook his head, smiling at Ariel, "you have your Queen to look after. Thanatos and I will be able to cover some ground by ourselves."

The rim of his ears turned a slight shade of pink as Eros winked at him and whispered, "And you said you didn't mess with her kind. Look at you now, threatening to fight the Titans if anyone hurts her."

Ariel blushed, standing next to Hades and he slid his arm around her waist, pulling her into him. "You all placed her in my care; I have to protect her."

Eros rolled his eyes, running his fingers through his hot pink hair and said, "Yeah, yeah, keep telling yourself that."

Hades glared at him, thanking his family for standing beside him and then guided Ariel to his room.

She sat on his bed quietly and unclasped her heels. She placed them next to his bed neatly and suddenly felt shy as he began pulling his armour off.

"Are you tired?" Hades put a white shirt on and comfortable pants.

Ariel nodded, standing up and said, "Thank you for today. I'll, um, see you tomorrow?"

Hades chuckled, raising his eyebrows as he watched and said, "Where are you going?"

She frowned, feeling confused. "To my room...? I want to take a shower and this dress looks like it'll be uncomfortable to sleep in."

He walked towards her, hugging her from behind and pressed a soft kiss to the underside of her chin. "Will you stay with me tonight?" He cupped her breasts, rubbing his thumbs over them and she nodded, knowing that if she spoke, she'd sound vulnerable.

Hades unzipped her dress, letting it pool at her feet and handed her one of his white shirts. She took it, turning to look at him and stifled a moan as he captured her mouth with his. He swiped his tongue over her lips, savouring the sweetness of her mouth and entwined his fingers in her hair.

Ariel closed her eyes in pleasure, loving how she felt whenever he touched her. He slid his hand down to the dimples on her back and pulled her closer, feeling as if though time wasn't enough to allow him to do whatever he wished with her body.

"H-Hades," she moaned, biting her lip as he pressed soft kisses down her neck, "let me take a shower first."

He sighed, releasing her from his hold and pressed a soft kiss to her lips. "It's through those doors." She turned around to walk to the doors he pointed to and as she crossed the threshold, looked back at him.

"Would you like to join me?"

She didn't need to ask him twice.

17

— • —

CHAPTER 17

Hades took his sweet time kissing her, leaving her completely and utterly breathless; the good kind. She moaned, wanting to feel his hands all over her at the same time. Her body was in fire and she needed to be sated.

He could feel her trembling against him with need as he deliberately slid her bra strap off, kissing her tender skin as he did so. Her heart thumped inside her chest nervously as he unclasped her bra expertly, surprising her as he didn't struggle with it whatsoever.

Ariel pleaded in moans, not knowing how to voice her needs without sounding more desperate than she already felt. His hands on her were light and caring, making her feel a whirlwind of emotions twirling in the pit of her stomach.

She was afraid of looking deep into his actions for they were loving and she didn't want to put that thought in her head. She was just Hades' release; he couldn't possibly love her the way she was beginning to feel towards him.

Her head tilted back into his chest as he slid his hands towards her breasts, cupping them in his hands lightly as he rubbed her nipples teasingly. She gasped as he slipped his hand down to her core and grunted at the moisture gathering in her centre.

"Hades..." It was a low growl, almost inaudible, but desperate enough that he abided to her needs.

Hades parted her lower lips, seeking for her nub and began to fondle her femininity, eliciting moans from her mouth. Ariel gasped, grabbing unto his neck as his mouth found the soft spot, between her ear and neck, and he began kissing it with his tongue.

Her legs shivered as her underwear slid past her calves and he grabbed unto her waist, lightly picking her up so she could kick them off. She tried to turn her body to face him, but he shook his head and held her in front of him.

Ariel groaned, feeling high off desire and bit her bottom lip hard enough to draw blood as he skidded his nose down her jawline, leaving behind a ticklish but sexual sensation. He breathed in deeply, muttering something in his native tongue and then whispered, "Love, I've been dying to kiss you all day."

"Then why the hell," she huffed, "are you not kissing the breath out of me?"

He chuckled, wrapping his arms around her waist as he turned her to face him and gently kissed her lips. He almost did it in a seductive fashion, brushing his lips against hers teasingly, leaving her wanting for more.

The God pulled away, smirking down at her as she slowly fluttered her eyes opened and whispered, "How the hell can someone kiss so freaking good?!" She groaned, wrapping her arms around his shoulders and kissed him deeply.

She swiped her tongue over his bottom lip, earning grunts from him and she suckled deeply on his sweet tongue. His flavour was addicting; he tasted of sweetness, nothing like what she'd imagine death to taste like.

She figured that since he was the God of death, he'd taste bitter and gross, but Hades was far from bitter or gross. He even smelt evocative and more masculine than anything a fancy perfume company could concoct.

"I just," she breathed in between kisses, feeling the need to speak, but not wanting to break the passionate and desperate lock of their lips, "I just want you naked, Hades, dammit!"

He gave a light, husky laugh, bowing down to kiss her and against her lips murmured, "Your wish is my command, milady."

Suddenly she could feel his strong arms wrapped around her waist, holding her up and her legs were locked around his naked torso. She groaned, grinding herself closer to him and tightened her legs around him, loving the warmth of his skin.

Hades began walking towards the shower, locking the door behind him as he pressed her against the wall and continued kissing her, feeling as if though he couldn't get enough of her. She had become the source of life he needed in his existence.

As the God of Death, Hades didn't have a heart. He had only felt his heart beating twice in his lifetime. The first was when he initially laid eyes on Persephone; she was dancing on a field of flowers, calling to all the gods who dared watch her–but only he was brave enough to take her.

He tried to woo her into staying with him and she began to return the feelings for the god, turning him into a nicer being. But Demeter, his sister, became enraged that she was with Hades, when she could've been with someone like Ares or Apollo.

She believed that her brother was never good enough, who'd want to reign over the dead? When they could control music or bring honour to the family. No matter that he was one of the three major figures; Demeter did not want Persephone with him.

So she 'grieved' and refused to let the crops on Earth grow so Zeus would allow her to take back her daughter. Persephone didn't want to leave, so she deliberately ate from the pomegranate fruits Hades had advised her not to eat from, and stayed with him.

As Demeter's grief began affecting more gods, Hades persuaded her to leave him for third of a year.

Ariel pulled away from their kiss, heaving out a sigh and lightly touched his jaw. "What's wrong?"

Hades smiled, wiping the crease between her eyebrows with his thumb and whispered, "Nothing could be wrong at a perfect time like this," she giggled, shaking her head and he said, "you are truly beautiful, Ariel, how you are not one of us; I still don't know."

Her cheeks heated up as he kissed her tenderly and began to trail debauched kisses down her collarbone. She moaned, tilting her head backwards as he kissed hard enough to leave love-bites behind and slid a hand in her front again.

An eager mewl bubbled out of her throat as he began to gently play with her lower lips, bringing about waves of passion that wouldn't allow the others to topple over each other; she felt that she'd burst by how wonderful he was making her feel.

"There is something I want to try," he whispered huskily, placing her on her feet and she watched with curious eyes as he began kissing her body, lowering his lips to her stomach and then thighs.

Ariel widened her eyes as he kissed her calves, then move upward to the space in between her legs and kneeled before her. Hades smirked up at her wickedly, lightly pushing her legs apart and she leaned against the wall to support herself.

As he pressed soft kisses to the inside of her thighs, he muttered, "I have never done this before, so forgive me if I–"

"–Hades," she interrupted him, her green eyes blazing with an undying hunger, "you're about to –holy shit!" She gasped, arching her back of the wall as his lips met with her centre and began lapping at her as if she were the source of eternal youth.

She grabbed her hair, biting her bottom lip roughly and muttered an incomprehensible string of words as he pushed her closer to the wall as he continued to lick her core. His tongue snaked around her bud, teasing her and she silently thanked Aphrodite for reminding her to wax earlier that day. The Gods of sexual desire definitely knew what they were doing.

Hades widened his mouth, trying to suckle her entire core into his mouth and she shuddered, crying out in unbelievable pleasure. His tongue brushed past her clit, making her breathe in sharply and she arched her back, curling her fingers in her hair.

"Dammit," she whimpered, as he ran his tongue down the length of her slit, "holy fuck, mother of Popeye and the damn peas, Hades!"

He chuckled at the strange words leaving her mouth and the vibrations of his voice sent her over the edge. She blacked out for mere seconds, barely able to breathe as he continued to assault her drenched püssy with his divine tongue.

Ariel looked down, almost feeling her legs giving out underneath her as she locked eyes with Hades. He was watching her, loving the sexual expressions she displayed. He was obviously bringing her pleasure and it filled him with lust and pride.

Her love for fruits was definitely coming through as he lapped at her feminine juices, tasting the strawberries she adored. Eros was not lying when he advised the God on pleasuring her; Ariel seemed to be soaring through the heavens as he continued suckling on her centre.

A loud groan escaped her lips as Hades pushed her legs further apart and twirled his tongue in painfully slow strokes, leaving her breathless and jittery. Her fingers wrapped around his hair, pulling him closer as he began to flick the tip of his tongue on her nub and she almost begged him to stop.

Almost being the keyword.

Eros had also advised the inexperienced god that if she begged him to stop, he was doing something well. At the time, Hades couldn't understand; how could she enjoy something and tell him to stop at the same time?

But as he continued licking her almost clean, he noticed what the god meant. Ariel couldn't decide on what to scream louder; "Faster!" "Stop!" or "Don't stop!" He determined that continuing until she reached her fifth climax would be enough.

Hades slowed his strokes, sliding his entire tongue up and down the length of her slit as she bucked her hips into his face and finally released her sore centre. She sighed in relief, moaning once he trailed a soft pattern of kisses up her stomach and towered over her.

She smiled up at him, feeling completely dazed and whispered, "How did you even...wow...like, I've never felt anything like that in my life! How did you even do that, if it was your first time?!"

Hades chuckled, turning the faucet on and faced her. He tucked back her hair behind her ear and felt the rim of his ears turning a light shade or rose. "Eros suggested I'd do that. Apparently you mortal women find that really pleasurable."

She leaned back on the wall, closing her eyes to regain her breath and said, "Damn. I am freaking speechless! If I knew öral sėx was that amazing, I'd come here sooner!"

He laughed, grabbing the showerhead and began to pour warm water on her shoulders. Ariel closed her eyes, leaning into his strong chest and said, "You really haven't done that before? Not even with Telephone?"

"Tele–oh," he grinned, shaking his head, "no, we never did anything that...pleasurable. The sėxual intercourse between us was very..." he trailed off, frowning as he tried to find the right word.

Ariel smiled, feeling content and triumphal; she brought Hades more pleasure than Persephobitch could ever. "Dry? Boring? Repetitive? And she never did it for you?"

"No, she didn't. Now don't get cocky," he continued to laugh, "it wasn't horrible, but it was nothing compared to ours. As I said before, you have a very high libido; I am surprised you can keep up with me. I like it."

She grinned, turning around to press a soft kiss to his lips and whispered, "Oh, babe, my sėxual beast is never fully satisfied. You're going to have to do more than that if you think you can get rid of me that easily."

Hades grinned, a devious smirk growing on his lips as he closed the faucet and stepped towards her. "Is that right?" She nodded, biting her lip to keep from smiling, "Well I guess I'm just going to have to kneel before you, my queen."

"Mm," she moaned, biting his lips sensually as she whispered, "I like that. I've been called 'bitch' before during sėx, never 'queen'."

He snorted, shaking his head as he hoisted her up to wrap her legs around his waist and said, "You've never been with a king in bed, milady."

Ariel threw her head back, giggling uncontrollably and said, "You're such a geek…but it's turning me on! We're going to have to work on your dirty-talk, but right now I want you to do something else."

He opened his mouth to argue with her, but grunted in pleasure as her warm fingers wrapped around his hard shaft and she slid herself down on it. Hades hissed in through his gritted teeth, pinning her to the wet wall behind her and growled out at her tightness.

No matter how many times they'd do it, she still made every inch of him burn with unspeakable desire.

She jerked in his arms as he slid his full length in her and clamped her teeth down on his shoulder to prevent herself from allowing the rest of the castle's personnel hear her throes of passion.

Hades quickened the pace of his hips at her request, filling every right spot that she yearned to be completed. He held her waist with his left hand and entwined their right hand together, pressing it against the wall as he continued pleasuring her.

Ariel closed her eyes, feeling feeble as waves of climax shattered throughout her body, leaving her completely exhausted. She never wanted the addicting feeling of Hades inside of her to end. She felt complete as they shared a carnal amalgamation.

One couldn't tell where the god began or where he ended; their bodies were moulded so perfectly together it was as if the Fates had created her solely for him.

He pressed his wet forehead against her heaving chest and kissed her damp skin sensually as he slowed down his strokes. It was almost deliciously painful as he slid his entire shaft from her and in one swift motion, penetrated her once more.

Her jaw went slack as he continued the pattern a few more times, until he found his release dancing above his fingertips, he just needed a few more encouraging moans from the beautiful young woman underneath him and he'd reach it.

She swore white stars were twirling above her eyes, making her desirous for her release and she suddenly went limp in his arms as an earthshattering sensation exploded throughout her body.

Ariel cried out, swearing loudly as Hades whispered delicious fantasies next to her ear, brushing his lips against her earlobe as he slammed his erection so deep into her wet cavern, she almost lost it and passed out from passion.

She stood corrected; the God of the Underworld could definitely talk dirty.

Hades breathed loudly, trying to recuperate the air exiting his lungs and gently placed her on her feet. She swooned, almost collapsing and he heaved out a chuckle as he held her up against him, struggling to keep himself upright.

"Will you call me crazy," she sighed as her breathing returned to normal, "if I say that I want to do that again?"

He bursted out laughing, opening the faucet once more and began to rinse away their sexual fluids. "We have time for anything you want to do, ayann, but right now we reek of sex; we have to shower."

She grinned lazily, as he began to wash her hair gently and she returned the favour. They spent less than three hours in the shower, just tending to each other's needs and she made a mental note to return one of his favours. It was only fair, since his idiot of an ex-wife never gave him the pleasure of oral sex.

"I don't understand," Hades frowned, popping a piece of popcorn into his mouth, "how can they think I look like that?!"

Ariel giggled for the umpteenth time, snuggling closer to him and said, "I told you, a lot of people think that death is scary. Plus you're the villain of the movie, you can't be attractive."

"They gave me blue hair," he whined, staring at the animated version of Hercules with pure disgust. "And I would never allow the Titans to escape Tartarus."

She grinned, kissing his cheek lightly and said, "I know, King Jelly. But it was a good movie, wasn't it?"

He shrugged, smiling at her as she got off the couch and searched for another Disney movie they could watch. "It was okay. I just find it humorous that Megara and Hercules are walking down to Earth all happily, when in a couple of years, he's going to murder her and their kids."

"Hades!" She chastised, shaking her head as she plugged in Mulan, "That is such a horrible thing to say!"

"What?" He laughed, "That Disney man got everything wrong! The Fates are not ugly nor do they share one eye; those are the Graeae. And I'm not ugly."

"You're not, King Jelly, you really are not." Ariel shook her head at his immaturity and sat next to him. He placed the bowl of popcorn next to him as he grabbed her waist and pulled her onto his lap. She smiled at him, pressing a kiss to his lips and licked the saltiness off her lips.

"What did you say this buttery maize was called?" He ate more, licking his lips and smiled at the delicious but salty taste.

"Popcorn," she chuckled and patted his thigh as the Mulan began to sing about her reflection, "sometimes you're so old fashioned it scares me. How can you not know what Disney or popcorn are? This place has kept you in the dark for too long, I'm going to have to take you out and keep you up to date."

"That's funny," he mused, "your people think my kingdom is ugly and dark, but it's not."

She raised a perfectly arched eyebrow. "And?"

He furrowed his eyebrows in confusion, his smile fading as he slowly said, "You said this place has kept me in the dark for too long...? I thought...never mind."

Ariel laughed, leaning back into his chest and wrapped the wool blanket closer to them. Hades wrapped his left arm around her and continued to eat popcorn with the other hand, feeding her some whenever she opened her mouth.

She felt like a queen in his arms and it was only logical; Hades was the King of the Underworld, she was going to become his and spend eternity with him–for only his Queen could live forever.

As Ariel giggled at Mushu's clumsiness, Hades smiled. He loved her smile. He loved her laugh, her moans, her eyes, her face; her.

The second time his heart ever pulsated was when Ariel came into his life, he could only hope she wasn't like Persephone and she'd actually stay.

18

⸺ ◆ ⸺

Chapter 18

At the dawn of morning, when the ersatz sun shone lightly against the side of her cheek, Ariel began stirring on the bed, slowly wakening from her slumber. She turned on her side and covered her mouth as she giggled at Hades' expression.

The God had woken up almost seconds before her and was struggling with something in his mouth. Ariel propped herself on her elbow, turning to look at him and said, "What are you doing?"

He frowned, sliding his nail in between his teeth and muttered, "There is something stuck in my teeth, it's that maize thing—popcorn?"

She grinned, keeping some distance between them as to not suffocate him with morning breath. "I told you to brush your teeth last night, silly!"

Hades narrowed his eyes, standing up and said, "You fell asleep on my arm last night, I didn't want to wake you so I went to sleep with you. It is very uncomfortable; it feels like my teeth are separating."

She pointed to the door, smiling at him with mirth shining in her eyes and said, "Go brush your teeth. It'll take out the little popcorn chips. You should've brushed your teeth when I went last night."

He huffed, muttering curses under his breath as he entered the bathroom and walked over to the sink. He stared at himself in the mirror and smiled in satisfaction. He hadn't seen his eyes shining so brightly in a long time; surely Ariel was good for him.

Heaving out a sigh, Hades grabbed his toothbrush and began ridding his teeth off the strange sensation of the chips stuck in between his teeth. Afterwards, he splashed cold water on his face and looked at himself in the mirror once more.

"Blue hair," he huffed, "out of all the hair colours they could've given me, they chose blue." He shook his head, running his fingers through his hair and walked out of the room.

A bright smile grew on his lips as his eyes landed on Ariel. She was lying down on his bed, a content grin on her face as she tapped her fingers against her stomach, rhythmically and as she became aware of his presence said, "I could so get used to this."

"Oh really?" He smirked, crawling on the bed towards her, "What could you possibly get used to, milady?"

"Oh nothing," she sighed nonchalantly as he grabbed her legs and wrapped them around his waist, "earthshattering orgasms, movie nights...you."

His smiled, if possible, widened, almost peeling his cheeks apart as she rested her hands on his chest. "I could definitely get used to this too, love. What would you like to eat for breakfast?"

"Mm," she let her hands fall on the plush pillows underneath her and said, "fruits!"

Hades laughed, pressing a soft closed-lip kiss to her mouth and said, "Do you have any preference?"

"Nope," she shook her head, snuggling closer to the warm blankets and said, "whatever you pick out is fine with me."

"Alright, I'll be right back, don't go anywhere." he nodded his head and grabbed a robe from his closet. She loved seeing him in casual clothes. She had forced him to wear grey sweatpants and a V-neck shirt, and he looked simply edible.

As he went to gather her breakfast, Ariel hopped off the king sized bed and made her way to his grand bathroom. If she thought that Persephone's bathroom was nice, she definitely had never seen Hades'.

It was large, enough to fit about fifty people in the room. The décor of the bathroom was simple yet elegant. Black and grey but even then, he somehow managed to pull that off as well. She grabbed a new toothbrush, humming to herself as she glanced over at the glass doors of his shower.

The imprint of her backside was still faintly outline on the doors and she blushed, remembering the wicked things that ran through her mind whenever Hades did anything as much as look at her. She just wanted to be in his bed forever⬚she could only hope he wanted the same as well.

After she brushed her teeth, she rinsed her face, wanting to cleanse her face and tied her hair up in a bun. She then climbed back on the bed, purring⬚yes purring⬚at the feel of the luxurious bed silks.

As he neared the room with the fruits, a heart wrenching shriek thundered from the suite and he dropped the food running to Ariel. His eyes widened in fear as he pushed the door open and ran to her, preparing himself to battle anyone who tried to harm her.

But she was alone.

Hades frowned, stepping towards her and she gasped, widening her eyes in terror as she tried to explain the exorbitant sensation burning throughout her body. "Ariel, what's wrong? Are you hurt?"

She opened her mouth to speak, but the pain became so unbearable that she could only moan in pain. Her eyes searched the room frantically for something, yet even she didn't know what she sought for.

Her fingers tightened around the silk sheets and Hades cursed under his breath as she began to turn a deathly pale colour. "Hermes! Apollo!" He frantically called for his nephews, fearing that whatever was hurting her, would eventually kill her.

Ariel felt her eyes water as she continued shrieking in pain. Her backside felt as if someone was burning her with a hot iron whilst at the same time tearing her skin apart with a knife. A gurgled cry rasped her throat as she arched her back and Hades took a hold of her hand, falling to his knees as he watched her helplessly.

She tried to gulp back her fear, but it simply worsened her pain. Her eyes began to flash brightly and she held unto Hades' fingers as tight as she could; it was the only thing keeping her alive. She felt as if though she were drowning, a massive force crushing her chest and preventing oxygen to flow through her lungs.

Hermes ran through the door, hearing the desperate cries of his uncle and widened his eyes in fear at the scene before him. Ariel seemed to be possessed by a deadly demon; there could be no other explanation for the ear-piercing cries leaving her mouth.

"Where's Apollo?!" Hades growled, turning back to her as he began stroking her hair out of her face. "I need him, dammit!"

"I'm here!" A young handsome man entered the room and widened his eyes at his uncle's lover.

Ariel arched her back off the bed, digging her heels unto the sheets as she fought with all her might to keep the shrieks within her. Whenever she cried out, Hades seemed to tear himself apart. He did not like seeing her in pain and not knowing how to help only worsened the situation.

Apollo blinked, his bright blue eyes glancing down at his uncle and he said, "What happened to her?"

Hades snarled, curling his lip over his teeth and said, "If I knew, do you think I would have called for you?! I cannot help her and she is dying!"

He sighed, running his fingers through his blond hair and walked towards the bed. The pain radiating off the young woman, made his stomach churn and he widened his eyes. "Holy shit!"

"What?" Hades felt his heart thudding slowly in his chest, fear making him think of the worst.

"The pain she's experiencing," Apollo shook his head, placing his hands over her body, "it's incredible! I am surprised it hasn't killed her yet."

Hades growled, making the God of healing roll his eyes as he tried to lessen her pain. "Uncle, it made me feel pain. I've never felt anything like it before."

He turned to look at her and kissed her knuckles as she looked at him with despair shining in her green eyes. She gritted her teeth, groaning as she fought to stay strong in front of the god and suddenly wished with all her might for death.

Apollo didn't seem to be helping much and she was becoming desperate. He sighed, shaking his head as he tried to figure out how to help her and said, "What was she doing before this?"

Hades shrugged. "I don't know. She was fine this morning, I went to get her breakfast and on my way back I heard her screaming. Then I saw her like this."

He nodded, waiting for his uncle to step away and took a hold of her hand. His eyes widened as the excruciating pain echoed throughout their slight touch and he gritted his teeth as he looked down at her. "Ariel, where does it hurt?"

She rolled her eyes, breathing in deeply as she tried to speak and sputtered out, "Every...where."

"I need you to be more specific, I can't heal you unless you tell me where the strongest pain is coming from."

"Back," she hissed, closing her eyes as another cry fought past her lips.

Apollo nodded, slowly turning her around and gasped, "Holy crap! I didn't know she had tattoos!"

"She doesn't," Hades frowned, walking over to get a better look and slowly widened his eyes. "What in the world is that?!"

Hermes stepped forward, his eyes glancing over her naked back. "They're moons."

Apollo rolled his eyes, numbing the pain erupting on her back and said, "We can see that, Hermes."

"No," he shook his head, stepping closer and lightly traced one of the patterns, "these are Hecate's moons. This is a mark, uncle; look at the moons." He trailed his finger down her spinal cord at all the moons that were covering it and said, "They're changing. It starts off as a full moon and then it goes through the entire cycle until it disappears."

Hades frowned and said, "What does Hecate have to do with this? Is she trying to hurt Ariel?"

"I don't know," Hermes shrugged, still frowning at the intricate pattern of swirls that adorned her smooth back.

Although Apollo managed to numb the pain that was coursing through her body, Ariel couldn't take much of the pressure she felt, and passed out from exhaustion. Hades sat next to her, stroking her hair and turned to Hermes. "Go and get Hecate for me, if she refuses to come, tell me and I'll personally go and get her."

Hermes nodded, quickly disappearing to search for the goddess. Apollo looked down at the immobile girl and said, "Uncle, the pain," he shook his head, feeling at a loss for words, "it was crazy. It made me feel discomfort; it must've been hell for her."

Hades sighed, covering her back as he began to feel uncomfortable that another man was seeing Ariel semi-naked. She seemed so beautiful in her slumber, but he was afraid that it wasn't going to stay that way.

Her screams of despair where etched into his mind for the rest of his eternal life. "I am so sorry I cannot help you, Ariel, I do not know what caused this, but I promise you that I will find out who did this and make them suffer ten times worse than the pain you felt."

The Goddess of magic entered the room confusedly and stood waiting for Hades' questions. "Brother, what happened to Ariel?"

"I don't know," Hades stood up; his eyes flaming with a dangerous anger that made her cower in fear as he faced her, "why don't you tell me?"

She frowned. "I-I don't know what happened to the mortal. I certainly wished her no harm if that's what you're trying to get at!"

Hades took a deep breath, pointing to her back and said, "Then explain why her back is covered with your mark."

Hecate covered her mouth, gasping in surprise and quickly ran to his side. Hades watched with curious eyes as she began to mutter words that only she could comprehend. "This is bad, this is really bad."

The God frowned, waiting for further explanation and said, "What is it?"

"She's cursed, Hades," Hecate stared at him with pitied eyes as she began trailing the patterns of the moon on her back. "This is a timetable; whoever cursed her must've done the curse with a deadline."

Hades gulped, watching as Ariel began to stir on his bed and whispered, "Do you know who cursed her?"

"I did," she whispered in return.

His eyes snapped to hers and he almost wrapped his hands around her neck to suffocate her, but she held her hands up in surrender and said, "Wait! Wait!"

"What?" He snarled, fighting the urge to lock her in Tartarus.

"I didn't do intentionally!" Hecate stepped away from Ariel as she turned to look at the four gods in the room and the goddess whispered, "I didn't know it was her when I helped my daughter!"

Hades gritted his teeth in anger, clenching his fists at his sides and hissed, "Then, explain to me how this came to be!"

"Hades?" Ariel croaked, frowning at how rough her voice came out and Hermes handed her a cup of cool water. "Thank you." He nodded, stepping away from her and turned to Hades. "What happened?"

"Ariel," Hecate interrupted, "when's your birthday?"

She raised her eyebrows, wiping the corners of her mouth after she finished the glass of water and said, "Uh, November 30th...why?"

"Today is November 30th, child," she whispered, making all of the people in the room frown at her in confusion. Hecate sighed, clearing her throat and spoke louder. "The curse was supposed to begin once you turned 17, which is why you were able to take life away so early. But the reason curse was completed whenever your birthday fell on a full moon. That was today."

Ariel frowned, shaking her head and said, "I don't understand. What do you mean I'm cursed? I mean, I don't exactly call my ability to kill people with my hands a "power," but you're referring to is is as a real curse."

"That's because it is," Hecate ran her fingers through her jet black hair, tucking it back behind her ears and sat beside the young woman, "but I believe that someone else should explain this to you." She turned to Hades and said, "Hades, do you think you can summon a soul?"

"Who?" He raised his eyebrows as he crossed his arms over his chest.

"Vera Aglea Lockhaven," her eyes flickered over to Ariel, whom was too dizzy to understand what was happening, "Ariel's great, great, great, great, great, great, great grandmother."

"I'll go get her," Hermes offered, disappearing before them once more.

Apollo turned to them with an amused look on his face and said, "As much as I'd like to stay here and figure out what is wrong with Hades' dear, I've other duties to attend to. If you need me, just call me, uncle."

Hades nodded, his eyes shining with appreciation and he said, "Thank you, Apollo." He nodded, smiling a boyish grin and vanished, leaving a light blue mist cloud behind.

Ariel rubbed her temples, swallowing back her fears and whispered, "You guys were saying something about my back; what was it?"

"You have ink on your skin, a□á□□," Hades lightly stroked the side of her cheek with his thumb and she frowned in confusion.

"How?"

"It's a mark," Hecate cut in, "like I was telling Hades, it's a timetable. It will let you know how soon your curse will end."

"Wait," her green eyes lit up, "my 'powers' will go away?"

The Goddess bit her bottom lip, shaking her head and said, "Not exactly...but I believe your ancestor should explain it to you."

Ariel nodded, scooting closer to Hades as Hermes brought forth a barely visible woman. She was young, but looked older than Ariel. Her hair was long and black, reaching past her behind. Her eyes were bright and blue and for a moment, Ariel felt jealous at how beautiful the woman was.

Until she realised that the spirit was her great, great, great, great, great, great, great grandmother.

"Ariel," she whispered, smiling at the girl with affection, "you truly have grown to be beautiful. I didn't think that Apollo was being truthful when he said you'd be as beautiful as you are right now. Edmund and I did a wonderful job, don't you think?"

Hades stood up, bowing his head in respect and said, "Vera, my name is□"

"□not to be rude," Vera interrupted him with a sly smile on her lips, "my lord, but everyone knows who you are; King Hades."

He smiled, feeling smug that he was so acknowledge and said, "You are correct."

The spirit turned to look between them and smiled widely, "Are you taking care of her, my lord?"

The rim of his ears turned slightly pink and he nodded as Ariel dropped open her jaw and blushed darkly. "I am."

"Good," she sighed, turning to her granddaughter, "so, I am guessing you are curious as to why you are cursed—and I must apologise for it was my fault."

"W-what do you mean?" She managed to stutter out, still not believing that her great, great...grandmother was standing before. Yet she was completely fine with believing Hades existed. She should be placed in an asylum.

Vera smiled at her sorrowfully, pulling on the white long sleeves that covered her arms and said, "When I was alive, I used to be a witch. Now, I wasn't an evil witch, I only used my powers for good and to help those who needed my help. I met your grandfather Edmund and we instantly fell in love."

She pursed her lips, her eyes darkening as the memory of her enemy came to mind. "There was another woman who was in love with him; Desdemos. Edmund though, didn't return the feelings and tried to let her know in the nicest way possible. Desdemos grew furious that he chose me over her and placed a curse on me and my generations."

Ariel was intrigued as she listened to the story, her imagination running wild as she imagined everything that her grandmother spoke of. "The curse, as cliché as it sounds, was that we would kill those we loved. The night that I got the curse, I had become pregnant and as my husband," she bit her bottom lip, blinking away her tears, "entered our home, he embraced me. As I returned the gesture, he fell in my arms, gasping for the life that I was taking from him."

"Oh my god!" She covered her mouth, feeling pity for her, understanding how horrible the situation was.

"The curse could only be broken by love, but how can you fall in love if you kill the person before you can break it? I tried to break it and prayed to Hecate to allow me to somehow cast it off, but since she had already helped Desdemos in creating it, she could only help me postpone it. That's why none of my other children had it. I managed to put it off until your time. I am sorry I couldn't have done more, Ariel, but...magic is a dangerous thing. I couldn't risk losing any more lives to it."

"So," Ariel whispered, feeling her heart shattering in pieces as she glanced at Hades, whom was watching Vera, "I can't break the curse because only love can and I won't be able to fall in love because I'll kill that person?"

Vera nodded, flickering as her time with them became shorter. Hades nodded, dismissing her and sat down next to his beloved. Ariel looked at him with watery eyes and whispered, "I can't fall in love."

19

CHAPTER 19

"**A**riel," Hades knelt before her, taking her cheeks in his palms and rubbed his thumb against the corners of her lips, "don't say that. Everyone can-"

"-not everyone is cursed like me," she replied bitterly, looking away from his pleading blue eyes. She took a deep breath and whispered, "It's a small price for what I've done, really."

He shook his head, gritting his teeth in annoyance, "You haven't done anything, Ariel."

Ariel looked down at her hands, biting her bottom lip as tears began to cloud her vision and muttered, "I've killed."

Hades sighed, running his fingers through his hair and said, "Ariel-"

"No," she pushed him away, but he didn't move an inch. He tightened his hands around her face, wiping away her tears and she whispered, "I can't do that. I can't kill someone else; especially not someone I love."

"You won't-"

"You don't know that," she snapped, more salty tears sliding down her cheeks, "I can't do this!" Her speech became slurred as she spoke faster, "I-I can't! The curse says that it can only be broken by true love, but I will kill that person and I know I can't kill you; our sexual rendezvous have clearly proved otherwise. But I can't lose you, Hades. I love you and I can't kill you."

The god stepped back, staring at her with wide eyes and dropped his hands to his sides. Ariel continued sobbing and a small smile broke through Hecate's face. She nodded approvingly, wanting to give them some privacy to sort their feelings, but Hades prevented her from doing so.

"Y-you what?"

Ariel frowned, sniffling and wiped the back of her hand against her lightly pink nose. "I can't-"

"No," he shook his head, inching closer to her so that they were touching once more, "the thing you said after that."

Her frown deepened and she scratched the back of her neck awkwardly. Hades laughed, taking her jaw in his hands and brushed his lips against hers as he whispered, "The thing about loving me."

"Oh," her eyes widened and she felt a heat of embarrassment crawling from her back up to her entire face, "that?" He nodded, biting his lips to keep himself from smiling. "I do," she mumbled, "I love you; which is why I have to stay as far as I can from you; I don't want to kill you."

The light shining in his eyes was bright enough to lighten any blackout in the world. His smile widened, making him feel like his cheeks were going to peel apart and he caressed her face, "You won't kill me."

She shut her eyes, desperately trying to believe his words and said, "Hades, I can't lose you. You don't understand." She threw her hands up in the air, feeling frantic for words to express what she felt,

"I can't kill you. I wouldn't be able to live with myself if something happened to you because of this stupid curse."

"Ariel," he grinned, "there's no way you can kill me."

"But," she frowned and he shook his head.

"No, buts." Hades stood up, to sit next to her and took her hand in his, tracing her knuckles gently as he said, "The curse states that you will kill your lover before you get the chance to fall in love. What the curse didn't count on was you falling in love with the God of Death."

He watched her face as she slowly came into realisation and her eyes widened in glee. "So," he continued, "you cannot kill me. My title, my being is of the dead. You cannot kill what is already dead."

Ariel scrounged her nose in disgust and whispered, "Wait, you're dead?"

He laughed, shaking his head and said, "It's just figuratively speaking. This is my realm, my power, who I am. If I were to disavow my title as King of the Underworld and god of death, then I could be killed." Her heart fell to the pit of her stomach in fear, but he smiled reassuringly, "But there is nothing in this world that could make me demit what is rightfully mine."

"So," she whispered, looking at him with hopeful green eyes, "we can...?"

Hades nodded his head, pulling her jaw towards him with his index finger and whispered, "I am in love with you, Ariel. I did not think it possible, but the Fates must've graced me with you as a gift. It must be their way of apologising for letting me lay eyes on Telephone."

She giggled, placing her arms around his broad shoulders and said, "Really?"

"I am madly in love with you," he eyed her lips, wanting to taste them desperately and then up at her eyes, "I would fight an entire army if you merely asked. At the snap of your fingers, a□á□□ µ□□, I would sit like Cerberus does when I command him to."

Ariel laughed, caressing his cheeks and said, "I wouldn't ask you to do that."

"Then, what would you like? Ask for anything," his grin widened as he inched closer, his minty breath fanning against her lips gently, "anything you want and I'll get it for you, a□á□□ µ□□."

Her green eyes became slightly crossed as he moved closer to her and she pressed her lips against his lightly. "I just want you, Hades—I'm not hard to please, just promise me you'll be mine and I'll do the same."

Hades kissed her softly, his lips moving almost seductive against her own as he kissed her passionately. "I do not have to promise you that, a□á□□ µ□□, for I am already yours."

His fingers entangled in her hair, pulling her closer as he swiped his tongue over her bottom lip, urging for her to open her mouth. He grunted once she pulled him closer and wrapped her legs around his waist.

Hecate widened her eyes, feeling her cheeks heat up uncomfortably and turned around to give them their needed privacy—with or without Hades' consent. If he needed her, he could go find her for she had nothing to hide.

Just as she was crossing the threshold of his room, a gurgled gasp escaped his lips and the goddess quickly spun to freeze in fear.

Ariel's green eyes were bright, almost completely white as she stared up at Hades and held unto him as if he was the only thing keeping her alive. In a way he was. Hecate gulped, not knowing what to do as she watched with horrified eyes as the young woman stole the god's energy.

Hades groaned, holding himself upright with his arms on either side of her. There was no way to describe the feeling he was enduring; Ariel was literally sucking the vigour from him. She tried to let go of him, to control whatever beast had taken over her, but the hunger that had suddenly taken over her, was being sated.

"Ariel!" Hecate cried out, knowing that if she touched any of them, the succubus within Ariel would take her life and she was too selfish to give that up. "You have to let go of him!"

Tears slid down the sides of her cheeks as she fought with all her might to release her hold on the god's life-force, but she couldn't. Her beast was winning. It felt as if though her throat was being cleansed with cooled, heavenly water.

She wanted more of what he was willingly giving her. Her body felt alight, she felt satisfied as she continued sucking more air from his lips. A blue, almost clear, mist was being exchanged between them.

Ariel had her back arched; the sprightly power coursing through her veins was giving her an inexplicable rush. She was becoming addicted and the swine within her didn't want to release her beloved. It didn't matter to it that it would cost her Hades' life. It just wanted to be sated.

Hades smiled down at her, not minding that she was satisfying herself in such a deadly way. Whatever she was doing to him, he was content with it. She had asked him to give himself to her and he had acquiesced. He just didn't know it would be so literal.

With a disgruntled cry, Ariel threw Hades off her, gasping as she held unto her throat and stared at the goddess with terrified green eyes.

"Ariel," Hades croaked, breathing in heavily as his body fought to regain his lost energy, "don't look at me like that."

She shook her head, holding unto the covers around herself protectively and whispered, "What did I do? Oh my god, Hades...I..."

"No," he shook his head, gritting his teeth as his muscles complained once he stood up. His head swayed and Hecate quickly helped him stand up. He stepped away from her, his stubbornness making the goddess roll her eyes and he stumbled towards his bed.

Ariel crawled backwards, breathing in rapidly as her back hit the headboard and she sought for a way out. Hades growled, grabbing her ankles and forcefully said, "Ariel, look at me!"

"I-I," she blubbered, feeling terrified that she almost killed him, "don't touch me!"

He rolled his eyes, walking towards her and she struggled against his hold. She pleaded with her eyes, begging him to let her go as her mind began to create the most horrible scenarios and even though there were many, they all had one thing in common; Hades' death.

"Please Hades," she whispered, choking on her tears as he held her clenched fists, "please, just let me go. I can't hurt you." Suddenly, she felt angry, as if a light switch had been flipped inside of her, twisting her emotions all over the place, "Y-you lied to me! You told me that I wouldn't kill you—so what the fuck was that?!"

He sighed, pulling her in for a hug and held her against his chest tightly. She trembled, wanting to hold him and feel protected but she was also afraid of what had just occurred. "I don't know. But it's okay."

"It's not!" She hissed through gritted teeth.

Hecate cleared her throat and they both looked at her. "I know what happened."

Hades raised a perfectly arched eyebrow, tightening his hold on her and pulled her closer whenever she struggled. "What?"

"The curse," she sighed, "when I created it, Desdemos wanted something lethal and never-ending. The first thing that came to my mind was a succubus, but she thought that if the curse was entwined with sexual desires, Vera wouldn't remember what she did. Desdemos wanted Vera to feel everything, to watch as she killed her beloved. And if I turned her into a succubus, she wouldn't be able to remember or experience pain as harsh as she did by killing Edmund with her hands."

Ariel frowned, finally relaxing against Hades' touch and whispered, "So I'm a succubus?"

"No," Hecate smiled at her confusion, "well not really. There is no specific name for what you are. I simply named the curse áthiktos or untouchable. If you would like to call yourself áthiktos, then I guess you could."

She shook her head, glancing down at her hands and whispered, "I'm not athi-whatever, I'm Ariel. What I still don't understand is why that happened."

Hecate sighed again, looking up at her brother and said, "Well you're not a succubus, but the curse was completing its cycle. Therefore some of the succubi effects had to be completed. I guess you could call that a finishing touch."

"Punny," she muttered bitterly and rolled her eyes.

Hades narrowed his eyes and said, "And you couldn't warn us about it, Hecate?"

She held her hands up in defence and said, "Hey! I didn't know that was going to happen! I'm just letting you know what ensued.

The upside is that it will never happen again," she turned to Ariel, "so you don't have to worry about it, alright?"

Ariel looked up at Hades, standing and hugged him tightly. She placed her face in the crook of his neck and held him as if her life depended on it. "I am sorry, Hades."

He smiled down at her, kissing the top of her head and said, "You have nothing to apologise for, a□á□□ μ□□. Now please don't push me away, I swear to you on the River Styx that I will do everything in my power to make you happy. You just need to let me."

Her lower lip trembled as she fought her tears and she nodded, closing her eyes as Hades kissed her forehead. He lowered his lips, brushing them gently against her skin as he whispered something under his breath and she frowned. "Philo se, Ariel."

"What?"

He grinned, pressing a soft kiss to her lips and said, "It's 'I love you' in my native language."

"Stop showing off, brother," Hecate laughed, "it's Ancient Greek, Ariel. Hades is the most fluent in languages out of Poseidon and Zeus so he tries to show it off as much as he can. Did you know that Hermes and Hades had a competition during the Olympics to see which god spoke better dialects? Obviously Hermes won since that's his forte, but Hades was pretty close."

Ariel grinned, caressing his red cheeks and said, "I didn't know you and Hermes were rivals."

He shrugged. "It was decades ago. Believe it or not, I didn't have much to do with my time since Persephone helped me with my kingly duties. We finished early and she'd want to do her own things; I'd go to the library and just...learn."

She ignored the sentence with his ex-wife's name and said, "I didn't know you liked to learn!"

"Oh," Hecate laughed, "he has a huge library! You should check it out sometime. Some of the best writers have written things for him during their afterlife."

She widened her eyes, nodding quickly and said, "That would be so fun! Can we, please?"

Hades laughed, kissing the tip of her nose and said, "Whatever you wish, a□á□□ μ□□."

"What does that mean?"

"My love."

Hecate rolled her eyes, unable to wipe the smile off her face at her brother's happiness and said, "Alright, brother, I'll bid you farewell. Goodbye, my Queen and happy birthday."

Ariel blushed waving her thanks and turned to Hades. "Why does everyone keep calling me 'queen'?!"

He laughed, entwining their fingers together and said, "Come, I've something to show you."

"Hades," she said in a sing-song voice, "answer my question."

"You are my queen; therefore they acknowledge you as one. We can talk more about it later, but right now I want to give you something. Sit," she sat on the bed, crossing her legs as she watched him, "what's your favourite colour?"

She shrugged, biting her bottom lip as her eyes raked over him. He had slight bags underneath his eyes, but even then he managed to look beautiful. His blue eyes were shining brightly with excitement as he waited for her to answer him.

"I don't really know. I like a lot of colours."

He sighed. "Fine, I'll choose." He closed his eyes, muttering an enchantment under his breath and she watched with wide eyes as a green mist began to twirl around in his hands.

Ariel frowned, inching closer but stayed on the bed. Hades clenched his fist, hiding the green mist and opened his eyes, a sly smirk growing in his lips. "There is more that I want to give you, but this is the first of many gifts, a□á□□ µ□□."

He motioned for her to open her hands and she giggled nervously as he placed a green gemstone on her hands. "I chose this shade of green because it's the exact colour of your eyes and it's beautiful."

She grinned, tracing how smooth it was and whispered his name in awe. He sat beside her, smiling at her as she continued tracing the miniature diamond and he said, "I made it extra small because I told Hephaestus to create a necklace with one of his best metals. I wanted to give you it for your birthday, but I didn't know it was going to be this soon."

Hades widened his eyes as she threw her arms around him and hugged him tightly. "Thank you. I would've been fine with just a movie and cuddling all day long."

He chuckled, shaking his head and said, "You do not know me very well if you think you will not be showered with gifts whenever I can give them to you. I am the god of riches; I can do this for all eternity."

"Show-off," she playfully smacked his arm and said, "but thank you, Hades, this is really sweet of you." He flashed her a boyish grin, making her laugh. "Can I ask you a question?"

"Of course," he nodded.

Ariel continued to play with the gemstone in her hands and said, "Do you have another name?" He frowned in confusion. "It's just that since we watched Hercules, every time I call you 'Hades' I picture you with blue hair."

He rolled his eyes, muttering under his breath and said, "If he hadn't brought so much joy to kids worldwide, I'd send him to Tartarus." She giggled and he smiled at her. "I have many names; I am known as Pluto."

She stared at him, aghast. "That is a dwarf planet and that's Goofy's dog in Mickey Mouse."

"Mickey Mouse?" he frowned.

"Disney," she laughed as he rolled his eyes.

Hades muttered, "Of course. What about Aïdōneus? It was very popular back in Ancient Greece."

"Aidon-what?" She laughed, shaking her head and said, "How about Aidon? It's short and sexy."

He nodded, smiling at her and said, "Aidon it is."

Before she could say anything else, her stomach grumbled loudly, making him laugh. "It's not funny," she frowned, stroking her aching stomach.

"I will be back, a□á□□ μ□□. Freshen up and come down to the dining room when you are finished, the gods want to give you presents later on today."

Ariel nodded, knowing that Eros and Aphrodite would be one of the most unusual gifts. She was excited to get something for her birthday. Ever since she ran away from home, she never received anything—and that's when she missed her mom the most.

Her mother would always write her a beautiful poem, describing how much she adored her daughter and how proud she was of her. But then she'd remember what a disgrace she was to her family and forced herself to forget.

After four years, she would be content with just e frowneHe a red rose, but Aidon gifted her with love and a beautiful gemstone. She smiled up at him, kissing him on the lips lightly and whispered, "I love you, King Jelly."

He smiled, his eyes shining brightly and he caressed her cheeks as he whispered, "Se latrevo." She frowned, puckering her lips as she crossed her arms over her chest and he kissed them before saying, "It means I adore you."

With one last kiss, Aidon sent her to get cleaned up. Ariel took a quick shower, unable to stop smiling in the bathroom as she realised that there was a way to be happy with the curse after all.

After she finished, she wore a simple sundress and combed her hair into a tight ponytail. Then she slid on a pair of comfortable flats and made her way to the dining room. As she entered, she swallowed back a gasp and laughed at her idiocy.

She was stupid for even thinking that a god like Aidon could love her. She was a mortal, a weird, cursed mortal—and he had been married once.

He had been married to the woman he was passionately kissing—Persephone. As if noticing her entrance, the lust-filled couple pulled away and Ariel clenched her fists at her sides as she waited for the clichéd "It's not what it looks like" line.

But she was surprised for the umpteenth time that day.

Aidon smirked, clearly noticing her presence, turned away and continued kissing the redhead in his arms as if the words that he swore to her had meant nothing. Ariel swallowed back her pride and turned on her heels, walking away with her head held up high, but emotionally tearing herself apart.

20

CHAPTER 20

arling, tell me what more can I do? Don't you know that I was meant for you? You say I feel like heaven on Earth-

"But you'd never know what heaven was if it wasn't for her!" Ariel slurred, falling to her knees as she continued singing to the music replaying in the radio. Her hair fell around her face, sticking to her cheeks from the sticky tears that were drying on her skin.

She sniffled, raising her bottle of liquor and continued slurring words with Beba Rexha. She had become addicted to the upbeat song. It was as if she wrote it knowing what she'd feel after finding Hades' making out with Persephone.

Her heart couldn't withstand the amount of pain it felt. Her mind couldn't process it correctly and she felt dizzy with pain the more she thought about it. So she decided that numbing out the pain was the best way to go.

Tears clouded her vision as she released the bottle of liquor and she stared up at the ceiling. Her life wasn't a fairy-tale, that much she knew, but it was turning out to be a complete and utter tragedy.

She finally allowed herself to love again after four years of fear, to only be shattered by the one person who could break her curse. A loud sob exploded through her chest, echoing around the empty dance room and she curled her legs into her chest, holding her knees tightly.

Half of her had wanted to confront them on the spot, but she feared that she wasn't strong enough. There were certain things that Ariel didn't believe she could do—and standing up to the man that she had professed her undying love for, was one of them.

The other half wanted to grab Persephone and watch as she writhed away to death like the malevolent goddess she was. Never would she have thought that hating someone could be so grandiose, but in that moment her love for the god had turned into complete hate.

She hated him for making her love him, for promising something he couldn't uphold to and managing to have definite control over her emotions.

But she hated herself more. She hated that she wasn't strong enough to face him and tell him off. She hated that had met him and fell for him harder than ever before. Loving someone the way she loved Hades shouldn't have been possible and she doubted that Eros would waste his time shooting arrows at them.

A loud growl rumbled past her lips as she clutched at her aching heart. Whenever someone mentioned heartbreak she thought it was figuratively, but now, as she lay on the hardwood floor, she could see where the term originated.

If her heart was capable of hurting any more, she'd have to rip it out herself.

"Well, well, well," A soft voice spoke from behind her, making her gasp as her eyes met with Derick's, "what do we have here?"

She whimpered, not having the strength to fight him and returned to her previous, foetal position. "What are you doing here?" Her voice cracked at the end, but she didn't bother repeating herself.

Derick shook his head, kneeling next to her and brushed his cold fingers down the side of her face. "Why are you crying so much, Ariel? He's just a god—or wait, you love him? You actually fell in love with him?" He cackled, throwing his head back as she shrugged his touch away. "You know," he mused, "I think it's even funnier that you thought he would love you back."

"Shut up," she whispered, hiding her face in her arms as she tried to drown away his comments.

"No," he began walking around her in loops, circling her like an animal would its pray. "I think you need to hear this. After all, you did take me out of my misery of being with you; don't you think I should repay you?"

"Please," she begged, her nose burning as more tears continued to spill down her cheeks.

Derick pressed the tip of his steeled-toe boots against her arms, but she didn't bother to look up at him. "No, if I suffered, then you should too." He got down on his knees again, his rough cold fingers trailing her jaw as he continued speaking, "If I went through all that pain, you should feel it a thousand times worse than me.

"Derick..."

"You are so weak, Ariel. So fucking worthless too. Do you remember what you did after killing me?" She whimpered, "You left me there! You fucking left my body behind and didn't even have the decency to give me a proper burial."

"I was scared," she whispered, tearing open old wounds. "I didn't know what to do! I panicked and left you there and I'm so sorry I did."

"That's not the worst part," he whispered, twirling his finger around her black locks, "no. The worst part is that you got all the money that I was planning on taking from you. That was supposed to be our money, Ariel, and after you got rid of me you spent it all on yourself. I bet you that that was your plan all along, wasn't it?"

Ariel shook her head, feeling more vulnerable than ever before. She didn't feel like her normal, strong self. At that moment, she was weak, broken and helpless. No one could save her; not even herself.

"Not only that," Derick tightened his hold around her hair, making her wince in pain, "but you are a murderer! How could you possibly think that that god would fall in love with you—a murderer?" He caressed her cheek, then grabbed it and forced her to look up at him. "You don't deserve to be loved, Ariel. You don't deserve to be alive!"

"I know," she sobbed, realising that Derick was only speaking the truth. "Kill me? Do it," she sat up, looking deep into his dark, lifeless eyes, "do it for me, Derick? Take your revenge."

He laughed, shaking his head down at her in mockery and said, "And take you out of your misery? I don't think so, dear. I'm going to let you live, that way you can cry yourself to sleep every night and watch as the man you fell for toys with your feelings like a kid on Christmas day."

Derick smiled down at her, malice shining in his eyes as he grabbed her throat and pinned her to the floor. "But I think that the satisfaction of watching your eyes lose their light will be enough for me." He tightened his hold on her throat, making her eyes widen as she began to lose oxygen and he laughed maniacally.

He suddenly released her, leaving behind dark red fingerprints and whispered, "Don't you think that I should finish what I started before you killed me though?"

Ariel widened her eyes, fear crawling up her throat and she shook her head, crawling away from him on her hands. He grinned, quickly unbuckling his jeans and began to walk towards her.

"I'm going to have so much fun with you," he whispered, his voice bringing chills to the back of her spine. His voice sounded so ethereal that she could swear it was all a part of her imagination, but everything felt too real to be fake. He had to be there in the same room with her.

"Think of this," he straddled his legs on either side of her waist, "as a payment for killing me and Adrianne. Don't you think she'd be happy," he leaned down to brush his lips against her jaw, "if you let me take advantage of you the way her boyfriend did. I think she would, I mean, let's face it. All those times that I forced you to be with me, you liked it. It's only logical that she felt the same."

She glared up at him, the mention of her friend bringing about an exuberant hatred that managed to fuel her with some type of morality. "Get the hell off me!"

He laughed, sliding his hands over her breasts and squeezed them roughly, making her grimace in pain. "You women are all the same, no means yes and yes means no. So in the end, you wanted me to take advantage of you and so did your friend."

Ariel cried out, struggling against him as he bowed his head down to kiss her and she began kicking her legs violently. Forgetting about her curse as fear filled all the thoughts in her mind. "I'm going to kill you!"

Derick grinned, his lips curling over his teeth as he whispered, "You already did, dear." He pressed a soft kiss to her jaw and she growled, wanting to strangle him to death, "And guess what? You can't kill what's already dead."

"ARIEL!" Hermes cried out, shaking her violently as she continued muttering incomprehensible words under her breath.

She snapped open her eyes, holding her arms in defence against the god and whimpered at the pain in her head.

"Are you alright?" His blue eyes scanned her head for any wounds and he took a step backwards to give her some space. "I found you here screaming and I thought someone was hurting you."

"Where is he?" She whispered, holding her head, hoping that the massive ache spreading throughout would pass.

Hermes frowned. "Where's who?"

"Derick," she licked her bottom lip, looking around the dance room for traces of her ex-boyfriend.

He shook his head, handing her a glass of water and said, "No one was here with you, Ariel. You were hallucinating."

"No," she shook her head, "he was here! He gave me these!" She pointed to her unscathed neck and widened her eyes as she looked at herself in the mirror. Her reflection was the exact same way it was before Derick had entered the room. "I swear he was here."

"Ariel," he whispered, pressing the back of his hand against her forehead gently, "you were hallucinating. A couple of spirits were searching for Hades—their powers must've affected you."

"I wasn't-"

He shook his head, glaring down at her and said, "They were spirits of fear, blame and deceit. Their names are Deimos, Momus, and Apate. Their presence must've triggered something inside of you and you thought that man was here. But believe me, there is no way he would be with you unless he went past Cerberus—and no one gets out alive from there."

She nodded, looking down at her immobile hands and whispered, "It felt so real; everything he was saying made sense to me. Everything he was doing...it just...it was real to me."

Hermes nodded, waving his hand in the air to fill her cup with more cooled water and said, "Drink up; you kind of dehydrated yourself from all that ambrosia you drank. Where did you even get that?"

She shrugged. "I wished it and it appeared." He sighed and eyed her hands. "I'm wearing my gloves." He nodded and took her hand in his to help her stand up. Ariel sighed, running her fingers through her hair and said, "How long was I like that?"

"About two hours," he led her out of the room carefully, watching her as if she'd break. It was slightly irritating her, but she ignored it and breathed in deeply at the fresh air that seemed to come out of nowhere. "I really freaked out when I couldn't get you to wake up; I thought Hades was going to kill me."

She bit back the tears that were building within her at the mention of the deceitful god and cleared her throat. "Hermes, can you do me a favour?"

He raised his eyebrows, his blue eyes watching her carefully. "Depends on what you'd like."

Ariel forced out a smile. "Nothing big; I promise. It's just that since you're the god of travel, I was wondering...well," she sighed,

"I was wondering if you could take me to the beach." He frowned, about to say no but she rushed out her last card, "For my 22nd birthday? Please! I haven't gone for years! And now that Hades is…busy, I wanted some time to myself. It's just been a stressful day," she rambled on, "I kind of want to get away from everyone and just enjoy myself."

He seemed reluctant, but he was also considering it. He didn't want to exactly babysit her for he had souls to search for with Thanatos, but he also knew that Hades would hang his head above his fireplace if any harm came to her. "How about-"

"Please?" She pressed, "I promise that I'll stay out of trouble! I just want to relax for a bit. Heck you can even take me to a beach that not a lot of people know. Although, the beaches around Hawaii are gorgeous…"

Hermes laughed, shaking his head in disbelief and sighed. "Very well, but if something happens to you, you take off your gloves and kill yourself a son of a bitch, okay?!"

She laughed, standing on her tiptoes to kiss his cheek and whispered, "Thank you so much, Hermes! You just gave me the best 22nd birthday present ever."

"I know," he winked. He stood outside her bedroom, swaying back and forth on the soles of his feet with his hands in his pockets as he waited for her.

"Let me just get some clothes and we'll be on our way."

"You have a bathing suit?" He frowned.

Ariel shook her head, rummaging through her drawers for something to wear. "Nah, but it's okay. I have panties and a bra; it's basically the same thing." She stuffed an extra set of clothing along with her towel in a plastic bag she found in one of the top drawers and turned to Hermes with a bright smile on her face. "Shall we?"

He chuckled, taking her arm in his and nodded. "We shall."

Ariel sighed in relaxation, closing her eyes as the warm rays of the sun warmed her legs. During the hour she was tanning, her legs had turned a nice creamy colour, and she loved it. She was always able to tan fast.

Her skin was glistening with drops of moisture from the suntan lotion and small particles of san. The water before her was crystalline and there weren't many waves crashing on shore. Small seagull croaks were heard throughout, but not loud enough to be unpleasant.

The smell of seawater was surprisingly fresh along with the soft breeze that brushed her black hair around her shoulders. Everything felt serene and perfect.

Ariel sat up, placing her feet on the cool sand and turned on her chair to grab a beer. The drink wasn't as strong as the ambrosia but it was serving its purpose; to forget everything that happened in the damn castle of the Underworld.

Someone whistled from behind her and she raised her eyebrows as she looked at a fairly attractive young man. He seemed around her age, maybe a couple of years older. He was darkly tanned with dark curls and piercing green eyes. They seemed a bit eerie on him, but he managed to pull it off.

His shoulders were broad and muscular, the appropriate size for his strong torso. "Dude, your tattoo is fucking awesome!"

Ariel laughed, raising her bottle in a 'toasting' manner and said, "Thanks."

"My name's Jesse," he extended his hand out to her and she took it hesitantly. He noticed, cracking a grin and displayed a row of perfect straight white teeth. "I don't bite—well I don't bite girls."

She snorted, taking a sip of her beer and said, "What?"

"I like guys," he shrugged, pointing at a guy standing next to the tiki bar, "that over there is my boyfriend."

"Okay..." she blushed, unable to stop herself from smiling at his forwardness.

Jesse shrugged again, running his fingers through his curls. "Just thought I'd let you know before you freaked out about a sexy guy like me talking to you."

Ariel laughed, her sides aching as she let her head fall back and wiped her tears away as she pushed her sunglasses to the top of her head. "I like you."

"How can you not?" He wiggled his eyebrows playfully as he motioned to the empty seats next to her and said, "Mind if we sit here? You seem like cool people."

She shrugged, squinting her eyes to look at Jesse's boyfriend, "Knock yourself out."

"Awesome," he muttered, sitting down and turned on his chair to wave his friend over. "Grant cooks the best pasta in Honolulu so if you want some, let me know."

She smiled, shaking her head and leaned back into the chair as she closed her eyes. Jesse watched her intently, his eyes falling to her fingers and noticed that she wore no ring. "Are you single?"

Ariel laughed, opening her eyes and said, "I thought you were into guys?"

"I am," Jesse grinned, "but I know a beautiful girl when I see one, and you're here all alone. So you're either avoiding all the male population or your boyfriend couldn't come."

"Mm," she tapped the tip of her beer bottle against her lip and said, "I don't have a boyfriend and I'm kind of avoiding all guys right now. No offense, but all of you are assholes."

"Amen, sister!" A voice said from behind her. Jesse turned around, grinning at his boyfriend and they shared a quick peck. "Bothering the poor girl, I see, Jesse?"

Jesse shrugged, smacking his butt as he walked around him to introduce himself. "I'm Grant, this idiot's boyfriend."

Ariel laughed, taking his hand and said, "I'm Ariel...this idiot's new acquaintance...?"

Jesse threw his fist in the air. "Yes! And that's cool; your name sounds like The Little Mermaid's except with a Jamaican accent." He then proceeded to pronounce her name in different accents.

She laughed at his goofiness and shook her head as she relaxed back against her chair. "So why are you guys here?"

Grant smiled, handing his boyfriend a non-alcoholic drink and said, "This is our third year together; we've spent it at the beach we met ever since."

"Aw," she cooed, "I'm here for my 22nd birthday. I wanted to get away from drama for a while."

"Ah," Jesse nodded, sipping back his drink, "trouble in paradise? We understand. Grant and I used to have such a bipolar relationship when we first moved in together. It was crazy! One minute we were fighting and the next we were fucking like rabbits."

"Jesse!" Grant blushed, smacking his arm playfully and Ariel laughed at his embarrassment. "Sorry, he doesn't know how to filter his mouth when he goes on a rant."

"It's fine," she grinned.

"Anyways," Jesse continued, "but we loved each other. So at the end of the day it was okay. If you're having troubles with your boo thang, just know that it'll eventually die out and it'll become a funny memory."

Ariel raised her eyebrows and said, "I didn't say anything about a guy."

"Honey," he narrowed his eyes, "you've been listening to I Can't Stop Drinking About You by Beba Rexha for the past twenty minutes; I'm pretty sure it has to do with a guy or girl, whatever you're into."

She laughed again, shaking her head and said, "It's a good song!" Her cheeks heated up a bit and she mumbled, "And you're right. But I don't want to talk about it."

Jesse smiled sympathetically, patting her hand in a caring manner and said, "Whatever he did to you, honey, make that son of a bitch pay!"

They continued speaking for hours, just sharing memories and although Ariel mostly listened, they were becoming good friends. For a brief moment, she felt normal. She felt as if though she had friends and was capable of living again.

But as Grant and Jesse decided to check in at their hotel for some business, she realised that her life was nothing but normal.

Demos, the creature that had tried to abduct her the dreadful night she was taken to the Underworld was trying to take her again.

It all happened so fast she couldn't process it quickly enough. One minute she was standing up to throw away her empty beer bottles and the next, Demos was twisting her ankle until it broke. She cried out in pain, noticing that they were no longer near the part of the beach she was in.

How they got away from the people in the beach was a mystery that she wasn't willing to find out for the pain coursing through her leg was far too great.

Ariel kicked her legs, hoping to cause Demos some pain and grabbed a bunch of sand in her knuckles. She turned around, throwing it at his face and he hissed at her as it fell into his eyes. She kicked his stomach and cried out as she struggled to crawl away from him.

Her ankle ached, making it harder to stand and she fought the urge to look down at it. It felt like a thousand little needles were pricking her foot, adding a sickening twisting sensation. She coughed, feeling her bikini top filling with sand as she began to crawl towards the water and forced herself not to look back.

Demos continued hissing, clawing at his eyes as he blinked the sand out. His eyes watered and burned immensely, making him curse in his native tongue and startle her to move faster. The demon rubbed the back of his hand against his eyes and breathed in profusely. "You filthy bitch!"

Ariel squealed, digging her nails deep into the sand as he grabbed unto her broken ankle and spun her around. "Let go of me, you piece of shit!"

He laughed, eyeing her hands so that she wouldn't grab more sand. She bit her bottom lip, trying to take the gloves off, but it felt as if though they were stuck to her skin and wouldn't move an inch.

But Demos didn't know that. For all he knew, her hands uncovered and she could kill him.

"Ah, ah, ah," he shook his head, stepping on her ankle as she tried to touch him, "we wouldn't want to break your ankle now would we?"

She hissed in a breath, gasping sharply at the pain that she felt and whispered, "Fuck you!"

"I've courtesssansss for that," he smirked down at her, his sickening yellow eyes glowing in amusement as she continued struggling underneath him.

"What do you want, you snake?" She glared up at him, discreetly searching the beach for her newly found friends, but Jesse and Grant were nowhere to be found. That part of the crystalline beach was as deserted as certain teenage girls during Valentine's Day.

Demos chuckled, trailing his calloused fingers up and down her calve. "Humour me, little mortal, but is it not true that you're supposed to be under the care of the King of the Underworld?"

Ariel rolled her eyes, kicking his hand away and spat, "Is it not true that your mother dropped you down a blender when you were a baby?!"

"What?" He scowled, his eyes flashing a bright colour. "Never mind," he shrugged, "what matters is that you are no longer under his care, which means that I am able to take you to a nice-"

"Fuck off, Gecko," she snarled, kicking her heel against his shin and throwing sand into his face again.

Demos growled, blindingly searching for her, but she turned around and grabbed unto the wet sand. She couldn't say why, but as the salted seawater splashed against her fingertips, she could only think of one person.

One god to be more specific.

"POSEIDON!" Her voice came out growled, almost hoarse as she used most of her upper body strength to get closer to the water. She felt as if though the closer she was to the water, the safer she'd be. "POSEIDON, DAMMIT!"

Ariel screamed, a bloodcurdling shriek, as Demos tried to grab her once more, but the current seemed to wrap around her and pull her further from shore. She gasped as Demos cursed out, screaming for her, but she could only focus on the turmoil of water wrapped around her feet.

Her eyes widened in fear as she stared at the bubbles emerging around her feet, pulling her deeper into the sea. As he returned from his car, Grant dropped the box of beer and began running towards his friend.

Jesse ran after him, both men terrified as they watched Ariel struggling against the current. Massive waves began crashing against her, as if fighting each other to pull her, but were actually suffocating her.

She tried to keep her head above water, spitting out the seawater whenever it entered her mouth and fought to keep her arms in the surface.

"Ariel!" Jesse kicked his sandals off, yanking his shirt over his head as he ran towards the water with the fear of losing his new friend to the sea; the exact way he had lost his sister.

"Jesse!" Grant ran after him, mirroring his movements as he tried to help his boyfriend save the drowning girl.

Ariel coughed, fear bubbling inside her chest as she realised that she'd die a slow, painful death. The water entering her lungs was building her panic and she didn't know how long her feet were able to keep her afloat.

Her legs were aching in exhaustion, urging her to simply float to her death. There was sliver of hope in her, whispering in her ear to keep kicking her legs in the water, that she still had plenty of things to tell Hades.

But she was tired, heartbroken and felt more hopeless than anything. No matter how much her heart begged her to continue fighting, her mind was numbing with pain.

Jesse fought against the waves that crashed against his knees and felt tears sliding down his face as he begged any gods that would listen to help him help her. "Ariel! Ariel swim this way!"

Their eyes met and for a second he swore he saw determination flashing through them. But it wasn't will to live, it was will to die.

"Grant!" He cried out, the veins at the side of his neck popping out as he screamed, "Help me! I can't lose someone else!"

Grant grabbed his hand, helping him fight against the water that now reached their torsos, but they watched helplessly as Ariel's hands slowly began to turn into a small dot in the distance.

Ariel pushed the water down with all her might, gasping for air as her head broke through the surface and began to cough violently. Her throat burned from all the coughing she was doing and the salty water travelling down them wasn't helping the cause whatsoever.

"When I asked for your damn help," she gasped, "I didn't mean it like this, Poseidon!" She tried swimming away from the current that was still swirling around her feet, pulling her deeper into the ocean and turned to look at the shore.

Jesse watched with wide brown eyes as a massive wave began building, reaching heights of about eight feet and made its way to

Ariel. His heart shattered as he realised that there was nothing that could save her from the wave; not even the gods. "ARIEL!"

She turned around, just in time to watch the crystal blue water heading her way. Ariel opened her mouth to release a shriek of terror, but that was a clear mistake as the wave enveloped her, pulling her deep into an abyss of pure, chilling darkness.

Salt water rushed into her lungs, leaving a burning sensation behind as she choked and felt her body flailing around. As she percolated away to meet her death, she fell with a smile on her face. Her name was Ariel, like the mermaid, but there was a difference.

The Little Mermaid could swim and breathe underwater but she could feel her lungs crushing from the massive pressure of the ocean.

21

CHAPTER 21

They all stood watching her silently. The grand throne room was so quiet; one could hear the slight noise of waves crashing above. Amphitrite bit her bottom lip, shaking her head condescendingly whenever her eyes fell upon Galena, the sea nymph that rescued Ariel.

Although, the way she saved her wasn't exactly safe; she managed to get her away from Demos.

Galena bit her bottom lip tightly, squeezing her fingers nervously and whispered for the umpteenth time, "I'm sorry! I didn't know she was King Hades' consort. She just called father..." she trailed off when Amphitrite gave her a stern look.

Apollo sighed, kneeling over Ariel and said, "Her lungs are completely filled with water. There's no way she survived that. They're filled with water and crushed; she's dead." He pushed a strand of wet hair off her face and shook his head. "I can fix her damaged limbs and bones, but the water will still be there."

Galena's green eyes brightened and she looked at the goddess of the sea as if she were ready to burst. Amphitrite sighed, motioning for her to speak. "What is it, Galena?"

"We can pull it out of her."

Hera grimaced staring at Ariel's pale body and said, "That sounds oh-so pleasant."

She held the urge to roll her eyes and turned to Amphitrite, "I can do it! I watched Leucothea do it to a sailor once."

"That's Leucothea's job," Hera rolled her eyes, "she's the goddess that helps sailors. That's what she's good at. Have you ever dealt with magic like that?"

"No," Galena mumbled, feeling her slightly blue cheeks turn a dark shade of pink, "but I'm sure I can do it if you let me try!"

Hera shook her head. "I'm not putting Ariel's life at risk."

"She's already dead," she muttered, quickly biting her lips nervously when Hera gave her a sharp look.

Apollo shook his head as he picked up Ariel's immobile hand and said, "Her soul is still attached to her body. Until Thanatos or Hermes come to pick her up, we have a chance."

"So," Hera snapped, "you're agreeing with Galena?"

"No," Apollo snapped in return, "I'm saying that we can try what the nymph has suggested. Calm down, Hera, the girl hasn't done anything to you."

The queen of the gods gritted her teeth and pointed to the nymph accusingly, "Because of her we might have a war in our hands!"

Amphitrite frowned, stepping forward. "A war? With who?"

"Hades," Hera rolled her eyes, "do you really think that he's going to be calm after this? One of your people killed his Queen and do I need to remind you of what happened to those idiots that tried to take Persephone?"

"Yes," Galena blurted out, making Hera's grey eyes burn in lividness. "Sorry! I just," she shook her head, covering her mouth and whispered, "I'll shut my trap now."

"Remember when Theseus and Pirithous tried to take Persephone? Hades gave them the option of living in the Underworld the rest of their lives or being eaten by dogs. They chose to live in the Underworld and he fed them to the dogs for the rest of their life in his kingdom."

"So?" Apollo shrugged, "What are you saying?"

"Hades actually loves Ariel. The Moirai confirmed to me that they are soul mates. Put two and two together, Apollo, I know you're not an idiot." She narrowed her eyes and hissed, "If he did that to Theseus and Pirithous because they tried to take Persephone, do you know what he'll do to Poseidon?"

Amphitrite frowned, crossing her arms over her chest defensively and said, "My husband didn't do anything!"

"Hades doesn't think when he's angry, Amphitrite! We all know that! He will just want revenge and because Ariel was killed by water, he'll see Poseidon as his enemy. If Ariel is dead there's nothing left for him to lose, he will call for a war and you know that will be the bloodiest one of them all."

She gulped, turning to Apollo and whispered, "Hera is right. We need to do something and we need to do it fast. No matter how strong Poseidon is, Hades reigns over the dead. He can call for millions of his soldiers and they won't die because they're already dead!"

"Err," Galena raised her hand slowly, "not to interrupt or anything...but shouldn't we decide on what we need to do? I'm pretty sure that Hermes is coming to get Queen Ariel's soul soon..."

Apollo nodded, smirking once Hera rolled her eyes at Galena and said, "She's right." He knelt over Ariel's body closing his eyes as he searched for the spots to heal and began to literally work his magic.

The two goddesses and Galena watched with anxious eyes as Apollo reconstructed her crushed bones. Her shattered ribcage suddenly pushed forward, giving the body a look of normalcy. Her skin was still extremely pale and her veins were dark in contrast, but she at least looked human.

As if her body was a balloon, it began to inflate, returning to her normal weight and look. Apollo stepped back after finishing and turned to them. "If Galena can't cleanse her lungs from the water then we're screwed."

"Can't we call Leucothea?" Hera groaned, running her fingers through her blonde curls.

Amphitrite shook her head and said, "Already tried; she's on the other side of the ocean. It'll take her at least an hour to get here and I'm sure that Hermes won't wait."

Galena bit her bottom lip, stepping closer to Ariel and whispered, "I can do it; I'm a water nymph I just have to call the water to me."

They watched in silence as Galena began to mutter chants under her breath whilst moving her hands around the air. It seemed like she was performing an exotic dance, but as Ariel's body arched forward and water began to glide from her mouth, one could tell that it was far greater than a dance.

Hera sighed in relief as Amphitrite smiled at the nymph proudly and they waited for her to finish the extraction. Galena opened her eyes after all the water was removed and said, "That's all the sea water."

Amphitrite bit her bottom lip, watching Ariel with worried eyes and they all waited in a painful silence. The atmosphere was so thick that a knife wouldn't be enough to cut it.

Suddenly, the young woman gasped, opening her eyes in fear and began to cough. Water gurgled out of her mouth as Hera looked at Galena, who shrugged and muttered a sorry; apparently not all of the water had been removed.

Ariel turned on her side, feeling worse than she had ever felt in her life. Her lungs ached, her feet felt like they had ran a million miles and even her nails ached. She sat back, groaning at the gross taste of saltwater rasping against her throat and croaked out, "Poseidon isn't very good at his job, is he?" She closed her eyes, trying to clear her throat to take out the taste of salt, "Idiot tried to kill me!"

Hera laughed, kneeling quickly to hand her a cup of fresh water. Ariel groaned, taking the cup from her hands and slowly began to drink it. It was cool and extremely refreshing; it seemed to take away all of her internal pains. "Poseidon didn't answer your prayer."

She frowned, breathing in slowly and holding unto her stomach. "Then what the hell was that thing that almost killed me."

"It actually killed you," Galena blurted out, feeling her cheeks turning pink as Ariel stared at her confusedly. "And that thing was me. Sorry!" She smiled brightly, "I was just trying to help; it wasn't my intention to hurt you."

"Darling," Ariel closed her eyes, shaking her head as the horrible memory of the turmoil of water suffocated her, "you should really work on your technique."

She nodded, running her fingers through her long blue hair and said, "I really do and I am really sorry! Please don't execute me!"

She frowned, shaking her head again and said, "What? Why would I do that? You saved my life!"

"Well," Apollo chuckled, "that was actually me."

Hera rolled her eyes, handing Ariel a warm towel and said, "Here, wrap this around yourself and get warm. I'll go send someone to get you something to wear."

Ariel nodded, sighing in relief as the towel seemed to work its magic quickly and turned to Amphitrite. "Wait," she frowned, "why didn't Poseidon answer my 'prayer'?"

The sea goddess smiled, her light blue eyes shining knowingly and said, "He's with your King."

Her frown turned into a scowl and she muttered, "I have no 'king'. If you're talking about Hades, I don't know where he's at."

Amphitrite frowned as Hera said, "Hades didn't tell you where he was going?" Ariel shook her head. "Strange," she muttered, "they all get called by Gaia to a meeting every year, right before their birthdate. They consult the primeval goddess on their ruling over the kingdoms and such. She warns them about upcoming wars and possible threats to the gods; that's how we found out about you."

Ariel shrugged, feeling grateful when Apollo handed her another glass of the refreshing water. One would think that after being almost drowned, she would've been tired of water, but she just wanted to cleanse her throat of the salty bitterness that was left behind.

"That's weird," Hera mumbled to herself, "they all tell us before they go; and Hades is way too crazy to leave you without knowing."

Because he was too busy sucking face with his witch ex-wife, she thought, but decided to stay quiet and continue drinking her water.

Apollo scratched his neck awkwardly and said, "Alright, I'm leaving; I'm going to start charging you for the amount of times I have to heal you."

Ariel laughed, waving as he disappeared and turned to Hera. She crossed her arms over her chest, handing her a chiton and said, "Spill the beans, darling."

She frowned, blushing as she realised that the only thing that was covering her was the semi-broken bathing suit and that Apollo had basically seen her in all her glory. The three women turned around, giving her some privacy and waited for her to change attires.

The chiton was coloured a light blue and had a brown leather belt wrapped around her waist. It was nice and somewhat elegantly sexy. "Spill the beans on…?"

Hera turned back around, rolling her eyes at Ariel and said, "I'm the goddess of marriage and all this other marital crap; I know when there are problems in a relationship."

"I'm here!" Aphrodite entered the throne room, with her hands in the air as if she were the reason they breathed. "You may gaze in awe at my beautiful dress!" She spun around, showing off the red cocktail dress and winked at them.

As her eyes landed on Ariel, she widened them and whispered, "What happened to you?!"

Galena raised her hand, grinning and blurted out, "I did."

"What?" Aphrodite frowned.

"Long story short," the nymph sighed, "I killed her by trying to save her from Demos. Apollo helped me by fixing her body and I took out the water that she had swallowed. Now here she is all safe and sound."

The goddess blinked slowly, puckering her lips in thought and said, "I love me some drama, but damn girl! Your life is crazier than an episode of The Hills."

Ariel laughed, shaking her head bitterly and said, "You've no idea."

"Wait," Aphrodite frowned, "why were you with Demos in the first place?"

"Yeah," the four women spoke in unison, "why were you with Demos?"

She rolled her eyes, crossing her arms over her chest and said, "I wasn't with Demos. I was at the beach, relaxing for my 22nd birthday when that Gecko tried to kidnap me."

"Where was Hades?" Aphrodite snapped.

Ariel shrugged. "Don't know, don't care."

Hera raised her eyebrows, clicking her tongue in distaste and said, "And this is where you tell us what happened with him."

"Nothing," she groaned, wanting to finish the interrogation, "hey! What happened to those two boys that were with me at the beach? Are they okay?"

"Boys?" Galena frowned. "Oh!" She smiled, "The cute couple? Oh they're fine! I sent one of my sisters to erase their memories of you."

Ariel pouted her lips, feeling somewhat sad that they would no longer remember who she was. "Oh."

"Hey!" Hera snapped her fingers, growing more impatient by the second, "What did Hades do, Ariel?"

"She doesn't have to tell us if she doesn't want," Galena mumbled, twisting her fingers idly.

The goddess took a deep breath, rubbing her fingers on her temples and said, "Yeah, you're right; I'm sorry. I just...this is my gift, my job. I care too much about marriages and I know something is wrong with you and Hades; I can feel it. I just don't understand how because Hades is-"

"-he was kissing Persephone," Ariel muttered bitterly, scratching her head as the remainder of sand began to bother her, "I saw them before I had this mental breakdown."

Aphrodite frowned, shaking her head and said, "Hades would never cheat on you, Ariel."

"Yeah well," she snapped, "and unicorns exist."

"Actually," Galena began, but closed her mouth when the three women turned to look at her with piercing glares. "I'm just going to go..."

Ariel smiled at her. "Thank you for saving me."

"No problem," Galena grinned in return and literally evaporated into the air.

She shook her head, closing her eyes and wished to be sitting down. Suddenly there was a comfortable couch underneath her and she breathed out in amazement. Amphitrite smiled, proudly and said, "It was a gift of Hecate's; anything you wish will appear, but it can only be material."

"Yeah," Ariel nodded, "Hades has a room like this too, but it's not his throne room."

"So," Hera sighed, "explain how my brother was kissing his ex-wife."

She shrugged. "I don't know! I just saw them sucking lips like toads," her eyes began to water as she reminisced and whispered, "He even saw me standing there."

Aphrodite gasped, shaking her head in disbelief and said, "And what did he do?!"

"Nothing," Ariel replied bitterly, "he literally smirked at me and went back to kissing her—and to think that minutes before that happened, I had confessed how much I loved him."

Amphitrite shook her head, like the other goddesses and said, "That doesn't sound like Hades. Are you sure it was him?"

Ariel gave her a deadpanned look, narrowing her eyes and said, "I'm not a liar, Amphitrite; I know what I saw. I'm not blind either."

Hera sighed, muttering something under her breath and Aphrodite groaned. "My ship!"

"Your ship?" Amphitrite raised her eyebrows in confusion.

The goddess of beauty nodded, resting her chin on her hand as she fell back into the couch that Ariel was sitting at. "Just like the Titanic; it sunk."

They all shook their heads at Aphrodite's remark and suddenly Hera grinned deviously. "I have a plan."

Ariel raised her eyebrows, somewhat interested. "On?"

"Revenge," she sat down across from them.

"We are not turning anyone into anything!" Amphitrite laughed.

Hera pouted her lips, slouching her shoulders a bit and then said, "Fine, but we can still do it."

Aphrodite grinned evilly, throwing her arms in the air and said, "I'm all for revenge!"

Ariel laughed, nodding and said, "What's your plan?"

"Next week Hades, Zeus, and Poseidon return from their week with Gaia. When they get back we throw them a birthday party and whatnot. I say that Ariel dresses up all sexily and doesn't pay attention to him the entire party; that always pisses Zeus off."

She widened her eyes, the corners of her lips turning upward into a smile and she said, "That sounds awesome!"

Aphrodite nodded, letting out a squeal and said, "I already have the perfect dress for you! It's a bit revealing, but we want Hades to be looking at you, right?"

She nodded, high-fiving the cunning goddesses and said, "I just have one request."

The goddess titled her head in wonder and said, "Yes?"

"It has to be a backless dress."

A week went by surprisingly fast and the closer his return would get, the more anxious she would feel. No matter how many times she replayed it over in her head, the actual look on Hades' face when she descended from the marbled stairs in Olympus was priceless.

He couldn't stop staring at her in awe, as if her beauty completely captivated him, which it did. His heart almost ran out of his chest and he could feel the imaginary drool sliding down his jaw and through the entire night he fidgeted in his throne, waiting to finally embrace her.

Ariel smirked, knowing that Hades was watching as she walked through the crowd of dancing deities. She wanted his eyes to be on her the entire time; she wanted him to watch as she completely brushed him away the same way he did when he was with Persephone.

Aphrodite tapped her shoulder, handing her a glass of ambrosia and muttered, "He hasn't stopped looking at you ever since you came in. In any other occasion I would've thought it to be sweet, now it's just creepy."

She laughed, turning away from Hades and said, "I'm surprised he hasn't come over."

"That's because he can't," the goddess took a sip of her drink; "none of them can leave their throne until midnight. It's a strange tradition, but they're supposed to be honoured and what not. Sitting down for a certain amount of time represents their wealth and status."

Ariel tapped her nail against the glass and shrugged, "My butt would be hurting so much." Aphrodite laughed and nodded. "But I'm glad he hasn't tried to talk to me yet. I don't think I'll be able to restraint my anger."

The goddess pursed her lips, smiling brightly at Hephaestus and said, "Don't count on that for too long; they're going to be able to leave their thrones soon. In about twenty minutes."

She sighed, watching as Aphrodite's husband began approaching them. "Good afternoon, beautiful women." Aphrodite grinned, pressing a light kiss to his cheek and Hephaestus said, "How has your evening been, Ariel?"

She shrugged, placing the cup on the tray of a passing servant and said, "It's been good. My feet are hurting a bit, but it's been fun. The food was amazing and the Muses surprisingly have good taste in music."

Hephaestus laughed, his perfect straight teeth dazzling her a bit. The colour of his skin was beautiful, almost a warm caramel and his black suit adjusted nicely to his toned muscles. She still couldn't understand how Aphrodite would cheat on him for he was an extremely attractive god.

"Hestia does an amazing job with the food and Dionysus picks the best drinks in the world."

Ariel nodded in agreement and turned around as a loud trumpet echoed throughout, silencing the Muses and the gods. She turned to Aphrodite with a frown on her face and the goddess smiled in return. "The cup-bearer will bring Zeus, Poseidon and Hades prosperous drinks to honour their marvellous reign over the main three realms and they will interchange their thanks to the other gods."

"Why don't they honour you guys too? I mean, you're all related and what not..." she whispered back.

Aphrodite shrugged and said, "We all hold equal power and status in Olympus, but Hades, Poseidon and Zeus reign over large kingdoms; they uphold the most responsibility out of all the deities. So they get a little extra recognition on our 'birthdates'."

She nodded, watching as a handsome blonde haired man walked up the grand marbled stairs. He wore traditional Ancient Greek attire with olive leaves crown woven around his head. His eyes were a striking green colour and his muscles were slightly toned. He was extremely attractive.

As if noticing Ariel's interest in the guy, Aphrodite smirked and whispered, "That's Ganymede, he was a Trojan prince that Zeus abducted to..."

Ariel widened her eyes, feeling her cheeks turn completely red and blurted out, "Zeus is gay!?"

Aphrodite laughed, shaking her head and said, "Not really; I guess bisexual is more of the word. Anyways, Zeus was so in love with him that he turned him immortal and now he's the cup-bearer of the gods."

"How did Hera react to this?"

A sly smile grew on the goddess lips and she waited until Ganymede gave the final cup to Hades before whispering, "Do you really think that Hera was going to stay out of the loop? No offense, but look at Ganymede, he's not exactly hideous."

Her jaw fell open and she watched as the three main gods spoke in their native tongue. "So she...with him too?"

Aphrodite leaned closer, grinning as she whispered, "No, darling, she sleeps with both. At the same time."

Ariel felt her cheeks turning a darker shade of red and almost died of hysterical laughter when she noticed that Zeus winked at Ganymede. She bit her bottom lip hard enough to draw blood and hid her face with her hands. Aphrodite giggled next to her and Hephaestus frowned at them in confusion.

"Oh my god!"

"It's actually pretty fun," Aphrodite whispered and Ariel turned to her with wide eyes. "What?" She held her hands up defensively, "Don't judge me! I'm the goddess of sexuality and pleasure; I have to experiment!"

Ariel continued laughing; fanning herself as her cheeks turned so red she almost looked like a tomato. Hades raised his eyebrows in confusion as he noticed her struggling to keep her laughter to herself and shook his head in amusement. Her laugh riveted him in more ways than he could explain.

The gods exchanged words of encouragement and thankfulness in their autochthonous dialect and then raised their cups as they said a toast. Ariel rolled her eyes as Hades grinned at her and she turned away from him to make talk with Aphrodite, but she was busy slow dancing with Hephaestus.

She turned to look for Athena, but she was busy speaking to a god that Ariel didn't recognise. Pouting, she crossed her arms over her chest and began walking over to the table with snacks.

She walked over to a plate filled with what seemed to be round, powdered donuts and stared at them for a while, trying to figure out if they were as good as they looked.

"Kourabiethes," Ares said smoothly as he took a slice of cheese from a nearby plate.

Ariel jumped, turning to look at him with wide eyes and said, "What?"

He pointed to the donuts and said, "Those are called kourabiethes."

She nodded, looking back at them and said, "What are they?"

"Cookies," he shrugged, "they have crunchy pieces of almond inside and are covered in white powdery icing. They're good, you should try some."

Ariel grinned, nodding again and said, "I will." She picked one from the plate and sniffed it, making the god of war chuckle at her expression. The cookie was soft and smelled wonderful. She took a hesitant, small bite and closed her eyes as the sweetness of the cookie spread through her tongue.

"Mm," she moaned, "this is freaking amazing!"

Ares laughed, nodding and took a sip of his wine. "Hestia outdoes herself every year."

After finishing the baked good, Ariel licked her lips slowly, not realising that two gods were watching her. Ares and Hades. She cleaned her fingers on a napkin and then threw it away as she made her way to the drinks.

The god grabbed a pint of iced fruit punch and poured it for her. She smiled cheekily, raising the cup in thanks before taking a much needed gulp. She sighed after her throat felt refreshed and squealed when the Muses began singing a song she recognised.

Ares raised his eyebrows in question and she said, "This is one of my favourite songs; I didn't think the Muses would know them."

"Ariel," he chuckled, "the Muses are known for their creativity and ability to create music. Of course they know every song there is in this world."

She shrugged, bobbing her head along to the beat of the song and he smiled at her. "Would you like to dance?"

Her eyes found Hades' and a sly smirk grew on her lips as she nodded her head, taking Ares' hand. He led them to the dance floor and placed his hands on her hips. She closed her eyes, letting her body sway to the beat of the music and grinned when Ares spun her around.

For someone who was so brutal and violent, he moved with grace—and it simply enhanced his attractiveness.

'Cause if you want to keep me, you gotta, gotta, gotta, gotta, got to love me harder. And if you really need me you gotta, gotta, gotta, gotta, got to love me harder. Oooh, ooh, ooh love me, love me.

Hades gritted his teeth, watching as Ariel turned around, pressing her naked backside to Ares' torso and slid down, twisting her hips in a circular motion. The jealousy coursing through his body was hot enough to melt Tartarus and he was tempted to crush the golden goblet in his hands to dust.

Ariel laughed as Ares began to sway his hips with hers, pressing his growing bulge against her backside. She threw her head back against his chest and slid her hands around neck as she continued gyrating her hips against his.

The god spun her away from his body, wanting to calm his growing erection and licked his lips as she turned back around to face him.

Ariel placed her hands on his broad shoulders, sliding her leg in between his and started grinding into him.

Ares growled, pulling her closer and whispered, "Hades is going to kill me."

She grinned, standing on her tiptoes to brush her lips against his earlobe and whispered, "He doesn't own me, Ares, and I clearly don't mean anything to him."

"I don't want to be your pick-me-up, little one," he chuckled, sliding his hands over her well-rounded butt.

Ariel bit his earlobe gently with her four front teeth and pressed herself closer to him. Half of her brain was screaming at how slutty and childish she was acting, but the other half was jumping with joy as she could feel Hades' blue eyes burning daggers onto the back of her head.

It sucked to be on the receiving end of things, didn't it?

"You're not my pick-me-up," she laughed sultrily; "you're just my partner in crime."

"Mm," he raised his chin, allowing her to spin around in one circle and he pulled her back in to dip her, "and what is our crime?"

She flashed him a flirty smile, shrugging as she took his hands and placed them on her hips. Ares growled, bowing his head to kiss the curvature of her neck lightly and she breathlessly moaned the lyrics for effect. "Love me, love me, love me."

Ares raised his dark eyes, smirking as Hades tapped his hand on his marbled throne impatiently and scanned the dance floor with pitch-black eyes. He tried to think of anything to keep his mind occupied and away from Ariel and her sensual dancing with his nephew—even if it was watching the hands of the clock tick away slowly.

He clenched his hands, refusing to allow his anger to get the best of him, but his eyes would persist on travelling towards the couple. He couldn't understand why she was dancing so sinfully with him, when he was dying to see her.

It had been an extremely long week for him and all he wanted to do was embrace her and be in her presence; she clearly had other things in mind—as well as other people and it was killing him inside. The jealousy was churning away in his stomach, twisting any positive emotion he had into anger.

As soon as the hand of the clock fell on the number twelve, Hades, Poseidon, and Zeus stood up to join the other guests. Ares and Ariel continued dancing, laughing at nothing to simply infuriate the god.

"He's coming this way," Ares whispered near her ear as Hades stalked past dancing gods.

Ariel smirked, pressing a soft, closed-lip kiss to his lips and whispered, "Thank you, Ares."

He nodded, just as Hades grabbed her forearm and pulled her away from him. Ariel rolled her eyes, feeling triumphal as he continued to push drunken gods out of their way.

"What was that?!" Hades growled, his blue eyes nowhere to be found; in their place were stormy pitch-black voids.

She widened her eyes innocently. "What was what?"

"Ariel," he growled lowly, the anger ringing clearly in his voice, "do not test me."

Ariel rolled her eyes, crossing her arms over her chest when he released her and said, "I was just dancing with him; I don't see why you're so pissed."

"You kissed him!" He spat.

"So?" she shrugged, turning away disinterested, "It's not like you give a crap about me."

Hades frowned, not understanding her sudden childish actions. "What?"

She waved her hand around, as if waving away his question and said, "You know what I mean, Hades."

"Hades?" His frown deepened.

"That's your name, is it not?" She narrowed her eyes, growing impatient as her anger fought to pour out. There were so many things she wanted to say to him, but watching him get jealous was satisfying for her. She was going to be able to hurt him as much as he had hurt her.

"I thought..." he trailed off, shaking his head and ran his fingers through his jet-black hair, "never mind."

"Is that all?" Ariel sighed, "You kind of took me away from my date—rudely might I add."

"What are you talking about, Ariel?" He sighed, sliding his hand down his face tiredly. "Of course I care about you."

She laughed, cold and humourless. "That kiss with Persephone, clearly proves otherwise."

"Kiss?" He frowned, looking genuinely confused, "With Persephone? Are you out of your mind? I haven't seen that woman in months. And if I had, the last thing I would be doing with her is kissing."

"Save your lies for someone who will believe them, Hades." She snapped, turning back around to walk away from him.

22

CHAPTER 22

Hades growled, grabbing her forearm again and hissed, "Do not walk away from me! We are not done."

Ariel glared at him, shrugging his hand off her arm and said, "I think we are. Like I said before, your kiss with Persephone shows that you still have feelings for her. I'm not going to stand in the way of that. I just wish that you wouldn't have gotten involved with me because now I'm the one that ends up hurt."

"Ariel," he sighed, rubbing his temples tiredly, "can you please explain to me what you're talking about? I am genuinely confused."

She stared at him, her green eyes scrutinizing his face for a sign of a lie, but she felt her heart dropping when she saw none. She cleared her throat, lowering her voice to a whisper and said, "My birthday. The day of my birthday you told me to get ready, that you were going to get breakfast for me and that when I finished to go to the dining room."

He nodded, gritting his teeth as he watched her eyes grow watery and clenched his teeth. She clearly didn't want him to touch her, but watching her eyes flash with pain made him want to comfort her. To wipe away the hurt that she felt.

"So," she sniffled, trying to keep her voice steady and not cry over her pathetic heart, "I did. I did what you asked me." Ariel gritted her teeth, feeling her nose burning with tears and hissed, "And then I saw you making out with Persephone. I stood there waiting for a damn explanation, but do you know what you did?!"

Hades stood quiet, waiting for her to finish.

"You looked at me." She pointed to her chest, making a thudding noise when her finger came into contact with it, "at me, Hades. You just stood there, smirked and went back to kissing that," she scrounged her nose up in disgust and spat, "that wench!"

"Ariel," He whispered, raising his hand to touch her, but she shook her head and stepped away from him.

She shrugged, taking a deep breath to try and compose herself and cleared her throat. "There you go. Does this ring any bells now?"

The god shook his head and stared at her with pleading eyes. "Ariel, I would never do anything like that to you."

She rolled her eyes, crossing her arms over her chest and said, "What are you saying? That I imagined the whole thing?"

"No-"

"-can we just drop it? I told you, I don't care what you do with your life. Really, I understand. Persephone came before me and even though she's an idiot, you still love her. It's okay, just please leave me alone."

"Ariel-"

"Hades!" Poseidon called him over, "We're lighting the torch now, you need to come."

The agitated god turned to her and opened his mouth to beg her to listen to him, but she forced out a smile and motioned for him to follow his brother. "I swear, Ariel," he rushed out, "I didn't do what you think I did."

She sighed, tucking back her bangs and whispered, "That's what I was afraid of, Hades. When I told you I loved you, I was afraid that you still loved Persephone. You simply proved my fears right, now just go light that torch and tell someone to take me back to the Underworld. My feet hurt."

"Hades!" Poseidon hissed more urgently.

Hades sighed, glaring at his brother and said, "I'll tell Hermes. Wait here." She nodded, releasing a breath that she didn't know she was holding and gritted her teeth, trying to hold back her tears.

It was pathetic. When she first saw him she only wanted to hurt him, to make him feel what she felt. But when they finally spoke, she couldn't bring herself to hurt him anymore. She really was in love with him.

Although kissing Ares showed otherwise, but it was her scorned side taking over. Ariel let out a loud groan, smacking her forehead and muttered, "Stupid!" underneath her breath multiple times.

Hermes raised his eyebrows, tilting his head to the side and said, "Want to talk about it?"

She jumped, turning around to look at him and sighed, "Not really, I just want to go home."

He grimaced, walking over to her and said, "You know I can't do that."

She nodded, wiping away a tear that rolled down her cheek and whispered, "The funny thing is," he looked at her questionably as she muttered, "that I was thinking of the Underworld instead of New York."

He widened his eyes, running his fingers through his hair and then pulled her in for a tight hug. She held him tightly, wanting to erase the ache in her heart and closed her eyes. Hermes stroked her hair gently as he transported them to her room in the Underworld and she wiped away her tears.

Hermes stepped away from her and took her cheeks in his hands as he stared deep into her eyes. "I know you're not lying; I can see it in your eyes, you did see Hades kissing Persephone. But I also know my uncle and I know that he would never cheat on you. He loves you Ariel. There has to be another reason for what happened."

She shrugged, lightly taking his hand from her face and stepped down from her stilettos. "I just want all of this to end. I want to go back to my dull, boring life. I want to wake up every morning and wonder why I was cursed with this thing and listen to Gabrielle Aplin. I want to forget about Hades, about Persephone about the gods, about killing Adrianne...you; everything."

The god sighed, nodding and said, "And that's understandable; but also know that some wishes may come true and it may be too late to undo them."

Ariel walked over to her bed and sat down, playing with her fingers idly. "Thank you for bringing me here, Hermes. Actually...just...thank you for everything you've done for me."

He grinned, his boyish dimples growing and he said, "That's what friends are for. Now I have to go, I'm supposed to give some eloquent speech."

She smiled, waving at him as he turned around and left. Ariel sighed, standing up from the bed and walked over to the mirror. That night, she looked spectacular; Aphrodite had outdone herself.

Her black dress hugged her curves nicely, outlining her feminine figure. The backless portion of the dress gave her a look of incredible sensuality and her tattoos gave her a touch of ruggedness. The moons were slowly fading, not exactly in the pattern she'd expect, but they were disappearing.

She'd figure that since they were moons, they'd follow the lunar pattern they represented. The moon cycle took about two weeks to finish and a week had passed since she was marked and she still had the full moon, it was slowly vanishing. Very slowly.

Ariel looked down at the bureau and breathed out. The miniature sized diamond Hades had given her was sitting there, mocking her. She picked it up, placing it in the palm of her hand and bit her bottom lip tightly, to keep herself from crying.

She was tired of crying, she had done it for too long. Now she just wanted to be happy—and the person, who could bring that happiness to her, didn't feel the same way.

She sighed, clenching her fist and started walking out of her room. She would stop being so dramatic about things, she would stop caring and in order to do so, she had to let go of the things Hades had given her.

She was symbolically ripping herself from him. As long as she was in the Underworld, she'd act like he always treated her; a guest. Well, after she entered his room because no guest would dare enter Hades' chambers.

Ariel took a deep breath as she entered his room, loving the evocative smell that lingered behind. She closed her eyes, trying to calm herself and quickly walked over to his bed. She placed the pinkie-sized diamond on his pillow and turned around to walk away.

Just a guest.

"Ariel!" Hades pushed the doors open, his eyes searching for Ariel urgently and he ran to her bed. She was on her side, sleeping peacefully and not gone. He sat on the edge of the bed, caressing her cheek gently and sighed.

She didn't know what she did to him. She didn't know how much he loved her and wanted her to stand by his side as his Queen.

Ariel slowly stirred underneath his touch, snuggling closer to the pillows and then groaned, unable to go back to sleep. Her eyes snapped open and she squealed in fear once she saw him. Her heart thudded quickly in her chest, making her breath rapidly and she held her hand to her chest.

"Hades!" She breathed out, "You scared me. What are you doing here?"

He looked down at the diamond he had given her and then at her. His blue eyes shone brightly, fear clear in them. "I thought you had gone when I found this on my bed."

She sat up, holding the covers around herself and frowned at him. "What?" She yawned. "What time is it?"

"Doesn't matter," he shook his head, ready to explain whatever doubts she had of him, "what matters is that I love you and you need to believe me."

"Hades," she sighed, pushing her unruly hair out of her face.

Hades shook his head, taking her hands in his and said, "No. I let you speak; now you hear me out." She sighed again, but nodded, biting the inside of her cheek as she waited for him to speak. "First I want to apologise, I completely forgot about my yearly trip to Gaia's abode. I should have told you that I was going to leave for a week, but my mind was too focused on you to think of other things."

"Ariel," he looked down at her hands, "I would never leave you for Persephone. You are who I love; I am madly in love with you. And I don't think you understand." He guided her hand to his chest, where his heart was beating wildly, "This muscle," he whispered, "has never beaten. Only twice, the first time I saw Persephone and then when you came into my life. I know that doesn't make you feel better, but as soon as I was with Persephone, my heart went back to its slumber."

Hades gulped, watching as she looked at her hand above his heart. "But with you? My heart...it hasn't stopped acting this way. I am the god of Death, but I feel so alive when you're with me; it might sound cliché, but it is the truth. You've given me life, a reason to live; love. And for me to throw it all away for Persephone would be incredibly stupid. I am not saying that you're lying about seeing me with her, but I am telling you that it wasn't me."

She opened her mouth to beg him to stop lying, but he was on a roll. He needed to express what she did to him, what she made him feel.

"I spoke to Hermes and he told me that Momus, Apate and Deimos were here searching for me. He also told me that when he found you, you were screaming and seemed to be hallucinating about something. Can you tell me what it was?"

"Derick," she whispered, "he was telling me that I was worthless and what not. He was reminding me of what I tried to forget when I killed him. He made fun of me for thinking that you actually loved me."

"Momus," he clenched his jaw tightly, almost shattering his teeth in the process. "He's the spirit of mockery. What else?"

Ariel frowned, still not letting go of his hands. "Um, he reminded me of Adrianne's death and his. He told me that I didn't deserve to be alive and tried to...finish what he began the day I killed him."

Hades breathed out slowly, trying to calm himself down and said, "That was Apate, he's the spirit of deceit. Deimos is left," he looked up at her, his blue eyes burning with intensity as he watched her and said, "He's the spirit of fear. What are you afraid of, Ariel?"

She bit her bottom lip, looking away from him and said, "A lot of things." He chuckled and gently tilted her jaw so that she was looking at him. She sighed. "I was afraid that after I told you I loved you, you'd leave me. That you'd go back to Persephone and just trick me."

Hades pulled her in for a tight hug, his muscular arms enwrapping her waist lovingly. "Ariel, I love you, a□á□□ μ□□. I want to spend the rest of my eternity with you; I would never cheat on you, please believe me."

She returned the embrace, closing her eyes as she relished in the warmth that enveloped her. "Then where were you? If it wasn't you kissing her?"

He pulled away, caressing her cheek and said, "I did go to get you those fruits, but then Gaia called me. I asked her to give me a couple of seconds to just warn you, but she's impatient and I decided that angering her was not my best choice at the moment."

"So," she lowered her eyes, staring at her hands as she blushed deeply, "I should apologise then...I went and tried to make you jealous with Ares."

He sighed, tucking her hair back behind her ear and said, "Let's just start fresh, alright? No more Persephone, no more Ares, no more Derick; just us two. Deal?"

"Hades," she whispered, "I'm serious; I'm sorry."

He kissed her cheek lightly and said, "So am I."

"Do you forgive me though?"

He chuckled, nodding and kissed her knuckles. "Of course I do, a□á□□ μ□□."

"Ugh," she groaned, "I'm so stupid!"

"Ariel," he cajoled.

Ariel shook her head, hiding her face in her hands and pouted her lips. "If I were you, I wouldn't take me back. I would be so pissed and just make this huge deal about trust."

Hades chuckled, standing up from the bed and knelt in front of her. "But are not the same and that's one of the many reasons why I love you. Now," he sighed, taking her hand as he looked up at her, "I wanted to give you this the day of your birthday, but things didn't go as I planned."

She frowned down at him, trying to understand his actions. Hades took a deep breath, kissing her hand lightly and said, "Ariel Marie Lockhaven-"

Her eyes widened and her heart began to beat quickly in her chest, so quickly she thought she'd pass out. "Hades," she croaked, her throat going dry from emotion.

"In my time your family would give me a dowry for this, but that was centuries ago and since you're always saying I'm very old fashioned, I decided to do this your way." He slid his hand in his pocket, taking out a thin golden ring and held it up for her to see. "You were supposed to find this in your fruit and place the diamond on yourself, to see if you liked it, but like I said; things didn't exactly go the way I planned."

"Hades," she squeaked, almost feeling herself go lightheaded and had to remind herself that breathing was an essential part of living.

"So," he continued, placing the diamond on the delicate ring before holding it out in front of her, "will you give me the honour of standing by my side as my Queen? I want to spend the rest of my eternity with you, Ariel. I want to wake up every morning and have you sleeping next to me. I want to hold your hand in front of the other gods and show you off. Will you marry me?"

She blacked out for a couple of seconds, falling into his arms.

Hades widened his eyes in fear, his smile disappearing from his face as he took a hold of her and caressed her face. "Ariel? Ariel, what's wrong?"

Ariel blinked slowly, then began to giggle hysterically. He frowned down at her, making her laugh even harder and she wiped away her tears. Then she proceeded to sob, feeling worse than a pregnant woman with bipolar disorder.

The confused god stared at her with wide eyes and held her closer to his chest. "Shhh, it's okay."

"No," she shook her head, trying to calm the turmoil of emotions that were rushing through her, "oh my goodness, it's not okay! I can't calm down," she continued laughing, then sobbed a bit.

Hades chuckled and said, "So is that a yes or a no?"

Ariel breathed in deeply, closing her eyes and bit her bottom lip to keep from laughing again. After she thought she was in control of her emotions, she opened her eyes and said, "Are you sure you want to spend the rest of your eternity with someone as crazy as me?"

He grinned, cupping her cheeks in his hands and pressed a soft kiss to her lips. "I wouldn't have it any other way."

She squealed, making him laugh as she threw her arms around him and kissed him deeply. Hades moaned, tightening his hold on her hair and pulled her even closer. His lips brushed against hers, sensually and lovingly, making her groan in delight.

Ariel slid her fingers through his hair, wanting to feel every fine line of his body pressed against hers and widened her mouth as he licked her bottom lip, demanding entrance to her lips. She moaned, suddenly feeling hotter than the dark pits of Tartarus and stared at him hungrily.

Hades placed her on the floor, pulling his shirt over his head and leaned over her body, caressing her thighs lovingly. She shuddered underneath him, tightening her legs around his waist and pulled him down for another ravenous kiss.

Once she began to run out of breath, Hades pulled away from her lips, lowering his mouth to press kisses down her throat. A gurgled noise escaped her mouth as he teased all the right places and she grinded her front into his growing bulge.

"You still haven't answered my question, a◻á◻◻ μ◻◻,"he whispered against her neck.

Ariel moaned, sliding his hands all over her body and stared up at him seriously, her eyes burning with passion and sincere love, "If you kiss me like this every day, there's no way in hell that I'll say no."

He chuckled, pressing another breathless kiss to her mouth and against her lips murmured, "So...?"

"Yes," she gasped as he slid his hand down her body, lightly tickling the fire growing between her legs. "Hell yes!"

Hades laughed, sliding the ring on her finger and then stared down at her with devious eyes. At that moment, he could only think of two things.

He was madly in love with the woman underneath him—and he had been a long week without tasting her. That night, they didn't sleep; they'd have all eternity to do that.

23

— ◆ —

Chapter 23

Ariel stirred, accidentally smacking her hand against Hades' face and he furrowed his eyebrows, grimacing in pain. She still didn't notice, for she wasn't fully awake. Her hair was sprawled all over her face and a bit of drool had moistened the corner of her lips.

Slowly she began to awaken, a slight feeling of disorientation engulfing her brain and she turned to Hades with a lazy smile on her lips. She wiped her mouth and tucked her hair behind her ears, letting out a quiet yawn.

"Good morning," Hades smiled, holding his nose carefully.

She yawned again, stretching her hands over her head and turned on her side to look at him. Sliding her hands under the pillow, she snuggled close to it and mumbled, "Good morning. What happened to your nose?"

He chuckled, sniffling and then turned to look at her on his side. "Nothing, you just accidentally smacked me."

Ariel widened her eyes, pouting her lips and mumbled, "I'm sorry."

"It's fine," he slowly sat up, grabbing his robe from the floor and shrugged it on.

"Where ya going?"

Hades turned to smile at her and said, "I have to go take care of some things, but it will not take me more than an hour. Would you like to have breakfast with me?"

As if on cue, her stomach growled, making them laugh. "Yes, please?"

He nodded, tying the robe threads around his waist. Their previous night had been amazing. One of the many things he loved about her was the ability to keep up with him sexually, at times he was even afraid that he wouldn't be able to satisfy her needs, but Ariel voiced differently.

Every single time Hades finished pleasuring her, she wouldn't be able to move from the bed for minutes until her legs regained their ability to move. He even left bruises and love bites—not hickies. Those were two entirely different things.

Hickies were given to one's sexual partner; love bites were given to the person that you adored—and he more than adored Ariel.

Hades closed the door gently behind him and made his way to his throne. A content smile playing upon his lips as he realised that once Ariel became his wife, she'd become immortal. Only the bearer of the Underworld's royal crown could become immortal, that of course, wasn't immortal before.

As he entered his throne room, his smile widened. He truly had been a successful god. His vast and beautiful throne room was a simple display of his infinite wealth. The pillars were made from the finest stones in his realm and had diamonds encrusted around for décor.

He stood in front of his throne, admiring the large but elegant settee and couldn't help himself but smile at the realisation that it would no longer be one throne, but two.

Ariel finally managed to pry herself from the bed. As much as she loved sleeping, she had to clean herself up. She still reeked of sex and an embarrassed giggle escaped her lips as she scraped the dried residue of Hades' sexual release off her stomach.

Sleeping with Hades had become an addiction; she couldn't get enough of him. Even after he finished her off, she was already fantasizing for more. There was something addictive that radiated off him, made her want to devour every bit of him.

She couldn't explain it nor did she care; she was just content that he seemed pleased she wanted him so much and was glad to give her whatever she wanted.

A satisfied yawn escaped her lips as she entered the shower and quickly opened the faucet. She closed her eyes as warm water began pouring down on her, washing everything away. Her mouth fell open as she gently washed her scalp, giving it a much needed massage. She then proceeded to wash her entire body with the fruity body wash Hades had placed in his shower.

Spending nights with Hades in his room was incredible; she never wanted them to end and as she glanced at the chic, but elegant ring on her finger she squealed knowing that she'd be able to spend eternity with him.

She wasn't exactly sure how everything would go about, but she knew that it would happen; she was certain of it.

After she finished her shower, she reached into the drawers and pulled out a blow dryer. Ariel hummed happily to herself as she tried to manoeuvre her unruly curly hair. Once it was dried, she combed it gently and braided it.

A sly grin grew on her lips at the robe on the bed; it was identical to Hades' except hers was smaller and feminine. She quickly slid it on, loving the smoothness of the fine silk and walked out to the dining room with a content look on her face.

As she entered the room, her face brightened even more as she watched Hades reading a couple of papers. "Whatcha reading?" She sat down next to him, pulling her leg underneath her. It was very unladylike but she didn't care and Hades didn't seem to notice.

Hades looked up, smiling at her and placed his hand over hers, caressing her knuckles gently. "Just reading some papers Hera sent; Aphrodite and her are preparing our wedding."

Ariel laughed, waiting for him to give her the papers and said, "Are you making them?"

"Ha!" He snorted, "If I didn't let them prepare the wedding, they'd throw a hissy fit. Of course," he lowered his voice to a softer, gentler tone, "you can prepare it if you desire. I know you mortal women love to do so."

She shook her head, handing him the papers and said, "Nah; I know they'll do an awesome job. Besides there's this disease that takes over brides when they prepare these things."

"Oh really," he smiled, "and what is it?"

"Bridezillas," she shrugged, sliding her finger around the rim of the porcelain plates before her, "and I don't want to turn into one of those, believe me; you'll leave me at the altar before anything else."

Hades laughed, shaking his head and kissed her knuckles gently. "I wouldn't leave you in the altar. Also, they asked what colours you would like the decorations to be, but they did warn me to tell you that they won't necessarily choose them."

She snorted, muttering under her breath and began playing with a napkin.

"What would you like to eat?"

Just as she opened her mouth to respond, Persephone walked in. Ariel clenched her fist, ready to prepare herself for a battle and waited impatiently for the wench to speak.

"Um," the goddess began, playing with her fingers nervously, "can I speak to you privately?"

Hades shook his head, raising a perfectly arched eyebrow and motioned to Ariel. "Whatever you have to say to me, you can say to my Queen."

Persephone smiled, it was small but it was a smile nonetheless. "I was actually speaking to Ariel, but very well."

Ariel raised her eyebrows, turning to look at her and waited for her to speak.

She took a deep breath, looking down at the floor and then at her. "I want to...I want to apologise; I haven't been one of the nicest goddesses to you and you haven't done anything. Well, I mean, yeah you're with Hades, but we don't love each other. I see the way he looks at you," she smiled at the god, "and he never looked at me like that."

Ariel widened her eyes, feeling her cheeks turn completely red as Persephone continued speaking. "I'm really sorry about what happened to your friend, Adrianne, was it? Anyways, I'm sorry that you were stuck here with Hades. I know he's a bit of a grouch at first, but he grows on you. Well," she chuckled, "in your case he loves you."

Hades tightened his hold on Ariel's hand and nodded thankfully at Persephone. "I just...I wanted to let you guys' know that. I don't want to fight anymore or make you feel uncomfortable every time I'm near."

Ariel stood up, swallowing the lump forming in her throat and croaked, "It's fine, Te—Persephone. I'm glad that we can leave that behind us."

"And," she scratched the back of her neck nervously, "I'm really sorry about that time I came here drunk. It was definitely not my week."

She cracked a grin, shrugging and said, "We've all had those; it's fine, and thank you."

Hades stood up, taking Ariel's hand in his and said, "You're welcome to attend our wedding, if you'd like…?"

Persephone widened her eyes brown eyes, blinking slowly and then said, "You're uh," she gulped, "you're getting married?"

"Yeah," Hades beamed, kissing Ariel's knuckles gently, "I proposed last night."

She smiled, at first it looked somewhat forced, but she eased into it. "Congratulations! You both deserve to be happy." The goddess opened her mouth to say something else, but thought better of it and shook her head. "I'll uh; I'll see you guys around? Again, congratulations!"

Ariel bit her bottom lip, noticing the goddess' discomfort and said, "Persephone?" She turned around to look at her and she released Hades' hand.

Persephone widened her eyes in surprise as Ariel slowly wrapped her arms around her and whispered, "You deserve to be happy too."

She blinked her tears away, feeling her heart twist inside her chest and whispered, "Thank you." She turned to Hades and waved, "Bye! And thank you for listening to me after that episode…"

After she was gone, Ariel turned to look at Hades and whispered, "Well…that was unexpected."

Hades chuckled, shrugging his arm and said, "Definitely was...you still haven't told me what you want to eat," he pouted his lips, "and I'm getting hungry."

Ariel laughed, sitting back down and shrugged. "Let's eat pancakes?"

"Sure!" He sighed in relief, "Wait, those are the fluffy, round, flat cakes, right?"

She nodded, suppressing a laugh. "They are."

"They taste delicious, especially with that sticky substance you pour on them."

"That's called syrup, Aidon," she sighed, giggling as she shook her head. Hades grinned, staring at her intently until she blushed and looked away. "What are you looking at?" She muttered.

He leaned back as a servant poured water in one of the cups in front of them and then continued to survey her, until she groaned. Hades pulled his chair closer to the table and said, "You called me Aidon."

"Yeah," she poured some water in her cup, "and?"

Hades sighed, unable to hide the smile growing on his lips and said, "It's the first time you call me that since our fight."

"Oh," she felt her cheeks turning dark again, "I actually like to call you both."

"And that's completely fine with me," he leaned towards her, cupping her jaw in his hand as he pulled her close and kissed her gently. Ariel closed her eyes, feeling utterly breathless as he kissed her softly, "as long as you let me love you for the rest of our lives."

She grinned, smiling with her eyes closed and whispered, "You can do more than just that."

He chuckled; winking at her so sexily she bit her bottom lip hard, trying to concentrate on the breakfast that the servants were placing before her. At that moment, Hades could be her breakfast and she wouldn't complain. "Oh and what would that be?"

Ariel let out a squeal as he grabbed her leg and began to caress her skin seductively. She stared at him with wide eyes and grabbed unto the table tightly. "Hades," she hissed, grinning at the servant as he walked away. She turned back to Hades, biting her bottom lip as he pulled her leg closer, brushing it past his growing bulge. "Stop!"

He grinned, wickedly, his blue eyes glowing with mischief as he continued to touch her sensually. "You said that I could do with you more than just love you, I'm guessing this is included."

"Hades!" She whined, forcing her eyes to look down at the warm pancakes on her plate. The steam rose, disappearing in the air just like Hades' desire to listen to her.

"What?" His voice came out growled, but soft, making chills run along her arms.

"Please?" She squeaked, grabbing the fork so tight in her hands, her knuckles were turning white. "I will let you do anything you want to do to me after we eat breakfast."

He laughed, releasing her leg and said, "I'm holding you to that."

Hades wrapped his arms around her waist, pulling her closer into his chest as he pressed a chaste kiss against her cheek. "Do you like it?"

Ariel grinned, entwining her fingers with his over her stomach and said, "I can't believe this is actually happening. We're going to get married and I'm going to spend the rest of my life with you; how crazy is that?!"

He nuzzled his nose against the soft curvature of her neck and continued pressing soft kisses. Her skin was almost as soft as silk and he was becoming addicted to touching her. "Well get used to it, because eternity is a long time."

She laughed, turning around to press a soft kiss to his lips and whispered, "You're going to explain the ropes and whatnot to me, right? I'm not exactly Queen Material and that throne up there is just making me extremely nervous."

Hades laughed, rubbing his thumbs against the dimples on her back and said, "Love, you're more than Queen Material. You're caring and passionate—and you're intelligent. Besides, you'll have me sitting next to you all the time."

Ariel leaned her head against his strong chest, mumbling, "It's just scary, in exactly one week I'm going to be married to you and sitting on a throne."

"Not just any throne," he kissed her forehead, "but your throne. This kingdom is yours as much as it is mine."

She grinned; standing on her tip toes to press a kiss to his lips and then turned around to look at the throne next to Hades'. After they had finished their breakfast, all sexual tension was gone and Hades decided that he wanted to show her where she would spend most of her days with him.

The throne was almost identical to Hades' sleek back settee, except hers was smaller and somewhat chic. Diamonds were encrusted on the top, adding an elegant and different touch to her new settee.

"Hades?" She asked as they walked down the castle's corridor, no destination in mind.

"Mm?" He turned to her, rubbing his thumb against her knuckles lovingly.

"Do you remember when I got here you told me that I couldn't whistle; why is that?"

He chuckled, giving a light shrug and said, "Cerberus has very good hearing and when he was smaller I would whistle to him whenever we could play. If you were to whistle from the castle, he'd either find it as a threat or be very playful. Either way, he would leave his post before the gates of Tartarus and millions of souls would flood out of the Underworld."

"Oh," she muttered, "I thought it was because it would annoy you; I was tempted to do so, but Adrianne told me that the last person who whistled didn't enjoy the ripped leg he had to carry to Apollo."

"I actually don't remember that..." he mumbled.

Ariel grinned as he opened the grand obsidian coloured doors. Her jaw fell open as they entered the room and she looked at the millions of stacks and rows of books. "This is your library?"

Hades shook his head. "This is just the first floor; I have three more floors and the third one is getting filled, I'm going to have to make another one."

"Hades," she gasped, turning around as she looked at all the rows, "this is freaking gigantic!"

He laughed, placing his hand on her lower back. "I've read every single book in this library. Shakespeare and Poe just finished a contribution; they're working on a heptalogy."

"A what?" She frowned, breathing in deeply. There was nothing better than the smell of old books. It was a strange scent, but she adored it. She'd definitely spend more time in that room.

"It's a book series containing seven books."

"Oh," she mumbled, "but wow! Poe and Shakespeare? Don't they have different styles of writing?"

He nodded. "Yeah, but they managed to merge them and I'm really excited to see what they come up with; they're both great author's."

"You're such a nerd," she giggled, wrapping her arms around his waist as she pressed a kiss to his jaw. "I love it."

"You better," he grinned peppering her lips with kisses, "in one week you're going to be married to a nerd."

24

— ◆ —

CHAPTER 24

Chaos.

Chaos broke out everywhere in the castle. Aphrodite and Hera's helpers ran around, trying to add the final touches as gods began to enter the garden. The after party would be held inside the castle, in the grand dining room that Ariel didn't even know exist.

All through this chaotic time, she was sitting in front of a vanity mirror, watching as Aphrodite twisted her hair in braids and around her head.

When the Goddess first began the hairstyle, Ariel wasn't very enthusiastic; she thought it was strange, but the final look was breath-taking. She looked beautiful, like one of their own; a goddess.

Aphrodite added an olive-leaves crown on her head and stepped back to admire her work. She grinned at Ariel through the mirror and said, "So? Do you like it?"

"Yes!" She gushed, tilting her head to look at the intricate braids circling her head. "It's so pretty! At first I didn't really like it, but the final result is definitely gorgeous."

"Girl," she narrowed her eyes, placing her hands on Ariel's shoulders, "this was like a girl going through puberty. At first she's ugly and everyone makes fun of her, but then I come in and voila! I make her so drop dead gorgeous that they're all grovelling at her feet. Of course, there's a lot of those, so for some it takes longer than others."

Ariel laughed, standing up when Athena entered the room with a large white bag. She placed it on the bed, grinning at them as she locked the door behind her.

"It took me all night to figure out what colour I wanted your gown to be...and I realised that gold looks beautiful on you. I know, I know," she waved her hand in the air, "the traditional colour is white; but you're not a virgin and we all know that."

Aphrodite snorted, shaking her head and Ariel blushed, flashing her a nervous grin. "Hey, sex is good! But you wouldn't know...being a virgin and all."

"I like being a virgin, thank you very much!" Athena snapped her fingers in a sassy manner, making Ariel laugh and she sighed. "But whatever. So! I know it's a bit cheesy and cliché and what not, but I figured; ever since you came into Hades' life you've brought him light. You're literally the light to his darkness, so why not show you off today that way?"

She held the dress up in her arms, slowly unzipping it and Ariel and Aphrodite gasped in utter awe as the dress slowly cascaded out of the bag. It seemed like gold was pouring from the bag, glittering and glowing.

"This is beautiful, Athena!"

She blushed, handing her the dress and said, "Here! Try it on. Hera thought it was gorgeous and that you would look beautiful in it. She was a little mad that she couldn't come and help you get ready, but she can't leave the servants alone because she's gone a little crazy."

"Of course, Hera would turn into a bridezilla," Aphrodite muttered as she unzipped the dress and waited for Ariel to unwrap her robe.

Ariel grabbed the dress gently; as if she were afraid it would break and with the help of Athena stepped in the dress. It slid up her body softly, tickling her smooth skin like smooth silk. Athena zipped the dress in the back, waiting for Ariel to adjust her breasts and they looked at her through the mirror.

The dress hugged her curves naturally, adding a sensual look to her elegance and the breast padding made her breasts seem full and sturdy. Aphrodite handed her a pearl necklace along with pearl studs and she let out a giggle as she put them on.

The excitement coursing through her body was tremendous; she was ready to run down the aisle and kiss Hades before anyone could tell them.

"You look fantastic, Ariel!" Aphrodite gushed, "I don't know how Hades is going to keep his hands off you for today!"

Ariel giggled, smacking her lips together after she added ruby red coloured lip stick and the goddess of beauty motioned for her to sit down again. She closed her eyes as Aphrodite added the final touches to her make-up and waited nervously for Hermes to pick her up.

Since he was one of the gods that had gotten really close to her, he was the one walking her down to Hades.

The doors flew open and Hermes walked in. He seemed nervous and like he was ready to drop bad news.

"Hermes," Athena frowned, "What's wrong?"

"It's Hades," Hermes gulped, avoiding her confused stare.

"What's wrong with him?" she frowned.

"He's not at the altar."

Ariel raised her eyebrows, feeling her heart beating quickly inside her chest and she bit her bottom lip. "Do you know where he is?"

Hermes nodded, nodding his head towards the door and said, "He's in his room, I tried getting him to leave, but he's not having it."

Ariel sighed, picking her dress skirts up and started walking towards his room. "I'll talk to him." Hermes opened his mouth to say something else, but thought better of it and continued watching out the door.

He didn't expect so many gods would show up to the ceremony, but Hades was getting married. After Persephone left him it didn't seem like he would be looking at another goddess let alone a mortal woman.

Hermes was happy for him; he finally seemed happy with someone and was more relaxed after Ariel warmed up to him. Now he was just worried that Hades would find a way to fuck it all up.

"Hades?" Ariel knocked lightly on the door, feeling her emotions go frenetic and bit her bottom lip nervously. "Are you alright?"

"Go away," he responded in a slur, his voice bitter and unhappy.

She frowned, jiggling the door handle and a little louder said, "Hades? Come on, honey, open up. Tell me what's wrong."

After a couple of minutes, she thought he was ignoring her; he was angry and refused to speak, but the door slowly opened and she gasped. Hades was sitting on the floor, his back leaning against the foot of the bed and he was drinking from a bottle of alcohol.

Ariel frowned, slowly entering the room and stood before him. "Hades?" Her voice was barely above a whisper, fear crawling up her spine as she took in his drunken state. "Hades, honey, what's wrong?"

"Everything," he chuckled bitterly, "everything is wrong."

She knelt before him, slowly taking the bottle from his iron-grip and caressed his face softly. She tucked his soft hair behind his ears, making him close his eyes at her feather-like touch. She was treating him like he was delicate and would crumble beneath her touch and he didn't like it.

He didn't deserve it.

"Stop," he croaked, holding her hands away from him.

Ariel nodded, placing her hands on her lap and whispered, "What's wrong, Aidon?"

"Don't call me that," he bit out, his bloodshot eyes glaring at her forcefully.

She gulped back the urge to fight him, but that wouldn't exactly be the best way to begin their married life. Neither was a drunk husband, but there must've been a reason. "Can you tell me what's wrong?"

"I already did," he snapped, sliding his hand down his face and hissed, "everything is wrong; we are wrong."

She blinked slowly, feeling taken aback and stood up. "What the hell does 'everything' mean then?!"

Hades stood up, standing before her and looked down at her as he towered over her. His eyes were red, as if he had spent the night crying, but it could not be, because he was too busy making love to her to even think about crying.

He walked over to the window, pulling the curtain back to glance down at the hundreds of gods filling his garden. He clenched his jaw, growing irate and turned back to Ariel. "Let me ask you something, Ariel."

She nodded, watching him carefully as he walked over to stand in front of her again.

"Can you still kill anything you touch?"

Ariel frowned, glancing down at her hands, which were covered in the golden gloves and said, "Y-yeah, but what does that have to do with anything?"

"It has to do with everything!" He snapped, running his fingers through his unruly hair, "Do you remember how it breaks? How the curse breaks?"

"Yeah," she nodded, "true love."

"Then why," he hissed, "are you still able to kill things with your hands?"

"I-I don't," she shook her head, feeling dizzy with confusion, "I don't understand what you mean."

Hades threw his hand in the air for emphasis and said, "What we have isn't true love, Ariel! If it had been true love, you wouldn't be cursed still! What we have isn't real; there must've been a mistake. The Fates are probably fucking with us and getting a kick out of this whole ordeal."

"Hades," she whispered, trying not to let his words get to her, "of course it's real! I can't fake what I feel for you and I certainly hope that neither can you!"

"No, I can't," he chuckled humourlessly, "but this can all be an illusion. The feelings that we thought we had for each other can be fake. This is probably just a game to all the gods. They're probably all laughing down there at my idiocy."

"Hades," her eyes watered as she struggled to keep herself together when his words were hitting all the wrong places, "listen to me; I love you. My love for you isn't fake or an illusion. If you don't want to get married now, we don't have to! I just thought that's what you wanted because-"

"That's not the issue!" He cried out, his eyes flashing an ethereal bright blue, "Why hasn't your fucking curse ended if what I feel for you is real?! Hecate clearly said that your curse could only be broken by true love! If I can't break the fucking curse then what does that make my feelings for you?!"

Her bottom lip trembled and soon, her vision was blurred by tears. She had never felt so vulnerable in her entire life. What Hades said sounded reasonable, but maybe it could've been broken a different way.

What she felt for him wasn't a game or fake, as he was desperately trying to get her to see. She loved him, she really did. She had never felt such an emotion for someone, not even for Derick and she had willingly snuck out of her house to be with him.

"Hades," she whispered, her voice breaking with emotion as she stepped forward to touch him, "please tell me this is an illusion. Those spirit things are roaming the castle again and I'm imagining all of this."

"It's not," he snapped, recoiling from her touch, "it's the real thing, Ariel. Why would you want to get married to me when we're not going to love each other? You're probably going to get bored of us like Persephone did and find pleasure amongst the other gods. Like you did with Ares."

She slapped him, loud and forceful, leaving behind her handprint, bright and red. Hades growled, obviously not pleased with her disrespect, but she no longer care. He didn't need to right out say what he meant; he was calling her a whore.

"You clearly don't know me very well, Hades. Yeah, I kissed Ares and it was a mistake. I'm sorry for that, but you weren't paying attention to me. It was stupid of my part to do so, but that doesn't make me a whore."

He snorted, gritting his teeth. "You sound just like Persephone before she left me. Always blaming it on me because you're not woman enough to admit it was your fault."

"I admitted it was my fault!" She cried out, no longer feeling broken by his words; now she felt irate. "And I am nothing like Persephone; I didn't sleep with Ares or any of the other gods and I truly did love you."

Ariel angrily wiped away a single teardrop that slid down her cheek and yanked her gloves off. She took the ring off her finger, tracing the ridges delicately and then looked at him with blurred eyes. "I guess I do have something in common with her." She placed the ring on the bed, bowing her head as she stood before him.

"We both left you. Good bye, Hades." She opened the door, slamming it behind and walked towards the throne room.

As soon as Aphrodite saw her broken expression, she widened her eyes and stomped over to her. "What the hell did he do?! What did he do?!"

Ariel forced a smile out, walking towards the grand obsidian doors and whispered, "It just wasn't meant to be."

Hermes widened his eyes, staring at Athena and Aphrodite with a confused look as she pushed the doors opened and all the gods turned to look at her simultaneously.

"Hello," Ariel spoke loudly and confidently, putting up a strong front, "welcome to the Underworld. I thank you all so much for coming today to join King Hades' and I for this…day, but I bring forth unhappy news."

A quiet wave of mutters broke through and she inhaled exasperatedly, "Hades and I finished our engagement today. There will not be a wedding today or any day for that matter between the God and I. I am truly sorry for having to interrupt your daily doings for this, but we have both decided that it is for the best. A couple cannot be united in marriage if there is no love—and Hades made it clear that what we have isn't love."

"That is a bunch of bullshit!" Eros stood up, stalking over to her. "If what you two have isn't love then I will gladly resign from my fucking position! What the hell got into him?!"

Ariel shrugged, playing with her fingers nervously. "As you all know, I am cursed. Whatever I touch dies. However, the curse can be broken by true love. Hades feels that because my curse isn't broken, we do not love each other."

"I'll show him what the fuck love is," Eros growled out, walking past her and slammed the grand doors behind him.

She sighed, not having the strength to fight against it and turned back to the gods. "Again, I am so sorry for bringing you out here for nothing. I…don't have anything else to say, so good bye and thank you for your patience. Also," she looked at Zeus, who was holding Hera back from running up to beat some sense into Hades, "you do not have to worry about me."

"My curse will not be used against any of you, no matter what I have to do; no harm will come to you. So please, respect my decision," she looked them all in the eye, "I will be returning back to my home in New York and we will never have to see each other again."

They all watched as Ariel picked her golden skirts up and walked over to the castle, holding her head up high like a true Queen would. Hades truly was blind; he more than loved Ariel and the feelings were reciprocated.

"Ariel," Athena whispered as if she were afraid that the girl would collapse, "I am so sorry. I know you were-"

"It's not your fault," she interjected, "so don't apologise. Now," she turned to Hermes, "I would really appreciate it if you could take me home. I'll just change out of this and meet you here?"

"Ariel," he sighed, "don't leave. Hades is probably feeling nervous, he doesn't-"

"Please stop," she whispered, not having the strength left in her to cry. She could not cry even if she wanted to, it was as if her body couldn't produce tears for her to release the excruciating pain her heart was enduring.

It was like a pressure was growing in her chest, pushing her heart to the extent of shattering it. She wouldn't be surprised if thin lines were the only thing holding it together. Her brain had stopped every other emotion and simply placed tired in her mind. She just wanted to sleep and not wake up for the next millennia.

"It's for the best," she cleared her throat, "I don't think I can be here any longer after today. I just want to go back home and forget all of this was about to happen. You guys have a god for that, don't you? A god to erase memories? That could be my goodbye present...?"

"Absolutely not," Aphrodite spat, "you are not forgetting me! And you're not going anywhere; we're going to make Hades' life a living hell."

Ariel cracked a smile, looking at the three gods before her and held herself back from hugging them. "Please stop, guys. I want this and if you guys don't take me, I'll find a way to get myself there."

Athena sighed, shaking her head and said, "This is absolutely crazy. I can't believe that one minute we were all excited about this damn wedding and now we're saying goodbye to you."

"Maybe it just wasn't meant to be," she shrugged, turning back to Hermes and said, "I'm going to change. Wait for me here." He nodded, feeling sorry that she had to endure the pain she was feeling.

Ariel quickly walked to the room where she slept, not wanting to call it hers for it never was. Even Hades' heart wasn't hers. She stepped out of the gorgeous dress, carefully placing it on the bed as well as the sandals.

She walked over to the drawers, where she kept the black dress she wore the night Hermes brought her to the Underworld and pulled it on. She wanted nothing of Hades, not even the necklaces or clothes he gifted her.

Since she had left her flats back in her apartment, she left barefoot. Ariel looked at herself in the mirror, feeling in awe at how beautiful Aphrodite managed to make her look like. She would have truly made a beautiful bride.

The black necklace Hades had given her when they first went to party with the gods sat in the jewellery box and she lightly traced the red ruby pendant. He had said that it would glow when she was near danger and it would take her back to her room in the Underworld.

It had lied.

It didn't glow when she was near him.

Ariel breathed in deeply, turning around to look at the room once more and gently closed the door. Leaving would've been all the harder if Adrianne had still been alive. She knew that if her friend were still there, she would be stronger and face Hades to make his life miserable.

But she was alone and she didn't have the strength left in her to see him anymore.

"Are you ready?" Hermes asked, watching her curiously as she slid on her leather gloves.

"Yes," Ariel nodded, smiling at them. Aphrodite pouted her lips, pulling her in for a tight hug and whispered,

"If you ever need me, just call me. I'll be literally a second away."

"Thank you," she whispered, closing her eyes to try and keep the good memories of the goddess.

Athena smiled at her, kissing her cheek lightly and said, "I am in awe at how wise you are sometimes, Ariel. At this moment, I'm not thinking you're very wise, but it may be because I want you with my uncle."

She shrugged, forcing out a smile and said, "The Fates work in mysterious ways, right?"

"Now you sound like my father," she rolled her eyes, pulling her in for a warm hug. "Goodbye, darling and I hope you change your mind and come back to us."

"The chances of that happening are negative," Ariel chuckled, "I'm a big girl, Athena. I can take care of myself and all of you can rest assured that I am of no threat. That group that was trying to kill you will have to find another girl because I'd rather kill them than attempt anything against you guys."

Athena nodded, sighing as she walked over to Hermes and he took her arm in his. "Close your eyes," he whispered and in a flash, they were in her apartment.

Ariel looked around, widening her eyes as she realised that everything was the same as she had left it. Even the wilted peony was sitting in the middle of the table. She walked around and turned the TV on.

Hermes had taken her to the Underworld around late August and it was December 31st; New Year's Eve and she would spend it sleeping.

"Ariel?" Hermes whispered, not wanting to leave her alone afraid that someone might try to harm her again. "If you ever need my help just call me, okay? If anyone tries to harm you, say my name and I will bring Ares to smite them."

She giggled at the word and nodded, standing up to walk towards him. Ariel hugged him, closing her eyes as he enveloped his arms around her waist and hugged her tightly. He felt like an older brother—a very old brother. "Thank you for bringing me here, Hermes. And I hope you find Adrianne. Come visit me when you do, okay?"

He nodded, blinking his tears away and whispered, "I'll make sure to bring her once I find her."

"And take care of her, okay? Don't you ever make her cry because I will find you and torture you."

He chuckled, nodding and lightly kissed her forehead. "Sleep, Ariel."

It wasn't a request, it was a command. She fell in his arms, exhaustion taking over and he swung her in his arms to tuck her in her bed. She wished for someone to take her memories, but Hermes couldn't bring himself to do so.

It would hurt her, but it would also strengthen her in the long run.

25

— • —

CHAPTER 25

"**W**hat the hell was that?!" Eros cried out, clenching his fists at his side angrily. "You literally threw your damn future away for no reason!"

"Shut up," Hades snapped, wiping the side of his mouth as he glared up at him. "I did us both a favour. That was clearly not-"

"Don't you dare say it wasn't love," he hissed, his features turning dark, "I would fucking know; I'm the damn god of that shit. We both know you would do anything to make her happy. So why the hell did you leave her?!"

The drunken god shrugged, placing the bottle on the floor next to him. "I already told you; I was doing us a favour. Her curse was going to be broken by true love, but it wasn't me that loved her truthfully. The Fates must-"

"You're so pathetic," Ares snarled, slamming the door behind him, making the hinges tremble under the force. "You made her cry! You never deserved someone like her."

"And you did?" Hades snorted, smiling at him evilly, "Or do I need to remind you of Helen? We're both the same, Ares, I just let her go before I ki-"

Ares stalked towards him, swinging towards his face and Eros winced at the noise that the impact made. Hades stumbled backwards, holding unto his aching eye, but Ares grabbed his collar, his knuckles turning deathly white. "Don't. You. Ever. Speak. Of. Her. Again. Do you understand me? I might not be able to kill you, but I can find ways to hurt you."

Hades pushed him off, glaring at him as he stumbled towards the bed and said, "Fuck off, Ares."

"You know she died, right?!" He spat, his anger taking over him so much he wanted to punch Hades' skull out. "She fucking saw you kissing Persephone."

"That was Deimos, it was one of her fears; I never did that."

Ares rolled his eyes, clenching his fists at his sides and said, "No matter, it was your fault. Hermes took her to the beach and Demos went to attack her. She drowned and to keep the peace between the three major kingdoms, Apollo saved her and tried to keep her living. But it was for nothing, because you're not worthy enough for her."

"A-Ariel died?" Hades whispered, the news hitting a nerve within him.

"Yeah," Ares spat, "and you didn't even know. So I guess you were right; you didn't truly love her. And for that, you'll pay. You're going to have to watch as she falls in love with someone else and they'll take care of her the way you never did. And I'll be damned, if you try to hurt her again, Hades."

"I didn't..." he choked on his words, not knowing what to say.

"If I could," he continued, "I would make her fall in love with me. Because I would take care of her and show her that what you gave her, was nothing in comparison to what I could give her. As a matter of fact, I'm going to go see her right now; is there anything you want to say to her?"

Hades glared at him. "Don't you dare-"

"-you don't?" Ares interrupted him, "Very well, goodbye Hades. I'll make sure that you regret this day for the rest of your damn eternity."

After waking up, Ariel realised that she couldn't be alone. She was a danger to herself more than she was to those around her. Her thoughts were her biggest enemy.

She tried to work out why he left her, to try and make up a reason for his sudden outburst. But there was none. And she realised that she simply had to let him go. Yeah, he had been drunk when he spoke to her, but alcohol had a way to bring out the truth from people.

She sighed, zipping up the last suitcase and sat down on the couch, staring at the dead flowers on her table top. After Hades' words continued to echo through her head, she made sure that her curse was still intact and it was. She could still kill whatever she touched.

When she woke up, she felt a longing for someone; someone who would care for her when she was the sickest she'd ever been.

Ariel missed her mom. She had been the only person that had loved her unconditionally and at that moment she needed that. She needed the warmth and caring of a mother.

Her father had left them at a very young age, she barely remembered him. And her mother, Karen, simply told her good stories of the man, not wanting to damage the image she had of him.

The broken hearted young woman took a deep breath, standing up to get something to drink, but on her way to the kitchen a soft knock came from the door. She frowned, glancing at the clock. 10:27pm. Who could possibly be looking for her?

She walked over to the door and looked through the small peep-hole. She frowned again, blinking to make sure that the man on the other side was whom she saw and not a figment of her imagination.

"A-Ares?" Ariel widened her eyes, letting him walk in her apartment and frowned. "What are you doing here?" Her eyes were puffed and red from all of the crying she had done. She had tried to stay strong and tell herself that it was for the better, but she was tired of lies.

The God stepped close to her, his chocolate brown eyes losing a bit of their anger and he cupped her cheeks in his hands. "You've been crying," he murmured, as he rubbed his thumb against her cheek.

She closed her eyes, not wanting to cry in front of him and whispered, "I...yeah."

Ares surprised her, pulling her in for a tight warm hug and she breathed out slowly, feeling his warmth spread throughout her. "I'm so sorry." His muscled arms squeezed her tightly, and he slowly released her, not wanting to make her feel uncomfortable. "If it makes you feel any better, I gave him a black eye."

A soft smile spread across her lips as she motioned for him to sit down on the black coloured couch and she said, "You didn't have to do that."

He opened his mouth to tell her otherwise, but frowned at the suitcases lying on the opposite side of the couches. "You're travelling?"

Ariel nodded slowly, playing with her hands nervously and said, "I can't be by myself…I don't think I'm strong enough right now to be alone; I'm going to see my mother."

"Ariel," Ares stepped towards her, his heart beating wildly inside his chest. He didn't love her, but he was attracted to her; strongly attracted to her. Physically and emotionally wise. If she would give him the time of day, he'd treat her like she deserved to be treated. "Come with me," her eyes widened in surprise, "you can live with me in my castle and I promise to take care of you."

"I-I…"

"I will protect you from anything and anyone; I will crown you a princess if that's what you want." He began to speak faster, desperate to convince her that being with him would work out for her. "I will never make you cry and I'll make anyone who hurts you pay."

Ariel stared at him for a couple of seconds, her green eyes wide with surprise as she let all of his words sink in. "Ares…"

"Please?" He knelt before her, a position that he had never done for any woman, "I don't think I can bear the thought of you being hurt. If you stay here you will be vulnerable, but if you come with me, I'll protect you with my life."

She knelt in front of him, taking his chin in her hand and caressed it gently. Her covered fingers ran over his old scars and his light 5 o'clock shadow and her eyes flickered towards his pink lips. "Ares, the gesture is really sweet, but I was just jilted by someone I thought loved me and I loved him."

He stared at her lips in return; the want to kiss her lips burning so deep it was making his skin itch.

"There's nothing left of my heart to give, if I do go with you, one of us will end up hurt. And I'd rather not hurt myself again."

Ares closed his eyes, placing his hand over hers and whispered, "I wouldn't hurt you."

"But I could hurt you," she whispered in return, breathing in quickly once his eyes opened and he leaned forward.

She closed her eyes, anticipation bubbling inside of her as he inched closer and she whispered, "Ares..."

But his lips were already on hers.

It was a soft, feather-like touch. If his hands hadn't been against her cheeks, she would've thought it was a part of her imagination.

The kiss had been merely a test, as if he were testing the dangerous waters he was stepping in and Ariel was craving company and another feeling rather than pain. What she was doing at the moment would be frowned upon by society, but as her senses began to acknowledge Ares' zesty, warm scent, she couldn't give another shit about what people would think of her.

She just wished that she could take her gloves off and touch his skin properly. She wanted to feel his warmth under her fingertips, but having him touch her should be enough.

Ares tilted his head, his four front teeth scraping her bottom lip teasingly and she trembled against him. He pulled her closer, kissing her with more confidence and tangled his fingers in her soft hair.

Ariel wrapped her arms around his shoulders, loving the broad and taut muscles that were mounted on him. She wasn't one to compare, but he was more built than Hades ever was. It did go well with his appearance; he was the god of war. He needed to look intimidating.

As for Hades, he wasn't as built as Ares, but he had toned muscles that made her mouth water. They were both proportionated according to their realms and powers.

Ares slid his tongue in her mouth, making her gasp at the sensual sensation and she allowed him access to her mouth. His hand slid down to her thigh slowly, but he never moved an inch closer to her naval area; he merely kept his hand over her thigh.

It was driving her mad with desire, but it also showed his respect for her. He wouldn't do anything she wasn't willing to do.

"Ares," she breathed, her voice wheezy and almost light, "this is wrong."

He nodded, but they continued kissing each other. His taste was addicting, it was like a pyromaniac playing with fire. They knew it was wrong, but it felt so good they couldn't stop. Ares was her fire and she was a pyromaniac for the time he was there.

After minutes of kissing, Ares pulled away. His eyes were dilated and dark and he was breathing deeply. He helped her to stand up and she pulled her hair into a ponytail, feeling too hot to have it around her face.

It was awkward as they stared at each other, not knowing what to say after their passionate brush of lips. Ares cleared his throat, opening and closing his mouth but couldn't release the words that he wanted to say.

Ariel breathed in deeply, sliding her hands down her face and said, "I know this is probably going to backfire, but...can you stay the night? I need someone to keep me sane and so far you're the only one that cared enough to come."

He nodded, letting her guide him to her room and she pulled the covers back. "When you came in I just finished my bags. I was going to try and watch some TV and sleep, but I don't really feel like watching anything."

Ares hesitantly sat on the bed and she boldly slid close to him and placed her head on his chest. His arms slowly rested on her waist and he relaxed.

"I wish it had been you I fell in love with," she whispered, looking out the window.

"You don't," he whispered back, "falling in love with me would've been a mistake."

She frowned. "Why do you say that?"

The god shrugged, not wanting to speak about his past, but found the words blurting past his lips. "The last person, who did, ended up dying."

Ariel widened her eyes, hissing in a deep breath and said, "What?"

"A very long time ago," he cleared his throat, "I was in love with a woman. She was beautiful and she just made me want to be a better person. Mind you, I am the god of war so I am a brute when it comes to anything. Helen and I..." his voice cracked, with emotion but not sadness. It was more longing for her than anything else. "We were getting ready to consummate our marriage and...I forgot how fragile she was."

"I didn't mean to, I was completely in love with her, but I somehow managed to suffocate her. I-I don't know exactly how, but she died in my arms. I've never been so enraged, I begged the Fates to bring her back. I even asked Hades and they warned me that if they did bring her back, it might not be the same Helen I fell in love with."

Ariel felt her heart clenching in sadness for him, she wanted to erase the pain he was feeling and make him feel better. But she was just as equally hurt. No wonder they sought company within each other; they were correspondingly broken-hearted.

"When I saw Helen again, she was afraid of me. She wanted nothing to do with me; she said I was a monster and I didn't deserve to love. So I took out my rage the only way I knew how, I began a war. I killed so many people, just to relieve the pain I felt. Athena tried to get me to calm down, but I couldn't. I was bloodthirsty and I wanted everyone to pay for what I felt. My father, Zeus, told me to stop, but I influenced the Trojans to enter a war they couldn't win. Athena supported the Greeks and beat me. I fled and hid for years, not wanting to involve myself in bloody wars again. Of course, it's my nature to start them so I didn't hold my ground for too long."

"Ares," she whispered, propping herself on her elbow to look at him and caressed his cheek caringly, "you're not a monster; even the most fucked up people deserve to love and be loved in return. There will be a person that will come into your life and heal those wounds; they'll soften you so that you will no longer remember what being a brute is."

He chuckled at her words, kissing her knuckles gently and said, "I will not hold my breath, but I do hope the Fates grace me with someone. Now sleep, little one, I'll watch over you for the night."

She yawned, nodding and rested her head on his broad chest again. He was warm and comforting, something she definitely needed. But she was too broken to heal him for she needed healing herself.

When she woke up, Ares was nowhere to be found. He left her a note, telling her that he was called away for business with the Olympians, but that he wished her a safe trip and that if she ever needed him, he'd be a call away.

Her cheeks turned slightly pink at the memory of their heated kiss and she looked down at her hands tightening around the wheel.

She had driven about an hour to get to her mother's house in Florham Park, New Jersey. As she passed the old school and café she would visit in her childhood, her heart clenched and she wondered whether it was a good idea to return.

She didn't even know if her mother still lived there!

Nonetheless, she had driven an hour there, the least she could do was check. She was currently parked outside her old home and everything looked the same.

White walls, large Oakwood tree in the backyard with the swing her mother had bought her. The beautiful flowers that her mother would tend to every Sunday were hidden beneath the snow, but she knew that her mother still took care of them. After her daughter, those were her babies.

The lights turned on, making a sudden wave of nostalgia hit Ariel like the blow of a train. She gulped, staring at the door and waited to see if someone opened it. After a couple of minutes, she sighed and forced herself to walk up the familiar steps.

Her flats made a crunching noise as she stepped over the salt that was melting the snow and she shoved her hands in her pockets, watching puffs of white escape her mouth whenever she breathed.

She practically pep-talked herself into ringing the doorbell and her hands shook more from nerves rather than the cold. It must've been at least 6 degrees outside and she suddenly wished that she was wearing something warmer.

"David, I told you not to forget your-" Her green eyes widened in surprise, her heart thundering inside her chest like the engine of a locomotive as she stared at her daughter. "Y-you're not David."

Ariel forced a smile, shrugging lightly and whispered, "I'm not…"

"Ariel," Karen breathed, her long black hair framing her face in a way that she didn't look a year over 30. It still amazed her, how her mother was almost 50 and she didn't even seem it. She didn't' even wear make-up or surgically scar her body.

"Baby," she gasped, her hands flying towards her mouth as her eyes began to fill with tears, "you're home! You came back!"

At the realisation that her mother wasn't going to kick her out, Ariel smiled, tears quickly welling in her eyes. Karen grabbed her daughter, pulling her in for a tight hug and coughed, "Come in, come in; it's freezing outside."

She stepped aside, letting her go in and she shuddered at the warmth that quickly enveloped her.

"Sorry if there's a bit of a mess, David and I just finished having lunch."

Ariel narrowed her eyes. The house was perfectly clean, her mother always exaggerated when it came to cleaning. Maybe that's where she got her urge to clean whenever she was on her period. "Mom, it looks fine."

Karen widened her eyes, trying to keep her emotions collected and cleared her throat, "Would you like some hot chocolate? I had the milk heating up already. You can put your coat in the closet, honey."

"Sure," she nodded, turning around to take it off and hung it next to hers. Ariel walked over to the hallway adjacent to the kitchen and felt herself going crazy with emotions as she saw her baby pictures still hanging on the wall.

It was like a timeline of her life. First were the baby pictures and they gradually changed until she graduated. Since Ariel's birthday was on November, she was one of the few girls that were the youngest of their class. Whilst everyone was already 18, she was 17.

Karen poured the milk in a mug, her hands shaking with emotion. She wanted to grab her daughter and hug her and tell her how much she loved her. To let her know that the moment she decided to return was the happiest time in her life.

And that she knew why she ran away.

"Here you go," she handed Ariel the cup, smiling sheepishly at the pictures; "you were such a cute little baby. Now look at you, all grown up and beautiful. Your father would be proud."

"Thanks," she smiled, chuckling a bit as she blew her hot chocolate. There was a moment of awkward silence and Ariel cleared her throat, wanting to desperately speak to her mother about the past four years of her life.

Karen nodded to the living room. "Come, come, let's sit down."

Ariel followed her into the living room, sitting down on the soft brown couch and turned to her mother.

"How have you been?"

She looked down at the cup, hoping that her mother wouldn't ask her to take her leather gloves off and whispered, "I've...I've been better."

"Ariel," Karen whispered, placing her hand over her daughter's arm, "honey, you can tell me anything. I can see it in your eyes, you're about to burst. Before you tell me what's wrong," she cleared her throat, "I have a confession to make."

Ariel frowned, watching as her mother walked towards the bookcase across the fireplace and she pulled out a weathered old, brown leathered book. "This was your great grandmother's. Apparently they passed this down from generations and I was supposed to give it to you, but you left before I had the chance."

"Mom I am so sorry!" Ariel exploded, her heart unable to keep her mother from talking, "I just...I've-"

"Ariel, sweetie," Karen sat down next to her, placing their cups on the table, "listen to me. I know about the curse, alright? I know why you're hiding your hands and why you left. You have nothing to apologise for."

"Y-you knew?" She stuttered, almost falling off the couch.

"Sweetie," she pushed Ariel's hair behind her ears, "that's what the book is about. It gives you a descriptive version of the things that will happen and why you have to be careful about what you do. It said when your curse would begin and how it could be finished. I was a little excited because I wanted you to have children, but-"

"Children?" Ariel frowned, blinking away her tears. "W-what are you talking about?"

Karen frowned, grabbing the book and opened it. She flipped through a couple of pages until she found some notes that Vera had left. "It says here that your curse can be broken by true love, but because that is extremely hard to prove, the offspring of true love would break the curse as well."

"But Hades can't have children," she whispered, making her mom look at her in confusion. Ariel cleared her throat and began telling her everything that happened. From the moment she killed Derick, to the moment she met Hades; every single thing that happened, she told her mother.

Even the sexual moments she shared with the God.

After she was done, Karen widened her eyes, her cheeks red with embarrassment and she whispered, "But he said he loved you...why would he just leave you at the altar? That makes no sense."

Ariel shrugged, leaning back on the couch and breathed out in relief. She finally told someone her crazy story and felt truly free. Her mother didn't judge her or interrupt, she simply listened and nodded for her to continue when she would reach certain points in the story that she wasn't certain she'd want to listen.

But it was her mother; she wanted to know everything.

"I didn't think it made sense either...but it happened. I don't think I've ever cried so much in my life before, mom. Not even when Derick died."

"He's a scumbag; he didn't deserve your tears. Neither does Hades, but you said he had problems with his ex-wife. Maybe they came to bother him and he lashed that out on you...?"

"It doesn't matter," Ariel sniffled, taking a sip of her hot chocolate, "I'm never going to see him again."

Karen pursed her lips, nodding and then said, "What about Ares? Do you like him?"

"No," she smiled and felt her cheeks warming up, "he's extremely handsome, though. I know you would consider him eye-candy."

She laughed, patting her hand and motioned towards her empty cup. "Would you like some more?"

"No thank you," she shook her head, standing up to take the cup to the kitchen. Her mother followed her and she said, "Isn't it crazy, though?"

"What is?"

"I thought I was normal, you know? I thought that I was going to graduate and become a teacher or something. But instead, I find out that I'm cursed. I killed my ex-boyfriend and fell in love with the god of the Underworld. I am not even sure how you believe me."

Karen smiled, leaning against the counter as she watched her daughter washing her cup and said, "If I had never read the book your grandmother told me to read, I wouldn't have believed you. And at first, I didn't believe it either. I thought it was just a book to scare me...but I started having dreams and somehow it clicked. It was like my human side didn't want to accept it, but my Lockhaven side had already agreed to this curse. Believe me, baby," she squeezed her hand, "I wish that it had been me instead of you, but then I wouldn't have had you. And you are the best thing that ever happened to me."

Her eyes watered and she blinked her tears away. "I remember holding you for the first time in the hospital. Your eyes were tiny and your head was covered in hair. I never thought a baby could be born with so much hair and then your back was hairy like a little peach."

Ariel's face morphed into an expression of disgust and she said, "Mom, that's creepy!"

She laughed, shrugging and said, "But to me, you were the most beautiful little bundle of joy ever. You stared deep into my eyes," her eyes watered and her voice cracked, "and just looked at me. You had me captured under your gaze and I knew from that day on that you were everything I lived for. You held unto my finger and squeezed tightly and I started crying."

Karen waved her hand in front of her face, as if trying to recollect herself and she whispered, "I got so emotional that the doctors had to take you from me. I started crying but it was happy tears. It was such an amazing feeling! I had given birth to something so beautiful and I was in total awe at how perfect and meaningful my life seemed at that very moment. And when you left me, Ariel, I swore that I would always be here for when you came back."

Tears slid down her cheeks and a sob broke through her chest. Ariel grabbed her mother, hugging her tightly and allowed her tears to spill onto her mother's blue blouse. She returned the embrace, running her fingers through her hair gently and whispered her apologies over and over until it was like a mantra.

"I am so sorry, mom, you don't even understand how ungrateful and just horrible I am. I am probably the worst daughter in the universe and you still stand here and hug me and tell me you love me. How can you even do that?!"

Karen smiled, tears sliding down her cheeks and she wiped her daughter's cheeks clean. "Baby, I'm your mother. I will be here whenever you need me. I am probably the only person in the world that will always take you back no matter what you do. And I know you're going to leave again, children always do, but I'm just grateful that you came back and shared with me what's been happening in your life."

"How can I be so lucky?" Ariel sobbed, her shoulders shaking uncontrollably, "You're such an amazing mother, mom. You don't understand how much I love you and how much I needed you in my life all this time. I wish I could go back and stop myself from going with Derick and being stupid."

She shook her head, wiping away all the tears that spilled from her cheeks and said, "No, sweetie. Things happen for a reason. If you hadn't been with Derick that night, no one knows what might have happened to you. You are a beautiful, smart young woman and you turned out absolutely flawless. If it hadn't been for those hardships you suffered, you wouldn't be who you are today. They morphed you into this; they created that tough exterior that allowed you to keep your head held high when Hades said all those stupid things to you. And I am so proud to call you my daughter, you don't need to apologise anymore, baby."

"But I always needed you. I wanted to come back and beg you to take care of my when I was sick. I needed someone to love me because I certainly couldn't stand myself. I was stupid and young and I didn't allow myself to enjoy my teen years. I just wish I had listened to you."

"Ariel," Karen said stubbornly, "enough, honey. Stop beating yourself over your past. Look at the woman you have become, you're successful and Hades was an idiot to let you go. Now look at me," she took her cheeks in her hands, "where are you staying?"

Ariel shrugged, sniffling and rubbed the back of her hand against her eyes. "I was going to rent a hotel after I saw you."

"Nonsense," she smiled, "you're going to stay here with me. Your room is exactly how you left it, except I cleaned it up whenever I got bored. So let's go to the living room and we can talk about my life and how much it has changed over the years you've been gone."

She laughed, nodding her head and scratched her pink nose, following her mom into the living room. "Yeah," she giggled, "tell me who David is…"

It had been exactly a month that Ariel had been staying with her mom. Every day they spoke about life as if she had never left. Her mother brought her a type of comfort that she couldn't explain; it was true that a mother's love was unconditional.

She knew that if it had been another person, she wouldn't forgive them. She had been gone for four years without a warning or trace.

Not only that, but she wasn't even 18 at the time; her birthday was a month away.

Yet her mother waved it away, telling her she knew it would happen. She just didn't expect it to happen so quickly. No matter what Ariel did, her mother would always love her and support her.

Although she wanted to spend every second with her daughter, Karen had a separate life from her daughter's. She had friends and David, her boyfriend that she needed to attend to and Ariel wasn't going to keep her from them.

So she decided to make a trip to the old dance studio she used to dance in. There was a room for rent for dancers that wanted to practise, they just paid for the amount of hours they would occupy it and return the key once they were done.

She was surprised to see that the dance room was almost the exact way it had been when she went to practise during her preteen years.

Ariel sat down on the cold hardwood floor, taking her black flats off and slid her feet in her pointe shoes. She tied the ribbons around her ankles to secure the shoes and then stretched her feet out on the floor.

She closed her eyes, somehow enjoying the ripping sensation her muscles felt as she stretched her arms over her body. She turned her torso, splitting her legs in a split and then hissed as her body tried to accommodate her muscles into the forgotten sensation.

Soon after, she found herself practising basic moves across the barre. She stretched her leg across it, extending her hands over her head in an arc formation and repeated the motion for the other leg.

She jumped in the air, performing a brisé in which her legs crossed in mid-jump and landed en-pointe. Once she landed gracefully on her feet, she began pirouetting around the room.

A smile grazed her lips as she began to lose herself in the un-choreographed dance; it was as if all her worries were being wiped away with every different step she took. Her ponytail whipped back and forth with her movements and her arms adjusted to keep her balanced.

Ariel grimaced, reminded herself of a dance move she hadn't done in years; the arabesque.

She had to stand on her tiptoes on one foot and extend her other leg in the air behind her body. Her corresponding arm would be behind her body as well to keep her balanced and the opposite arm would be in front of her face, reaching towards the ceiling.

"You're really good!" A girl from behind her clapped her hands, startling Ariel and she lost her balance.

She turned around, smiling at the blonde young woman and said, "Thanks!" Ariel stretched her hands over her head, turning away to look at herself on the mirror again and hoped with all her might that the girl wouldn't scare her again.

"I'm Diana," She walked up, standing next to her as the danseuse continued stretching.

"Ariel," she grinned, standing en pointe and raising her leg on the bar. "Are you a dancer?"

Diana pursed her lips, moving her hand in the air in a "half and half" manner. "Kind of...? I definitely don't do the routines you do, but I like to dance. I used to take Hip-Hop and Jazz."

"That's cool," Ariel stood straight turning her body to face her. "Are you going to dance now? I can leave, I just lost track of time."

"Nah," Diana shook her head, her bright hazel eyes twinkling in delight, "I was just leaving the music room and saw you dancing. I thought it was awesome how you were literally jumping across the room and thought I'd let you know."

Ariel laughed, shrugging modestly and said, "I kind of stopped for a bit, so my moves are a little rusty. My toes feel like they're going to break in half."

She widened her eyes in shock and said, "Really?! You look like you've been dancing for years!"

"Practise, I guess?" She laughed again, shaking her head as she wiped her forehead.

The girl looked young, maybe in her late teens or early twenty's. She was very pretty, with blonde curly hair and rosy pink cheeks. Her eyes were bright and seemed to be shining with life. And the more that Ariel looked at her, the more she felt like she knew her.

She gave out a light chuckle, making Diana frown in confusion and said, "What?"

Ariel shook her head, shrugging one arm and said, "You kind of remind me of someone; do you have any brothers?"

"Just one," she beamed, "he's in college."

"I knew this guy named Apollo, you remind me of him for some reason. Not that you look like a guy or anything, but I don't know...there's something about you that screams 'Apollo' to me."

Diana laughed. "Apollo? Like the Greek god? Wow, I didn't know that people named their kids that, it's kind of sad."

"It is a pretty strange name to call their child," she muttered thoughtfully and then shrugged, not wanting to talk about the gods any longer. Half of her didn't want to remember the pain she felt after being jilted by Hades and the other half was simply afraid that Apollo would hear them and decide to visit her.

"So," Ariel began, "what do you play?"

"Huh?" She frowned, as she looked around the room strangely. It was as if she was searching for something or someone. Whatever it was, it didn't look like Diana was comfortable.

"You said you were in the music room, I thought that maybe you played an instrument," she trailed off unsure.

Diana continued looking around the room, appearing more and more uncomfortable as they continued speaking. Something didn't feel right; there was malevolent spirit near them or something that was making her feel distressed. "Uh, no...my brother's the musical one. I was leaving some papers for my professor in her office."

"Oh," she frowned, looking around as she tried to figure out what she was looking for. "Are you okay?"

She turned to look at her, a frown etched on her features and then she relaxed. "Oh, yeah. Sorry I just...I don't know, doesn't it feel weird here? Like maybe it got colder or something? I don't know maybe I'm just paranoid."

Ariel shrugged, going over to her bag and picked it up from the floor. She switched her pointe shoes out and grimaced at the slight burning sensation she felt on her toes. Then she slid her feet in her black flats and smiled at Diana. "Nah, I feel normal. Maybe it's because I was dancing-"

Diana placed her arm over her chest, pushing her behind her protectively as she glared at the darker corner of the room. Ariel frowned, pushing her hand away lightly and said, "Excuse me, what are you doing?!"

"Show yourself, dumbass, I can feel your presence." Diana snarled, her voice sounding way too powerful for a girl her size.

"Uh," Ariel tapped her shoulder lightly, trying to see what she was doing, "Diana...there's no one there."

"Demos," Diana growled, curling her lip over her teeth in a primal manner, "stop playing games with me. Unveil yourself so we can have a fair fight...unless you want me to veil myself too."

Her frown deepened. How did she even know..."D-Demos?" She stuttered, "What are you-"

A dark shadow stepped out of the corner of the room, slowly making their way to them and Ariel hissed in a breath, her heart thudding in her chest faster than ever. "You godsss are no fun," he hissed, rubbing his hands dramatically.

Diana rolled her eyes, muttering something under her breath and suddenly she was wearing battle armour. Ariel widened her eyes, looking at her in shock and said, "W-wait...Diana," she looked up at her and whispered, "you looked like Apollo because you're...Artemis."

"Bingo!" Demos clapped his hands, "Took you long enough to figure that out, dearie."

"Shut up, you reptile," Artemis spat, holding her sword in front of them defensively, "leave before I hang your head above my fireplace like the rest of you slimy creatures."

"Ah, ah, ah," Demos shook his head, stepping closer to her, "I wouldn't do that if I were you."

She rolled her eyes, gritting her teeth and said, "You know what? I won't even spend my time on you; I'll just call Ares and let him deal with you."

He chuckled maliciously. "Call whomever you want, darling, they won't answer."

"What-"

"Ariel!" The doors were pushed open and Persephone ran in. Her red hair was flying around her face and her cheeks were scathed. "You have to help me!"

"Persephone?" Artemis frowned, still eyeing Demos. "What are you doing here?"

"There's no time to explain," she panted, grabbing Ariel's hand, "chaos broke out through the Underworld. All the Olympians are nowhere to be found and I think that that's why this thing is trying to get Ariel. They're going to-"

"Take her?" Demos interrupted, grinning as he ran his slimy tongue over his crooked yellow teeth, "That's exactly what I'm planning on doing."

"Over my dead body," Artemis spat, swinging her sword in front of him and Demos stepped back. "Take her somewhere safe Persephone; I'll try to see what's happening with the Olympians."

Persephone nodded, tugging at Ariel's arm as she pulled her away from the dance room. They ran out of the room, although Ariel wanted to make sure that Artemis was alright, but Persephone reminded her that she was the one in danger. Artemis was a goddess; she could take care of herself.

"You have to help Hades, Ariel," She pleaded, taking huge gulps of air as they continued sprinting towards the exit, "he's been a mess since you left."

"I'm not going back to him," Ariel panted, "he made it clear when he said our love wasn't true."

"He's stupid!" Persephone rolled her eyes, "He needs you. Heck we all need you, without you we can die. Hermes and Ares are missing too if that makes you want to help."

"Hermes and Ares?" She whispered, fear knotting in her stomach. "Ares will be okay, he's the god of-" But she never finished her sentence.

The last thing she heard before a wave of black consumed her was Persephone screaming her name.

26

CHAPTER 26

The Olympians watched as Demos pushed an unconscious Artemis into one of the cells; he kicked her in when she slumped to the side and slammed the barred door behind him. He left the room and a couple of seconds later he entered with Persephone, slung over his shoulder.

Her eyes were slowly opening as she regained some consciousness, but she wasn't strong enough to fight Demos yet. She groaned as he dumped her on the floor and her body hitting the floor made a thudding noise.

Demos left yet again, whistling under his breath and this time entered the room with Ariel over his shoulder. Her stomach was on his hard, bony shoulder and her head kept smacking into the back of his thigh.

Her long black hair reached the floor, sometimes getting caught in the things that were scattered across the floor, but she wasn't conscious enough to notice the pain shooting through her scalp. Demos dumped her next to Persephone, groaning as he snapped the iron handcuffs on her wrists.

Soon after he was gone, leaving the rest of the gods in darkness and fear.

Hades was leaning against the iron bars, completely sober as he watched Ariel's back move up and down. At least he knew she was alive and breathing, but it would most likely not be for long.

He needed to tell her that he was sorry. He needed to let her know that he was an idiot for letting her go and that he understood if he hated her, but his love for her would surpass his death. The death that was coming no matter who fought or who got in the way.

To protect Ariel, he'd do anything he could.

Slowly Persephone began to wake up, her eyes gazing over the darkness and she groaned. The side of her head was aching tremendously and she touched it, grimacing at the sticky substance pouring from it. She looked at her fingers, biting her bottom lip at the dark blood that suddenly covered her fingertips.

She looked up, frowning at the hands that were tied above hers. They were both tied to a pole with ringlets to tie the handcuffs from. Ariel's hands were hanging above hers and she looked to be in the most uncomfortable position.

"Ariel?" Persephone whispered, touching her foot with her own. But she received no answer. She cleaned her bloody fingers on her chiton, taking a deep breath and forced herself to move closer to the mortal. "Ariel?" She whispered louder, moving her shoulder with a bit more force.

Ariel groaned, recoiling from the goddesses' touch slowly and hissed at the pain on her wrists. They burned, as if she had cut her skin and poured salt over her wounds. She slowly sat up, adjusting herself so that she was leaning against the iron pole and moaned at the ache of her joints.

"Persephone?" She croaked, blinking rapidly to try and adjust her eyesight. "Where are we?"

She shrugged, leaning her back against the pole as well so they were looking at different directions. "I don't know; I think it's the Underworld, but I wasn't looking when that thing brought me in."

"You're in the Underworld," Hades whispered, startling both of them.

"Hades?" Persephone frowned, "What's going on? Where are you?"

He cleared his throat, shifting against his cell and said, "Right across from you guys and I don't know what's going on." He suddenly wished that he was drunk again, like all those times after Ariel left.

"Apollo?" Zeus croaked, slowly releasing Hera's hand to move his son's shoulder. "Can you bring so light in here?"

Apollo groaned, sitting up and said, "The cell is taking most of my energy; I can only light it up for a couple of minutes and that's pushing the limit." He took a deep breath, snapping his fingers and groaned once the light in his hands flickered away. He tried again, this time with much more force and waved his hand on Ariel's and Persephone's direction.

Ariel blinked, squinting her eyes to adjust them to the new light and gasped. All of the Olympians were sitting in mediocre-sized cells, which looked weak enough to kick over. But none of them moved; they all looked like they had been drained of their looks and energy.

She sat up, getting on her hands and knees and slowly crawled towards Ares. He was the closest god to her, but it still tore Hades' heart. She didn't even glance at him for more than a couple of seconds.

"Ares?" He forced his head to look up at her and she took a hold of his scarred, bloody cheeks. "What happened to you?"

He coughed, his teeth covered in blood and he whispered, "These cages are made with some type of magic stronger than any of ours. I tried breaking them, but the more I fought, the weaker I became. It's like I am almost human."

She caressed his cheeks, thankful for Hephaestus' gift; her neon coloured gloves. "Who did this? Who put you all in here?"

The doors slammed open dramatically and Ariel jumped startled, quickly crawling back to the pole. "I did," A soft female voice whispered. It was almost sweet, but the darkness underlying it brought shivers to run along Ariel's back.

"Mom?!" Persephone gasped, suddenly standing up, but forgot she was tied to the pole and fell back to her knees. "What's going on? What are you doing?"

Demeter sighed, pushing back her reddish-brown hair and turned all the lights on. They were in Hades' throne room, surrounding the two sleek black thrones. "You know why I am doing this, Persephone, don't act surprised."

"Momma," she whispered, fear glinting in her eyes, "I told you not to go through with this! You cannot take the Olympians on by yourself and dealing with Cronus is not good. Please, momma, please just let them go and maybe they'll spare your life."

She rolled her eyes, walking around Hades' throne room and ran her fingers up and down the settee. "Persephone, please cut the act. Ever since you met that man Ass or whatever his name is, you've changed."

"Axon, momma, his name is Axon," she whispered, lowering her eyes in shame, "and I've changed for the better. When you love someone you're willing to do anything in your power to make them happy."

"This is exactly what I am doing for you, Persephone!" Demeter howled, anger blazing in her hazel eyes. "Nonetheless, he is a mortal. A weakling, he cannot provide you like one of the gods can. When you married Hades I was pissed, but at least you were a Queen. I wanted you with Poseidon or Zeus, but Hades? He reigns over the dead! There's nothing prosperous in death."

"But now," she hissed, grabbing Persephone's jaw and yanked it up so they were looking deep into each other's eyes, "you fell in love with a mortal man. He has nothing to offer you!"

"I have things to offer him!" She hissed, pushing Demeter's pale hands away. "And his love is enough for me!"

Demeter glared down at her, standing with her hands on her hips and said, "A woman should never have to offer herself to a man. Look at how far that got me with Zeus. I had you and that's all I received. He didn't love me or give me anything."

"He gave you me, momma," Persephone whispered, her heart breaking at the realisation that her mother's greed was greater than her love for her.

She narrowed her eyes. "I meant materialistic things, Persephone. He always had Hera and the idiot always took him back, even though she knew that he would cheat with anything that walked and had a beating heart."

"Don't insult my wife," Zeus spat, his voice sounding stronger than what he felt.

Demeter waved him away, rolling her eyes and said, "Shut up, Zeus." She turned back to Persephone and whispered, "Now, honey, stop this nonsense talk and join me. We have the mortal now, we can use her powers to kill them all and take over Olympus."

Persephone shook her head, tears sliding down her cheeks and she whispered, "I can't do that momma. I don't want to take over Olympus. I just want to be happy."

"Having Olympus will make you happy!"

"No, momma," she shook her head, "it'll make you happy."

Demeter pursed her lips, taking a deep breath and whispered, "Very well. You leave me no choice." She turned to the door, speaking to no one in particular, "Demos, bring the mortal in."

"Momma," Persephone whispered, panic crawling up her throat, "what are you doing? Who are you bringing in?"

Demos entered the room, yanking behind him a dark-haired man. He was attractive with kind green eyes and full pink lips. His skin was a light caramel colour, sweet and sun-kissed. His eyes looked all over the room in fright and when they landed on Persephone, his eyes softened; love clear in them.

"Persephone," he whispered, his voice had a thick accent that Ariel couldn't recognise, "what is going on, my love?"

Tears welled in Persephone's eyes, turning them into a pool of chocolate and her bottom lip trembled. "Momma," her voice broke, "momma, please don't do anything. Don't hurt him, momma, he's kind!"

Demos pushed Axon towards Demeter and he fell in front of her feet. He looked up at the malevolent Goddess and frowned.

"You are, my love's mother? She has pictures of you in our home," he smiled, not realising what Demeter's dark intentions were.

"Momma," Persephone begged, her voice raw with emotion as she fought the handcuffs preventing her from protecting her beloved. "Momma, please I am begging you! Leave Axon out of this. I'll do anything you want, but please leave him out of this."

"You don't understand," Demeter whispered, taking a black dagger from the inside of her chiton. She looked up at her daughter, grabbing Axon's neck and held him in her arms. His eyes met with Persephone's and she sobbed desperately, shaking her head as she continued begging for her mother's mercy.

"Persephone, sweetie," she placed the dagger over Axon's stomach and whispered; "love makes us weak."

"Momma no!" Persephone bellowed, falling to her hands once her mother dug the dagger into the mortal's stomach. She fought the chains, severely damaging her wrists on the process as she pulled and clanked them, crying for her beloved. "Axon!"

Demeter grimaced, stepping away from the gurgling man and motioned for Demos to release Persephone.

As soon as the chains fell from her wrists, she ran towards him, picking his head up and placed it on her lap. Sobs broke through her chest and all the gods, along with Ariel, watched as she cradled his head to her chest and whispered in his ear.

Axon looked up at her with wide eyes and caressed her cheek with a bloody hand. "Don't cry, my love, it is alright."

"No," Persephone shook her head, her tears falling on his cheeks, "it's not! I can't bring you back. That dagger destroys souls and without your soul I can't bring you back."

The love in his eyes was tremendous, even as he was slipping away to meet his eternal death, he gazed at Persephone with adoration. She sobbed, holding unto him tightly and cried out in anger. She took the dagger from his stomach and pulled it out gently, her hands shaking as she caressed his cheeks.

Axon's head tilted to the side, his last breath wasted on his proclamation of love towards the goddess and Persephone lost all rationality.

It was for him that she was willing to change her cold bitter heart. It was for him that she wanted to live a better life and it was for him that she apologised to Ariel and Hades for trying to break their bond.

But now he was gone. Now she had nothing to live for and if she couldn't have the love of her life; no one else could either.

Persephone closed his eyes, slowly standing up and walked towards Hades' throne room. A gold pot was sitting next to it. It was like Pandora's Box; the object containing the insides was beautiful, it almost drew anyone in. But what it held inside was deadly to the gods.

It was Cronus' poison, the one he would use to kill his children.

The goddess of spring growth slowly opened it; grimacing at the horrid stench it gave off and dipped the tip of the dagger in. It sizzled a bit when it came into contact with the dagger and she closed it, slowly standing up to look at her mother.

Tears continued to slide down her cheeks and Demeter pulled her in for a hug.

"Oh honey, it's alright, he was just a man. You can get yourself another one any time you want! Now," she smiled, brightly, "let's kill these idiots and get on with our plan, yes?"

"He wasn't just any man, momma," Persephone replied in a monotone voice, all emotion gone from her facial features, "I loved him."

Suddenly Demeter gasped, widening her eyes as she looked up at her daughter and then down at the dagger that she was holding. It was deep into her stomach and Persephone held herself back from moving the dagger to cause her more pain.

"You're right, momma," she whispered, watching as her mother fell to her knees, gasping for air, "love does make us weak."

Persephone stepped away from Demeter, watching emotionlessly as she tried to grab her daughter's feet, but she was growing weaker with all her movements. The dagger fell besides her, making a clanking noise once it connected with the marbled tiles and she breathed in slowly.

She turned to Demos, motioning with her hand to clean up the two bodies on the floor. "Take them to my mother's castle; I'll clean them once I finish here. Come back right away."

He nodded, fear flashing across his eyes as he realised that Persephone could be worse than Demeter. Her mother had just been greedy, but Persephone was broken-hearted and bitter. She would have no remorse, for she had no one to love.

"You," she pointed to Ariel, "get up."

Ariel blinked her tears away, wanting to tell Persephone her condolences, but her words caught in her throat and fear replaced them. "Persephone-"

"Shut up," she hissed, cleaning her bloodied hands on her chiton. Demos entered the room, quietly, looking at Persephone with cautious eyes. "Let her go," he pointed to Ariel. He nodded, opening the handcuffs and released her.

Ariel grimaced; rubbing her scathed wrists and stood quietly, not knowing what do to. She wanted to run and never look back, but she knew that was impossible. The look in the goddess' eyes told her otherwise.

"Bring me a dancer, Demos, I don't care who as long as he's a male."

"Yesss, milady," he bowed his head, quickly leaving the room.

Persephone walked towards Ariel, eyeing her up and down and whispered, "You know? I was trying to be good. I tried so hard to be good because Axon wanted me to be good. He told me that you and Hades were in love so that I shouldn't get in the way." Tears blurred her vision and she clenched her teeth, trying to hold them in, "But that didn't stop my mother, did it? Our love for each other wasn't strong enough to make my mother let him live."

"Persephone," Ariel whispered, "I am so sorry."

She held her hand up, glaring at her and said, "I don't want your meaningless apologies. Shut up and listen to me. I met Axon in Egypt. I was travelling there to meet Ra, the sun god of the Egyptians because my mother was trying to set up a deal with him. I was supposed to go, please the god however he wanted and make sure that my mother's plans went accordingly."

"Axon was an archaeologist, excavating a tomb he found. I thought he was cute and he looked interesting. I went over to talk to him and he freaked out because he thought he was the only one there. I assured him I meant no harm and we began speaking about what he was doing. He thought he had found some Pharaoh's tomb, I wasn't really paying attention. He was so beautiful and I couldn't stop looking at him, at that moment I thought that maybe Eros had shot an arrow at me or something." A soft sad smile grew on her lips, "And he was so sweet. I cleared up his confusion on the Egyptian gods and explained to him what their roles were and the right versions instead of what the humans had written."

Persephone bit her bottom lip, holding back her tears and whispered, "He offered to buy me lunch to keep talking about the gods and we spoke for so long, I forgot about my meeting with Ra. My mother grew furious when she heard that I didn't uphold her end of the bargain, but I didn't care because I spent time with Axon. We continued to meet up, until one day I boldly kissed him. He kissed me back and it was the most glorious moment of my life. We moved in together and I told him about my past with Hades and you. Of course, he thought you guys were mortals and I didn't want to scare him away, so let him believe what he wished. He told me that I had to apologise to you, that I had to let you know that I wouldn't get in the way of your love. And I really wouldn't have because I loved him. I never loved Hades, I might've had an infatuation with him, but it was never love."

Tears slid down her cheeks and she wiped them away angrily. "I was expecting his child. I was going to have Axon's child, but now I cannot bring him into this world without his father. Especially now that I know what type of woman I am. I do not want my children to grow up the way I did with my mother. And this is where you come in; I cannot be with the love of my life? Well neither can you."

"Persephone," Hades spoke up for the first time since Ariel spoke to Ares, "please leave her out of this. She's done nothing to you."

"Did Axon do anything to my mother?!" Persephone lashed out, "No! But she took him from me! So I will do the same to the rest to all of you. I will make all of you watch as I kill your beloveds and then I will kill you myself."

"Persephone," Zeus whispered, "Honey, it doesn't have to be this way. We can find a way to bring Axon back."

"You don't understand, do you?" She snorted, "You can't bring a mortal back without his soul! That dagger that my mother used destroyed his soul the moment it touched him!"

Demos entered, pulling in the soul of a dancer and motioned towards Persephone. "Here you go, milady."

Persephone smiled, nodding in approval and said, "You like dancing, don't you, Ariel?"

"Yes," she whispered.

"That's good. Now, how ironic would it be, if you died doing something you loved?"

"Persephone-" Hades growled out.

"Shut up, Hades!" She hissed, glaring at him and turned back to look at Ariel. "You're going to entertain me, human. You're going to dance until I tell you to stop and if I don't like what you do, I will make you regret it." Persephone looked at Demos and said, "You know what dance I feel like watching? Tango; you can do that, can't you, human?"

She nodded quickly, fear making her throat go dry.

The goddess smiled and said, "Splendid; choose a song, Demos." She turned to the spirit and whispered something in a language that Ariel couldn't understand.

Hades growled, punching the bars that confined him and cried out, "Persephone, ☒x☒!"

She rolled her eyes, waving him away and said, "Now dance, human; entertain me."

The spirit grabbed Ariel, his translucent hands holding her tightly. She grimaced, biting the inside of her cheek to prevent herself from complaining and frowned as the music slowly began to fill the throne room.

It was soft, almost inaudible until the singer cried something out, his voice gruffly and hoarse. The guitar was strummed repeatedly in a minor chord, along with the piano. The violin began playing, giving the beginning of the song an almost sensual sound.

The spirit began twirling Ariel around, moving his hands over her hips as they skidded across the floor. El Tango de Roxanne began to play louder, until it was booming through the speakers and vibrating across her body.

Ariel grimaced as the spirit grabbed her hand, spinning her away from his body and spun her with such force her arm almost came out of her socket. He picked her up, throwing her in the air and she squealed, widening her eyes in fear once he grabbed her and threw her again.

As the music became more intense, so did his movements. It was as if he was really feeling the song and forgot that she was merely human. Her joints felt like they were going to be ripped as he yanked her back against his chest and she began breathing harder, her body trying to let the oxygen flow through her lungs.

The song ended and Ariel breathed out, relieved, but was surprised when it began again. She groaned as the spirit holding her, dipped her, almost making her head hit the marbled floor.

"Love...it will drive you mad!"

He continued jerking her around, making her feel like her arms were going to break from her body and she widened her eyes as he forced her to stand on her tiptoes. They danced more dramatically, mixing ballet dance moves with the tango and she gasped for much needed air.

Suddenly her legs slipped and she looked down at the floor, gasping at all the blood that was smeared from her feet. The spirit spun her around until she thought she would vomit her intestines out and held her right leg out, extended in the air.

After the third time the song replayed, Ariel lost count. She was growing weaker and lightheaded by the second and her dance partner wasn't helping her. He threw her in the air without warning and spun her around the room so much she was going to fall to her knees and cry.

He grabbed her hand, literally throwing her away from him and her hand slipped from his grasp. Ariel huffed, smacking her head on the floor and groaned in pain. She couldn't stand up, her legs refused to support her and her hands ached from all the yanking they had experienced.

Persephone stood up from Hades' throne, clapping slowly and said, "That was marvellous! Really, just splendid!"

Ariel pressed her cheek on the cool floor, gasping for air and felt her eyes tearing up at the excruciating pain her entire body was experiencing. She had never experienced something like it; it was utterly agonizing.

"Now," Persephone slowly walked down towards Hades' cage, "you know what I'm going to ask you for, right?"

"Leave her out of this, Persephone," he begged.

She smiled, maliciously and ignored his plea, "Renounce your title, Hades. Step down from your throne and crown me the new Queen."

He snorted, "No."

27

CHAPTER 27

An amused smirk grew on her lips and a strange glint shone in her eyes as she stepped forward, clasping her hands before her. "That's cute," she tilted her head, "you think you have a choice." Persephone glared at Hades, "You don't, Hades. Renounce your throne if you know what's good for you."

"No," he repeated, his gaze never wavering from hers.

Persephone sighed, pinching the bridge of her nose and said, "Really, Hades? You're going to make me do this?" She walked over to his cell, kicking the door open and he fell on his side, not strong enough to uphold his own weight. "This metal," she said thoughtfully, "was made with metals from grandfather's time. That's why all of your powers are basically useless. It was made to suck the life source out of the caged animal—in this case, it would be you guys."

Hades growled, pushing himself to sit up and groaned at the pain his joints were experiencing. "When I can stand, Persephone, I will make you regret ever doing this."

"Hades," she sighed again, "hasn't Rhea ever thought you not to make promises that you cannot uphold to? Like," she glanced at Ariel who was still struggling to stand up, "you swore on the River

Styx to make everything in your power to make her happy; yet on your wedding day, you left her."

The God looked down at the floor, shame clear in his eyes and he whispered, "I had my reasons."

"Yeah," Her eyes grew teary, "my mother. She went to you, didn't she? She told me that she was going to try and put doubts in your head so that the mortal would fall into this damn trap. I tried to stop her, but your idiot guards thought that I came to interrupt the wedding."

She shook her head, looking down at Hades with a sudden anger blazing her watered brown eyes. "Did you know that all you had to do was marry Ariel and the curse would go away?" Her jaw clenched in anger and she bit her bottom lip to keep herself from crying, "All you had to do was show her how much you loved her, that you would stick with her through it all and she would be fine! But no! You had to let your damn insecurities get the best of you!"

"You caused those insecurities, Persephone!" He bit out.

"I apologised!" She hissed in return, "But what do I get in return? The love of my life stripped away right before my eyes! Axon was the only one who ever cared for me. Even my mother didn't give a shit about me, she was always too greedy; comparing the things she had between the other goddesses belongings. My father? He simply adored Athena! She was his favourite child and he never gave me the time of day." She snorted, wiping away her tears, "But I never complained! And then I chose to stay with you; it was my way of rebelling and I thought that for the first time, someone cared for me."

"But my mother told me that you wouldn't make me happy, she planted seeds in my brain. Evil thoughts and she ripped the love I had for you away. You know she's the reason we never had kids?" Her bottom lip trembled as her eyes spilled tears, "My mother made sure that any living egg inside of me would be killed before I could have your child; I had two abortions Hades. Two fucking abortions because of her and I thought that you would notice. I was waiting for you to notice when I started distancing myself from you and that your love for me would come through and you'd tell me that it would be okay. But you never did; you demonstrated that you didn't love me. So I got my pleasure from other gods and ended up leaving you."

Hades looked up at her, his eyes wide with surprise, "We...I can have children?"

She glared at him, angrily wiping her tears from her cheeks and ignored him, "Then I met Axon and everything turned upside down. He made me turn into a better person and I was willing to do it because I loved him. And ever since I became good, things began to spiral out of control. I lost the little bit of love I had from my mother, but it was okay because Axon's love made up for it and I reminded myself that being good would eventually compensate me." Her voice rose in irritation, "And what did that get me?! What did trying to be good get me?! The love of my life died! The only fucking person who ever gave a shit about me died and I couldn't do a fucking thing because I went to get help! I went to get Ariel to keep her out of harm's way when I should've kept Axon safe."

"Persephone," Hades whispered, remorse filling his heart.

The Goddess shook her head, holding her hand up to stop him and she whispered, "If you had simply married Ariel, Hades, none of this would've happened. My mother would've postponed all this shit and Axon wouldn't be dead. But your fucking imbecile-self couldn't go through with it!" She kicked her foot into his stomach, clenching her fists at her sides as she cried out, "Why couldn't you just marry the goddamn human?! I would still be trying to be a better fucking person and not dying to rip all of you fucking idiots to shreds!"

"Persephone," Ariel croaked, "you can still be good, you don't need Axon-"

"-don't tell me what I need and what I don't need," she spun around, glaring at her with blazing bright eyes. "I didn't need Axon to be good. I needed him to remind me why I was being good. But it doesn't matter to you because you always had it. Your mom adored you and Hades loved you like no one could. Hell even Ares grew a liking towards you and all I wanted was one person to pay attention to me. One fucking person to show me that I was worth something; Axon was that person. And now he's gone," she turned back around, wiping her tears again and hissed, "so, Hades; renounce your fucking title and hand it over."

He shook his head, grimacing at the pain she left behind on his stomach after kicking him and coughed, "N-no."

Persephone groaned, walking over to Ariel and yanked her head upwards by her hair. Hades quickly froze and Ares sat up in his cell. "Hades," she whispered, her voice dripping with no emotions, "renounce your title or I will slit her throat; I don't need her to kill you. I have Cronus' poison, but that's more painful than a simple touch from her."

"N-no," Ariel shook her head, widening her eyes as she looked at Hades, "don't you dare do it."

He gulped, his eyes flashing with sadness and he licked his lips. "Please let her go."

The Goddess took the dagger, pressing it to the mortal's neck and hissed, "You have exactly two seconds to make up your mind, Hades. I will slice her jugular and let her bleed to death right before your eyes."

"Ariel," he choked, his eyes speaking the words he couldn't say.

She shook her head, as much as she could under the goddess' tight grip and whispered, "Hades, no, please, please don't!"

"I..." he breathed, a single tear sliding down his cheek as he whispered, "I renounce my title as King of the Underworld and god of death; Persephone I crown you the new holder of these names."

She breathed in deeply, releasing Ariel and stepped back from the mortal before she could realise that she could take her gloves off and kill her. No matter what, it was too late; Persephone was now the new Queen of the Underworld and the goddess of death.

A low groan came from the ground beneath them, making Ariel cover her ears in pain and the ground gave a sudden tremor in complaint. They all looked around in fear as Persephone grimaced at the scorching hot power coursing through her body.

"Do you know what this means?" She whispered, looking down at Ariel.

"What?" she whispered.

A malevolent smile grew on her lips, resembling that of a snake and she whispered in return, "You can kill Hades."

Ariel gulped, hiding her hands underneath her stomach as she looked at Hades and relaxed her body against the cold floor. "I'm not going to touch him."

Persephone rolled her eyes, "You guys were really made for each other, weren't you? It's cute how both of you believe that you have a say in this. Now," she walked over to Hades with the dagger that had killed the two important people in her life, "you can either kill him yourself or watch as he drowns in his own pool of blood."

"Persephone," she whispered, her chest constricting in pain, "please...please stop."

"Mm," she looked down at Hades as he stared at Ariel as if trying to memorise her face for the last time he would see her, "where would this," she twirled the dagger in her fingers, "make him feel the most pain? Here?" She pointed to his heart, "No...that would be too quick."

Her vision got clouded by tears as she forced herself to sit up and she quickly blinked, growing angry at Hades' defeated expression. "I am not going to kill him! You need to stop acting like a damn bitch and get over it! Boo hoo, they killed your damn love, but we had no part in it! Just let us go!"

"You had no part in it?! The reason Axon was fucking killed-"

"-was because your mother was a psychopath! She told you to join her in her crazy plan but you said no and you said no because there was some good in you! So please stop this and let us go."

Persephone gritted her teeth, kneeling closer to Hades and said, "You don't understand, Ariel. The only reason there was some good left in me was because Axon was still alive. I didn't know my mother had him; if I had known, all of them," she pointed at the cages, "would be dead."

"No," she said forcefully, "I know there's some good in you-"

"Just stop!" She snapped, "Are you going to kill him or do I have to dirty my hands again!?"

"No-"

"Ariel," Hades whispered, forcing a smile, "honey, it's okay. I got to spend these couple of minutes memorising every inch, every mole, scar, smile, laugh of yours that I will ever need in my eternal slumber. Just do me the honour of dying by your hand; it'll be a bittersweet death."

"Shut up," she sobbed, shaking her head in denial as she clenched her fists in fear, "don't you dare say your fucking good-byes; I'm not killing you."

"Ariel," he crawled towards her, lowering his hand once she re-coiled from his touch and said, "a□á□□ μ□□, please, I know I hurt you. I didn't mean to leave you stranded on our wedding day, what I said…I didn't mean it. I was drunk and insecure; I did love you and I love you now more than ever. You changed me for the better, you gave me a reason to wake up every morning and smile at the day because you were there and without you I don't know what I would do. So please, I am begging you for selfish reasons, but begging you nonetheless, take me out of my misery."

Her bottom lip trembled as a sob shattered through her chest, making her shoulders shake in despair as she looked around the room for any help. No one dared to look at her; they were all too worried about their own undoing to spare her a look of hope.

Ariel cried out, sobbing desperately as Hades embraced her. He pulled her in for a tight hug, the warmth from her body making him shudder. His hands slowly stroke her hair behind her ears and he whispered sweet nothings near her ear.

"Stop," she sobbed, choking on her tears, "please stop and wake me up. I can't kill you Hades. No matter what you've done to me, my heart belongs to you, so please I am begging you; do something. Don't just make me kill you when I've given you all I am."

"I am doing something," he whispered, taking her hands in his and kissed her forehead. "Persephone," he spoke louder, "you will not hurt her after this, right?"

"No," she spoke quietly, looking away from them as she knew first-hand the pain they were both feeling; yet it didn't stop her from making them go on.

"Please?" Her face contorted painfully as tears spilled down her cheeks and Hades rubbed them away with his thumb.

"Smile, a□á□□ μ□□, give me the pleasure of seeing you smile one last time?"

Ariel gritted her teeth, shaking her head and sniffled, wiping her red runny nose. "Do something," she smacked her hands against his chest, "don't just fucking give up."

Hades entwined their fingers together, caressing her knuckles gently and whispered, "I told you I am doing something." He looked down at their entwined fingers and smiled as he looked up at her.

Her eyes widened in terror as she realised that whilst they spoke, he had managed to take her gloves off and was now touching her caringly. A terrified shriek escaped her lips as Hades pulled her hands up to his cheek and he pressed her palm against his skin, closing his eyes in pleasure.

"H-Hades," Ariel sobbed, her hands shaking uncontrollably as he stumbled into her arms, "Hades, no." Her lips trembled as tears streamed down her face and she held unto him tightly, "please, get up."

She ran her fingers through his jet black hair, sobbing painfully slow and hugged him tightly against her chest. "Please," she rocked him back and forth, whispering incomprehensible things as her mind went into a state of denial. "I'm sorry! I'm so sorry, but please,

please come back to me! I'll do whatever you want, but please get up! Open your fucking eyes!"

Persephone rolled her eyes, crossing her arms over her chest and said, "I actually have other things to do today, so I would love it if you could hurry up and move to the next one. You can keep crying over him later."

"You fucking bitch," she croaked, hugging Hades in her arms, not wanting to let him go because she wanted to believe he was merely sleeping.

"What did you say to me?" She hissed.

Ariel looked up at her, her bloodshot red eyes holding no emotion but hate in them. "I said, you fucking heartless cünt."

The goddess snorted, opening her mouth to say something else, but Ariel gingerly placed Hades on the ground and pressed a soft kiss to his forehead. She stood up, the anger coursing through her veins allowing her joints to ignore the pain they were feeling.

"I am going to fucking murder you."

Persephone smiled, clicking her tongue against her teeth, "Well you see...when Hades handed his title over to me, I became the goddess of death. Therefore, you can't kill me."

"Do you want to fucking bet?" Ariel hissed menacingly, walking towards her.

She blinked, frowning at the colour of the mortal's eyes; they were now pitch-black. She looked like a demon; a demon thirsty for blood. "You're a mere mortal; you can die with a flick of my wrist."

"You don't know me very well do you," Her voice came out growled, a legion of voice speaking as one, "I am going to enjoy ripping you apart, Persephone. There won't be anything left of you by the time I am done, no one will be able to recognise your body and I will make sure to destroy your soul whilst I'm at it."

"You dare threaten a goddess?!" She spat, growing irate with her.

A scorned, emotionless laugh echoed past her lips and she stood before her, no longer feeling pain coursing through her, but an endless wave of hatred. Hatred and so much power that she thought it would end her on the spot.

Ariel grabbed Persephone's throat, her teeth curling over her teeth as she whispered, "You made me kill Hades and for that you will pay. I would gladly let you live to endure the pain of losing the one you love, but that won't satisfy me." She pulled her closer, whispering near her ear, "I'm going to rip your limbs one by one, you little cunt."

Persephone growled, pushing her with so much force that she flew across the room. Ariel huffed, smacking into the wall and slid down, slowly forcing herself to stand up and dusted her tattered jeans.

Hera gasped as the goddess of death slapped Ariel with so much force it seemed as if her head was dislocated from her shoulders. "The baby!"

Ariel widened her eyes, confusion growing within her, but she had to stand up and dodge Persephone's incoming blows. A growl rumbled in her chest as she kicked her leg into Persephone's stomach and made her stumble backwards.

"You cannot kill me," she taunted, wiping the blood dripping from her mouth, "we've already established this. You're simply walking into your own death."

A sadistic smile grew on her lips as she jumped on the goddess, knocking her down unto the marbled steps that lead to Hades' throne and she smacked her cranium unto it. Persephone hissed in pain, incapable of using her powers against the mortal for she had no idea on how to use them.

"You," Ariel smacked her head on the floor harder, "entered a fucking fight," smack, "that you cannot fucking," smack, "win, you bitch!" Her eyes, if possible, darkened and her voice became more demonic as she continued smacking the goddess' head on the marbled steps.

"I told you," she hissed, grabbing Persephone's throat in her hands and tightened her fingers around the slender column, until her fingers were turning a pasty white colour, "I am going to fucking kill you."

Persephone laughed, her pearly white teeth covered in blood as she tightened her hold on her and began to cough. Ariel wiped away the blood on her cheek and gritted her teeth as the source of power bubbling in the pit of her stomach began to be released through her fingertips.

It felt as if an electric wire had gone haywire within her, releasing immense amounts transcendent power that she couldn't manoeuvre.

The goddess underneath her widened her eyes in fear as she felt flickers of power touching at her mere source of light, as if it were tugging away her life source.

Blood began to drip down Ariel's nose, dripping unto the goddess jaw as she struggled against her hands, no longer believing that she couldn't kill her. But Ariel wouldn't let go; her hands were ironed around her neck like a clamp.

Persephone coughed, her eyes almost bulging out of her skull as she writhed under her, squirming like the lowly worm she was. "Let...me...g-go," she spluttered, clawing at her fingers.

Ariel held her down with one hand, punching her face with the other hand and smirked at the sickening crunch that came from her nose. Persephone spat blood on her face, crying out in pain and she growled, angrily wiping the disgusting fluids off her face.

More power coursed through her, making her dizzy and weak as she began to strip the goddess of her divinity. Ariel could see as she killed the vile woman underneath her, the life was literally draining from her and the fear and surprise crossing her facial features, pleased her greatly.

Persephone gasped, arching her back off the floor and whimpered as Ariel grabbed the dagger inside her chiton and stabbed it into her heart multiple times. Red blood splattered on her face from the gory act, but she simply stood up once she knew the goddess was dead and wiped it away, mixing it with her own.

Ariel turned to the other gods and they all cowered away in fear, not daring to meet her eyes. She glared at them in disgust as she fell to her knees in front of Hades' immobile form and caressed his cheek with a shaking hand.

A slight smear of blood was left behind from her fingers as she placed her head to his chest, a quiet sob trembling through her and she held unto him tightly. "I'm so sorry," her voice was normal, quiet and pained, "I want to bring you back, Hades, but for every life we try to save, another one has to pay."

Ares stood up in his cell, kicking the door open, no longer afraid that Persephone would use his weakness against him and whispered, "Ariel, don't do it."

"I have to," she whimpered, "the Underworld needs a king and no one looks sexier than the god of death than Hades."

"There has to be another way," he pled, holding his bloody arms from all the force he had done to get out of the cage, "you can take my life instead."

A humourless chuckle left her lips and she shook her head as she caressed Hades' face, "It has to be me, Ares. That's the reason why the Fates brought me to Hades. This was my purpose all along; not to fall in love with him."

"Please," he closed his eyes, wanting to desperately change her mind for he knew that if Hades awoke without her, he'd be tormented, "don't do this, Ariel."

"All my life," she whispered, "people have told me what to do and what not to do, I think I can take this damn decision by myself. Now leave me alone."

Ares opened his mouth to beg her, but shook his head and went to help his family out of the cages. They were all speechless, watching with wide eyes as Ariel muttered her goodbyes to Hades and called forces that she never knew were inside her.

She caressed Hades' cheek one last time, trying to memorise his face, like he had done, before she would close her eyes for the rest of her eternal slumber. Ariel felt heavy tear drops sliding down her cheekbones as she pressed a soft kiss to his smooth forehead and whispered her undying love for the god and managed to whisper her life into his.

No one knew how; not even her. But she collapsed in his arms, her head falling right on his heart and a sob shattered Aphrodite as a smile grew on Ariel's lips. It only grew for the last thing she heard was Hades' heartbeat.

28

CHAPTER 28

Hades gasped, widening his eyes as his entire body trembled with energy and blinked slowly as he slid his hand down his face. "W-what happened?" He groaned, slowly sitting up to look up at the Olympians circling him.

"H-Hades," Aphrodite whispered, her face turning into an ugly expression of heartbreak.

He raised his eyebrows looking down at his hands and clenched his fists, not believing that he was living. The last thing he remembered was looking into Ariel's dark green eyes to keep a memory of her in his everlasting sleep. But now he was awake and felt powerful.

"I'm...?"

"You're alive," Hera whispered, sniffling and Zeus pulled her in for a tight hug. His heart broke at the sight of his wife crying, but he knew it would be worst once Hades realised why he was alive.

"Why's everyone crying?" He frowned, looking behind him and slowly pulled himself up to look around his throne room.

His eyes widened at the gruesome sight. Persephone was lying on the marbled steps that led to his throne with blood smeared all over. A black metalled dagger was stabbed into her chest and blood pooled underneath her.

He grimaced, crinkling his nose in disgust at the thick stench of blood and turned to his family. "Where's Ariel?"

They all looked away; not having the courage to tell him and Zeus decided to speak, assuming his role as leader.

"Hades..."

"What?" He looked around at all the blood that was smeared in the ground. It looked like a bloody battlefield had taken place, but the victor was nowhere to be found.

Slowly realisation dawned on him and he shook his head. Fear crawled up his throat as he walked around the vast throne room and his voice cracked, "Where's Ariel?"

"W-we had to clean her up," Athena whispered, twisting her fingers nervously.

Hades frowned, running his fingers through his hair and said, "Can I see her?"

"Aw come on," Ares growled, "let the man know! He has a right!"

"Know what?" He gritted his teeth, clenching his fists at his side.

Thanatos entered the room with Hermes and they widened their eyes in fear at Hades' look of desperation. They slowly walked closer to them, not knowing how to tell Hades that his beloved was in another room—clean and non-living.

"Tell me what?!" He spoke louder, growing angrier by their silence.

"Uncle," Athena spoke quietly, "you know how the balance of life works?"

He narrowed his eyes, "I would like to think I do."

"Then," she continued, "You'd know-"

"Ariel's dead," Aphrodite sobbed, falling to her knees as she hugged herself. Hephaestus kneeled next to her, picking her up and muttered words of comfort near her ear. She snuggled close to him, sobbing painfully and trembled in his arms.

"N-no," Hades stuttered, "Persephone said that after I died, she would leave Ariel alone."

"And she kind of did," Ares hissed, "but she taunted Ariel and she killed Persephone."

"Persephone was the goddess of death, there's no way that Ariel could've killed her," he whispered, knowing in the back of his mind that Ariel was capable of more dangerous things; like bringing him back.

Ares glared at him, gritting his teeth and whispered, "How can you question her? She gave up her life to save you and you question her ability to-"

"Ares," Zeus interrupted him, "son, that's enough."

"No," he spat, "it's not! All he ever did was hurt her and now he's trying to dirty her name even when she gave her damn life for his! He didn't deserve her."

"Ares!" Zeus hissed, glaring at him but the god couldn't control his anger and decided that leaving to mourn Ariel's death alone would be best.

"She's not dead," Hades whispered, looking at them as he searched for a sign that would tell him she wasn't. "S-she can't be dead," he stood up, turning to Hermes and said, "Where is she?"

Hermes looked at the other gods, waiting for confirmation and Thanatos bowed his head in respect. "She's in her old chambers, my King."

Hades nodded, slamming the doors out of his way and ran up the stairs, completely forgetting that he could summon himself anywhere he'd wish with a snap of his fingers. As he reached her door, his hands shook nervously and he held them over the door tentatively, not knowing whether he wished to disturb her or allow her to sleep; but the need to know that she was well gnawed at him, pushed him to knock on the door.

"Ariel," he whispered, leaning his forehead against the door, "a□á□□ μ□□, open the door, please?" No noise came from the other side and he grew restless. Hades jiggled the doorknob in his hands, exhaling in relief once the door opened slowly.

"I know you dislike it when I enter your room without your permission," he whispered, entering the room slowly, "but I had to see you; I have to make sure you're alright."

Ariel lay on the bed, a calm expression on her soft features. Her hair was no longer dirtied by blood or sweat and her face was clean, her once rosy cheeks were now pale and dark circles were underneath her eyes.

She wore a white silk chiton, the customary dress to bury a person of high ranks. They would also bury her with her most prized belongings so that she could enter the Underworld and entertain herself as she waited to be judged and two drachmas were placed over her eyes to pay Chiron.

"A-Ariel," Hades whispered, walking towards her bed hesitantly. "Ariel?" He whispered louder, taking her hand from her stomach and felt his eyes watering at the coldness of her fingers. "Please?" He pressed a gentle kiss to her knuckles, "If this is your way to get even with me for leaving you at the altar, I just have to tell you it's cruel. Take your revenge any other way, a□á□□ μ□□, but please don't play with death."

"Hades," Hermes spoke quietly, "the Fates are on their way; I figured you'd want to talk to them and ask to-"

"-she's not dead!" He interrupted, caressing a locket of her hair behind her ear, "she can't be dead."

"Uncle," he began, but the God shook his head and he decided that it was best to leave him alone.

Hades grabbed her in his arms, cradling her body into his as he tried to wake her. "Please," tears slid down his cheekbones, staining her white chiton, "please, do not trick me like this. I beg you to open your eyes, your beautiful green eyes, open them please."

More tears blurred his vision as he caressed her cheeks and his shoulders shook as a sob rumbled out of his chest. She was really gone and there was nothing he could do. The Fates would cut her life string and he'd be left alone for the rest of his miserable eternity.

It was selfish of his part, but he would rather her be living without him than be alive without her. He knew she was strong and could move on, but he knew he wasn't. He had never loved anyone like he loved her; he didn't know how he would be able to live without her.

Her soul was still attached to her body, but it was all a matter of time. The Fates had to cut her soul away and Hermes or Thanatos would take her away.

As he rocked her, sobbing desperately, he realised that she had died before—and like Ares had stated, it had been his entire fault. Every wrongdoing that occurred to Ariel, Hades had some sort of part in it.

The only thing in her life that he had no control over was her curse; he didn't create it. But even then, he could have saved her; he just had to marry her and even that he couldn't do. All of the bad incidents that happened to her because of him, outweighed the good he ever did for her.

Hades pressed a kiss to her lips, desperate to wake her. He kissed her again and again, waiting for her to wake up and show him the smile he grew obsessed with. But she didn't.

Her lips didn't move an inch, they remained closed and temperate.

"What are you doing, Hades?" Clotho murmured, frowning at her sisters as they glanced at the King of the Underworld.

His tears fell down his cheeks, ending their journey on her hair as he looked at her desperately and said, "She believes in these kinds of things! That's how all of those films we watched went," he whispered, "they'd awaken by a kiss."

"Hades," Atropos sighed, shaking her head in displeasure, "you had your chance to show her your true love for her."

"And you ruined it," Lachesis whispered, touching his shoulder gently.

"N-no," he sobbed, shaking his head in denial and kissed her with more force, "I'm just not doing it right, t-there has to be another way."

"Hades!" Atropos spoke with authority, wanting to let him know what would happen, but the god refused to listen.

"Bring her back!" He suddenly cried out, his hands shaking as he placed her back on the bed and grabbed her hand. He looked up at them, his bloodshot eyes blurry with tears and he pointed at them accusingly, "You brought her to me! And now you're going to take her away?! I won't let you do that! You have to bring her back."

Clotho sighed, "Hades, we can't-"

"-you're the damn Fates! You control all life; you determine who gets to die and who gets to live!" He cried out, "Don't you fucking tell me that you can't bring her back. We were able to bring back Helen and even Adrianne, why is she any different?!"

"If you would allow us to explain," Atropos hissed, "you'd understand why!"

Hades swallowed, wiping his tears angrily and said, "Then explain yourselves."

The Fate reached into her cloak, pulling out a string. It was a mixture of a red and sheer silver string; they seemed to be entwined. "Ariel," Atropos pointed to the string, "is the red thread. You are the silver thread. Now, do you see what's different between these two threads?"

"No."

"They're entwined, unlike your previous thread. You are now bound to her and she's bound to you. If we were to separate her thread from yours, we'd destroy yours and kill you. But you are the god of death, we cannot kill you."

"And?" Hades frowned.

Clotho sighed, pushing back her dark hair and slowly said, "Hades, we cannot separate the bond. We cannot kill her, but we cannot bring her back. It would cause a great unbalance in our books and you know better than anyone else that great chaos erupts when we do not work by the book."

"So," Lachesis whispered gently, "the mortal will be bound to you for eternity, but she will not be living."

Hades shook his head, looking down at her and whispered, "Please don't tell me that. I-I can't live without her; my heart, my mind, my soul are hers. Without her I am nothing, you must bring her back, even if it destroys our bond."

Atropos took a deep breath, sliding her hand down her face tiredly and said, “Hades, we cannot break your bond. Once two threads entwine themselves together nothing can tear them apart; not even death. You must live with this; consider it a small punishment for breaking her heart.”

He looked down at her, his bottom lip trembling as he placed his head on her chest and cried out. The sound was so raw and powerful that even the Fates were afraid of his actions. Yet he wasn’t strong enough to do anything; Ariel was his strength, his love, his everything—and he had managed to lose it all.

“I-I can’t do this alone,” he whispered, hugging her body tightly, “I need you, a⊠á⊠⊠ µ⊠⊠, without you I am nothing. You brought life to death and I repaid you with the latter. If you wake up, I promise to do anything you wish. I will move mountains and oceans if you desire. But please,” his voice cracked, “I need you.”

“Hades,” Clotho began, but the god shook his head and held his hand up.

“Let me mourn in peace; you are dismissed from my presence.”

They gritted their teeth at his stubbornness and left the room angrily. If he had only listened to what the future upheld, he wouldn’t have to mourn.

Hades pressed a soft kiss to her forehead and susurrated, “Stay with me, Ariel, but come back to me. You need to wake up so that I can beg for your forgiveness; I need to show you how much I regret not marrying you.” He wiped his tears away and cleared his throat, “Persephone was right; if I had only married you none of this would’ve happened. You would have been Queen of the Underworld and we could’ve tried having children.”

"Where is he?!" An unrecognisable voice rang throughout the castle, making the god frown and stand up from the bed. "Where is Hades?"

Suddenly the doors flew open and Hades frowned at the woman. She was a mortal and Ariel resembled many of her features; she was beautiful and in her younger days, must've looked like his love.

"Who are you?" He glared at her, bothered by her intrusion.

"I'm her mother," Karen spat, stalking into the room and felt her bottom lip trembling as she glanced at her daughter lying on the bed. "My baby," she sobbed, turning to him and smacked her hand against his cheek.

She didn't care that he could kill her or torture her, the rest of her life for disrespecting him, but that was her daughter. There wasn't anything that she wouldn't do in order to save her daughter, but now she was too late.

"This is your fault!" Tears fell down her cheeks as she smacked her knuckles against his chest, "All your fault! You killed my baby and all she ever did was love you!"

"Stop touching me, mortal," he grabbed her hands, holding them at an arm's distance and glared at her with bright blue eyes.

Karen gulped, a slight hint of fear growing inside of her, but the loss of her daughter was causing her a greater pain. "Not only do you break her heart by leaving her stranded on the altar, but now you take her life."

He was growing irritated by the woman with every word she spoke. "I didn't take her life-"

"-I know she traded hers for yours," she snapped, glaring daggers at him that managed to silence the god, "Ares told me everything."

"Ares?" He frowned.

"I let her in," Ares spoke from the threshold of the room, his arms crossed over his chest as he leaned against the doorframe.

"Why would you let the human in here?! Do you know what she can-?"

"Ariel told me all about the gods," Karen narrowed her eyes, "she told me everything. And my name is Karen, not human; learn your manners."

Hades widened his eyes in incredulity, turning to Ares and the god of war shrugged, feeling a slight twinge of pride for Ariel's mother. She was speaking to a godly King like if he were her son.

Karen walked over to Ariel and kissed her forehead. Her nose burned as more tears threatened to spill past her cheeks and she whispered, "Oh baby, you had just come back to me. After four years you finally returned and now you're gone again. Now you're gone for good and we didn't spend enough time together."

"I remember," she caressed her hair, "when you were little, you were running around in the garden and you fell and scraped your knee. It was the first time I ever saw you get hurt so badly and I panicked. I remember I ran into the room with you in my arms and cleaned if before putting a Band-Aid on. Through it all I was crying like it had been me who was hurt, but you were simply trying to comfort me. It should've been the other way around," Karen sobbed, "but you were always so strong and you told me that it didn't hurt. That I shouldn't cry because you were going to be okay."

Ares took a deep breath, not feeling strong enough to listen to stories about the woman he had grown so attached to. He slid his hand down his face before nodding in Hades' direction and left him to deal with Ariel's mother.

Hades turned to the woman, watching her tentatively as she continued whispering to her daughter between sobs.

"You were my first and only baby and I vowed that I was going to protect you from all evil and I didn't keep my promise. I let that Derrick man hurt you and now Hades. And now there's nothing I can do because you're gone. You're gone again and now you won't come back. You were supposed to be my maid of honour because David proposed yesterday. We were in this cute little restaurant in Little Italy and he popped the question; I knew you liked him so I was more than happy to say yes. But now," she sobbed, her shoulders shaking as an incredible pain broke through her chest, "now you're gone and I won't get to see you live your life."

"I remember when you told me that you wanted me to walk you down the aisle because your father wasn't there and now I can't do that. And no one is going to walk with me down the aisle to meet David." Karen placed her head on Ariel's chest, not wanting to leave her side, "Come back to me, Ariel. Don't leave me again, sweetheart, don't leave for good this time."

"Karen," Hades whispered, "I am sorry; I already tried speaking to the Fates and they can't-"

"-I know," she interrupted him, sitting up to look at him, "Ariel explained the whole balance of life titbit when we spoke about Adrianne. I just wish that she had lived her life a little more before death took her from us. Why didn't you marry her, Hades? She loved you more than anything in her life."

"I was insecure," he cleared his throat, "my previous marriage had been a disaster and I was afraid that Ariel didn't love me enough because of her curse."

"Do you know that if you had had a child with her, the curse would've been broken?" She eyed him, "Because it was so hard to prove someone's love for another, the birth of a child from true love would break it."

He frowned. "How do you know that?"

Karen shrugged, standing up from the bed and said, "My mother gave me a book that explained the curse and whatnot. Where am I going to sleep? I'm not leaving you alone with the burial of my daughter."

It had only been a day that Ariel was gone and Hades felt like multiple trains had crashed into him. He couldn't concentrate on his duties as King of the Underworld and the guilt he felt whenever he saw Karen, destroyed him.

The woman was somewhat strange. When they first met she was about ready to rip him to shreds, but in one day she managed to warm up to him. She would tell him stories of Ariel when she was younger and he found herself missing his love more and more.

He sat down on his throne, turning away from the settee next to his and leaned his elbows on his knees to hold his face in his hands. He was tired and extremely sad, but no matter what gods he asked, no one could help. He even went to Egypt to ask Moat for help; no one could bring her back.

"HADES!" Karen gasped, startling him out of his tangled thoughts, "HADES!" She ran into the throne room, gasping for air rapidly and managed to wheeze out Ariel's name.

"What's wrong?" He frowned, walking down the steps to stand in front of her.

"She...something...wrong."

His frown deepened. "What?"

"Something," she hissed, holding unto her chest, "is...wrong."

His heart skipped a beat and he summoned them both to Ariel's room. Karen had wanted a glass coffin instead of the traditional Greek burial. She insisted that her daughter had to be buried like the queen she was and in her mind a glass coffin was needed.

Hades walked towards her slowly, fearing that someone had tried to tamper with her body. "What's wrong?"

"Her stomach," Karen whispered, no longer out of breath, "touch it; it's warm."

He walked towards the side of the coffin that was opened and lightly placed his hand over Ariel's stomach. A frown grew on his features for it was more than warm; it was burning. "What in the world?!"

"I know!" She said, "I was cleaning the glass when I swear I saw her hand twitching; it didn't happen again so I thought it must've been my imagination. But then her stomach started glowing like an orangey colour? Yeah and I touched it and it was warm. Now it's not glowing but I-"

Hades held his hand up, stopping her from rambling any further and said, "You said her stomach was glowing?"

"Yeah," she nodded her head quickly, "I know I look crazy, but I'm not. I know what I saw."

"I didn't," he shook his head and sighed, "I wasn't calling you crazy." His eyes widened in surprise as a cough came from the coffin, but Ariel's eyes were still closed.

They suddenly opened, wide and in panic and she gasped, hyperventilating from the confinement of the coffin. Hades pushed it off, hoping with all his might that it wasn't a dream; that she was really awake.

"Mom?" She croaked, sitting up slowly and turned to her mom. Karen squeaked, blinking slowly at her daughter and then collapsed on the floor.

Ariel widened her eyes, coughing in displeasure at the raspy sensation in her throat and looked at Hades. He blinked slowly, holding his hand out to touch her, but she recoiled from his touch.

"A-Ariel," he whispered, lowering his hand and tried not to show how much pain the rejection caused him, "y-you're awake?"

"I'd like to think so," she frowned, pinching her hands and hissed at the sensation. She placed her hand over her stomach and bit her bottom lip. She couldn't explain how it felt when she was dead; it was just black. She felt as if though she were floating in a black void. There were no feelings or emotions, she just slept.

She knew she should've been dead, but there was something keeping her at bay, sending bits of life into her. And through it all, she remembers the warm sensation in her stomach. It was like if someone had placed their hand over her belly and warmed her up.

It began coursing through her body, starting in the pit of her stomach and rushing through her fingers. And then she heard her mother speaking. She didn't know how she got there or why she was allowed entrance into the Underworld, but she was glad. It would make leaving easier.

"Ariel," Hades gasped, his eyes lighting up with happiness, "a□á□□ µ□□, you're alive."

Ariel nodded slowly, turning her body to stand up, but he held her back and said, "The glass is shattered, let me carry you."

"No," she recoiled from his touch again, widening her eyes in fear and whispered, "don't touch me."

"What?" he frowned. "Why?"

"Because," she whispered, "I just want to go home and eat; I'm starving."

He smiled reassuringly, "That's fine, I'll take you to the kitchen and you can ask for anything you want."

Ariel shook her head, pressing her lips into a thin line and said, "You don't understand, Hades; I don't want you to touch me. Get Hermes, when my mother wakes up, I want to go home."

"But," he began.

She glared at him, her voice dripping with ice as she whispered, "Do me a favour, Hades, think of it as a payment for bringing you back to life; stay away from me."

"Ariel-"

"Forever, am I clear? I never want to see you again. Ever since I met you," she gave out a chuckle, "my life has been chaos. Now that there are no more threats to the gods, I want to go home and never see any of you again. There's just so much pain I can endure."

29

— • —

CHAPTER 29

Ariel awoke with a jolt. Thick, heavy droplets of sweat were sliding down her forehead, drenching her entire body in perspiration. She gasped, trying to control her erratic heartbeat and looked around the room in fear.

Everything was like she had left it.

It had just been a dream.

She laid back on the pillows, breathing in deeply and ran her fingers through her sweaty hair, pushing it back as she fanned her face. She felt hot and her eyes glazed over the entire room as shadows began to turn into her biggest fears.

A shaky chuckle rumbled past her lips and she rolled her eyes at her frivolousness. She was twenty-two, living with her mother, and she was currently unemployed. Not that the money mattered much, for her grandmother's inheritance would sustain her for another lifetime. But nonetheless, she was still living with her mother, whom was soon to be married.

She breathed in deeply again, closing her eyes as her heartbeat began to slow down to normalcy and she rubbed her index fingers against her temples. It had just been a dream; nothing more.

After the incident with Persephone, her death and resurrection, Ariel decided that she needed a lifetime-vacation from the gods. She wanted nothing to do with them, not even in pictures. Just the mere thought of stumbling paths with any of them, brought shivers to run down her spine.

Thinking about Hades brought about an inexplicable pain to her chest. She knew that she should've stayed with him. After all, she had given up her life for his; it only proved how much she loved him.

But he had broken her, broken her trust and most importantly her heart. She couldn't just throw herself back into his arms and allow the hurt to return. If it occurred again, she would be titled an imbecile.

Nonetheless, she was afraid. And he had thankfully listened to her when she begged him to never look for her again. He had upheld his promise – only three days had gone by, but she had gotten no signs of the gods and she was utterly content.

Some parts of her wished that he would fight her, that he would show up at her doorstep with a mariachi band and serenade her, but he wouldn't do that. Besides, she really wasn't into Mexican music; she didn't understand Spanish.

Ariel shook her head, rolling her eyes at her absurd thoughts and glanced at the neon clock on her dresser. The clock read; 9:16pm. It wasn't early, but it wasn't extremely late.

Ever since she came back from the Underworld, she found herself tremendously tired, which was kind of ironic, seeing that she had slept for almost two days straight. One would think that the last thing in her mind would be sleep, yet her body proved that it overruled any of her thoughts.

It was like her body was slowly shutting down. At times she feared that she would go to sleep and never wake up again, but whatever greater being out there had brought her back, must've done it for a reason. They weren't just going to bring her back to take her back. Right?

She sighed, kicking the slightly wet covers off her legs and slowly sat up, as to not cause herself vertigo. Ariel blindly searched for her slippers and then grabbed her towel, to head into the shower.

For the past two nights she had the strangest dreams she'd ever have. She didn't tell David or her mom because she was afraid they'd send her to a nuthouse. She knew that if she could, she'd do so herself.

The dream would begin with her running through a clearing. She didn't understand it or recognise her surroundings, but she heard a childlike voice calling for their mother. In her chest, she'd feel panic. She was younger, around seven and she was running, looking for her mother.

She slowly realised that the childlike voice belonged to her and once she looked up, she'd see her mother waiting for her at the end of the clearing. She felt afraid that whoever it was in her dream was in danger. To make matters worse, near the ending of her dream things would change. She would suddenly find herself in her mother's place.

The child was running towards her, running away from a danger that she couldn't fight off. And it frightened her more because that was her child. He'd shriek out her name and the dream would end – she would wake up alone, scared and confused.

She sighed, opening the faucet and closed her eyes as hot water poured down over her head. It slid over her shoulders, down her collarbone and over her breasts. She tilted her neck, allowing the water to reach every place of her body and leaned her head backwards to wet her entire hair.

After thoroughly washing her hair with lemon-scented shampoo and conditioner, she began lathering herself with soap, careful with the healing wounds on her wrists. The indents from the shackles were a slight reminder of what she had gone through; of what she had survived.

Ariel opened her eyes, watching the soap swirling down the drain and then pushed the curtains away. She stepped out of the shower, grabbing a towel from the rack and dried herself completely.

Once she was done, she grabbed a long camisole and stepped into her slippers. She leaned over the sink, wetting her toothbrush before she added toothpaste and ran her hand over the fogged mirror to look at her reflection.

Her eyes widened in fear and a whimper rasped past her lips as she looked at her reflection. The young woman in the mirror had a deformed face. Her eyes were slowly drooping and blood was dripping down her nose.

Ariel stepped back, dropping the toothbrush on the sink and quickly touched her face, trying to see if her eyes were really sliding down her cheeks. But they felt normal. She glanced at herself in the mirror again and only saw the blood dripping down over her lips.

She grimaced, grabbing a piece of toilet paper and quickly dabbed her nose, but no blood came out. Her heart began to speed up and she quickly opened the door, fear troubling her thoughts with gruesome images.

"Mom!" She cried out, yanking the door open and cupped her nose. She didn't know if there was blood, but if there was, she didn't want it to ruin her mother's carpet.

Karen walked towards her daughter's room quickly, David trailing behind. They had been watching a movie in the living room because she didn't want to leave her daughter alone. Ever since she lost her and got her back, she knew it was a gift that she couldn't afford to lose.

"What's wrong, honey?" She frowned at Ariel, whom was sitting on the floor with her back against the wall and her knees pulled close to her chest.

Tears slid down her cheeks and she looked up at her mom with desperate eyes. "I-I don't know. One minute I'm going to brush my teeth and the next my face is all deformed and-" she hiccupped, trembling as she lost control over her emotions and began to sob hysterically.

Karen knelt down beside her, carefully taking her into her arms and hugged her tightly. "Shhh," she whispered, pulling her wet hair away from her face, "honey, it's okay. It was just a mirage, nothing to worry about."

"That's the thing," Ariel whispered, trying to focus her attention on her mother's rhythmic heartbeat to calm her nerves, "I've been having nightmares for the past two nights and they're not like what I had when I was little. They're really weird and I feel like they mean something, b-but they make no sense."

David knelt before her, pushing his glasses up the ridge of his nose and in his soothing, doctor voice said, "What are the dreams, Ariel?"

She shrugged, sniffling as she snuggled closer to her mom, finding the comfort that she needed. "I don't know...I start out in this clearing, running to my mom. I'm screaming and I'm scared because something is chasing me, but I don't know what. Then it goes all crazy and it changes. I'm in my mom's place and there's a kid running towards me. I just," she looked up at him, "I know it sounds crazy, but I know he's my baby. And he's afraid and I know there's something after us and I'm scared because there's nothing I can do – and I just..."

"Shhh," Karen kissed her forehead, eyeing her daughter's hands as she tightened them around the towel, in order to keep them concealed, "it's okay honey. It's just a dream."

"I wake up all sweaty and scared and it's disgusting." She whispered, closing her eyes as a couple of tears slid down her cheeks.

David nodded. "Have you thought about having children? Maybe this is what's causing your nightmares? You might be suppressing some memories as well?"

"No," Ariel quickly shook her head, "the last man I was with was sterile; so I didn't really think about kids."

"Ariel," Karen slowly pulled herself away, standing up to get her leather gloves from her closet and handed them to her, "honey, when I was pregnant with you, I had similar dreams."

David frowned, nowhere in his years of studying psychology had he heard of that. He had been a psychologist for almost fifteen years and he'd never heard of pregnant women having the same dreams as their mothers.

"Mom," she narrowed her eyes, clasping the gloves on and said, "H-Aidon was sterile; we couldn't have kids. And I didn't sleep with other men, so the possibility is out of the question."

She sighed, nodding and helped her stand. "Do you want to go to the hospital? Maybe they can give you pills or something to help you sleep at night and whilst we're there, we can eliminate the pregnant question?"

"Mom," she began, slouching her shoulders in dislike, but Karen gave her the look. No matter how old she was, when her mother gave her the look, she had to obey her. It was like she had some sort of power over her even when she had been gone for four years. "Fine."

"Thank you," Karen smiled, turning to David, whom was confused at their silent exchange, "David, sweetie, can you go and turn the car on?"

He nodded, turning around to walk down the hallway and grabbed the keys from the counter. After they heard the door opening and closing, Karen turned to her and seriously said, "Ariel, you said so yourself, Hades could have children. What if you got pregnant from one of the many rendezvouses?"

Ariel shook her head and said, "Mom, my period is scheduled to come next week. I'm already having cramps. I missed it last month, but my cycle was always a bit irregular."

She sighed, opening her mouth to say something, but decided against it and said, "Go put some sweatpants on or something. I'll get your coat from the closet and then we can go to the hospital."

"Fine," she muttered, walking into her room and slid some grey sweatpants on. She combed her wet hair and tied it into a sloppy bun.

Only her mom had the ability to calm her down so quickly and convince her to visit the doctor because she could possibly be pregnant from sleeping with a sterile god.

"You ready?" Karen beamed, trying to unsuccessfully hide the excitement she felt. If Ariel was pregnant, her baby would be the outcome of true love and end her curse.

Ariel nodded, huffing in annoyance as she buttoned up her coat and they turned all the lights of the house off, locking the door behind them.

They had been waiting in the room for almost two hours. Ariel was slowly falling asleep on the bed and Karen was using David's shoulder as a pillow. He had his arm wrapped around her securely, and was reading a sport magazine with his other hand.

Ariel tapped her fingers against her stomach, waiting anxiously for all the results that the doctor would bring her and she tried not to fall asleep. She was afraid that if she did end up sleeping, the nightmares would return and they'd have to sedate her.

A soft knock on the door startled her out of her hazy thoughts and her mother sat up straight. The doctor smiled at them happily, her curly hair framing her face nicely and she slid her glasses to the top of her head.

"Ms. Ariel Lockhaven, right?" Ariel nodded, smiling at her and shook her extended hand. "I'm Dr. Kelly; sorry I took so long, I was supposed to have the day off, but another doctor fell ill and we're short on staff members."

"It's okay," she croaked, eyeing the papers in her hands nervously.

Dr. Kelly smiled, brightening up her face and said, "Well I have some really good news. Would you like me to tell them to you in private or...?" She glanced at Karen and David.

Ariel shrugged, smiling at her mom and said, "They can stay."

The doctor nodded, looking over the papers on the clipboard and said, "Well, you're very healthy. Your sugar levels are neutral and your haemoglobin is a little bit over the normal number, but it's nothing serious. However," she looked at her, "there is something else..."

Ariel licked her lips nervously, playing with her fingers and said, "What? Is there something wrong with me?"

"Well," She began slowly, closing the clipboard and said, "Ms. Lockhaven, have you felt strange over the past couple of weeks? Maybe your period came later or you've felt unusual cravings?"

"No," she frowned, "my period is a bit irregular so I don't freak out much if I miss a month. I should have it next week; I've been having the worst cramps these past couple of days."

Dr. Kelly smiled at her naivety and said, "Honey, it's not necessarily cramps; it's your uterus."

"What?"

"It's your uterus," she repeated, "it's expanding to accommodate the foetus growing in you."

"But-" Ariel began and widened her eyes in surprise, "no; I-I can't be..."

The doctor quickly widened her hazel eyes and said, "Oh if that's the case there are other options. You can-"

"-no," Ariel interrupted, shaking her head slowly, "you don't understand. The only man I've been with is sterile; I can't be pregnant."

"Your urine sample shows-"

"He's sterile," she pressed, feeling hysterical and in her chest, bubbles of terror began to suffocate her, "he can't have kids!"

"Ms. Lockhaven," Dr. Kelly tucked back a curl behind her ear, "the blood tests show you're positive as well. You're half way into your second month. Is the father still with you?"

"N-no," her bottom lip began to tremble as tears welled in her eyes and her mother quickly stood up to comfort her.

"They had a big fight," Karen whispered to the doctor, hugging her daughter's head against her chest, "but how's that possible, doctor? Aidon was sterile."

She shrugged, standing up uncomfortably and said, "Some men take pills to become fertile, maybe he was? There are other reasons, but I don't think we should discuss such a delicate matter right now."

"Ariel, honey?" Karen whispered, tilting her daughter's chin so she was looking into her eyes, "What's wrong? Are you okay? Do you need me to get you something?"

Ariel shook her head, slowly turning away from her and whispered, "Can I just be alone for now? I-I need time to think."

Karen nodded, heaving out a sigh and kissed her forehead. "Whatever you decide to do, baby, I'll support you, okay? No matter what, I'm here for you, do you understand me?"

Before she released her, Ariel whispered, "Don't tell anyone, mom! Not even him!"

She sighed, nodding and kissed her again. "I won't. Just don't do anything stupid, okay?"

She nodded, gulping back the urge to cry uncontrollably and David mentioned his support for her as well. She couldn't exactly make out his words because her ears were ringing loudly. After the door closed and she was sure she was alone, she let out a despairing sob and covered her face.

She couldn't be pregnant! Hades had said he was sterile. And they had sex plenty of times before for her to get pregnant, and she hadn't! What made that certain time any different?!

Ariel placed her hand over her stomach and shut her eyes tightly, hoping to wake up from the terrifying nightmare. Because that's what it had to be, there was no way that she could really be pregnant; especially since the baby's father was not with her.

Her shoulders shook violently as she leaned on her right side and hugged her arms around her body tightly. Part of her wanted to keep the baby and bring him into her world and love him, but the other part was scared.

What if she wasn't good enough of a mother? What would she tell him when he'd ask about his father? Oh he's a god; the god of death to be more exact. It wouldn't really do.

No matter, what would she do?! She couldn't touch her own child without taking his life! There was no way that she would allow herself to do such a crime.

Another heart wrenching sob exploded out her mouth, shattering her heart as a feeling of loneliness washed over her and she held unto herself tighter. She wanted to cry herself to sleep, but she knew that if she slept, she'd dream. And her dreams weren't her best companions so far.

"Ariel?" A soft voice spoke from the corner of the room and she quickly sat up, wiping her tears away in alarm as she looked for the owner of the voice.

Hades stepped out of the shadows tentatively, his eyes taking in every inch of her slowly and he cleared his throat.

"W-what are you doing here?" She finally found her voice, and although she sounded like she almost choked, she managed to speak.

"Hera told me," he said carefully.

Ariel frowned, curling her fingers around the blue hospital sheet and said, "What did Hera tell you?"

"She spoke to the Fates," Ariel rolled her eyes, but he continued, "and they affirmed that you're having my child. That's why – well it's correlated with your resurrection."

"It doesn't answer my question; what are you doing here? I thought I told you-"

Hades clenched his fists at his sides, gritting his teeth angrily and hissed, "You can't exactly expect me to sit around after being told that I can have children, right?! Ariel, I thought I was sterile; I've wanted kids for centuries and now that I can have one, you want to keep me from him?"

She glared at him, but her anger was nowhere near the high level his was in. "I don't even know if I'm keeping him."

"What?" He thundered, his eyes turning a bright shade of blue and he lowered his voice so that strangers couldn't hear him. "You cannot be serious! I am not going to allow you to dispose of my child."

She gritted her teeth, rolling her eyes and touched her stomach. "You have no right to tell me what I can or what I cannot do; you lost that chance the moment you left me at the altar and even then, I am not your toy. You can't boss me around."

His blue eyes softened considerably and his expression relaxed, making regret clear on his face. "Ariel..." he cajoled.

Ariel waved him away, shaking her head and said, "I don't want to hear this, Hades. Just please leave; I told you that I never wanted to see you again."

He sighed, running his fingers through his hair and slid his hand down his face. He looked tired, as if he hadn't slept in decades, but even then, he managed to look handsome. Only Hades could have dark circles under his eyes and look like a god. "Please hear me out. I know you hate me, I know you regret saving me and I know there's nothing I can do to change that. But please, Ariel, I will get down on my knees if that's what you wish, but I am begging you, let me be the father of this child."

Her eyes widened and she felt tears threatening to spill out her eyes. She quickly blinked them away, sniffling and said, "I don't hate you, I just...you hurt me, Hades. You swore you loved me and swore that you'd do anything to keep me happy. But when the time to prove yourself came, you failed. You couldn't even leave your past behind you. I was and am nothing like Persephone. I loved you with every fibre of my being; I willingly gave my life for you. But that wasn't proof enough for you."

"And you don't think I loved you?!" Hades seethed, "Ariel, I lost my fucking mind when I woke up and you weren't there. I made mistakes, okay? I know I hurt you, it'll haunt me every day for the rest of my eternity; I think that's punishment enough. I don't know what you want me to do to show you that my feelings for you were and are real."

She held her hand up, shaking her head and said, "I don't want to hear this, please. If it's being a father to him, then yeah; I'll allow you to be with him and anything you want. But that's it. I don't want you to talk to me about anything that doesn't involve him; we're going to be strictly friends."

"Ariel," he pleaded, his eyes showing the remorse that his heart felt.

But she shook her head and gritted her teeth. As much as it pained her, she couldn't go through the heartache again. She needed stability in her life, someone that would love her no matter what and although Hades was willing to do so, he had broken the bond of trust they shared.

It could take him decades to reconstruct it.

"Very well," he croaked. Hades looked down at the floor, zoning out and she sighed, placing her hands over her stomach.

It was slowly sinking in; she was pregnant. Inside of her was growing the product of her carnal joining with Hades.

"There is one last thing," Hades began, "Gaia wishes to meet with you."

"Gaia?"

"Yes," he nodded, "she has urgent news to inform you of."

Ariel sighed, leaning her head on the pillow and said, "What could Gaia possibly want to inform me of?"

"Why ask him," A soft, melancholy voice spoke from behind Hades and he stepped aside, allowing Mother Nature to present herself to Ariel, "when he's simply the messenger of my command?"

Ariel widened her eyes, then slowly frowned at the person standing near her bed. It was a child; she looked to be around 8 or 9. Her head was covered with thick, luscious blonde curls and her eyes were a vibrant green. Freckles were splattered across her nose and long, full eyelashes adorned her pretty eyes.

"Ariel Marie Lockhaven," she spoke quietly, but with such authority that it brought chills to Ariel's back.

"You're a child," she whispered.

Gaia rolled her eyes, shaking her head and said, "I am not a child. It is merely the form I chose to present myself to you. You have been dreaming of children have you not?"

She nodded, trying to swallow the lump in her throat and her green eyes followed the girl as she sat on the plastic blue chair.

"I have been trying to communicate with you, but it seems that your powers are protecting you. Nonetheless, I am not going to strain my powers over you. If I wanted to invade your dreams and get my point across, I would. But you are a peculiar one."

Ariel raised her eyebrows, completely forgetting about Hades and said, "W-what do you mean?"

"Well," she tapped her chin, swinging her legs back and forth, "you gave your life for my grandson, yet you push him away. I understand that he broke your heart...but you bear his child. And when I tried to communicate with you, it was Hades' name you called out."

Her cheeks turned a crimson red colour and Hades bit the inside of his cheek to prevent himself from smiling. His heart swelled with hope and he made a mental note to ask Gaia about what Ariel thought of him.

"Nevertheless," Gaia sighed, "let us speak of the subject at hand, shall we not?" She nodded. "Very well; you were supposed to die once you gave your life for Hades. That's how the balance of the Fates works. They kill a person and another one is automatically born; it's how the cycle works. Yet you," she spoke curiously and interestingly, "you came back. Would you like to know why that is?"

"I-I..."

"Of course you do," Gaia clasped her hands together, pursing her pink lips, "that's how human nature works. You want to know everything, yet you do not realise that knowledge comes at a price."

"Gaia," Hades sighed, "just tell her, please?"

She rolled her eyes, but they crinkled at the sides in affection. She always had a special spot for Hades. He was one of her favourites; he always listened to her and made careful decisions. Of course, the time where Persephone was involved with him was excluded from it.

"You're no fun, Aïdōneus," Gaia muttered, turning to look at Ariel with piercing green eyes, "so, as my grandson says; let's get to the point, shall we? You killed two of my goddesses and one of them had a seat in Mount Olympus. I know Demeter wasn't suited to be a goddess with such power, so I am glad you were able to rid of her without my involvement, however, there is no balance in Olympus now. Minor gods are fighting amongst themselves for the empty seat and I figured that since you were cursed by a god, that you would be rewarded by one too."

Hades glared at the girl, making a girly giggle escape her lips and Ariel shuddered. It was so strange watching a child speak to her so seriously and authoritative. She felt as if though she couldn't listen to her because it felt out of place.

"I am rewarding you with a high honour, Ariel. I saw in you a fire and determination that I hadn't seen in many women for a long time. I decided to save you and your child and gift you with the power of reincarnation. If you were willing to fight for your life, then you'd stay with the power – and you have demonstrated that you want to live. I have titled you the goddess of reincarnation and you will sit amongst the Olympians as one of them."

"What?!" She blurted out, broadening her eyes wide enough to allow them to fall out of their sockets.

Gaia sighed, hopping off the chair and walked over to her. She placed her hand over Ariel's stomach, smiling a bit at the power that radiated off the girl. Ariel stared at her with wide, petrified eyes, but dared no movements. "Do you really need me to say all of that again?"

"N-no," Ariel squeaked, watching Gaia walk back towards Hades' side.

"Good," she beamed, "because I want to go home. Now, I will allow you to stay in the mortal world but with Hades as your companion. What better suitor than the love of your life and father of your child. Once two moon cycles are complete, you must leave with him to the Underworld, where you will reign the rest of your life."

"Why the Underworld?!"

"Because it'll be a nice contrast; death and life all in the same place, splendid, no? Besides why would you want to stay far from Hades?"

Ariel gritted her teeth, feeling angry that the Titaness thought she could just enter her life and control it, but was smart enough to not speak against her.

"Oh," Gaia turned around, smiling at her and said, "do not worry, Αν□□□□□□μ□□□□, your child will be as beautiful as he is healthy." Then she disappeared.

"Ana—what?" Ariel frowned at Hades, making him chuckle at her expression.

"Αν□□□□□□μ□□□□, it means "reborn." It is your new name as a goddess. When people begin to worship you or when we address you, that's what we will call you."

"I can't even pronounce that!" She exclaimed, shaking her head and said, "Why can't it just be Ariel."

He laughed, shoving his hands in his pockets and it was then that Ariel noticed he wore casual clothing. He had a comfortable black shirt with dark jeans and boots. He looked...edible. She shook her head, trying to shake away her thoughts and Hades said, "I will let them know to address you as Ariel. Αν□□□□□μ□□□□, is only used for formalities. When you are crowned or presented as the new Olympian goddess, Gaia will call you that. You can let the minor gods know that you wish to be called Ariel, but that is deem as disrespectful, so I suggest you say Ana."

Ariel grumbled shaking her head and then stared at him with wide eyes. "Wait! I'm a goddess?! I don't feel any different." He nodded. "So does that mean...that I won't...that I can't kill things with my hands?"

"You won't feel different until the coronation day; Gaia wants it to be after our son is born." Hades walked over to a chair, pulling it closer to her and sat down, "You are now the goddess of reincarnation; your curse was broken."

30

— • —

Chapter 30

"Oh," Ariel responded lamely, playing with her fingers idly. She sighed, looking up at the ceiling and then closed her eyes when Hades' began to burn against the side of her cheek. She could feel his stare piercing through her skin and it was making her extremely uncomfortable. "What?"

He shrugged, straightening his back and said, "I do not know...you just...you're glowing."

She rolled her eyes. "That's what everyone says to pregnant women."

"No," he shook his head, "you're face; it looks more relaxed than when it was when I came in." His eyes grazed every inch of her face for a couple of silent moments and he concluded, "You are content."

"About as content as a turkey after Thanksgiving Day," she muttered.

Hades frowned, shaking his head at her strange comparison and bit his bottom lip to keep from speaking what his heart desired to say. He didn't like knowing that she didn't want to give him her heart, but he also knew what her reasoning was. He had hurt her and he would torture himself over it for all his life.

"Can you leave?" She whispered, suddenly feeling extremely drained as she turned on her side, snuggling closer to the pillow.

"Ariel," he began, his voice soft and pleading.

Ariel shook her head, shutting her eyes tighter and whispered, "Hades, no; please just go. I want to be left alone I need to process all of this. Because no matter how much I want to stay away from you and your crazy family, it seems that my destiny is to be part of that crazy family."

He sighed, running his fingers through his black hair and said, "Why don't you just let me speak?"

She was quiet for a couple of minutes, biting her lip hard enough to draw blood and looked at the heart monitor on her side. "Because," she whispered, "I'm scared that you'll convince me to love you again."

Hades nodded, swallowing back his words and said, "Was it that bad to be in love with me?"

"It wasn't..." she trailed off, "until you started doubting me."

"Ariel-"

"-Hades, please," she enunciated each word, "just let me think. Can you give me that? Let me sort my thoughts out and try to figure out what's happening to me."

He gritted his teeth, his jaw visibly clenching and he nodded, releasing a loud blow of air. "I'm sorry for what I did," he whispered, sincerity dripping from each word he spoke, "and if you can ever forgive me...well I'll be here."

"You know," she snorted, feeling angry with herself as she turned back to look at him, "I'm surprised you're not questioning whether this baby is yours or not. Do you remember what you told me when you cancelled the wedding? You told me that I was going to be like

Persephone and sleep with other men because of that one time I sought for Ares' companionship. You judged me for one mistake and now you want me to take you back like nothing happened. I can't simply forget how you made me feel Hades! You had my heart in your hands and you shattered it like it was worthless."

"Please," he spoke softly, his eyes never wavering from hers, "stop; I don't need-"

"-yes you do!" She interrupted him, her heart rate increasing significantly, "You need to know why I feel this way! You keep wanting me to forgive you and all this shit, but have you stopped to think of how that made me feel? You didn't trust me enough; you didn't think my love for you was enough because of the stupid curse. What if that was the test? What if you demonstrating that even though the curse wasn't broken you still loved me was the test? Then you failed it, Hades. You gave up when things seemed too difficult and I can't have that. I don't want that. I don't need that. If I am going to have this baby, which I am, I can't bring him up that way. I need to know that his father will be there through thick and thin. That even if I seem to lose my mind, you'll be there because I need stability. I just can't-"

"Ariel," Hades took her chin in his hands, cupping it carefully, "listen to me. I've thought about everything I made you go through. I know I hurt you and I know it'll be extremely difficult to gain your trust again, but I already had those insecurities drilled in my mind. I know you and Persephone are nothing alike, but my mind was constantly reminding me of the hurt I went through because of a woman. I spent years trying to figure out what I had done wrong and I came up with nothing, but I was blinded by my infatuation for her company and I developed that issue with women. Breaking your heart was and is unforgivable, but I swear to you that I will do anything in my power to make it up to you if you just allow me to."

"I need to-"

He shook his head, his blue eyes blazing with seriousness, "I need to know now. If you don't want to give me a chance to prove myself to you once more then it's okay, but if you do give me the chance; I'll make it worth your while."

"Hades," Ariel gulped, her throat suddenly feeling extremely dry. Maybe she was smart or maybe, just maybe she was really stupid. "If you mess this up," she whispered, her heart rate speeding in such a way that the nurses would enter her room in time, "I will make sure you regret it for all eternity. If you hurt me again-"

He pressed a soft kiss to her forehead, slightly shaking his head and whispered, "Never. I'll see you tomorrow; you need to rest for you and our nipper. I spoke to The Oneiroi and they will no longer meddle with your dreams to try and connect you with Gaia."

"The what?" She frowned, feeling her cheeks heating up as his familiar scent began to fill her mind and tried to think of anything to keep herself sane.

"The Oneiroi," he repeated, "they're the spirit of dreams."

A soft smile grew on her face and she shook her head. "No, I mean, yeah I wanted to know what the O-whatever's are, but I meant that n-word you said. Nipper?"

Hades laughed, his eyes crinkling at the sides and he said, "Our baby, Ariel. Now rest, I will visit you tomorrow."

"It's so tiny," Karen gushed, looking down at the photograph in Ariel's hand. She pointed to the blob in the left corner and said, "can you believe that's a baby?"

Ariel laughed, waiting for David to see the sonogram and said, "Mom, it's only my second month, of course the baby is still tiny."

"I know!" She grinned, still looking at the baby over David's shoulder. "But aren't you excited?! Next month you can figure out the sex of the baby!"

She shrugged, playing with her fingers nervously and said, "I guess."

David smiled, handing her the sonogram and said, "Have you thought of any names?"

"Well," she pursed her lips, "I kind of have a love for Ancient Greece or anything related to that, so I was thinking that if I have a boy, I want him to be named Alexander, after Alexander the Great. But if it's a girl, I'm thinking of either Phoebe or Selene."

"Ooh," Karen nodded her head quickly, "those are nice names."

"Those are Titaness, am I correct?" David frowned, feeling a bit out of the loop. Karen seemed to be into Greek history as much as Ariel was and he sometimes had to go home and look up the people or deities they spoke about so animatedly.

"Yup," Ariel nodded, "Phoebe is the Titaness of intellect and Selene of the moon."

"That's nice," he mused, pushing his glasses back as he sat back into the couch.

She smiled, placing her hand over her stomach and suddenly felt warmth erupting through her body. It made her giddy and nervous all at the same time. After Hades had left, she called them into her room to let them know of her decision.

Karen almost passed out from excitement and David congratulated her. The doctor told her that they could schedule an ultrasound for the next day and release her that very same night. After prescribing some prenatal vitamins, she was sent home.

That night she slept peacefully, but woke up nervous. Once everything was finally sinking in, she was jittery and about ready to explode with eagerness.

The doorbell snapped her out of her thoughts and she frowned at them. "Are you guys waiting for anyone?"

"Nope," Karen shook her head, turning to David, who shrugged.

Ariel sighed, standing up and placed the picture on the coffee table before walking over to the door. She opened it, widening her eyes in surprise and hissed, "Hades, what are you doing here?"

He smiled, revealing his pearly white teeth and whispered, "I told you I was coming to see you. I went to the hospital, but you were gone."

"You can't be here!" She shooed him away, stepping in front of the door. "I didn't tell my mom that we talked and her boyfriend is here."

"Splendid," he clasped his hands together, "then I can meet them."

"No," she hissed through gritted teeth, "you have to go, come back at a later time."

"Ariel," Karen called, "honey, who is it?"

"Oh no one," she said nervously, "wrong house."

Hades rolled his eyes, placing his hands on her shoulders and lightly pushed her into the house. "Karen?" Ariel widened her eyes, slapping her hands on his chest and muttered profanities under her breath as he locked the door behind him.

"H-Aidon?" Karen frowned, turning to Ariel with a questioning look. "What are you doing here?"

David walked in behind her, raising his eyebrows at the dark-haired man and suddenly felt jealous of his striking good looks. Karen seemed to be well acquainted with him and the power that radiated off him was hurting his manly ego. "Aidon?" He frowned, looking at his fiancée, "who is he?"

"I'm Ariel's-" He began but Ariel interrupted him.

"He's..." she frowned, glaring at the god as she looked for a proper word to describe him.

He raised his eyebrows, looking between Ariel and Hades and said, "Your...?"

She sighed, "The baby's dad."

"Oh," he widened his eyes in surprise, "oh; you were the asshole who hurt her?!"

Hades widened his eyes, surprised at the mortal's sudden anger and cleared his throat in awkwardness. "I didn't..."

David sneered, shaking his head in disgust and said, "Men like you sicken me. Y'all get a poor girl pregnant and then leave her to fend for herself. It takes balls to come show your face here; so you either have them, or you're wishing for a death sentence."

Karen pursed her lips, to prevent herself from laughing at the irony of her fiancé's statement and wrapped her arms around his bicep. "David, honey, he didn't know she was pregnant."

"Oh," he frowned, his cheeks turning a slight shade of red, "still."

Ariel smiled, liking that he tried to defend her and turned to Hades. "I told him yesterday that I was pregnant. I didn't think he'd actually show up here today."

Hades grinned, making her roll her eyes in distaste and said, "I told you I want to be a part of this baby's life. He'll never need anything as long as I live."

"Well come in," Karen waved her hand at him; "we just got back from the doctor's. Do you want to see a picture of the baby?"

He widened his eyes, turning to Ariel with bewilderment in his eyes and said, "Even we can't see children this early! Only the Fates are allowed to do such a thing."

David frowned at him, shaking his head at the gibberish he heard and said, "It's called an ultrasound. You know? The black and white pictures that look like x-rays?"

Hades turned to Ariel, his eyebrows creasing in confusion and she sighed, shaking her head and pulled him towards the living room. They sat down on the plush seats and she handed him the sonogram pictures. "This little blob here," she pointed to the photograph, "is the baby."

"He looks...strange," he muttered.

Ariel snickered, leaning towards him and whispered, "Hades, please try to act normal. That's just a picture of the embryo; he'll start looking more like a baby when I enter my third month."

"Oh," he smiled, a look of longing crossing his eyes, "he will be so beautiful."

"How do you know he will be a boy?" David questioned, feeling annoyed by his presence.

The god shrugged, oblivious to David's aggravation. "Hera told me."

Ariel nudged her elbow against his ribs, making him widen his eyes at her and she forced out a laugh. "Aidon is really...special. His family thinks they can see the future and whatnot. Hera is his sister and she's a sweetheart...but...yeah. Anyways!"

Hades raised his eyebrows at her strange behaviour and said, "Have you thought of any names? She said that your kind usually think of this at an early stage?"

She sighed, sliding her hand down her face and muttered, "I have thought of names, Aidon, can you stop talking that way. It's so unnatural!" She glared at him, begging with her eyes to watch what he said in front of Karen's fiancé. "If it's a boy I want him to be named Alexander, after Alexander the Great and if it's a girl, I'm stuck between Selene and Phoebe."

His eyes widened for a fraction of a second and his features softened. She wanted to name their child something that had to do with his history; it tugged at his heart in a sentimental but strange way. "I was thinking of Achilles," he said softly, "but I like your idea better."

Her cheeks turned a dark red and she muttered, "I am not going to let people make fun of my kid because I named him that. Alexander is my favourite and that's that."

It was quiet for a couple of minutes as Hades smiled and continued inspecting the picture in his hands. It brought him a sense of pride and happiness like nothing had ever. He wanted to speed time up and have the baby in his arms, but Chronos, the god of time, wouldn't allow it.

"So," David cleared his throat, making all eyes fall on him, "what are your plans now? Where are you going to stay and how are you going to provide for your child?"

"I'm staying with mom," Ariel blurted out before Hades could say otherwise, and although it hurt him to know she didn't want to be by his side, he accepted it. He could only hope that time would change her mind.

"I am pretty wealthy," Hades spoke cautiously, "and as I said before, as long as I am alive, he won't need anything; I'll give it all to them."

"Being a father isn't easy, you know?" David sighed, "There are diaper changes, sporadic naps and crying, he'll sometimes cry and you won't know why. It's not like you can return it to the store."

Hades chuckled, shaking his head and said, "You can rest assured that we will not be returning anything. If Ariel allows it, I will do anything that is needed in order for them to be well."

He nodded, liking his answer and Karen grinned at him, "Would you like to see some pictures of Ariel when she was younger? That way, if she's a girl you can see what she might look like."

"Mom," Ariel rolled her eyes, "Aidon doesn't-"

He stopped up, motioning for her to continue and said, "Lead the way."

She groaned, face-palming herself and pouted her lips. She wasn't an ugly baby, but there were embarrassing pictures of her. Her mom would take pictures of everything; she said she wanted to have memories of anything she ever did. She even took pictures of Ariel's first time using the toilet.

"So," Karen gushed, flipping to the first page and pointed to a picture where Ariel was still in the hospital incubator, "this was like two hours after she was born. Since she was a premature baby, the doctors wanted to keep her for a little more time just to make sure everything went according to plan and I wasn't able to take her right away."

Hades smiled, feeling a sense of euphoria as Karen continued speaking of her daughter animatedly. Her happiness was contagious and he found himself eager to look through the rest of the scrapbook.

"Here she turned three and I remember her walking into my room wearing lipstick all over her mouth. It was a disaster but she swore she looked like the 'girl in the commercial,' so I had to leave her make-up alone and take pictures." Karen smiled, different emotions going through her body and she said, "She wanted to be a model until she was 14, after that she wanted to be a nurse. I always told her she had the looks and confidence to be a model, but for obvious reasons she didn't go through with it."

"She is beautiful," Hades said, watching as Ariel muttered her complaints to David.

Karen smiled at him, lowering her voice just in case Ariel or David were listening and whispered, "Fight for her, Hades. She loves you and you're clearly crazy about her, but if you don't put an effort, she'll keep telling herself she doesn't love you and begin to believe it."

"I don't know how to demonstrate to her my love if she doesn't let me," he sighed, smiling slightly at a picture of her licking an ice cream. She seemed to be around seven or eight and was missing one of her front teeth.

"Bring her flowers, be there for her and be persistent. Now that she's pregnant she'll be going through an emotional rollercoaster; show her that even though she'll be a little psycho, you still love her and understand her."

Hades nodded, whispering his thanks and they continued flipping through the photo album.

"I can't believe them," Ariel hissed, glaring at her mom and ex-fiancé, "look at them all happy and cutesy; they're acting like in-laws."

David laughed at her bitter tone of voice and said, "They were going to be in-law's, Ariel and at one point you loved him, otherwise you wouldn't have this baby and allow him to be a part of your life."

"I haven't stopped," she whispered, picking at her chipped nails idly and said, "but he hurt me and I don't ever want to go through something like that again. So he'll just be the father of our baby and that's it."

He patted her hand fondly and said, "I don't like the guy," Ariel grinned, "but he does seem to care for you. I mean, it's not every day that you're pregnant. He's what? 25? 26?" About a million or more..."He could just leave and live his life as if nothing had happened, yet he came and asked to be a part of your life. If that's not love, then I don't know what is."

Ariel sighed, looking up as Hades' and Karen's laughter got louder and muttered, "You don't even know the half of it."

David gave her a crooked smile, slowly standing up and said, "As cliché as this sounds, listen to your heart. Let it guide you, but use your brain; it was given to you for a reason and you're a bright young girl. You'll figure it out. Now I'm going to leave, tell your mom I had to sort some things out with a patient; I don't want to interrupt her session with her son-in-law."

She chuckled, shaking her head and said, "He's not my husband."

"Do you want him to be?" He raised his eyebrows.

She shrugged, feeling her cheeks heating up and said, "Yes...but he doesn't need to know that."

He chuckled, nodding his head and saluted her before walking over to the closet to bundle up. Ariel sighed, walking towards the kitchen to get something to drink and made sure the door was securely locked before going back to the living room.

"You were adorable," Hades smiled up at her, closing the book before standing up.

She smiled quickly, looking around the room for her mom and said, "Where's my mom?"

"She went to talk to David really quick."

"Oh," she mumbled, "okay."

He nodded. "Yeah; he's...something else. He clearly doesn't like me."

"Well you did just show up out of nowhere," Ariel rolled her eyes, "and my mom likes you. Even though I know it'll feed your humongous ego, you are good looking; any guy would be jealous."

Hades grinned, his eyes glowing happily and he playfully said, "You think I'm good looking?"

She narrowed her eyes at him, but the corners of her lips were turning upward in a smile. "Don't make me kick you out of my house."

"Hey!" He raised his hands up in surrender, "You were the one that said it; I just wanted to hear it again."

"Hades?" She said quietly, standing in front of him and looked up at him. She bit her bottom lip into her mouth, swiping her tongue over it nervously and felt the urge to throw up. Not because she was pregnant, but because she was nervous.

Butterflies were erupting in her stomach, making her giddy and dizzy with emotion and her heart was beating about a thousand miles per hour. No matter how much she tried to fight off the attraction she felt for him, it was there.

She loved him to the point she was willing to give her life up for him again and although she wanted to make him wait for her more, she knew that the upcoming months were going to be rough. She would need his company and reassurance; she would need him.

"Yes?" He cocked his head to the side, watching her curiously.

Ariel stepped towards him, standing on her tip-toes and pressed a soft kiss to his lips. He widened his eyes, surprised that she was so close to him – let alone kissing him, but as soon as she did it; it was over.

"What was that for?" He smiled, hope glistening in his eyes.

She cupped his chin, pulling him closer and whispered, "You have exactly until our baby is born to prove to me that I am not being an idiot by giving you another chance."

Hades smiled, wrapping his arms around her waist and pulled her close to him. "That's all I'll need."

He kissed her tenderly, as if it were their first kiss ever and was afraid that she'd crumble under his fingertips. It made butterflies soar in her stomach and she almost passed out by how content she felt at that very moment.

He would torture himself enough every day for what he did to her; she didn't need to add to his torture anymore. But if he screwed up his second chance, she'd make him regret it.

Ariel entwined her fingers in his soft, smooth hair, pulling him even closer and tilted her head, allowing the kiss to heat up. She breathed against his mouth, feeling avid with emotions and poured her everything into their passionate lip-lock.

Hades pulled her closer, until she could feel the pronounced lines of his abdominals pressed into hers and kissed her as if she were the air he needed to breathe. It made Ariel want to curl her toes and melt in his arms.

"I'm gone for a couple of minutes and I find them trying to make another baby," Karen sighed, shaking her head.

Ariel quickly pulled away from Hades, leaving him wanting for more and grinned nervously at her mom. "Sorry..."

"Oh don't apologise!" She laughed, "I'm glad that you're finally letting the man-god – whatever, sweep you off your feet again. Now don't mind me, I'm just going to get my coat and head off to get some groceries. You take care of her and don't try to make another baby just yet."

"Mom," she laughed, feeling her cheeks get so hot they could almost melt off her face, "we're not going to do...that."

"Yeah, yeah," Karen waved her hand in the air, muttering under her breath about her coat and locked the door behind her.

Ariel turned back to look at Hades and he pressed a soft kiss to her forehead.

"I love you, a□á□□ μ□□," he whispered warmly.

She flashed him a grin and said, "I know."

He chuckled, kneeling down and pressed a soft kiss to her flat stomach. "And I love you too, little one."

A giggle escaped her lips at his affectionate tone of voice and she said, "Remember, Hades, don't make me regret-"

Hades stood up, kissing her quiet and against her lips mumbled, "When I first started falling for you I was afraid that I wouldn't be able to spend the rest of my life with you, but now I know that we will and I'm going to make sure that you fall in love with me every day like I will with you."

He sealed his promise with a breath-taking kiss, erasing any doubts in her mind as he placed his hand over her stomach, wanting to somehow let their child know that he would be loved equally – and even greater for the love he had for Ariel and the love he had for their child was different.

"Every day?" She whispered, placing her head on his shoulder as he hugged her tightly.

"Every day," he confirmed, sliding her hand up to his chest, where his once-again beating heart was going mad. Ariel smiled, pressing a soft kiss to his neck and pulled him to the couch to cuddle. He placed her on his lap, wrapping his arms around her as she placed her ear above his chest and slowly fell asleep to the melodious sound of his heart.

Slowly, things were falling into place. It wasn't exactly the way she pictured her life, but no one ever did picture their life falling in love with a god – and certainly not the god of death.

31

EPILOGUE

Aphrodite and Athena stepped back, twirling their hands in the air so that Ariel could turn around and she sighed, expressing her discontent. The Goddesses rolled their eyes and Aphrodite knelt down to fix the flowing long skirts.

"Mm," Athena tapped her bottom lip, "I think we should add some colour to her waist, it looks plain."

She nodded, running her fingers over Ariel's waist and added some nice golden accents. Athena nodded approvingly and said, "And for the final touch," she brought forward some small peonies and handed them to Aphrodite, "flowers to adorn her hair."

Aphrodite slid the miniscule flowers in between Ariel's braided hair, accessorising it nicely and patted down some loose strand until it was pure perfection. "Mm, we don't want to add too much because then the crown will look tacky."

Athena nodded, handing Ariel some bracelets and said, "Here, put these on and we'll be finished."

"Thank god," she muttered, clasping the bracelet on and flashed the goddesses a cheeky grin, "sorry guys, but whenever you play dress up with me, I feel sorry for all those Barbie's I tormented when I was little."

"We're not that bad," Aphrodite huffed indignantly.

Ariel shook her head, "You're not; I just feel like you guys have way too much fun playing dress up with me."

Athena chuckled, taking out a pair of sandals from a box and held them out for her to take. "That's because we are having fun. Here, take these. They're called krepis and they're our traditional sandals."

She took them, inspecting the leathered sandal and untightened the leather laces to wrap them around her ankle. She tied them like her pointe shoes and then held her foot out to admire the shoe. Her entire outfit consisted of traditional Greek attire; whatever the two goddesses were preparing her for must've been extremely important for them.

"These are cute," she murmured, wiggling her golden toes and grinned up at them.

Aphrodite nodded, quickly running her fingers through her hair before turning back around to face them and said, "It's time; we have to go."

"Are you ever going to tell me what this is for?"

"No," they replied in unison.

Ariel rolled her eyes, crossing her arms over her chest and said, "You know I can just ask Hades, right?"

Athena snorted, "He's the one that told us not to tell you."

"Darn," she muttered, letting out a sigh and turned to look at herself in the mirror. To say that she looked like a goddess would be the understatement of the century. Her hair was pulled up in elaborate, interlocking braids that were pulled back to open up her heart-shaped face. Her makeup was done lightly, accentuating her features and blurring out some blemishes.

To end her breath-taking look was the dress Athena and Aphrodite had designed. It was a simple traditional Greek gown, but with its own personal touch. A sensual yet elegant slid revealed her part of her leg, enough to leave anyone wanting more; being a dancer had its perks and strong, beautiful legs was one of them.

The dress was off-the shoulder, revealing her slightly freckled shoulder and some of her no-longer-tattooed-back. It hugged her curves, accentuating her body in all the right places and gave her the confidence to knock anyone off their feet.

"You look good, don't you?" Aphrodite chuckled, noticing her awed look.

Ariel nodded, flashing her a grin and quickly hugged the two goddesses, "You guys did amazing! I feel all pretty and whatnot."

"Because you are," Athena rolled her eyes, picking up her purse and motioned for her to walk out the obsidian doors. "Now come on, we have places to attend."

"And people to grace with our beauty," Aphrodite chimed in, winking at Ariel as she laughed.

The goddesses guided her down the dimly lit corridor until they reached a pair of beautiful, high golden doors. It seemed like if it had almost come from a movie; the room must've been lit up because the light was escaping through the doors almost making it look angelic.

Aphrodite let out an excited giggle, making Ariel bite her lip in nervousness and whispered, "Guys, please tell me where we are!"

For the past five hours, they had tied her up, thrown her in Athena's chariot and taken her to an unidentified location. They were sworn under the River Styx to not speak and even though Ariel knew, she wanted to know the place they had taken her to.

Anticipation made her heart beat faster and she let out a shaky breath once Athena waved her hands in the air and the door slowly began to open. Ariel closed her eyes, expecting the room to be brighter than the sun and Athena pushed her forward.

She glared at the goddess, quickly walking in and squealed once she saw her mother standing by the entrance of the doors. "Mom! What are you doing here?"

Karen grinned, feeling her content emotions taking the best of her and her eyes watered. She pointed to the room behind them and whispered, "Take a look, honey; I think you'll understand."

Ariel turned around and quickly dropped her jaw open. Thousands of gods were sitting, waiting for her to walk by them. Further into the room were 12 thrones and three were opened. The rest of the Olympians were sitting comfortably, smiling at her as if it were a welcoming party.

Hades stood up, walking down the grand marbled steps and stood at the end of the row. His hands were clasped behind his back and he radiated power and confidence. As soon as their eyes met, he smiled at her, making her suck in a breath and grab her mother's hand tightly.

Karen laughed, blinking away her tears and whispered, "Baby, you look so beautiful."

"Thanks, mom," she whispered back, slightly jumping once Apollo began to play a soft melodious tone. She widened her eyes, looking at her mom with fear and said, "What's going on?"

"Ariel," she narrowed her eyes, taking her daughter's arm in hers, "honey, you're smarter than that. Come on, Hades has something to ask you."

Ariel frowned, but followed Aphrodite and Athena as they walked down the aisle. The few gods she made eye-contact with bowed their heads slightly, acknowledging her with respect and she felt her cheeks turning a dark shade of red.

Soon after, she was standing next to Hades, who took her hands in hers gingerly and smiled down her with so much love she thought she'd pass out. Hera stood next to them, holding their five month old son and gushed at how "adorable he was."

The goddess of marriage had grown a loving infatuation with the little Alexander, justifying her love for the child's beauty. He was truly adorable and had all the gods and goddesses wrapped around his tiny finger.

"Ariel," Hades whispered, sliding his hand in his pocket and rubbed her knuckles gently, "I know I messed up a year ago because of my insecurities and it almost cost me the lives of everyone I care for. I know that I can't simply expect you to forgive me, but these past months I've grown to love you more than I thought possible. The way you care for Alexander and manage to give me the time of day is amazing. Sometimes I get jealous," he chuckled, "because you look at him with so much adoration, but then I remember that I look at you that way."

"You don't adore your kid?!" Eros gasped, making the gods erupt in laughter.

Hades rolled his eyes, grinning and said, "Of course I do! He's literally the centre of my universe, but the love I have for Ariel and the love I have for him are entirely different. I just never catch her looking at me the way she looks at Alexander and it's a funny bittersweet feeling."

Ariel laughed, glancing down at their baby boy and breathed in happily. He was truly beautiful; he looked mostly like Hades, with her green eyes, but his jet black hair. His nose was definitely his father's and his cheekbones were high like Ariel's.

"Nonetheless," He cleared his throat, "what I want to say is; will you marry me? This time I did it when we were both in the room so nothing could go wrong. If you say no, it's alright; I understand."

"I do," she whispered, quickly blinking her tears away and sniffled, making Aphrodite groan when tears began sliding down her cheeks, "ruining her makeup."

"There's no official ceremony for marriage between gods," Hera smiled, shaking Alexander in her arms as she moved her weight from her right foot to her left foot continuously, "but we hold them in Olympus."

She nodded, smiling through her blurry vision as Hades slid the ring in her finger and gently cupped her chin in his hands to press a soft kiss to her lips. Ariel wrapped her arms around his shoulder, letting out a quiet sob and against her lips, whispered, "I love you, Ariel."

"I do too," she grinned, wiping away her tears and breathed in deeply, before releasing a relaxing breath.

"So," Gaia clapped her hands together, snapping everyone's attention towards her and said, "thank you, Hades, for stealing the spotlight, but this ceremony isn't for you and Ariel. It's for Ariel."

Ariel blushed, turning to Hades with a quizzical look on her face as he pushed her forward.

"About a year and a half ago, I told you that I was taking your curse away and in return gifting you with something very honourable." She nodded, keeping an attentive look as she watched Gaia, "I told you that you were going to be the goddess of reincarnation; that's what we're here for."

She turned around, motioning to an empty, light coloured sleek throne next to Hades' dark one and said, "From this day forward you will sit amongst the 12 Olympians for you are now one of them." Gaia took her hand in hers, motioning for her to bow and said, "I am crowning you goddess of life; you will be honoured as such, listening to those who pray to you and keeping balance in the Underworld."

"We know Hades is just in his judgements, but you will now bring a greater balance to the life cycle. Those who have been killed wrongfully will be protected by you. You are their saviour and protector; their goddess. For all these callings, I shall rename you □□□□□□□□□."

Gaia placed a thin, golden crown upon Ariel's braids and helped her stand up as she motioned to the other gods. "□□□ □□□□□□□□□."

"Um, what?" Karen said, making the gods chuckle and Gaia grinned.

"Goddess Anagénnisi."

"Woo," she mumbled, "tongue-twister!"

Ariel laughed at her mom, grateful that she wasn't the only one who thought so and widened her eyes when Gaia led her to the throne room. She bit her bottom lip, definitely feeling too nervous to be a goddess and sat down once she was told to.

Everyone began to clap, saying her new name in unison and she felt her smile freezing on her lips. After a while of thunderous claps and congratulatory shouts, the chairs disappeared and servants began to fill the room with foods. The Muses entered the room, humming a melodious tune and the gods began to disperse through the room.

Hades slid his arm around Ariel's walking with her towards Hera and he took Alexander in his arms. Hera pouted, glaring at Hades and he chuckled, "You've had him for almost the entire day!"

"You get to have him all the time!"

"He's my son!"

She rolled her eyes, huffing out in annoyance and stomped away. Zeus laughed, shaking his head at his wife and said, "Congratulations, brother, you finally found the right wife and she turned out to be a beautiful goddess."

"Watch it, Zeus," Hades grinned, "I don't need Hera turning Ariel into anything."

Ariel rolled her eyes, cooing down at her son and slowly took him from Hades. "Hi, baby," she grinned at him, "I've missed you so much," he giggled at her and her grin widened, "yes, I did!"

"Stop talking that way," Eros rolled his eyes, "it makes me uncomfortable."

She laughed at him, kissing Alexander's little nose and said, "Oh shut it, Eros; you're just jealous that my son is cuter than you are in a diaper."

He gasped, looking appalled and said, "I have never worn a diaper! Humans just like insulting me."

Aphrodite laughed, messing up his blonde hair and said, "We can make another bet and you can lose again; then you'll have to wear a diaper."

"I lost once," he hissed, glaring at her, "never again! And you probably cheated!"

"Me?" She gasped, "Cheat? Heavens no!"

Hephaestus began to cough, making all the gods laugh and Aphrodite blushed, smacking his arm playfully. He grinned, pressing a soft kiss to her forehead and swept her away to dance.

"A□□π□ μ□□," Hades whispered near her ear, "can I have Alexander? Everyone keeps taking him from me."

She laughed, giving him the baby and said, "I thought you were going to ask me to dance or something!"

He grinned cheekily, taking his son in his arms and began to make playful sounds. Ariel shook her head, unable to wipe the smile off her face and jumped when her mother hugged her tightly.

"So do you feel any different?!"

"What?" She frowned.

Karen rolled her eyes, waving her hands in the air impatiently and said, "You're a goddess now! How does it feel?"

Ariel shrugged. "Not really different...just...I feel strong – and pretty."

"Of course," she laughed, "but you were always beautiful, honey, now your beauty was enhanced."

She grinned, watching as Hades cooed down at Alexander, making the cutest giggle leave his lips. "He's so adorable."

"Came out like his grandma," She joked, "what else would you expect?!"

"Mom!" She laughed, shaking her head.

"Ladies," Hermes bowed, kissing Karen's knuckles gently, before turning to Ariel, "do you mind if I take you away from your mom really quick?"

Ariel looked at her mom, who shrugged and walked away to the snack table. Hermes wrapped his arms around Ariel's waist, hugging her tightly and then began to move to the beat of the music.

"Why so happy?" She giggled after he spun her around.

"Guess what?" His blue eyes glimmered brightly.

She raised her eyebrows, shrugging and said, "Uh...I don't know. What?"

"I found her," he whispered, excitedly.

"No!" She widened her eyes, grinning widely.

"Yes!" He chuckled, nodding his head quickly, "I found Adrianne. She was born in Rome to some wealthy parents. She just turned 2 last week."

"Aw, Hermes," She gushed, "I'm so happy for you!"

"I know," he sighed contently, "she's so beautiful already."

"That's a bit creepy," Ariel laughed, ignoring his glare, "I mean, she's only 2! I get that you love her...but don't go and scare her away."

"I won't!" He replied, "I'm just watching over her. I'm making sure her parents take care of her and that no harm will go her way."

Her smile widened and she hugged him tightly. "You'll be like her guardian angel!"

"More or less," he chuckled, noticing Hades' presence nearing them.

"May I cut in?" Hades grinned, waiting for Hermes to give him his wife's hand.

"Bye, Hermes! We'll talk more later!" He nodded, turning around to talk to other gods. Ariel pressed her cheek against Hades' shoulder and after a while of silence mumbled, "Where's Alexander?"

"With Aphrodite," he muttered, rolling his eyes.

Ariel laughed, pressing a soft kiss to his cheek and said, "Let them have their fun! It lets me relax; as much as I love him, it's nice to take a break once in a while."

Hades nodded, kissing her forehead and said, "Speaking of breaks, I was wondering..."

She raised her eyebrows. "What?"

"Would you like to visit Greece with me this summer? It'll be for just a week and Alexander will be ten months old and Hera volunteered to take care of him."

"Mm," she pursed her lips, "I don't know...he's my little baby...I don't know if I'll be able to be away from him for that long."

Hades chuckled, nodding and said, "We can always take him if you'd like, but," he lowered his hands down her waist, reaching her butt and squeezed it lightly, and whispered, "I was thinking that we could give him a little sister."

She grinned, pressing a chaste kiss to his lips and said, "I basically just gave birth to Alexander and you want to make another one?! Do you think you'll be ready for another pregnant me?"

"Mm," he mused, "are you going to cry if you burn the pasta again?"

Ariel slapped his shoulder playfully, feeling her cheeks turning a dark shade of pink and muttered, "I was thinking that because I burned the pasta, I wouldn't be able to feed him."

"I told you I could cook for you," he laughed, loving the feel of his wife in his arms. She was his life; the one who brought a reason for existence.

"Yeah, but I was hungry," she huffed, "and you were in a stupid meeting with Poseidon and Zeus."

"No matter," Hades whispered, making goose bumps raise over her neck when his breath brushed past it, "you haven't answered my question."

Ariel shrugged, snuggling her face into his neck and breathed in deeply. He smelled of her favourite cologne; spicy and evocative. "I don't know, I don't want to give you a definite answer now, but if trying to give Alexander a little sister is what you wish," she nibbled on his earlobe, making his hold on her tighten, and she whispered, "we can do that tonight."

"Sounds like a plan," Hades whispered in return, his voice husky with lust and he had to try and hold himself back from taking his wife in front of his family.

She laughed, pressing a soft kiss to his mouth and whispered, "I love you, ugly."

He smiled, then quickly frowned at her. "I am not ugly!"

"Disney thinks otherwise," she replied in a sing-song voice as she walked away from him, to beg Aphrodite for her son.

"He's an idiot," he huffed, running after her as he tried to get her to call him handsome. She continued pushing his buttons, until Aphrodite smacked him upside the head and told him that Alexander was lucky he took after his aunt.

It resulted in a bicker between the gods, trying to determine why Alexander was so adorable. Hades ended the argument, stating that he looked just like his parents, making Ariel laugh and cough that he looked more like her.

He only kissed her and agreed, crying out his thanks to the Fates for bringing life to death.

www.ingramcontent.com/pod-product-compliance
Lightning Source LLC
Chambersburg PA
CBHW070734190726
48292CB00002B/264